A World of Difference

A World of Difference

Harry Turtledove

NEW ENGLISH LIBRARY
Hodder and Stoughton

First published in Great Britain in 1998 by Hodder and Stoughton
A division of Hodder Headline PLC
First published in paperback in 1999 by Hodder and Stoughton

A New English Library Paperback

10 9 8 7 6 5 4 3 2 1

A CIP catalogue record for this title is available from
the British Library

ISBN 0 340 71271 6

Printed and bound in Great Britain by
Mackays of Chatham PLC, Chatham, Kent

Hodder and Stoughton
A division of Hodder Headline PLC
338 Euston Road
London NW1 3BH

To the memory of my father-in-law Frank Frankos . . .
and for Barney the Frog.

Author's Note

Mars is boring. Turns out it's too damn small. But what if it weren't . . .

MINERVA *is the fourth planet out from the sun in the solar system, the first planet past Earth's orbit. At its nearest approach to Earth, Minerva is the brightest object in the sky except for the sun and moon. It then looks to the naked eye like a brilliant, gray-blue star of magnitude −5.9. Sometimes it may even exceed that brightness for a short period. This is the result of the famous "Minervan flash," which occurs when breaks in the cloud cover above the planet's surface allow the sun to reflect directly off ice or water. Long before the cause of the phenomenon was known, it gave the planet its name: the Greeks called it Athena, after their flashing-eyed goddess of wisdom. Minerva is the Latin name for the same divinity.*

Since the invention of the telescope, Minerva has fascinated observers. It is the only world in the solar system besides Earth where water can exist as a liquid, and the presence of oxygen in its atmosphere has long suggested that, like Earth, it is a home for life.

Since 1965, American and Soviet space probes have greatly added to our knowledge of Minerva. Despite the planet's thick, cloudy atmosphere, we now have reliable maps of almost its entire surface. Not until 1976, though, did the Viking I spacecraft actually land on the planet. The Viking analyzed Minerva's lower atmosphere, and the craft's biological experiment package and the photographs it returned to Earth confirmed that there is life on the planet.

Viking I's last photograph, arguably the most famous ever taken, confirmed far more than that. It proved humanity is not alone in the universe, for it shows a Minervan native carrying what cannot be anything but a deliberately manufactured artifact—whether a weapon or simply a pole remains the subject of hot debate. Transmission from Viking I ceased immediately after this photograph was made . . .

TABLE OF MINERVAN DATA

Equatorial diameter: 9,264 miles (14,909 km)

Mass: 8.35×10^{24} kg (about 1.4 times that of Earth)

Density: 4.81 g/cm³ (about 87% that of Earth)

Surface gravity: 1.02 that of Earth

Escape velocity: 7.60 miles/second (12.22 km/sec)

Greatest distance from sun: 154,800,000 miles (249,120,000 km)

Least distance from sun: 128,350,000 miles (206,560,000 km)

Sidereal day: 24 hr 37 min 23 sec

Mean solar day: 24 hr 39 min 35 sec

Sidereal period: 687 days

Synodic period: 779.5 days

Albedo: 45-50%

Surface atmospheric pressure: about 1,500 millibars

Atmosphere: Nitrogen, 80%; oxygen, 17%; argon, 1.2%; water vapor, 0.7%; carbon dioxide, 0.6%; other gases, 0.5%

Moons: 3 (Sophia, Parthenia, Arachne)

—From the *Encyclopaedia America* article, "Minerva." Reproduced by permission.

1

Irv Levitt pumped away on the exercise bike. Sweat clung greasily to his skin and matted his dark brown hair. He tossed his head. That was a mistake he still made after eight months in space. Little drops spread in all directions.

The anthropologist swore and mopped them out of the air with a soft, absorbent cloth like a big diaper. Without mopping up, the sweat would float around until it hit something—or someone. Jamming six people into a ship as cramped as *Athena* was tough enough without troubles like that.

Levitt worked the bike with grim intensity until finally, mercifully, the timer rang and let him off the hook. Then he toweled himself off and pushed himself out of the tiny exercise chamber and past the three sleeping cubicles.

On his way by, he stuck his head through the privacy curtain of his own chamber for a moment. The light inside was dim and red; his wife Sarah was tethered to the foam mattress, asleep. He smiled a little and went on to the control room.

Patricia and Frank Marquard were already there, watching the monitor as Minerva flowed by below at almost 19,000 miles an hour. Levitt saw the longing on their faces. It mirrored his own: like him, they wanted nothing more than to get down to the planet so they could start working. She was a biologist, her husband a geologist.

At the moment, the monitor showed mostly ice. That was not surprising; each of Minerva's polar caps reached about halfway to the equator, the northern a bit more, the southern a bit less. Sometimes the planet looked so frigid and forbidding that even a glance could make Levitt shiver.

Not now, though. The *Athena* moved north past the edge of the southern polar cap. Through cloud cover, Levitt glimpsed one of the long, deep gorges that channeled meltwater from the icecaps to the seas and lakes of the southern tropics every Minervan spring.

"I think I'd kill for a shower about now, even in water that cold," he said.

Pat Marquard nodded rueful agreement. "Disinfectant wipes just aren't the same," she said. "I'm sick of smelling like an infirmary. I'm sick of short hair, too, and even sicker of having it smell like an infirmary." Back on Earth, her hair had been a curly blond waterfall that went halfway down her back; she was vain about it. Keeping it only a couple of inches longer than Frank's had given her something to complain about ever since *Athena* left the American space station.

"I could go for a shower, too, but I'm not looking forward to gravity again," Frank said.

Levitt glared at him half seriously. "You have the nasty habit of pointing out things we'd all rather not think about. Just working the bike leaves my legs sore. Having to hold myself up again, walk, run—" He broke off, shaking his head in distaste.

"We may have to do some running," Pat said quietly.

She let it drop there, but her eyes, her husband's, and Irv's automatically went to one of the two pictures taped above the monitor: the *Viking* photo. It shared pride of place with Galileo's first sketch of Minerva through the telescope, but Galileo's drawing got short shrift. Sometimes Irv stared at the *Viking* shot so hard that he ignored the planetary view under it. That picture was the reason for *Athena*, and the reason it had an anthropologist—it had *him*—aboard: the only glimpse humanity had ever had of another intelligent race.

Ever since *Viking* was destroyed, people had been searching for words to describe Minervans—or at least *this* Minervan, Levitt reminded himself; nobody had any idea how typical he, she, or it was. "Fat hatrack" was about the best short phrase anyone had come up with, and even the learned articles in *Science* and *Nature* had not done much better than that.

The creature was essentially cylindrical, better than six feet tall, and about a foot and a half across through most of its height. Half a dozen short, stumpy legs were equally spaced around its base. A like number of arms ringed its torso about a foot below the top; a ring of six eyes sprouted from the bulge there.

No mouth was visible. Some people wondered if the Minervan had one. If so, was it on the side away from the *Viking*'s camera, or in the center of the top part? Levitt would have bet on the latter; the Minervan looked to be radially symmetrical, not built on the bilateral pattern more common on Earth. He was willing to admit he was just guessing, though.

Each of the Minervan's legs ended in three claws, each arm in three fingers. Two arms held the Artifact, as the anthropologists had dubbed it. Levitt had no idea what the thing was supposed to be for: it could have been a crook, a flail, a pole vaulter's pole, anything. He doubted it was intended as a wrecking bar, but it had done the job plenty well.

"Junior doesn't look as though it'd be very fast," he said musingly.

"Neither are we, relative to the rest of the big mammals," Pat said. "We have things besides speed going for us. So do the Minervans, I'll guarantee you that."

"That 'relative' is a good point, Pat," Frank Marquard put in. "Without knowing what the local competition is, we can't tell whether Junior's a sloth or a gazelle."

"You've been listening to your wife too much. Comes of sharing a cubicle with her, I suppose," Irv said. He tried to remember when they had started calling the Minervan Junior and failed. Sometime very early on in the flight, anyway. "Me, I don't care how fast Junior is by local standards. I just want to know whether I can outrun it if it decides to swing the Artifact at me."

"Now who sounds like me?" Pat said, and poked him in the ribs. "That's what I said a minute ago. You should spend more time with Sarah; then you and she would be echoing each other."

"She's asleep back there. Doing the last set of bloods and getting the data back to Houston took longer than she thought it would—that glitch showed up in the software again." Sarah Levitt was an M.D. who specialized in biochemistry but was out of med school recently enough not to have forgotten what people were all about, either: a natural for *Athena*. For that matter, Irv knew that being married to her had not hurt his own chances.

"By now, everyone on this ship sounds like everybody else," Frank said.

"In a pig's ear we do." Emmett Bragg glided through the cabin like a shark sliding through a tropical lagoon. If ever a man was made for free-fall, Irv thought for the hundredth time, Emmett Bragg was the one. The pilot was close to fifty, a decade older than anyone else aboard *Athena*, and the only real astronaut on the crew. Before NASA, he had flown Phantoms in Vietnam. Once he had stayed loose on the ground for three days until a chopper got him out after his plane went down south of Haiphong.

Frank laughed. "Nobody wants to imitate that mouthful of grits you talk through, Emmett. What do the Russians think of it, anyway?"

Still without a wasted motion, Bragg strapped himself into the commander's seat. "Matter of fact, the accent interests 'em. One of 'em said to me once I sounded like I was from Georgia. I told him, naw, Alabama."

Frank snorted, and Pat giggled.

"He meant Stalin country, Emmett, not where the Braves play," Irv said.

"I know," Bragg said calmly. "But it doesn't hurt any to have the boys on the other side take you for a natural-born fool." He checked the radar screen. A blip was showing: the *Tsiolkovsky*, coming up over the Minervan horizon.

"Right on time," Levitt said.

Bragg nodded. "They haven't been playing with their orbit again, anyhow." He had worn a crew cut when it was stylish, kept it through the years when it wasn't, and still had it now that it was in again. The only difference was that gray streaked it now. He picked up the radio mike. *"Zdrast'ye, Tsiolkovsky,"* he said, and went on in Russian that was accented but fluent. "All well aboard?"

"Very well, thank you, Brigadier Bragg." Colonel Sergei Tolmasov sounded like an Oxford don. Just as the Americans used Russian to talk to the Soviet ship, the crew of the *Tsiolkovsky* always replied in English. Tolmasov's dry wit went well with the slightly fussy precision he brought to the language. "Good to find you in your expected place, old fellow."

"We were thinking the same thing about you," Bragg said.

The *Tsiolkovsky* had changed orbits several times in the week since it and *Athena* had reached Minerva. Had each burn not taken place on the far side of the planet from *Athena*, Levitt would have been happier about believing the Russians when they said the maneuvers were just to enhance their observations. As things were, he had not been sorry when Bragg also started jinking. "Let them worry, too," the pilot had said.

Now Tolmasov remarked, "I will be glad when we are all on the ground, and this foolish maneuvering can cease."

"Agreed," Bragg said at once. "We'll be too busy cheating the natives to worry so much about each other."

"Ah—quite," Tolmasov replied after a moment's pause. "There are times, Brigadier, when I must confess myself uncertain as to how facetious you are being. *Tsiolkovsky* out."

Bragg chuckled. "Sometimes I wonder myself, Sergei Konstantinovich. *Athena* out." When the mike was dead, he fell back into English. "The other thing I wonder about is whether all this back-and-forth with the Russians will end up making a full-time liar out of me."

" 'Too busy cheating the natives,' " Tolmasov echoed. "I like that. I only wish I could believe it."

"We should send a recording of that remark back to Baikonur," said Oleg Lopatin, the only other Russian in the control room when Tolmasov spoke to *Athena*. "It shows how the Americans are already planning to exploit the people of Minerva."

"He was just joking, Oleg Borisovich," Tolmasov said. His Russian did not share the arid perfection of his English.

Lopatin's heavy eyebrows came down in a frown. "You did not seem so certain of that when you were talking with him."

"Never show all you know," Tolmasov said. He did not bother pointing out that that also applied to his dealings with Lopatin, who was KGB. Tolmasov sighed. Things being as they were, that was inevitable. At least Lopatin was also a perfectly able electronics engineer and, by Russian standards, computer man. That gave him some real use aboard *Tsiolkovsky*, aside from his value to Moscow.

Tolmasov looked around the control room and sighed again. He knew that, with its round analog dials instead of slick digital readouts, it would have seemed old-fashioned to Bragg. The panels full of glowing green numbers he had seen in pictures and tapes of *Athena* and other American spacecraft seemed—what was the American slang?—glitzy to him. All what you're used to, he thought.

But he did envy his opposite number the computer power under those panels. Every one of *Tsiolkovsky*'s orbit-changing burns had been calculated back on Earth. *Athena*, he was sure, had figured its own. Partly that was a difference in approach. Ever since the earliest days, the Soviet space program had relied more heavily on ground control than the Americans.

The technology gap did exist, though. The big Russian boosters let *Tsiolkovsky* carry a lot more weight to Minerva than *Athena* could. The engineering on the life-support system was solid, or he wouldn't be here worrying. But Bragg had a lot more data-processing capacity than he did, and down on Minerva there would be nothing but data to process. He worried some more.

While he was at it, Tolmasov spent a little while worrying about Bragg. Envy mixed in with the worry there, too. The colonel was out of Frontal Aviation; his flight experience before being tapped for cosmonaut training was all in MiG-27s and other attack aircraft. Without false modesty, he knew he was good. But he had never seen combat; he had left his squadron a few months before they flew against the Sixth Fleet's Tomcats during the Third Beirut Crisis. He wondered how much difference that made.

Not much, he tried to tell himself. He had done everything but. Still, Russian and English both had a word for somebody who had done everything but sleep with a girl. The word was virgin.

That turned Tolmasov's mind in another direction. He smoothed his short, light brown hair. It was not as neatly trimmed, of course, as it had been when *Tsiolkovsky* set out from Earth orbit. Eight months of amateur barbering had left everyone on the ship a little ragged. Tolmasov knew, though, that ragged or not he still kept his good looks: like so many Russians, he had a face that would somehow contrive to seem boyish and open until he was well into his fifties. And those evil days, fortunately, were a good many years away yet.

He gave his attention back to Lopatin. "I'm going aft for some rest, Oleg Borisovich. Call me at once if anything unusual happens, or if there is any unscheduled communication from Earth."

"Of course," Lopatin said. "Rest well."

His voice held no irony. Even with curtains, even with a bigger ship than *Athena*, privacy hardly existed aboard *Tsiolkovsky*. Tolmasov missed it less than most Americans would have. He had grown up with a brother and three sisters in a two-bedroom apartment in Smolensk, and his father was not badly off. It was, he realized wryly as he pulled himself from handhold to handhold down the corridor to the laboratory, good practice for the life of a cosmonaut.

He heard a centrifuge whir and looked into one of the chambers. "Well, Doctor," he said, smiling, as he glided in. "Are we healthy?'' The question was a way to start a conversation, but also seriously meant: if anything was wrong, Tolmasov needed to know about it right away.

Dr. Zakharova checked a reading, squinted, checked again, then nodded. "Healthy enough, after so much free-fall. The new calcium supplement seems better than the last one we tried.''

"That's good, Katerina Fyodorovna. I'm glad to hear it.'' Again, Tolmasov felt his words bearing two meanings. He was not looking forward to being under gravity again—even less so if he and his comrades suffered more than they had to from the weakened bones brought on by prolonged weightlessness. Moreover . . . "Have your tests reached a point where you can stop for a while?''

The doctor raised an eyebrow and smiled a little. "I think so,'' she said. She was a small, dark woman with startling blue eyes. Tolmasov was no longer sure whether she really was pretty. As the only woman on *Tsiolkovsky*, by now she looked good to him—and, he was sure, to the other four men in the crew.

Afterward, in his cabin, they sat in midair, her legs still wrapped around his back. Free-fall did not have many advantages, but sex was one of them. Tolmasov kept a grip on a handhold, so he and Katerina would not drift out through the curtain into the corridor. "A pleasant way to pass the time,'' he said.

"I'm glad you think so.'' She raised that eyebrow again.

He'd expected her to; after so long, few surprises were left between crew members. It had to be a lot like being married, he thought.

That brought *Athena*, always in the back of his mind, up to the front. The Americans had tried to solve the problem of sexual tension by putting three married couples aboard. They hailed it as a triumph of equality. Tolmasov could not see that—he doubted any combination of couples would get the Americans' best people to Minerva. And Minerva was too important for anything less than the best.

The Soviet selection boards had thought as he did. If that meant life aboard *Tsiolkovsky* sometimes got complicated, too bad. Fortunately, Katerina was as fine a woman—as fine a person—as she was a physician. He wondered if the boards had chosen her for that, too. Probably not, he decided. Otherwise they would never have come up with Igor Lopatin.

He grimaced. Had Katerina been as crabbed and dour as the

engineer, life aboard *Tsiolkovsky* would have been a lot worse than complicated. It would have been intolerable, and maybe dangerous. He ran a grateful hand down the smooth skin of her back, glad she favored him at the moment.

She stirred and detached herself from him. "Now," she said, "back to work." She retrieved her underpants and coverall from the little bag where she had stowed them. Tolmasov used a tissue to mop liquid out of the air. Katerina chuckled. "To the head first, then back to work," she amended with a doctor's practicality. As soon as she was dressed, she slipped out of the cubicle and away.

Tolmasov put his clothes back on more slowly. It was not animal lassitude; he was too disciplined to let that affect him. Calculation played a much bigger part in it. Someone besides Oleg Lopatin, he was sure, had KGB connections. That was the way things were. Katerina made the most obvious choice: if anyone on the ship could find out everything that was going on, she was the one.

Of course, the KGB did not have a reputation for being obvious. Tolmasov let out a snort of laughter. If Katerina was not what he suspected her to be, she doubtless had suspicions about him.

A drop of water fell from the castle ceiling onto Reatur's head. He extended an eyestalk and stared balefully upward at the ice. Was it starting to drip already? Plainly, it was. Summer was coming.

Reatur was not happy about summer. It would be too hot; it always was. Most of the tools made of ice would melt; they always did. The domain-master would have to see to getting the stone tools out of storage, as he did toward the end of every spring.

He did not like stone tools. They were hard to make and expensive to buy. His peasants did not like them, either. They were heavier than ice and tiring to use in the fields. He wished he lived in a land with a better climate, where ice stayed ice the year around.

Even his castle's thick walls would drip and trickle all summer long. He remembered the really scorching summer—how long ago was it? Seven years, that was it—when big chunks of the roof had melted and fallen in. Lucky his domain had been at peace then, and lucky the collapse had killed only mates.

Reatur's eldest son Ternat came into the great hall, breaking his chain of thought. Ternat thickened his body so the top of his head was lower than the top of Reatur's. "You are respectful," the domain-master said, pleased, "but I know you are taller than I."

"Yes, clanfather." Ternat resumed his natural height. "A male from the great clan of Skarmer waits outside. He would have speech with you."

"Would he?" Air hissed out through the breathing-pores under Reatur's eyestalks. "I wonder what he wants." Visits from the males who lived on the west side of the Ervis Gorge were never casual affairs; the gorge was too hard to cross for anything but serious business to be worthwhile. "Bring him in."

"Yes, clanfather." Ternat hurried away. He was eldest, but he knew better than to do anything without his father's leave. One day, if he outlived Reatur, he would be clanfather himself, and domain-master. Till then, he was as much in his father's power as a just-budded mate.

He led the Skarmer male up to the domain-master. The westerner politely widened himself before Reatur, though like most of his people he was already the shorter and rounder of the two. That peculiar combination of plump body and long eyestalks always made the males from west of the gorge look sneaky to Reatur.

Still widened, the Skarmer male said in trade talk, "I bring my clanfather Hogram's greetings to you, domain-master, and those of all the domains sprung from the Skarmer bud. I am named Fralk; I am eldest of eldest of Hogram."

Reatur felt like hissing again but refused to let this Fralk see his surprise. Not only did the westerner have plenipotentiary power—Reatur was not even sure how many domains there were on the far side of the gorge—but he was also in line to become clanfather of his domain.

"I am pleased to receive such a prominent emissary," Reatur said, more polite than ever. Then, still without abandoning his manners, he started to get down to business. "To what do I owe this privilege?"

"A moment, if you please, before I come to that," Fralk said. "I have heard from merchants and travelers of a curious—well, a curious thing that you keep here. May I see it? Travelers' tales are often wild, but the ones that have come to me have enough substance to be intriguing, I must confess."

"Odd you should mention the strange thing. When Ternat announced you, I was just thinking about the summer I found it," Reatur said. "Come this way. In deference to your rank, I will not even ask any price of you."

"You are generous." Fralk widened again, then trailed after Reatur and Ternat toward the side-chamber where the domain-master kept the strange thing.

That chamber's outer wall had much less sand and gravel mixed with its ice than was true of the rest of the castle. As Reatur had intended, more sunlight came through that way; the room was almost as bright as day.

Fralk walked all around the strange thing, looking at it with four eyes and barely managing to keep a polite pair on his hosts. Reatur understood that. When he had first found the strange thing, he had stared with all six eyes at once, lifting the stalk on the far side of his body over his head. He remembered that that had only made matters worse. He was so used to seeing all around him all the time that having a big part of his field of vision blank left him disoriented. He had wanted to lean in the direction his eyes were pointing.

Fralk was leaning a little himself. He noticed and recovered. At last he said, "This once, the tales are less than truth. I have *never* seen anything like that."

"Neither had I when I came across it, nor have I since," Reatur said, and meant it. He looked at the strange thing almost every day, and it still made no sense to him. With all those sharp angles—more than on any eighteen things he usually came across—it did not seem as though it had any right to exist. Yet there it was.

"How did you find it?" Fralk asked.

The domain-master had told the tale many times. Somehow, though, maybe because Fralk was a male who displayed extraordinarily good manners, it came out fresher than it had in years. "I was out hunting nosver."

"I've heard of them," Fralk said. "We don't have them in the Skarmer domains."

"You're lucky. They're dreadful pests. By the tracks, a male and his whole band of mates had come down to raid the fields. I trailed them back to the low hills east of the castle. That summer was so hot that when I felt dry, I couldn't find any ice or snow to pick up and put in my mouth. I had to lie down flat and dip my head in a puddle of water."

"Annoying," Fralk said sympathetically. "That always makes my gut itch."

"Mine, too. Miserable stuff, water. The nosver, curse 'em,

like it, you know. They splashed along a stream coming off a
tongue of ice till I couldn't smell 'em anymore, and I wasn't
having any luck finding their prints on the far side, either. You
can imagine how happy I was.''

''I don't blame you a bit,'' Fralk said. He really was a fine
fellow, Reatur thought.

The domain-master went on. ''So there I was, grouchy as all
get out and with the start of some really fierce indigestion. I
came round a boulder and almost bumped right into—that.'' He
pointed at the strange thing. ''I looked at it, and looked at it.
And then it moved.''

''It did what?'' Fralk said, startled.

''Moved,'' Reatur insisted. ''An arm came out of its bottom
and stuck itself into the ground. I tell you, I almost voided where
I stood—I daresay the damned water I'd drunk had something
to do with that, too. I never imagined the strange thing could be
alive. I didn't stop to think. I just took a whack at it with the
stave I was carrying.''

''I would have done the same thing,'' Fralk said. ''Or else
run.''

''I hit it over and over. What a racket it made! It was hard,
harder than anything alive has any right to be. Feel for yourself
if you like—it's like midwinter ice, or even stone. It didn't fight
back, and all I can say is that I'm glad. I only quit hitting it
when pieces came off. If it wasn't dead then, it never would
be.''

''Has it moved since?'' Fralk asked.

''No; I guess I did kill it. My sons and grandsons and I spent
days hauling it back here to the castle.''

''What a job that was,'' Ternat said, whistling with remembered strain.

''Yes,'' Reatur agreed. ''It made me wonder all over again
how the strange thing could ever have been alive. It's as heavy
as stone, and as hard to get from place to place. But it did move
by itself.''

Fralk turned an extra couple of eyestalks on it again. ''You
could tell me it sang songs and I would not argue with you. It
might do anything; it might do nothing.''

''It's done nothing since it's been here,'' Ternat said.

''Well, not quite,'' Reatur said. ''Most travelers I charge food
or tools to see it. Over the years, now that I think, it's earned
me a tidy sum.''

"That I do believe," Fralk said. "It's worth traveling a long way to see."

A well-spoken young male indeed, Reatur thought. "Guest with me tonight," he said expansively. "My ice is yours."

"I thank you," Fralk said. Then he proceeded to wreck the fine impression he had made, for he took the old proverb literally. He reached out a couple of arms, used his fingerclaws to scrape a good handful of ice from the wall, and put it in his mouth. "Very nice," he said.

Reatur saw Ternat turn yellow with anger. The domain-master glanced down at himself. He was the same color, and no wonder. "Envoy of the Skarmer domains, you forget yourself," he said. His voice was stiff as glacier ice in midwinter.

"No, domain-master, I do not. For this I was sent here." Fralk took more ice and put it in his mouth as calmly as if he were munching it from the walls of his own castle. Suddenly, his politeness seemed something he had assumed at will, not native to him.

"This is insolence," Reatur said. "Why should I not send you back to your clanfather without the arms you have used to prove it?"

Fralk spun round in a circle. "Which arms are those?" he asked when he stopped. Yes, he was mocking Reatur.

"Any two will do," the domain-master growled.

He had to give Fralk reluctant credit; the Skarmer envoy went neither blue from fear nor an angry yellow. "You would be unwise to take them," Fralk said. He was the very odor of good manners again. Reatur, whose moods ran fast and deep, began to see why this young male had been chosen ambassador. Like smooth ice reflecting the sun and hiding whatever lay beneath, he did his clanfather's bidding without revealing himself in the process.

"We come down to it, then," Reatur said, still trying to provoke a reaction from him. "Why should I not?"

"Because I aim to inherit this domain from you," Fralk said. "That is why I treated it as my home to be."

The chamber with the strange thing had no weapons in it. Reatur knew that. His encircling eyes glanced around it anyway, just in case. One of the things he saw was Ternat's eyestalks twisting in a similar search. Another was that Fralk had turned blue. He was afraid now.

If he had been standing on Fralk's claws, Reatur would have been more than afraid. "Shall I think you have gone mad, and

set you free on that account?'' he said. "I could almost believe
it. Why else would you speak so, in the presence of a domain-
master and his eldest?''

Fralk slowly regained his greenish tint. "Because the domains that come from the first bud of Skarmer grow straitened
in their lands. Just as mates must bud, Skarmer must grow.''

"How?'' Reatur thought about what he knew of the lay of the
land west of the Ervis Gorge: not much. But one piece of knowledge came to him. "Are not all the domains in the west Skarmer,
all the way to the next Great Gorge?''

"They are,'' Fralk said. "We will be coming to the east,
across the Ervis Gorge.''

"He lies!'' Ternat exclaimed. "What will the Skarmer domains do, send one male at a time across the rope bridge? Let
them. After we have slain the first warrior, and the second, and
if need be the third, they will grow bored with dying and all
will be as it has been before.''

"We will be coming,'' Fralk said. "We will be coming in
force. I do not think you will stop us. You may reckon me
witstruck, but a year from now the mastery of these lands will
be walking on its eyestalks, of that I assure you.''

"Suppose for the sake of talk you are *not* witstruck,'' Reatur
said slowly. "Why come to me to announce what you intend?
Why not simply fall on me one night when none of the moons
is in the sky?''

"Because your domain lies at the eastern edge of the Ervis
Gorge,'' Fralk said. "We would have you aid us, if you will.
We know you have no great love for either of your neighbors.''

"You know that, do you?'' As a matter of fact, Reatur thought,
Fralk had a point. As far as he was concerned, Dordal was an
idiot and Grebur a maniac, and both of them disgraces to the
name of domain-master. Still—"Why should I like your clanfather Hogram better, or any other Skarmer? Why do you have
the arrogance to claim my domain will be your own? I have an
eldest, and he an eldest after him. This domain is ours, and has
belonged to great clan Omalo since the first bud. Should I tamely
yield it to males sprung from a different bud?''

"Yield it tamely and you will stay on as domain-master for
your natural life. Your sons and grandsons will not suffer, save
that all mates henceforward will take no buds from them. Resist,
and I will become domain-master here as soon as your castle
has been melted to water. You and all of yours will die. The
choice is yours.''

Fralk sounded very sure of himself, Reatur thought. He thought the Skarmer domains could do what he said they could do. Reatur was convinced of that. Fralk was no clanfather, though; he lacked the years to have learned the difference between what one wishes, even what one is sure of, and what turns out.

"Your choice is no choice," Reatur said. "Either way, my line fails. I will defend it, as long as I may."

"Thank you, clanfather," Ternat said quietly. Then his voice turned savage. "Shall I now deal with this—this clankiller as he deserves?" He moved to put himself between Fralk and the one exit.

The Skarmer envoy went blue again. "The penalty I told you of will fall on you if I come to harm here," he gabbled.

"From what you say, it will fall anyhow," Ternat said. "So how are we worse off for punishing your filthy words?"

"Let him go, eldest," Reatur said. "Shall we make ourselves into hunting-undit, as the Skarmer seem to be?" He turned all his eyestalks away from Fralk, denying that the young male deserved to exist. Still speaking to Ternat, the domain-master went on. "If ever he shows himself on our side of the gorge again, it will be the worse for him. Now take him out and send him on his way."

"As you say, clanfather." That was as close to criticism as Ternat would let himself come. He escorted Fralk out of the little chamber; Reatur still kept his eyes averted from the Skarmer male. Ternat was a good eldest, the domain-master thought. Unlike so many, he did not stand around waiting for his father to die or, as also happened sometimes, try to speed the process along. A good eldest, Reatur thought again.

The domain-master walked slowly back into the great hall. Ternat soon returned. Some of his hands still had claws out. Reatur guessed that he had not been gentle in escorting Fralk away. He did not blame him for that.

"What now, clanfather?" Ternat asked.

"I don't know." The admission made Reatur unhappy. "None of my eyes sees any way the Skarmer could make Fralk's boasts good. Is it the same with you?"

"Yes. But he would not have been here boasting if they did not have something. War across a Great Gorge . . ." Ternat's eyestalks wiggled in disgust.

Reatur felt the same way. Wars against neighboring domains were rarely pushed to extremes. In the end, after all, everyone hereabouts sprang from the first Omalo bud. But the Skarmer would care nothing for that, would be aiming to plant their own buds on the local mates—Fralk, curse him, had come right out and said as much.

"We will have to set a watch on the gorge," Ternat said.

"Hmm? Oh, yes, eldest." Lost in gloomy musings, Reatur had almost missed Ternat's words. The domain-master's wits started moving again. "See to that at once. And I suppose we will have to send word to the rest of the Omalo domains, warning them of what may be happening. And if nothing does, what a laughingstock I'll be."

He paused. "I wonder if that isn't the purpose of this whole affair, to split me off from the rest of the domains and leave me alone vulnerable to the Skarmer." He hissed. "I dare not take the chance, do I?"

"Clanfather, the answer must come from you."

Reatur knew his eldest was right. So long as Ternat was in his power, the younger male had, and could have, no responsibility of his own. The domain-master's six arms had to bear that burden alone. "Send the messengers," he decided. "Better to be ready for a danger that does not come than off our guard to one that does. You tend to it, in my name."

"In your name, clanfather," Ternat agreed proudly. He hurried off.

Reatur started to follow, then changed his mind. Instead, he walked down the corridor to the mates' chambers. As they always did, they cried out with joy when he opened the door; they never failed to be delighted to see him. "Reatur!" they shouted. "Hello, Reatur!" "Look what we're doing!"

"Hello, Lamra, Morna, Peri, Numar," he said, patting each one of them in turn. He did not stop until he had named and caressed them all; he made a point of remembering their names. Unlike some clanfathers, he treated mates as people, as much as he could. They could not help it that the sardonic saying "as likely as an old mate" meant something that would never happen. They had a directness of their own, a beautiful openness males outgrew too soon.

"Look, Reatur, look what I did!" Numar proudly showed him some scribbles she had made with a soft, crumbly red stone on a piece of cured hide.

"That's very good," he said gravely.

"It looks just like Morna," Numar said.

"It certainly does," he agreed with a certain amount of relief:

now he would not have to ask what the marks were supposed to be. Numar might have told him, or she might have had a tantrum. He did not feel like coping with a tantrum at the moment. He wanted the mates to be their usual happy selves, to salve his anger and worry after the encounter with Fralk.

The mates were exactly as he wished them to be, and even that did not help. "See how big Biyal's buds are getting, Reatur," Lamra exclaimed.

Biyal stepped up to show the domain-master the six bulges that ringed her body, one not far above each foot. "I wonder which is the male," she said.

"So do I," Reatur said gently.

"I want to have buds," Lamra said.

"I know you do, Lamra." In spite of himself, Reatur felt worse instead of better. He knew that Biyal's buds would break free of her when they were ripe, and that she would die when that happened. She knew it, too, and so did Lamra, but it meant nothing to them. They were too young. That was the one consolation of the life of a mate. Now, to Reatur, it did not seem enough.

"I want to have buds," Lamra repeated. "Reatur, I want to have buds right now."

"I know, Lamra." The domain-master let the air hiss out through his breathing-pores. "Come here." She squealed with glee and came. They pressed together. The other mates cheered them on. In a part of his mind, the cheering made Reatur sadder, but the exquisite sensations running through his body pushed the sadness far away.

"Roger, Houston, we are set for coded transmission, as ordered," Emmett Bragg said. He clicked off the transmitter and looked around the *Athena*'s cabin. "First codes they've sent us since we got here," he remarked. He sounded casual, but even without weightlessness the words would have hung in the air.

Irv Levitt asked the obvious question. "What are they telling us that they don't want the Russians to hear about?"

"Secrets." His wife Sarah spoke the word as if it were obscene. She pointed to Minerva rolling by on the monitor. "That's the enemy, not the people on *Tsiolkovsky*. Compared to whatever's down there, the Russians are our next of kin."

She sounded absolutely certain. She usually did, her husband thought. A lot of MDs he knew were like that—they needed arrogant confidence to deal with their patients' problems, and it spilled over into everything else they did.

Bragg only shrugged. "Secret is what they ordered, Sarah. Secret is what they'll get." He glanced over at Sarah Levitt; in his quieter way, he was at least as stubborn as she was. His voice, though, stayed mild. "I expect that's why they handed the mission commander's chair to somebody like me. I've been a soldier a long time—I can take orders, not just give 'em."

Irv saw a dark flush rise to Sarah's cheeks, saw her purse her lips for an angry retort. Before she could get it out, Louise Bragg spoke. "Suppose we see what they sent us before we get ourselves all in an uproar."

"Sensible," her husband said. Sarah nodded a moment later, her short, curly brown hair fanning out around her face at the motion.

"Good," Louise said. She was a large, calm, blond woman, about fifteen years younger than Emmett.

Irv remembered that she was Bragg's second wife; they had not been married long when the selection process for *Athena* began. Would Emmett Bragg have dumped his ex and gone after an engineer to help himself get picked? Absolutely, Irv thought. That didn't mean they didn't care for each other. Had they not, the ship was too cramped to hide it.

Speed of light to Houston, time to react there, speed of light back. A quarter of an hour went by before the message came in. Bragg transcribed the code groups, one by one, and taped them so he would have a backup. "Roger, Houston, we copy," he said when the transmission was done.

He unstrapped himself. "Excuse me, folks," he said, and pushed himself out of the cabin and down the passageway toward his compartment. Irv saw him pull a key from a pocket on his coveralls. The cubicle he shared with Louise, unlike the other two, had a locked drawer.

Louise did not have a key for it. Once she had asked her husband what was in there. He had grinned a lopsided grin and replied, "My girlfriend." Nobody had asked since. Now they had at least part of the answer.

"I hate having someone else in charge of my fate this way," Sarah said.

"Now you know how patients feel," Irv told her. She glanced sharply at him, then gave a rueful nod.

Free-fall was relaxing anyhow, after the nausea went away, and Louise Bragg contrived to look almost boneless as she stretched herself in midair. "When there's nothing to do but wait," she said, "you might as well be comfortable."

They waited. After a while, Irv pulled a folding chess set with magnetic pieces out of his hip pocket. He opened it up, then shook his head. Two pawns was too far to be down to Sargon; the computer program was going to clean his clock again. He knew he ought to resign and have another try. He knew he was too stubborn to do it. He tried a knight move, thought better of it, and put the piece back.

He was still tinkering and not getting anywhere much when he heard Emmett call, "Pat, Frank, come forward for a bit, if you could."

A moment later, Bragg came gliding into the cabin. He stopped himself on the back of his chair. Within a minute, Pat and Frank Marquard had joined everyone else in the cabin.

"What's up, Emmett?" Frank asked. He sounded casual, but his expression belied his tone. He and Pat both could tell something was up: Bragg had the veteran officer's knack for turning ordinary words into an unmistakable order.

The mission commander glanced down at the sheet of scratch paper in his hand. He was also holding, Irv saw, a map of Minerva compiled from *Mariner* and *Viking* photos. "Interesting," was all he said.

Louise would not let him get by with that. "Come on, Emmett, out with it," she told him. "Suspense isn't funny."

"All right," he said, a little sheepishly. He held up the map. "We've all known since '76 where *Viking* landed, haven't we? Here." He pointed.

"Not far west of the Jötun Canyon, sure," Irv said. Everyone else nodded.

"Not sure. They've just done a pile of new computer work on the *Viking* data, and it turns out the lander actually came down *here*, about fifty miles east of where they thought. We'll have to adjust our landing site to conform to the new data. Louise, honey, it'll mean more time on the computer for you—sorry."

"I expect I'll manage," she said, which for a minute or so was the only break in the silence that followed her husband's announcement.

"How very—convenient," Sarah Levitt said at last. "Now we know, and the Russians don't." Both missions had intended to land as close to the *Viking* touchdown point as possible; only there could they be sure they would find intelligent life.

"There might be *anything* on the other side of that canyon," Irv said. Pat Marquard nodded vigorously. He knew they were thinking along the same lines. Minerva's big canyons were wider and deeper than anything Earth knew; each spring they carried meltwater from the south polar cap to the seas and lakes of the southern tropics—though on Minerva the word "tropics" had a strictly geographic meaning. The great gorges had to be formidable barriers to both ideas and genes.

"I reckon the Russians will tell us, same as we'll tell them what we come across on our side," Emmett Bragg said. His drawl had gotten thicker. That happened, Irv had noticed, when Bragg did not want to come out with everything that was on his mind.

"I think we ought to pass the word on to *Tsiolkovsky*," Sarah said.

Bragg raised an eyebrow. "If Houston had wanted *Tsiolkovsky* to know, they wouldn't have coded the information before they sent it." He sounded as though that closed the subject for him and expected it to for everyone else.

It didn't. "Houston is on Earth, umpty-ump million miles from here. The Russians are right here with us," Sarah said. "Right now, I have more in common with them than with a pack of chair-warmers back in Texas."

"Really," Frank Marquard agreed. "Is there intelligent life in Houston?"

"I think they're right, Emmett," Irv said. "This is going to be tough enough, even sharing what we have. It's too big for us not to." He spoke with some hesitation. He was anything but combative and did not relish the idea of getting into a shouting match when the mission commander blew a fuse.

But Bragg surprised him. Instead of losing his temper, or even pretending to for effect, he looked over at his wife and asked, "Honey, how many coded transmissions has *Tsiolkovsky* received since we assumed Minerva orbit?"

"Let me see." She fiddled with the computer. "At least twenty-nine, plus however many they got when we were on the far side of the planet and couldn't monitor them."

"How many of those have they shared with us?"

Louise did not have to check that. "Next one will be the first."

"Oh, but that's the Russians, though. That's just the way they—" Pat Marquard stumbled to a halt as she realized where her words were taking her. "—do things," she finished lamely.

Irv shook his head. Bragg couldn't have had that turn out better for him if he had planned it for weeks. And now the commander took the advantage, saying, "If you all"—he carefully made it two words—"think I'm not sorry to put some distance between *Tsiolkovsky* and us, I won't say you're wrong. Minerva's a big place. Why rub elbows with the Russians when we don't have to?"

"What if we end up needing something they have and we don't, or the other way round?" Sarah had not given up.

"Canyon or no canyon, we won't be that far from them," Bragg said. "If anybody needs anything that bad, he can holler for it."

"What if we need a ride home?" Sarah asked softly.

Frank Marquard winced; Irv felt himself doing the same thing. But Bragg said flatly, "Anybody who needs a ride home is dead, unless he can make it on Minerva until another expedition comes along. *Athena*'s life-support won't take more than six people home, and neither will *Tsiolkovsky*'s. For that, folks, we are on our own. We'd all best remember it, too."

The words hit home. Irv had lived on *Athena* long enough to have grown used to it, as he would have to, to, say, an apartment. Being reminded of how fragile a place it was hurt.

But *Tsiolkovsky* was just as fragile. "So the territory *Viking* saw was really on the east side of Jötun Canyon, then, not the west?" Irv asked. At Bragg's nod, the anthropologist went on. "What is the west side like, then? Are the Russians going to try to fly *Tsiolkovsky* down into badlands? If they are, I say we call them, and the hell with Houston. I wouldn't do that to anybody."

Bragg frowned, but then his face cleared as he thought it over. "That's fair," he said. "We'll find out." He folded the map and stuck it into a breast pocket of his coveralls. It was not nearly detailed enough to show him what he needed. He pulled the NASA *Photographic Atlas of Minerva* off a shelf; the Velcro that held the book in place let go with a scratchy sound of protest.

The mission commander riffled through the pages till he found the plate he needed. He held the book open. Five heads craned toward it. "Looks to be flatland and low hills, same as we'll be landing in. None of the miles and miles of scree and boulders you see around the edges of the polar caps, and no big erosion features. They aren't taking any worse chances than we are."

Frank Marquard studied the photo with a professionally appraising glance. When he said, "He's right," Irv knew that any chance to overturn Bragg's decision was gone.

So did his wife. "All right, Emmett," Sarah said. "But if they don't trust us once we're all down on Minerva, they'll have reason now."

"They don't trust us now," Bragg answered. "And you know what? I don't trust them, either. That's all right. The best way to deal with 'em is to keep one hand on your wallet. That way you never lose track of where it is."

Sarah snorted. The Marquards went back to the labs in the rear section of *Athena* to return to whatever they had been doing. And when Tolmasov called from the *Tsiolkovsky*, nobody said anything about code groups.

When she and her husband were in the almost privacy of their cubicle, though, Sarah Levitt said, "I still don't like it, Irv. Not just that we didn't tell the Russians, but that word about the changed coordinates came through today the way it did. It just seems too pat somehow."

"I know what you mean," he said. "That bothers me, too. It's almost as if Houston's known all along that the coordinates they gave out to everybody weren't the right ones, and just decided now to let us in on it."

He had meant the words as a joke, but once out they had an appalling ring of probability to them. He felt Sarah's slim frame stiffen. "I wish you hadn't said that," she told him. "I don't—want to believe it."

"Likely it isn't true," he said, though he doubted that himself.

"Give me one good reason why not." Sarah's tone said she did not believe he could come up with one.

But he did. "When was the last time the United States was able to hang on to a secret for thirteen years?"

"A point," she admitted at last. "Not a very consoling one, but a point. You pick the oddest ways to make me feel better."

"Did you have something else in mind?" he asked hopefully.

"No," she said after a small pause. "I'm tired, I'm grouchy, I wouldn't enjoy it much now, and I don't think I could make it much fun for you."

"You're very annoying when you make sense, you know," he said. That coaxed a small, almost reluctant laugh from her, but she went to sleep all the same. After a while, so did Irv.

* * *

Oleg Lopatin's face, Tolmasov thought unkindly, was made for frowning. Those eyebrows—the colonel still thought of them as Brezhnev brows, though the Chairman was seven years dead and thoroughly discredited—came down like clouds covering the sun.

"You should have asked the Americans about the coded message," Lopatin said.

"I did not see how I could, Oleg Borisovich. They have never asked us about any we receive. And besides," Tolmasov added, unconsciously echoing Emmett Bragg, "I did not think they would tell us. They would have sent it in clear if they did not care whether we heard it."

"You should have asked them, anyway," Valery Bryusov said.

"Why do you say that, Valery Aleksandrovich?" Tolmasov asked, more sharply than he had intended. The linguist did not usually speak up for Lopatin. If he did, he probably had a good reason. Tolmasov wondered if he had missed something.

Bryusov tugged at his mustache. The gesture had become a habit of his in the months since he had let it grow. It was red-blond with a few white hairs, a startling contrast to the hair on his head, which was about the color of Tolmasov's.

He tugged again, then said, "We send things in code because it is our habit to send things in code. Even Oleg Borisovich will agree, I think, that it would not matter much if the Americans found out what was in a good many of them."

Lopatin's frown got deeper. "I suppose that may be true in a few cases," he admitted grudgingly. Tolmasov knew it was true. He was a trifle surprised the KGB man did, too. Lopatin went on, "What of it, though?"

"The crew of *Athena* must know that, too," Bryusov said, ticking off the point on his finger like the academician he was. "They must have studied us as we studied them. They, though, boast of how open—to say nothing of prodigal—they are with information. If they send in code, then, it must be something unusual and important, and so worth asking about."

"You may have something at that," Tolmasov said. "Let me think it over; perhaps next time we talk with *Athena* I will put the question to Bragg. Hearing what he says could be interesting, I suppose." .

"My congratulations, Valery Aleksandrovich," Shota Rustaveli said. "Even a theologian would be proud of reasoning that convoluted. Here it may even have reached the truth, always an unexpected bonus."

"Thank you so very much, Shota Mikheilovich," Bryusov said.

"Always a privilege to assist such a distinguished scholar," Rustaveli replied, dark eyes twinkling. Bryusov scowled and floated off to find something to do elsewhere. Tolmasov smiled at his retreating back. If he didn't know better by this time than to get into a duel of ironies with the Georgian biologist, it was nobody's fault but his own.

"You would talk with the Americans, too, then, Shota Mikheilovich, and try to find out what Houston sent them?" Lopatin asked.

"Oh, not me. They find my English even worse than you do my Russian." Rustaveli deliberately exaggerated his slight accent. He hung in midair, upside down relative to Lopatin and Tolmasov. It did not seem to bother him at all.

"Will you ever be serious?" Lopatin growled.

"I doubt it." Whistling, Rustaveli sailed down the corridor after Bryusov.

"Georgians," Lopatin said softly.

"He's good at what he does." Tolmasov meant it as a reproof, but was not sure it came out that way. Down deep, he thought the KGB man had a point. Rustaveli was the only non-Russian on *Tsiolkovsky*. Everyone else found him indolent and mercurial, very much the stereotypical man of the south. He found them stodgy and did not try to hide it.

"Let us see how well he does in Minervan weather," Lopatin said. "Him and the Americans both." He chuckled nastily and mimed a shiver.

Tolmasov nodded. After Smolensk, no winter held much in the way of terror for him.

But Rustaveli had come back. "About the Americans I do not know, Oleg Borisovich," he said, exquisitely polite as always, "but I will do well enough. If I should have trouble, perhaps Katerina will keep me warm."

It was Tolmasov's turn to frown. Russians credited Georgians with legendary success with women. Shota did nothing to downplay the legend, and even though he and the doctor had quarreled, the way her eyes followed him made Tolmasov wish she looked at him like that. She gave herself to Tolmasov these days, and he was sure she enjoyed what they did together. Still, somehow it was not the same.

"Is your boasting all you want to tell us?" the pilot asked

stiffly. "We have more important things to do than listening to it."

"No, no, Sergei Konstantinovich." Rustaveli sounded wounded. "I just wanted to remind you that the odds are it will not matter in the long run whether you talk with *Athena* or not."

"And why not?" Tolmasov fought for patience. Maybe, once Rustaveli got the jokes out of his system, he would settle down for a while.

For the moment, the Georgian did not seem to be joking. "Because, very probably, Moscow has the code broken and will send us what it says."

"Hmm." Tolmasov and Lopatin looked at each other. "Something to that," the KGB man said after a brief hesitation—even here, so many kilometers from home, he wondered who might be listening.

"I am glad you think so, Oleg Borisovich," Rustaveli said. He lifted a finger, as if suddenly reminded of something. "I almost forgot—Yuri wants to see you."

"Me? Why?" Lopatin sounded suspicious, but only a little. Yuri Ivanovich Voroshilov spent as much time as he could in his laboratory. The chemist, Tolmasov thought, found things easier to deal with than people. It was quite in character for him to treat Rustaveli as nothing more than a biped carrier pigeon.

Smiling, the Georgian sank his barb. "He's all out of ice, and wants to borrow your heart for a few minutes."

"Why, you—" Lopatin grabbed for the buckle of the safety harness that held him in his seat.

Tolmasov brought his hand down on top of the KGB man's. "No brawling," he snapped. Lopatin kept struggling for a few seconds to open the harness, then subsided. Tolmasov turned his glare on Rustaveli. "I will log this incident. You are reprimanded. There will be no repetitions."

"Yes, Comrade Colonel." Rustaveli clicked his heels, a gesture only ludicrous in free-fall. "Reprimand all you like. But it means nothing."

"You will think differently when you get back to Earth," Tolmasov ground out. "Are you a mutineer?" He was a military man; he could not think of anything worse to call Rustaveli.

"No, merely practical," the biologist answered, quite unruffled. "If we get back to Earth, I will be a Hero of the Soviet Union, reprimand or no. If we don't, the reprimand certainly will not matter to me. Truly, Sergei Konstantinovich, you should think things through more carefully."

The colonel gaped at him. The worst of it was that Rustaveli even made a twisted kind of sense.

"There, there," the Georgian said, seeing his pop-eyed expression. "To please you, I will even accept the reprimand—provided you also log the KGB man, for mocking my people."

Lopatin let out a scornful laugh. He knew how likely that was. So did Tolmasov. Under Mikhail Gorbachev, the KGB might have been made to answer for misconduct. Too bad Gorbachev had only lasted nine months. Tolmasov still wondered if his cerebral hemorrhage had been of the 5.54mm variety.

"You've talked yourself out of your bloody reprimand," the colonel told Rustaveli. "I hope you're satisfied. Now go away."

Grinning, the biologist sailed off.

The male shoved Fralk toward the bridge. "Go on," he said harshly. "Never let us see you on this side again."

See me you shall, Fralk said, but only to himself. He stepped out onto the cables of the bridge.

"Once you are across, we will cut it," the male told him. "If you do not hurry, we will not bother to wait."

Fralk hurried. His toes wrapped around the lower rope; his fingerclaws gripped the upper one. He walked out over empty space. On the eastern side of the gorge, the one he was leaving, the males of Reatur's clan grew smaller.

The western side, though, the lands of the Skarmer clans, did not seem any closer. Even down close to its bottom, the gorge was too wide to yield him sight of progress so soon. And with one wall visibly receding while the other appeared fixed in place, Fralk had the eerie feeling that the canyon was stretching itself like a live thing as he traveled, that he might never reach the far side.

The wind whistled around, above, below. Over the heart of the gorge, Fralk let an eyestalk turn downward, and another up. The other four, as usual, looked all about. Only the thin lines of the rope bridge, extending in the direction he had come and toward his destination, gave his vision a clue he was not a mote suspended in the center of infinite space.

The sensation was so daunting that he stopped, forgetting the male's threat. If the gorge were infinitely wide, how could movement matter? He looked down and down and down, to the boulders far, far below. For a giddy moment, he thought they were calling to him. If he let go of the ropes, for how long would he fall?

That reminded him he might indeed fall, regardless of whether he let go. The Omalo males would know how long someone took to cross the bridge and surely would allow him no excess time, not when they knew he and his wanted to supplant them. Telling that to Reatur had perhaps been less than wise. But then, Fralk had reckoned there was a fair chance the domain-master would yield. How little folk on one side of a gorge understood those on the other!

Fralk hurried onward. Every tremor of the bridge in the wind set him to quivering with fright, thinking he was about to be pitched into the abyss.

At last the far side of the gorge began to appear closer, while the one from which he had come seemed frozen and distant in space: the reverse of the stretching he had nervously imagined before. The males he could see were his own solid Skarmer budmates, not scrawny easterners.

They helped pull him off the bridge and clustered around him. "What word, eldest of eldest?" called Niress, the commander of the crossing.

Fralk gave it to him: "War." A moment later, as if to underscore it, the bridge jerked like a male who had just touched a stunbush. Then, like that same imaginary male a moment later, it went limp and hung down into the gorge. Fralk feared its stone supports would give way now that it was not attached to anything on the far side, but they held.

Niress's eyestalks wriggled with mirth. "As if cutting the bridge will stop us," he said. He and Fralk began the long climb up to the top of the gorge.

2

The red numbers on the digital readout spun silently down to zero. "Initiate separation sequence," Emmett Bragg said.

"Initiating." His wife flipped a toggle.

Strapped in his seat, Irv Levitt heard distant metallic bangs and rattles different from the ones he no longer consciously noticed. After a while, Louise said, "Separation sequence complete."

We're on our own, Irv thought. As if to emphasize the point, *Athena*'s monitor gave him an image of the rocket motor package that had accompanied the ship to Minerva. While he watched, the motors slowly grew smaller as they drifted away. They would wait in orbit while the hypersonic transport that was *Athena* proper went down to the planet and—if everything worked exactly right—returned to rejoin them for the trip back to Earth.

He glanced over at his wife, whose seat was next to his in the cabin. Sarah's answering smile was forced. "Just another flight to a new research lab," he said, trying to cheer her by coming out with the most ridiculous thing he could think of.

"I hate them all," she said. "I don't like being in any situation where I don't have full control of things, and I can't do that in an airliner—or here," she added pointedly. "Once we're down, I'll be all right."

He nodded. A lot of doctors he knew felt that way, some of them much more than Sarah. That was, he supposed, why so many of them flew their own planes. He smiled. Sarah would get her chance at that.

The radio crackled to life. "Tolmasov here. Good luck, *Athena*."

"Thank you, Sergei Konstantinovich," Bragg said. "The same to you and *Tsiolkovsky*. Give our regards to Comrade Reguspatoff."

"To whom?" Puzzlement crept into the Russian colonel's precise voice.

"Nichevo," Bragg replied. "It doesn't matter."

"As you wish," Tolmasov said: an oral shrug. "We will see you on the ground, then. We also are about to uncouple."

"Expected as much," Bragg said. "We'll both be busy for a while, so I'll say good-bye now. *Athena* out." He cut the transmission.

"Reguspatoff?" Frank Marquard asked. He made a good straight man.

"Registered—U.S. Patent Office," Bragg explained with a grin that looked more like a wolf's lolling-tongued laugh than any gentler mirth. "Or do you think *Tsiolkovsky* looks so much like *Athena* just by accident?"

"It's bigger," Frank said. "Why don't we copy their rockets?"

"I wish we would," Bragg said. "Well, we do what we can with what we've got. Not too bad, I suppose: we'll be down ahead of them."

His wife broke in. "Or maybe we won't. Radar shows two images from *Tsiolkovsky*. I'd say that means they *have* uncoupled from their engine pack."

The mission commander's head jerked toward the screen. *"Son* of a bitch," he said softly. He picked up the mike, punched the TRANSMIT button, and started speaking Russian. *"Athena* to *Tsiolkovsky*."

"Tsiolkovsky here: Lopatin." The engineer's English was accented but easy to follow.

"Tell your boss he's a sandbagging bastard."

"Sandbagging? I do not understand this word," Lopatin said; Bragg had left it in his own language. A moment later, Colonel Tolmasov came on. He sounded like a man fighting laughter. "I do, Emmett. That is uncultured."

"You should talk."

"You will excuse me if I lack time for casual conversation, Brigadier. We are, as you said, rather busy at the moment. *Tsiolkovsky* out."

Growling, Bragg killed the circuit. Before he could ask her, Louise said, "Coming up on three minutes . . . mark."

"Damnation!" Bragg seldom swore; Irv could not remember his doing so twice in the space of a couple of minutes. The pilot twisted in his seat as if it were a cage and his shoulder harness bars.

Seconds crawled by on hands and knees. They had been going by slowly enough already, but watching Bragg writhe made Irv wonder if time itself was holding its breath. The last time he had felt that way, he had been walking up the aisle toward Sarah and the rabbi.

"One minute . . . thirty seconds . . . " Somehow, Louise Bragg's words kept coming out at normal speed, no matter how much everything else was slowed down. Irv wondered how she managed that. Then she was going, "Two . . . one . . . ignition."

"Ignition!" her husband said savagely. He stabbed at the button. The engines came to life, kicking *Athena* out of orbit and down tail-first toward the world waiting below.

"Kicking" was the word, Irv thought. He gasped for breath, fighting against the gorilla that seemed to have landed on his chest. After so long without weight, having it back was anything but welcome.

"Have the Russians started their burn?" Bragg asked. He sounded the same as always, Irv noticed a little resentfully.

"Yes." His wife had to work to get the word out.

"Just have to really fly this baby, then," Bragg muttered. He worked the attitude controls.

"You put the tail up too high for optimum reentry," Louise said. "We'll build up extra heat."

"We'll get down faster, though. I'll watch the skin temp, don't worry."

"So will I, don't worry," his wife answered. The effort she needed to talk made her sound even grimmer than she would have otherwise.

Sarah glanced over at Irv. "Hell of a time for Emmett to play like he's Richard Petty," she said. Irv admired her for trying to joke, but saw the worry in her eyes. He was surprised to find how relaxed he was, in spite of his discomfort. Bragg had flown against MiG-17s and glide-landed a shuttle twice. Compared to flying like that, getting *Athena* down should be a piece of cake.

Unless something goes wrong, a small voice said inside his head. Shut up, he told it. To his relief, it did.

"Temperature is up a little," Louise said. "We're starting to get into the atmosphere."

Her husband glanced at the gauge, then at the radar altimeter. "Still well inside specs. The carbon-fiber matrix can take more than shuttle tiles, and having a machine with a skin all in one piece means we don't need to worry about spending our Minerva time gluing those little suckers back into place."

Now there, Irv thought, was a really alarming notion.

A thin whistle began to fill the cabin and rose toward a shriek. "I thought by now I knew every noise *Athena* could make," Pat Marquard said nervously.

"It isn't *Athena*," Frank answered. "It's Minerva—the wind of our passage." His voice held awe. Irv understood why. No one but they—and half a dozen Russians, some unknown number of miles away—had heard the wind of another world.

His wife thought of something else. "I wonder what the Minervans will make of our noise coming down."

"When the shuttles landed at Edwards, we'd hear the boom in L.A.," Pat said. "And that's without the noise from the ramjet and turbojet sections of our motor."

Emmett Bragg chuckled. "They'll be hiding under their beds, if they have beds. And speaking of ramjets—" He checked the altimeter again and *Athena*'s velocity. "We're low enough and slow enough to fire it up and save our liquid oxygen for the trip back up. I'm shutting down the lox pump, Louise."

"Acknowledged," she said. A moment later, she added, "First time I ever heard Mach six called slow."

"Next to what we've been doing, honey, it's just a mosey in the park."

Irv sided with Louise. Mach six was no mosey, so far as he was concerned. Despite aggressive soundproofing, the noise was up, too. The pump was no longer thumping and clacking away, but the shriek of Minervan air coming in through the ramjet inlet more than made up for that. It reminded Irv of a dentist's drill the size of Baltimore. His teeth cringed at the very idea.

His seat was padded and contoured, but he still felt as though he weighed tons. "Are we really sure Minerva's gravity is only a couple of percent higher than ours?" he asked plaintively. "Or are we still decelerating?"

"Yes, we're sure and yes, we are," Emmett replied, but before Irv had a chance to be relieved, the mission commander went on. "But not enough to do anything about our weight." He sounded amused.

Irv groaned. So did Frank.

Sarah felt strong enough to raise an arm and point to the monitor. "We just passed something big. A castle, a temple, a barracks—"

"Could be anything," Irv agreed. "I wish we knew more about where the Minervans are technologically. They don't have atomic energy and they don't have radio, but there's a lot of difference between where we were in 2000 B.C. and in 1890."

"Or in 22,000 B.C.," Emmett put in. He enjoyed sticking pins in people to make them jump.

This time it didn't work. Irv had the facts to shoot him down. "No big buildings in 22,000 B.C.," he said smugly. Then he shut up as another whatever-it-was went by on the screen. Clouds blurred the view, but he still recognized the pattern on the ground surrounding the building. "Those are fields down there!"

"You're right," Pat said. "You see those grooved circles in the middle of nowhere when you fly over irrigated farms in desert country."

"But the lines—plow marks, would those be, Irv?" Sarah said.

"On Earth, sure. Here, who knows?" he answered.

"The lines aren't straight," she observed. "What does that mean?"

"Maybe contour plowing. Maybe the Minervans don't know what straight lines are. That's what we're here to find out."

Emmett said, "Yeah!" as *Athena* flew over a pair of volcanoes with glaciers snaking down from their peaks. "Those are Smaug and Ancalagon," he added. "Now I know where we are. We need to head just a touch further east." He made the adjustment.

They flew lower and lower, slower and slower. As they dropped below 45,000 feet and Mach one, Emmett cut in the turbines. The engines went from a shriek to a full-throated roar. "This is your pilot speaking," Bragg said. "Thank you for flying Minerva Air. The cabin attendants will be starting the movie shortly. Please keep your seat belts fastened."

"*Athena* does sound just like a 747 now, doesn't she?" Irv said; the mission commander's deadpan, dead perfect delivery made him realize consciously what he had been feeling in his bones. Not even a first-class seat on a big jet, though, had the padding and room this one did. On the other hand, airline passengers didn't need so much, either.

"How's she handle, Emmett?" Frank asked. He had flown

light planes before he went into astronaut training, and T-38 jet trainers since. If anything happened to Bragg, he would try to get *Athena* home. Neither he nor anyone else relished the prospect.

Bragg thought for a moment before he answered. "Depends on what you're comparing it to. It's no fighter, but it's a long way from being a mildly aerodynamic brick like the shuttle, too."

"More like fun, or more like work?" Marquard persisted.

"In space it's fun. Here it's work, but not pick-and-shovel work. White collar, you might say. I'm not really dressed for it." Grinning, he ran his hand down the front of the blue NASA coverall.

"Where's *Tsiolkovsky*?" Pat asked.

Louise Bragg checked the radar. "Well west of us, and a couple of miles higher."

Everyone in the cabin whooped—none of them wanted the Russians to beat them down. "In Baikonur our name is cursed, when they find out we landed first!" Irv sang, mangling Tom Lehrer in a good cause.

"I wonder what they think of our bearing," Louise said. "Why aren't they calling to ask us about it?"

"They figure we screwed up," her husband guessed. "Tolmasov's just gonna let us. Sitting in his chair, I'd do the exact same thing."

Sarah was still watching the monitor. She gasped. "Will you *look* at that?" Other gasps followed shortly.

Irv had seen plenty of pictures of Jötun Canyon taken from space. He had flown over the Grand Canyon half a dozen times. Neither did anything to prepare him for what he was seeing. Jötun Canyon was a great gouge on the face of the world. Three miles deep, a dozen miles across, even at jet speeds it took a minute and a half to cross.

"That's my spot," Frank declared. "Just start me at the edge, give me plenty of rope, and let me work my way down. If Jötun doesn't cut through a billion and a half years of stratigraphy, I'll eat my hat."

Bragg flew *Athena* south along the eastern rim of the canyon. "We swing inland when it jogs southwest," he said. "Then we start looking for a place to set down." He laughed a couple of syllables' worth of laugh. "After the shuttle, that looking-around time is a luxury."

They were down very low now, low enough to see individual

trees—if those tall, dark green, stationary things were trees—in the forests. Snow clung to them, though summer was about to start.

The canyon changed direction. Bragg flew *Athena* away from it. In a couple of minutes, he flew over some little rolling hills. Seeing them made Irv sit up, even against gravity's new and unpleasant grip. He was not the only one who recognized them. "That's where *Viking* set down!" Pat exclaimed.

"Sure does look that way," Bragg agreed. He flew on. Before long, he flew over another one of the large buildings and the fields that surrounded it. "Hate to rip a half-mile track in a fellow's crop," he said, "but I don't think we're gonna do any better. Anybody really want to try talking me out of it?"

Irv thought about it, but in the end he didn't. *Athena*, he hoped, would be strange enough—and big enough—to win the humans the benefit of the doubt. Nobody else said anything, either.

"All right," Bragg said. "I'm gonna do it. Let's go around for one more pass to kill some speed and get nice and lined up, and then we land."

Athena was so close to the ground that on the monitor Irv saw things moving around down there. Things . . . He felt the hair on his arms and the back of his neck tingle as the realization hit him. Those were not *things*. Those were *Minervans*.

"Altitude 500 feet, speed 320," Louise said as her husband swung *Athena* down. "Three hundred feet, speed 300 . . . 200 feet, speed 290."

"Arming the landing gear," Emmett said. He lifted the switch's cover, pushed it to the ON position.

Louise's reading never paused. "A hundred fifty feet, speed 260 . . ."

"Deploying landing gear." Emmett uncovered and pushed the switch next to the one he had just hit. *Athena* really seemed a plane to Irv now; the noises and bumps as the wheels came down were the same as the ones he knew from Delta jets.

"Ninety feet, speed 240 . . ."

"Landing gear down and locked." Bragg hesitated, then bared his teeth in what was almost a smile. "We owe the Russians this one—the undercarriage is borrowed from the Ilyushin Il-76. There's no better big plane in the world for getting in and out of unpaved fields."

"Fifty feet, speed 230 . . . 20 feet, speed 220 . . ."

There was a jar. "Down! Hot damn, we're down!" Bragg

said exultantly. "Wheels locked," he added a moment later. He reached out with his left hand and slammed the speed brake all the way forward.

"I hope you have something more historic than, 'Hot damn, we're down!' planned for when we step outside," Sarah remarked as they bounced along the ground.

"Did I say that?" Bragg sounded amazed.

So was Irv, at how gentle the landing was. He had experienced bumpier ones at Dulles. "Let's hear it for Russian undercarriages," he said.

They rolled to a stop. Pat was looking at an instrument cluster that had not had much to do since it was installed. "Temperature 39 degrees, humidity 48 percent, wind out of the south at . . . six knots. A lovely almost-summer day," she finished.

"If you're an ice cube," Irv said.

Emmett Bragg was on the radio. "Houston, this is *Athena*. We contacted the surface of Minerva at 2:46:35 P.M. Landing extremely nominal. Baby, it's cold outside. *Athena* out."

He got up and walked back to a panel just aft of the cabin. He might have been on parade; he conceded nothing to so many months of free-fall. Irv watched admiringly. Soon enough, he would have to start walking, too. He was in no hurry about it.

Like the meteorology package, the panel Bragg opened had not been important while *Athena* was in space. Now it was. The mission commander started taking out parkas, snow pants, boots, headgear . . . and pistols and ammunition pouches.

"Just in case," he said, holding them up. "Time to go meet the natives."

The scream in the sky faded a little—enough to let Reatur hear other screams in the castle. The mates and new-budded males were making an unholy racket. So were a good many adults. Reatur did not blame them. Were he without a domain-master's dignity to uphold, he would have screamed himself.

The first thud had slapped against the walls like a boulder of ice. When everything jumped, Reatur's first thought was, *quake!* He took an instinctive step toward the doorway, while his eye-stalks sprang upward to see if the roof was going to come down on him.

But only that one jolt came. "Funny kind of quake," he said out loud. He started to go on about his business, but then the roar started. Fear of a quake, at least, was a familiar kind of fear. The bellow overhead kept getting louder and shriller, until

Reatur wondered if it was the end of the world. He had not known how alarmed he was until he gauged his relief as the insane, impossible noise at last began to recede.

A male came running into the great hall. "Clanfather!" he cried. "There's a monster moving through the air, shrieking so that we're afraid to work."

"I don't blame you, Enoph," Reatur said, an understatement if ever there was one. "A monster, you say? What is it like?"

"Like—like—" Enoph tried twice, gave up. "Like nothing I've ever seen before, or heard. Horrible!"

Reatur pushed past him. Enoph was a sober and reliable male. If he could not describe the sky-monster, Reatur needed to turn his own eyestalks on it. As he neared the entrance, he snatched up a spear. He did not know what it could do against anything with a voice like that, but he had no better weapon.

It was warm outside, warm enough to melt ice, though very slowly. His spearhead was in no danger unless he stayed out for days. More males milled about in the courtyard, and others were heading toward the castle from the farther reaches of the fields.

The palace's thick walls had cut the din more than Reatur guessed; it smote him anew as he left their protection. "There!" males shouted, pointing east with two or three arms at once.

The domain-master let a pair of his eyestalks go that way. Sure enough, something was in the sky, a wedge-shaped something that looked to have no business in the domain of clouds and snow and sleet. It looked too small to be the source of the great noise, but that was undeniably coming from its direction.

To Reatur's mind, the best thing about it was that it was getting smaller. "Whatever it is, it doesn't seem to want to have anything to do with us," he said.

"That works both ways, clanfather," one of the males said. Everyone who heard waggled his eyestalks in a nervous laugh of agreement.

Afterward, Reatur often wondered if keeping his mouth shut would have averted what happened next. As it was, his words were hardly spoken when a male cried, "It's changing its path!"

Moments later, another said the worst thing any of them could think of: "It's coming back!"

The noise began to grow again. It tore at Reatur's hearing and left him almost too stunned to move. The monster drew closer and closer, dropping lower and lower in the sky. Legs came out of its belly. There was something worse to be said, after all. Enoph said it: "It's going to come down in our fields!"

Reatur had never seen legs like the monster's. They ended in clumps of fat, black, round things like no claws or sucker pads or hooves the domain-master knew. The deliberate way the legs descended from its belly was new to him, too . . . or was it? The arm that had come out of the strange thing had moved rather like that. Were they related?

He did *not* think the monster would be easy to kill as the strange thing had been. Too bad.

Dust and crops and a little drifted snow flew as the monster's legs touched the ground. Behind it, crops withered, as if it voided raw heat. Perhaps it did; even from some distance away, Reatur felt a lick of warm air as it went by the castle.

The monster moved ever more slowly. At last, not far from the edge of the cleared land, it came to a stop. The noise died. Reatur waited for the monster to notice him and his males—or at least his castle, the only thing nearby of a size to compare to it—and to approach. But it did nothing of the kind. It stayed where it was, as if waiting for him to come to it.

The domain-master wanted to run, to hide. He saw, though, that while half the eyestalks of his males were turned on the monster, the other half pointed toward him. These were his sons and sons of sons and sons of sons of sons. They were under his power and would be as long as he lived. A third son of a fifth son of a fourth son might dream of becoming clanfather and taking a clanfather's power one day and be safe in the dreaming, knowing it would never turn true. But Reatur knew he was as much in his males' power as they in his. What he wanted meant nothing here. He knew what he had to do.

"Let's go see what the cursed thing is," he said. He hefted his spear and started walking toward the—the thing, he told himself firmly. If he did not think of it as a monster, maybe it would turn out not to be one.

Pride flowed all the way out to the tips of his fingerclaws when he saw how many of his males followed him. Against an ordinary foe—even against the Skarmer males, curse them, if Fralk was not a liar since the moment he was budded—Reatur would have expected to find all his males coming after him. Here, though, he found he could not blame the few who hung back.

He muttered angrily as he came to the track of destruction the mon—no, the thing—had left behind. Its round feet made grooved tracks that pressed the ground down. How much did it weigh, to do that?

He looked at shriveled, sagging plant stems and muttered again. How much of his crop had he lost? Why did the monster have to choose him? Why not the Skarmer, who really deserved a monster's attention? Thinking of it as a thing was not working. He gave up.

"Shall I make a cast at it, clanfather?" a very young male asked.

"As long as it's content to just sit there, I'm willing to let it," Reatur said dryly. "What if you made it roar again?" He quivered at the very idea. At such close range, the noise would probably tear his eyestalks off. The youngster, who did not seem to have thought of that, lowered his spear in a hurry.

"Surround it," Reatur said. His males moved to obey. Unfortunately, they reminded him of so many little runnerpests trying to surround a nosver male. The monster's round feet alone were taller than any of his people.

Its size was not the only curious—no, more than curious, alien—thing about it. Every animal Reatur had ever seen was arranged the same way males and mates were, with limbs and appendages spaced evenly all around its body. The monster was different. Its front end was nothing like its back; the only pieces that matched each other were the ones that would have resulted from its being split down the middle lengthwise.

And even that limited symmetry was not absolute, for on the far side of the creature Ternat shouted, "Clanfather, a mouth is opening!" A moment later, the domain-master's eldest amended, "No, it's doorway! Beasts are coming out of it!" Reatur saw no such doorway on his side.

"On my way!" he yelled back. Greatly daring, he ran under the monster's belly. If it stooped, he would only be a smear on the ground, and Ternat the new domain-master. It did not stoop.

Breathing hard, Reatur emerged from its shadow. Only Enoph and a couple more of the bolder males had followed him. More were taking the long way around the monster. As with those who had stayed back by the castle, Reatur did not blame them. Only when he was back in the sunlight did he let himself think on what a fool he had been.

Fortunately, he had no time to brood about it. Ternat and other males were pointing with eyestalks, arms, and weapons.

"There, clanfather! Do you see them?" Ternat cried. "Aren't they the *oddest* things you ever looked at?"

"They certainly are," the domain-master agreed absently. He was too busy staring at the weird creatures to think much about what he said. The things were a mottled green and brown, all but one part of their—heads? Those were pinkish and had eyes that looked amazingly like people's eyes, except that they were not on stalks.

One of the creatures turned so Reatur could see the other side of its head. It had no eyes there. It only had two arms, too, now that he had seen all the way around it, and, like its fellows, only two absurdly long legs. How, he wondered, did the things keep from falling over?

"Smoke is coming out of them!" shouted the young male who had wanted to spear the giant monster out of which these smaller beasts had come. The worst of it was, the youngster was right. Smoke streamed from the openings just below the creatures' alarming eyes.

The young male waved his spear. One of the creatures reached for something it carried near where that ridiculous pair of legs joined his body. It held the thing in a paw—no, not a paw, Reatur saw; a hand, even if it had too many fingers. And the thing that hand was holding, whatever it was, was no random stone or chunk of ice; it had the purposeful shape of something made to carry out a specific task. Which meant, or could mean—

"Don't throw that spear!" Reatur shouted. Half an eighteen males had been ready to hurl their spears—the creatures walking on the monster made far more tempting targets than that huge thing itself. At the domain-master's cry, they all guiltily lowered their weapons, each sure that Reatur had shouted at him alone. "I think they're people," Reatur went on.

Had he not been clanfather, he was sure the males would have hooted him down. As it was, they respected his rank, but he knew they did not believe him. Even Ternat, who had a mind with more arms than most, said, "They're too ugly to be people."

"Ugly?" That had not even occurred to Reatur. The creatures were as far outside his criteria for judging such matters as was the strange thing back at the castle. "They aren't ugly. Fralk, now, he's ugly." That got eyestalks wiggling with mirth and brought the males back toward his way of thinking. "These things, they're just—different."

Up above him, the creatures were making noise of their own.

Some had voices that sounded much like his; others used deeper, more rumbling tones. None of their babble sounded like any language he knew, but it did not sound like animal noises, either.

"Quiet!" Reatur said. The crowd of excited males obeyed slowly. When at last silence settled, the domain-master turned four of his eyes on the creatures above him. "I don't want any trouble with you," he told them, pointing first at himself and then at them. To emphasize his words, he set his spear on the ground.

As he had hoped, his speaking when the rest of the males were quiet drew the strange creatures' attention to him. They turned their eyes his way—which brought on another thought: was that the only direction in which they could see? He decided to worry about it later—it was just one more weirdness among so many. Meanwhile, the creature that was holding the whatever-it-was put it back in the pouch where it had come from. Reatur chose to take that as a good sign.

The creature held up an arm. Reatur did the same. The creature stuck up one finger. Reatur did the same. "One," he said. The creatures rumbled a reply. Reatur tried to imitate the noise it made, then said, "One," again. This time, the creature came out with a rather blurry version of the same word.

"You were right, clanfather," Ternat said. "They *are* people—or they aren't animals, anyway."

"No, they aren't," Reatur said. "This reminds me of the language lessons we go through whenever a traveler comes from so far away he hasn't picked up trade talk."

The domain-master returned his attention to the creature above him. He hoped the byplay with his eldest had not distracted the thing. Evidently not—it was getting something out of an opening in its mottled hide; something flat and square. The side Reatur could see was plain white.

The creature came to the edge of the monster's back. It looked down at Reatur, then surprised him—(as if anything about it were anything but a surprise!)—by bending its legs and stooping. It reached down, holding the flat square out to him.

"Be careful, clanfather. It might be dangerous," Ternat said.

"Thank you for worrying," Reatur said. He held up an arm just the same. A goodly gap remained between his fingerclaws and the creature's hand. He waved in invitation, urging it to come down to join him and his males. He wondered if it understood and wondered what it meant by shaking its head back and forth.

Refusal, evidently; it did not come down. But it did let the flat square fall. The square thing flipped over and over in the air. Reatur saw that its other side was not just white. There was some kind of design on it, but the thing was turning too fast for him to tell what. He grabbed for it and missed. It fell to the ground. Naturally, it landed with the plain white side on top. He widened so that he could pick it up.

He turned it over—and almost dropped it in amazement. "The strange thing!" he exclaimed, holding it up so more males could see. It was a picture of the thing he had killed, the thing he and his males had dragged with so much labor back to the castle.

And what a picture! He had never imagined an artist could draw with such detail. With new respect, he used two eyes to look up at the creatures still standing on the monster, while he used two more to keep examining that incredible image. The creatures had more abilities than monster-riding, it seemed.

They were watching him, too. They were so peculiar, he realized, that they might not understand that he recognized the strange thing. He pointed at that unbelievable picture, at himself, back to the castle, and at the picture again.

By their reaction, they understood that. They yelled, leapt about, and hugged one another so tightly Reatur wondered if they were coupling. Then he laughed at himself for his foolishness. They were all about the same size, so they surely were all males. That made sense, he thought. Mates, by their nature, were not travelers.

Travelers . . . His thoughts abruptly turned practical. Travelers traveled for a reason. If these—people, he made himself think—were wandering artists, he wondered how much they would want for a portrait of him. No harm trying to find out.

Tolmasov clicked off the radio with a snarl of frustrated rage. "Not first," he growled. "That damned uncultured old American son of a pig beat us down." Despair lay on him, heavy as gravity.

"They may have been first, Sergei Konstantinovich, but we were better," Valery Bryusov said, trying to console him. "They are eighty kilometers east of where they should be, and across the chasm from us. They will not have an easy time returning."

Tolmasov only grunted.

He looked through the window. Seeing out only by way of monitors was one thing for which he emphatically did not envy *Athena*. Television, to him, was not quite real. It could lie so easily that even the truth became untrustworthy. Glass, now, a man could trust, streaks, smears, and all.

To the eye, the country reminded him of the Siberian tundra where *Tsiolkovsky*'s crew had trained. It was gently rolling land, with patches of snow here and there. From a distance, the plants looked like plants; Tolmasov was no botanist. Some were dark green, some brown, some yellow.

He did not see anything moving. He had set *Tsiolkovsky* down well away from the buildings he saw in the landing approach. It was not that he wanted to, or could, keep the landing secret—as well keep sunrise hidden! But if the Minervans came to him, he would have an easier time meeting them on his terms.

He got out of his seat and walked over to the closet full of warm clothes. "What's the temperature outside, Katerina Fyodorovna?" he asked.

She checked the thermometer. "One above."

"Brr!" Shota Rustaveli gave a theatrical shiver. The five Russians, even quiet Voroshilov, laughed at him. A degree above freezing—that was weather to be enjoyed, not endured, Tolmasov thought.

"It *is* early afternoon, at a season that is the equivalent of May, in a southern latitude that corresponds to Havana's," Dr. Zakharova pointed out, and Tolmasov felt his mirth slip. Russian summer was brief, but it was there. On Minerva, the weather did not get a whole lot warmer than this.

"Thank you for coming to my defense, Katerina, in these bleak circumstances," Rustaveli said. The doctor murmured something. So did Tolmasov, under his breath. Where had the Georgian learned to sound like a courtier from some perfumed court and, worse, to do it so well?

The colonel drew calf-length felt *valenki* over his feet and put his arms through the sleeves of his quilted *telogreika*. The rest of the crew, except for Lopatin and Voroshilov, crowded around to do likewise.

Next to the jackets, boots, and prosaic thermal underwear hung six full-length sable coats, for bad weather. Bryusov ran a loving hand down one of them. "Here is something the Americans cannot match," he said.

"And here is something else," Oleg Lopatin added. He had opened a locked cabinet not far from the protective gear. He started passing out weapons and brown plastic magazines.

Tolmasov took his gratefully. Even though it was the new model AK-74 with small-caliber, high-velocity ammunition and not the AK-47 he had trained with, a Kalashnikov was a Kalashnikov: a good friend to have if the going got rough.

"How long shall we wait for the natives to come to us before we start looking for them?" Rustaveli asked as all of them but Lopatin and Voroshilov stood in front of the airlock. Doctrine was two people on *Tsiolkovsky* at all times, one of them able to fly the ship, and Lopatin was backup pilot.

They went through the lock two by two, Tolmasov and Bryusov first. The pilot stood on *Tsiolkovsky*'s left wing and stared out at a world not his own. The view was broader than the one from the windows, but not much different—boring, barren, superficially familiar terrain. A thrill ran through the colonel all the same. He had been in his teens when Buzz Aldrin had first set foot on the moon. Well, Aldrin was envying him today.

The lock's outer door came open behind him. Katerina and Rustaveli emerged and looked around. The Georgian tugged his jacket tighter around him. Tolmasov smiled to himself.

Rustaveli was carrying a chain-link ladder. He fixed it to brackets on the edge of the wing and let it unroll. The other end landed on the ground with a metallic *whump*. The biologist cocked an eyebrow at Tolmasov. "I suppose you'd shoot me if I tried to go down ahead of you."

"I would try not to hit anything vital," Tolmasov said. Rustaveli laughed, bowed, and stood aside with a sweeping gesture of invitation. Tolmasov slung his rifle, stood, and started down the ladder. He was glad he had managed to keep his tone light. The way his hands had tightened on the rifle at Rustaveli's impudent suggestion made him know he was only half joking.

The ground felt like ground under his feet. He took a few steps away from the ship and away from the shadow of the wing. He glanced up at the sun. Did it seem too small in the sky? Hard to tell, the more so as he had got used to its shrinking as *Tsiolkovsky* traveled outward. He was sure though, that nowhere on Earth was the sky—or what he could see of it through patchy clouds—quite this shade of greenish blue.

The ladder rattled and clanked. Katerina Zakharova lowered herself down onto the Minervan surface. She took two heavy, deliberate steps, then looked at her footprints. "Humanity's marks on a new world," she murmured.

"Ah, but the other question is, what marks will it leave on us?" Shota Rustaveli came next. Tolmasov would have bet on that. If Bryusov had tried preceding the Georgian, the linguist likely would have arrived on Minerva headfirst.

A moment later, Bryusov did join the other three. He looked ill at ease and soon revealed why. "I am not of much use here, until we actually meet the Minervans."

That left him wide open to a sardonic retort from Rustaveli, but, rather to Tolmasov's surprise, it did not come. Instead, just as Lopatin shouted in his earphone, he heard the biologist say quietly, "I do not think you will be useless long, Valery Aleksandrovich."

Rustaveli was pointing; Tolmasov's eyes followed his finger. A Minervan had been hiding behind a stone big enough to make Tolmasov glad *Tsiolkovsky*'s undercarriage missed it. Now the native came out, moving slowly toward the waiting humans.

It looked like its picture. That should not have surprised Tolmasov, but somehow it did. What he did next was as hard as anything else in his life. He stepped aside, saying, "Valery Aleksandrovich, now I am not of much use. You and Shota Mikheilovich must go forward from here."

"The man who covers is as useful as the one who advances," Rustaveli said. Hearing an army phrase from him caught Tolmasov off guard. So did finding out the Georgian meant it literally; Rustaveli set down his Kalashnikov before he walked away from *Tsiolkovsky* to meet the Minervan. After a moment's hesitation, so did Bryusov.

The colonel automatically shuffled a few steps sideways, so his companions would not be between him and the Minervan. He turned his head to tell Katerina to do the same thing, but she already had.

She nodded at him. "You see, I was listening after all through those endless drills," she said. He dipped his head in acknowledgment.

Their gloved hands open and empty before them, Bryusov and Rustaveli stopped a couple of meters in front of the Minervan. It kept two eyes on each of them, while its remaining pair refused to hold still on any target, even *Tsiolkovsky*, for more than a couple of seconds at a time. The spectacle was unsettling. Tolmasov wondered how the creature kept from tying its eyestalks in knots.

Bryusov pointed to himself. "Valery." He pointed to Rustaveli. "Shota." He pointed to the Minervan and waited. For this, Tolmasov thought, we need a linguist?

It might have been simple, but it worked. The native pointed toward itself with three arms at once and said, "Fralk." Its voice startled Tolmasov again—it was a smooth contralto. To his way of thinking, nothing taller than he was, and unbelievably weird-looking to boot, had any business sounding like a woman—a sexy woman, at that.

Get used to surprises, the colonel told himself. Expect them. After all, you were just reminding yourself this is a whole different world. He wondered how many times he would end up giving himself that order. A great many, he guessed.

Bryusov was still talking at the Minervan, trying to pick up nouns. The tape recorder in his pocket would save the replies he got for more study later. Tolmasov chuckled to himself. The recorder was just as good as the Americans'. Both expeditions used Sonys.

While the linguist worked, Rustaveli walked halfway around Fralk so he could take some pictures of it—him? her?—and Bryusov. But when he pulled out his camera—also Japanese, again like the Americans'—the Minervan sprang away from him and Bryusov. Its body got short and plump, so its arms could reach the ground. A moment later it was tall again, and it was holding stones in three hands.

"Hold still!" Katerina shouted, startling Tolmasov and the Minervan both. A couple of Fralk's eyestalks whipped toward her. The native did not put down the rocks it had seized, but it made no move to throw them, either.

At the same time Fralk was watching Katerina, it was also keeping an eye on Bryusov, another on Rustaveli, and one more on Tolmasov. A Minervan, the colonel realized, was a creature that had no behind—one direction was as accessible to it as another. He wondered how the natives chose which way to go.

Worry about that some other time, he told himself firmly. First things first. "I think the photographs will have to wait, Shota Mikheilovich," he called. "At least until this Fralk understands that your camera is no weapon."

The biologist's thin, mobile features twisted in a grimace, but he lowered the camera, moving slowly and ostentatiously. The eyestalk Fralk was using to watch him followed the motion. The Georgian signed. "You appear to be right," he said mournfully.

"I will go turn over some flat stones. With luck, nothing I find under them will want to slay me for taking its picture."

Seeing Rustaveli go off to do something that had nothing to do with it seemed to reassure Fralk. It started giving long answers to Bryusov. It talked, in fact, at such length that the linguist threw his hands in the air. "This will be wonderful later, when I and the computers back at Moscow have a chance to analyze it," he said plaintively, "but for now it's only so much nonsense."

He had picked up a couple of rocks of his own, a small white one and a larger gray one. He held the white rock above the gray one, then below it. "Spatial relationships," he explained to Tolmasov, then turned back to Fralk, who was saying something or other.

Eventually, the colonel thought, he would have to learn Minervan. He ought to be just getting fluent in it when *Tsiolkovsky* lifted off. Then he likely would never use it again. Things worked that way sometimes.

The thought he had had before occurred to him again. "How are you going to learn the native words for 'front' and 'back,' Valery Aleksandrovich? This Fralk doesn't have either one."

For a moment, Bryusov looked scornful, as he did whenever anyone presumed to comment about his specialty. Then he must have realized he had no impressively crushing rejoinder handy. He tugged at his mustache. "A very good question, Sergei Konstantinovich," he admitted.

The alarm rang in the headsets of the crewfolk on the ground. Oleg Lopatin's voice followed it. "A large party of Minervans heading this way out of the northeast. They appear to be armed."

"Then we should have the one here on good terms with us, to speak well of us to its companions," Rustaveli said. He reached into a jacket pocket. The motion made Fralk turn an eye from Bryusov to him. The biologist pulled out a pocket knife and opened its blade. Fralk hefted the rocks it was holding.

"You are not endearing yourself to the native, Shota," Katerina remarked.

That had comebacks obvious even to Tolmasov, but Rustaveli was, for once, pure business. "Hush," was all he said. He bent, set the knife on the ground, and stepped back from it. Then he pointed to it and to Fralk and waved an invitation to the Minervan. "Go ahead; it's yours," he said, though Fralk could not hope to understand his words.

The gestures got through, though. Fralk moved toward the

knife, hesitantly at first but then with more confidence as Rustaveli and Bryusov backed farther away to show that it was all right. The Minervan grew short and wide and picked up the knife—by the handle, Tolmasov saw, which meant it knew what a knife was. Well, Lopatin had as much as said that.

Yes, Fralk knew what a knife was. It held the blade in one hand and tested it with the fingers of another. It must have approved of what it found. It pointed to the knife, then to itself, and made a noise that Tolmasov mentally translated as, "For *me*?"

Rustaveli must have read it the same way. "*Da, da,*" he said. When he did not try to take away the pocket knife, Fralk must have gotten the idea.

Tolmasov heard faint contralto cries in the distance. The Minervans sounded angry. His face quirked into a smile, almost against his will. Angry Minervans sounded like angry sexy women—an unexpected perk of the job. The American slang threatened to make his smile wider. He forced himself to seriousness.

Katerina also heard the locals approaching. She took cover behind one of *Tsiolkovsky*'s huge tires. That made such good sense that Tolmasov crouched behind another one.

He watched the Minervans approach. They were within a couple of hundred meters now, carrying spears and stones and other things less easy to identify. The Kalashnikovs could make bloody hash of them—and of the Soviet mission. If the Americans made peaceful contact while he got into a firefight . . . he shuddered. He would not end up a Hero of the Soviet Union when he got home. He would end up begging for a bullet, more likely.

Bryusov did not seem to have noticed the—army? gang? posse? He gestured vehemently, like a man in the grip of an overpowering itch. Maybe he was getting through to Fralk, though; the native had three eyes on him, for whatever that was worth.

"I suggest you come to the point, Valery." Shota Rustaveli was on his belly on the cold ground, behind a stone that would give him some cover. He knew the Minervans were coming. So did Fralk, who kept an eye on them.

Evidently Bryusov did come to the point. Fralk hurried out toward its—countrymen? Probably, Tolmasov thought. If they were enemies, it would have run the other way.

Fralk shouted something. The onrushing Minervans came to

a ragged halt. A couple of natives emerged from the crowd and hurried up to Fralk. They made themselves short and wide, then resumed their usual shape. If Bryusov had gone through contortions before, they were not a patch on the ones Fralk put on now. Of course, having six arms and eyestalks gave it an unfair advantage there.

One of the natives who had approached Fralk said something. Fralk broke in loudly. The other native went short and wide again. "That must be a token of submission, like a salute or a bow," Bryusov called.

Fralk shouted to the whole group of Minervans. They set their weapons on the ground. "Valery!" Fralk called in that thrilling voice.

The linguist had put down his rifle when he started trying to communicate with Fralk. "Cover me," he called to his companions, and walked, empty-handed, toward the Minervans. Fralk widened himself as the human came up. In delighted reply, Bryusov bowed from the waist.

That set the Minervans off again. "They're not used to anything that can bend that way," Katerina guessed.

"No," Tolmasov agreed. He knew he sounded absent-minded, and he did not care. The relief washing through him was too great for that. First contact was made, and made without bloodshed. History books—maybe history books on two worlds, he thought, blinking—would not bear his name as a curse.

No one with a lot of arms would try to ram a spear through his brisket, either, which also counted. He stood up, stepped out from behind *Tsiolkovsky*'s immense tires, and let the Minervans see him. He left his rifle at his side but did not put it down. Not yet.

"For me?" Hogram tested the knife blade with a fingerclaw and, like Fralk before him, was amazed at its keenness. "A most generous gift, eldest of eldest."

"Gift?" Fralk held his eyestalks very still, the picture of innocence. "How can such a thing be a gift, when all the clan possesses is in the clanfather's keeping?"

Hogram turned a second eye on the young male, who wondered if he had laid the flattery on too thick. Maybe he had. "There is a difference, you know," Hogram said, "between being in my keeping and being in my hand." But the domain-master's eyestalks twitched; he was more amused than anything else.

Fralk did not take another chance. He changed the subject, at least to some degree, saying, "These—strangers—may be valuable to us, clanfather." "Strangers" seemed a better word than "monsters," especially as he was trying to speak well of them.

"If they have more knives such as this, certainly," Hogram said. "Or, better yet, if they can make them with longer blades. Those would help us when we cross the Great Gorge. I would pay well for them."

"Of course, clanfather," Fralk agreed. "The trouble is finding what the strange males want. They are so—different—from us that much of what we find valuable may be of no interest to them."

Hogram's eyestalks were more than twitching now; they were wiggling with mirth. "That is the trouble with any trade, eldest of eldest, finding out what the other male wants and what it's worth to him." The clanfather's faded, sagging skin and the continual wheezing of his breathing-pores showed that he would never be young again, but with his years had come shrewdness. Clan Hogram prospered, even among the Skarmer clans, where a trading blunder could put a clan up to its eyestalks in trouble.

Fralk had learned a great deal, just watching and listening to his grandfather. Now to apply some of that learning, if he could . . . "Clanfather, have you chosen a male yet to work with the strangers, learn their peculiar words, and teach them ours?"

"Why, no." Hogram sounded a bit taken aback.

Good, Fralk thought. The domain-master had not had a chance to work through all the implications of the strangers' arrival, while he himself had thought about little else since the sky-box—(no, the sky-*boat*, he amended, consciously using the Lanuam word the Skarmers had borrowed)—almost fell on top of him.

"Surely it would be better to have a single male handle such matters than to scatter them piecemeal among several," he said.

"So it would, so it would." Hogram's fingers twiddled as he thought. "You see to it, if you care to, Fralk. You've been dealing with the creatures since they came here, so you know more about them than anyone else." The domain-master paused. "I've given you two hard tasks together now, first dealing with the Omalo domain-master and now with these strangers. You are still a young male. If you decline here, I will not think less of you."

"I will try, clanfather." Fralk did his best to put a doubtful tremor in his voice, but had all he could do to keep from dancing with glee. If he was the channel through which the strangers dealt with clan Hogram, some of what went by would stick to him, just as debris littered the sides and bottom of Ervis Gorge after the summer floods passed. He suspected the strangers had things much more interesting than the little knife. No trader with even the tiniest sense gave away his best stock as an opening present.

And Hogram, the young male vowed to himself, would not see everything the strangers had to offer. Some Fralk would keep or dispose of for himself. Though clanfathers' rights were as strong in theory among the Skarmer clans as with the Omalo across the gorge, in practice a male still under his clanfather's power could also accumulate a limited amount of wealth for himself. Or even, Fralk thought, not such a limited amount, so long as he was careful.

His musing made him miss something Hogram had said. "Your pardon, clanfather," he said, widening himself contritely.

"I wonder where these strangers—creatures—whatever they are—come from," Hogram repeated. "We've not seen nor heard of nor smelled their like." His arms waved in agitation. "Imagine not having eyestalks, being blind to half the world all the time. Imagine having only two legs, and two hands. Imagine wanting to stay so *hot*—"

"That is unnerving," Fralk agreed. The strangers had a device with fire somehow trapped inside it and had used it on the journey to the castle when night came. They huddled around it, though the evening was mild. The heat had been so savage that no one wanted to go near them, not even Fralk, who was curious about the fire. He knew of few things that burned readily; a new one would find a ready market among ice-smiths and also could be useful in war. When he got more words, he would ask about that.

"They follow strange gods, too, if what you and the others have told me of them is true," Hogram went on. "I've never heard of anyone worshiping the Twinstar."

"They do, clanfather," Fralk insisted. "They roused a little before dawn this morning, as did we, and through clouds low in the east they spied the Twinstar, the bright blue one and its little faint companion. As we watched them, they pointed to it, to themselves, and to it again. I cannot think of any reason for such a rite as that but worship."

"For all we know of them, they may have been trying to tell

us they're *from* the Twinstar," Hogram said. "They're weird enough."

Fralk's eyestalks started to twitch. Then he noticed that Hogram was not laughing. He thought about it. It made as much sense as anything else, he supposed. He said so. He was still thoughtful when he left the domain-master's presence a little while later. He was reminded he would have to be even more cautious in his dealings with the strangers than he had thought. Taking Hogram for a fool would never do.

3

"I hope they don't mind us watching as their young get born," Pat Marquard said as she walked along behind Reatur.

"So do I," Irv said. "From the way they keep their females so restricted, I'm afraid they might. But I hope Reatur will see we're so different from his kind that we don't count."

Though he had gloves on, he kept his hands in his pockets. He noticed himself doing that whenever he was inside Reatur's castle. Just the idea of being in a building made largely of ice gave him goose bumps. He glanced over at his wife. She was doing the same thing.

"Do you think it's being so restricted that makes the females here nothing like the males?" Sarah asked him.

"More likely just a universal constant," he said, which earned him a glare from his wife, a snort from Pat, and, at the noise, the brief honor of a second eyeball on him from Reatur. If it was an honor, he thought, and not simply a reflex.

He wasn't really sure about that. After two and a half weeks on Minerva, he wasn't really sure about much. Back on Earth, the people to whom *Athena*'s crew relayed data all sounded certain they knew what was going on. Irv would have had more confidence in them if the advice they sent agreed with itself more than two times in five. As it was, he was looking forward to the day when the Earth slipped behind the sun. Being out of radio contact for a while was beginning to seem a delightful prospect.

Reatur brought him back to the here-and-now by opening the door to the females' part of the castle. As always, the din that came from the other side of the door when the females saw him was impressive. "Reserved" was not in the Minervan female vocabulary.

The din redoubled when the females spotted the three humans behind the—baron? chief? Irv still had no sure feel for the best rendering of Reatur's title. One of the few things Minervan he did have a feel for was what the local females thought about humans.

They thought humans were hilarious.

They came crowding around, staring, falling over one another, prodding, poking, pulling their arms back in amazement every time they directly touched warm human flesh, then reaching out to do it again. "They're like a bunch of berserk puppies," Pat said as the wave washed over her. She was smiling; it was hard not to smile around Minervan females.

Irv jerked his head back, just in time to keep a female's fingerclaw from poking him in the eye. The female reached up and ran the finger under the earflap of his cap instead, then let out an almost supersonic squeal.

"Reminds me even more of my two-year-old niece," Irv said. The thought saddened him; Beth was three now, not two, and would be five when Irv got back to Earth. She probably would not remember Sarah or him.

"They *are* like toddlers, aren't they?" Sarah said slowly.

"Not the one named Biyal," Pat said. Sarah and Irv both had to nod. No toddler on Earth could have been so dramatically gravid as Biyal. The bulges above her legs made her instantly recognizable to the humans, where even with Reatur they had to pause and consider before they were sure who he was. Those bulges also made her move very slowly, so she was the last female to come out and see the humans.

"Hello, Biyal," Irv said, waving.

"Hello, Irv," she answered, and waved back with three arms at once. Except for that, both words and gesture were eerily accurate echoes of what the anthropologist had said and done. Such a gift for mimicry was something young children often displayed; Irv thought his wife might have put a finger on an important truth.

Biyal was still wading through the crowd of females toward the humans when she suddenly stopped. "Reatur!" she called, and followed the chieftain's name with a stream of what was still gibberish despite nearly sleepless efforts on the part of everyone from *Athena*.

Reatur and the females understood, though; they all turned

an extra eyestalk or two toward Biyal. The rippling motion reminded Irv of a wind blowing through a forest of snakes.

Reatur shouted something at the females between him and Biyal. They moved out of the way, clearing a path for him to go to her. The humans followed him.

Sarah's hand tightened on Irv's arm. "Look!" she said. "The skin over that bud has split vertically! Reatur timed it well—she must be right on the point of giving birth!" Irv saw that his wife was right. Excitement ran through him. Learning how Minervans were born surely would give him clues to other aspects of their culture, to say nothing of the importance the knowledge held for Sarah and Pat.

Reatur seemed like any other concerned father-to-be. He took two of Biyal's hands in his own and helped her waddle backward toward the passage out of which she had come. The other females did not go with them. Instead they called out Biyal's name and one of the few Minervan words Irv was certain he understood: "Good-bye!"

"Do we go on?" Pat whispered to Irv. "I want to."

"Let's," he said after a moment's thought. "If Reatur or Biyal don't want us along, they'll let us know about it." His first thought was that they would get far enough along behind Reatur's back that the chieftain would let them continue instead of sending them away. But of course Reatur had no back to be behind. With eyes all around, he saw the humans' first steps after him.

He hesitated, then used one arm to wave them on. This time Sarah and Pat both gave Irv a squeeze. "You were right," Pat said, her blue eyes glowing.

Reatur led Biyal into a small chamber. It was crowded when the humans also came in. There was no place to sit down except the floor; Minervans were not built for sitting. All the humans stayed on their feet. Their boots were much better insulated than the seats of their pants.

Biyal reached out with a fingerclaw, scraped some ice from a wall, and reached up to put it into her mouth. Reatur got her more. He gently touched her while she crunched it up.

"He takes good care of her," Sarah said approvingly. She studied Biyal. "She doesn't seem to be in much distress, does she?" Sarah laughed at herself. "Of course, I have no idea whether she's supposed to be. It would be nice if she weren't, wouldn't it?"

Pat moved around as best she could in the cramped space,

taking picture after picture. Biyal pointed at the camera. "Noise? What?" she asked. Females always spoke more simply than males, Irv had noted; Biyal simplified still more to get her meaning across to humans.

"Autowinder," Pat said: not an explanation, but at least a name to give to the thing that whirred. Reatur, by now, was used to the noise. Then Pat spoke to Irv and Sarah. "The splits in her skin above each bud are getting longer."

"Six babies born all at once?" Irv shook his head. "My cousin and her husband have two little kids, a couple of years apart, and they're ragged." Remembering the chaos at Victoria's house made him have trouble thinking like an anthropologist. Finally he managed, musing, "An enormous extended family like the one Reatur has here must make things a lot easier."

"Splits are longer still," Sarah said. "If things go on at this rate, either those babies will be born very soon or Biyal's going to fall apart in so many segments like an orange. And she's perfectly happy, too. When we send the data back to Earth, I think a lot of women are going to be jealous."

The splits were growing wider, as well as longer. Minervans, Irv saw, were born feet-first. Six young, each with six legs, plus Biyal's six . . . Irv began figuring out how many legs that was, and found himself thinking of the man with the wives and the cats and the rats, all on their way to St. Ives. Adding in arms and then eyestalks as they appeared only brought the nursery puzzle more strongly to mind.

"They're connected to their mother by their mouths," Pat observed. "Very neat; they get their nourishment directly from her, and never had to evolve anything fancy like a placenta."

"I wonder how they do dispose of their wastes, though," Sarah said.

"There." Pat pointed. "See those little tubes around the central mouth, the ones linking mother and infant? I'll bet they have something to do with it. Six of them, of course. That seems to be the pattern here."

"Yes," Sarah said. She sounded curious, eager to find out what would happen next, trying to guess along. "How do you suppose the babies are going to separate from Biyal, Pat?"

"I don't know, but I think we'll find out pretty soon. Look— the ring of little tubes has already come free. She's bleeding a little from where they went into her, do you see? Minervan blood is browner than ours, isn't it?"

"Yes," Sarah said again. She leaned forward for a better look.

Irv was watching Reatur watch Biyal. When the bleeding began, the male stepped closer to her. He reached out to pat her on the side, then said something to her. Irv thought he heard the word "Good-bye" again. He touched his pocket. The tape recorder would tell him for sure.

"Here we go," Sarah said. "Look, Pat—you can see the muscles loosening around the babies' mouths. Must be some sort of sphincter ring there—"

"Yes, like marsupial babies' mouths have, to keep them attached to the teat when they're in their mother's pouch," Pat broke in. "Here, though, I'd say the babies will just let go and fall plop on the floor."

The babies let go and fell plop on the floor.

Biyal's blood spurted after them, six streams of it, one from each inch-and-a-half-wide circle where a baby had been attached. With so much being lost so fast, the streams quickly diminished. Less than a minute after she had given birth, Biyal's arms and eyestalks went limp and flaccid. She swayed and started to topple.

"Good-bye," Reatur said; this time Irv was certain he recognized the word. The male eased Biyal down, making sure she would not fall on any of the newborn Minervans.

"She's dead." Pat's voice was shocked, indignant.

"She certainly is," Sarah agreed grimly. She lifted one foot. Minervan blood dripped from her boot; it was all over the ground. "Judging by this, I'd say giving birth for a Minervan is just about the same as getting both carotids cut would be for one of us."

"This can't be normal," Pat protested. "Something must have gone wrong—"

"No," Irv said before his wife could answer. She glanced at him sharply, but he went on. "This must be what always happens. Look at Reatur. He knew exactly what to expect. He's seen it before. He may not be happy about it, but he's going on about his business."

Reatur was doing just that. He was rounding up the six new little Minervans, which scurried about on the floor. Active as they were, they reminded Irv more of newly hatched lizards or turtles than of newborn human infants. Reatur caught them and picked them up, one after another. Finally he had three in one hand, two in another, and the last separately in a hand on the other side of his body.

"Why apart?" Irv asked him, pointing at the last baby; Reatur had carefully transferred it away from the others, as if he wanted to keep special track of it.

"Male," Reatur said. He held up the other struggling, squealing infants. "Females." He said something else that Irv didn't quite catch. The anthropologist spread his hands, a gesture of confusion Reatur had learned. The—baron?—paused to think for a moment, then lifted the females to show they were what he meant, saying, "Good-bye fast, like—" He used a free hand to point to Biyal's still, dead body.

"That's all females do here?" Sarah's back was stiff with horror and outrage. "Get pregnant and then die? But they're intelligent beings, too, and could be as much as the males, if, if—" She could not get it out.

"If they lived longer," Irv finished for her. She nodded, her head down; she would not look at him, or at Reatur.

"Biologically, it makes a certain amount of sense," Pat said reluctantly. "They reproduce, then get out of the way for the next generation."

"But who takes care of the babies?" Sarah said.

Pat watched them squirm in Reatur's grip. "They look like they're pretty much able to take care of themselves. If they can find their own food—and I'll bet they can—"

"Then males could nurture as well as females," Irv broke in. "Or maybe they leave the females in here with their own kind, knowing, uh, knowing they'll not last long, and take the one male out to train him up to be part of the bigger society."

"That's disgusting," Sarah said. She still was not looking his way.

"I didn't say I liked it." Something else occurred to Irv, with force enough that he whacked himself in the forehead with a gloved hand. "We'd better be careful about how we let Reatur and the rest of the natives learn that we aren't all males ourselves."

At that, Sarah looked at him, and Pat, too. "We'd better leave," his wife said in a tight, overcontrolled voice. "If I start laughing, I don't think I'll be able to stop."

Irv waited until one of Reatur's eyes found him. Then he bowed and said, "Good-bye," in the local language. Using the word after what he had just watched sent a chill through him that had nothing to do with the icy air in the room.

"Good-bye," Reatur said. Irv tried to read emotion in his voice and failed. In Reatur's grip, the babies made noise. Reatur paid no attention to it, so Irv supposed it was the kind of noise baby Minervans were supposed to make.

"Come on," the anthropologist said. The three humans left the females' chambers through the room where most of Reatur's—spouses? again Irv found himself stuck for a word—were still amusing themselves.

The females came crowding round, as full of curiosity as before. Irv was glad he could neither understand nor answer their questions.

Outside Reatur's castle stood three all-terrain bicycles. They could go places a four-wheeled vehicle could not, and six of them weighed a lot less than a rover would have. "I'm going back to the ship," Pat said, climbing aboard hers. "I want to get these pictures developed."

"I just want to get away and think for a while," Sarah said. She pedaled down the curved track that ran through Reatur's fields. Her breath streamed out behind her like a frosty scarf.

Irv hesitated. "Which way are you heading?" Pat asked. "Want to ride along with me?"

"I think I'd better see to Sarah."

"She'll be all right."

"I know. Even so, though—" He left the words hanging and started after his wife.

"Ah, well, see you later, then," Pat called to his retreating back. When he did not answer, she slowly rode off toward *Athena*.

"I didn't understand that, Valery Aleksandrovich," Tolmasov said. "Ask Fralk to say it again."

"He said—" Bryusov began.

The colonel raised a hand. "I thought you understood it. I want to make sure I do, too, and if you translate for me all the time, how can I?" Having decided to learn Minervan, Tolmasov was throwing himself into the project with his usual dogged persistence.

"Again, please," Bryusov said in the best Minervan he could muster.

"Slowly," Tolmasov added. That was one word he had used often enough to feel confident about it.

"You give me—" Fralk pointed to the hatchets, hammers, and other tools the Russians had brought for trade goods. "Some

I give Hogram, he—'' The word that followed was unfamiliar to Tolmasov. He looked at Bryusov.

"Trade, I think," the linguist said doubtfully. "Maybe context will make it clearer." He turned back to Fralk. "Go on."

"Hogram, he—'' That word again. "Then he use what he get to get you things. Some things you give me, I not give Hogram. I''—and again—''them myself. Some of what I get for them, I keep and save. Some I use to get other things; them, to get more things. Some I use to get you things you want."

"Not 'trade,' " Tolmasov exclaimed. "I know what that word means—it means *sell*. Fralk will sell some of what he gets from us, use some of the profits to acquire more goods, whether from us or his own people, and invest the rest." The colonel rubbed his eyes with the heels of his hands. "What does that make him?''

"A capitalist," Bryusov said in a small voice.

"Just what I was thinking." Tolmasov looked at Fralk, not altogether happily. As an alien, the Minervan could be studied for his own sake, without preconceptions. Thinking of him as a capitalist brought in a whole load of ideology. The colonel suddenly laughed out loud.

"What?" Bryusov said.

"He would look very strange, driving a large American car."

"So he would." Bryusov permitted himself a smile, but it was a nervous one. "Moscow will not find it funny," he warned. "I doubt Oleg Borisovich will, either."

"There is that," Tolmasov said. Still, he wanted to be there when Lopatin got the news, just to see his expression.

Fralk made a noise that sounded amazingly like a woman clearing her throat when the two men with whom she is at dinner have spent too much time talking about their jobs and not enough with her. Tolmasov shook his head at the irony of that marvelous voice being wasted on an alien, and, the Russians had learned, a male alien at that. The colonel bowed to Fralk in polite apology for his woolgathering.

The Minervan widened himself in turn. "Want more—'' He pointed at the hatchets and hammers again, and also at a box of little battery-powered lamps.

"Shall we give him more of the axes?" Bryusov asked.

"Well, why not? We brought them to trade, and the local tools and books and specimens we get in return will be worth a lot more than their weight in diamonds back on Earth. Still, I suppose you have a point, Valery." Tolmasov tried to use his tiny Minervan vocabulary. "These—" He pointed to the hatchets himself. "What you do with? Use for?"

"Use on Omalo."

Tolmasov took a certain small pride in noticing Fralk had chosen a preposition different from the one he had used. The object of the preposition, though, remained obscure. "Omalo? Omalo is what?" he asked.

Fralk said something. "Ervis Gorge" was all the colonel understood: the local name for Jötun Canyon. He turned to Bryusov. "Did you follow that?"

The linguist frowned. "The Omalo are something across Ervis Gorge."

Tolmasov frowned, too. That was better than he had done, but not enough to tell him much. "Again please, slowly," he said to Fralk.

The Minervan pointed to himself. "Skarmer," he said. He pointed to the castle where his—king? grandfather?—lived, the castle that was much the biggest building in this settlement. "Hogram Skarmer."

"A surname?" Tolmasov asked.

"We've seen no signs of such yet," Valery Bryusov answered. "And while he might use an ax on Hogram, he would not use one on himself. Besides, let him go on—I don't believe he's finished."

The linguist was right. Seeing he had not yet made his point, Fralk said, "Ervis Gorge—this side—Skarmer—all." He waved his six arms to emphasize his words. "Ervis Gorge—across—Omalo."

"*Bozhemoi,*" Tolmasov said softly. He was afraid he did understand that. "Valery, I think he's trying to tell us these Omalo on the other side of the canyon are another whole country. I think we should think three times before we go arming these folk for war."

"I think also, Sergei Konstantinovich, that we should consult with Moscow," Bryusov said.

The colonel made a sour face. Bryusov wanted to consult with Moscow to decide which pair of socks to put on in the morning. Then, reluctantly, Tolmasov nodded. "I am afraid you are right. The Americans, after all, are also on the other side of Jötun Canyon. War against them, even by proxy, would not be well received back home, I suspect. We came too close to falling off the big cliff, the nuclear cliff, in Lebanon."

"We need to learn more of the situation here as well," Bryusov said.

"So we do." They could not hope to learn enough, either, Tolmasov thought, not in the limited time they had on Minerva. In the end, they might act anyway. People did things like that.

"Shall we tell the Americans?" Bryusov asked.

"We'll let Moscow worry about that, too," Tolmasov decided. "If it were my choice, though, I'd say no, at least not yet."

Reatur finished cleaning the chamber where the new budlings had burst into the world. It was somber work. That was one of the reasons he did not give it to the mates. The other, of course, was simply that, being as they were, they would have done a bad job of it.

He dragged Biyal's corpse out of the room, toward the door that kept the mates in their own part of the castle. The evening was growing dark, and he hoped the mates would be back in the little rooms where they slept.

Seventeen evenings out of eighteen, they would have been. Even tonight, most of them were. But Numar and Lamra were still chasing each other up and down the hall. They came to a stumbling stop when they saw the domain-master and his burden.

"It's Biyal," Numar said.

"How sad," Lamra echoed. But she did not sound full of grief, no more than if she were speaking of a broken pot or, at most, a dead animal she did not care much about one way or the other. She was too young to grasp that Biyal's fate awaited her as well. As if to underscore that, she said, "Feel me, Reatur. I think I'm going to bud."

Reatur ran fingers along her body. Sure enough, the barest beginnings of bulges were there. "I think you are, too, Lamra," he said, as gently as he could.

"Good," Lamra said. No, Reatur thought, she did not understand the connection between buds and death that so abridged mates' lives. Sadness pressed on him. Lamra was a mate he cared for more than he had for any in years. She was more uniquely herself than most mates ever got to be in their limited spans. He would miss her when her time came. Maybe, he thought, a minstrel would be visiting the domain then, and he could pay the fellow for a song by which to remember her.

While he was musing, Numar was getting bored and annoyed

that no one was paying attention to her anymore. She poked Lamra with three arms at once, then raced off down the hall. Letting out a squawk loud enough to wake half the mates who were sleeping, Lamra dashed after her.

Reatur got Biyal out of the mates' quarters and barred the door behind him. He was taking the corpse to the fields when he almost ran into Enoph, who was on his way back from the humans' flying house. More questions, Reatur supposed; the humans asked more questions and poked their eyes—even without eyestalks—into more places than any people the domain-master had ever known. If they had not been so spectacularly strange-looking, he would have suspected them of being Skarmer spies.

Enoph peered through the gloom. When he recognized what Reatur was dragging after him, he asked, "Would you like me to take care of that for you, clanfather?"

"Eh? No, thank you, Enoph. Mates get all too little in life; I try to give them what I can, and to honor them as I can after they die, as well."

Enoph opened and closed a hand in agreement. "Yes, I think you act rightly, clanfather. I have two mates in my booth, and treat them as well as I can. For one thing, they're more fun to be with that way than when you don't try to train them and just leave them like animals."

"I certainly think so," Reatur said.

"Are the budlings well?" Enoph asked.

"The male is large, and seems sturdy. So do the five mates, come to that." Reatur let air sigh through his breathing-pores. "Time will tell." So many budlings died young. If a male lasted five years, he might well live a long life . . . if. Many mate budlings never lived to receive buds themselves. And those who did, no matter how strong and healthy they were, had only Biyal's fate to look forward to.

"How many males is it for you now?" Enoph asked.

Reatur had to count on his fingers and was not quite sure even when he had finished. "I think this puts me within three of filling my fourth eighteen," he said at last.

"A goodly sum," Enoph said. In the gathering darkness, Reatur could hardly see the younger male's eyestalks. "I've had four myself, only one still alive. The mates budded with them have not done well, either."

It was Reatur's turn to open and close his hand. "Few who aren't domain-masters have the food to spare to keep many mates alive even to budding age," he said sympathetically. "I daresay we'd run short of them if they didn't come five to our one."

"Something to that." Enoph widened himself. "I've kept you long enough from what you came out here for, clanfather. I'll leave you to it now." He started back toward the castle's outwalls.

Reatur let him go, though he had been glad enough of the interruption. Saying farewell to a mate was not a task he approached eagerly. He dragged Biyal's corpse to a part of the field where the humans' flying house had seared the crops. Scavengers, he knew, would make off with most of it, but the rest would decay and give fresh value to the soil.

Farther north, he had heard, were folk who, at least in summer, dug holes in the ground as resting-places for their dead. That was practical there, where the ground unfroze to a depth greater than a male's height and stayed soft half the year. In Reatur's domain, and those around him, burial was more trouble than it was worth.

He murmured a prayer, asking the gods to grant Biyal the long life she had not been able to enjoy here. He added a brief petition for the budlings' health, then widened himself in a last gesture of respect for their mother.

He was just returning to his full height when two of his eyes were suddenly blinded by a brilliant flash of violet light. He almost jumped out of his skin. Glaring afterimages filled those eyes even after he shut them, as if on a rare clear day he had looked straight at the sun.

Before he had the sense to tell himself not to, he had turned another eyestalk in the direction of the flash. He saw a human pointing something at him. "I might have known," he muttered. A moment later, the flash went off again, putting that third eye out of commission. "Enough!" he shouted.

"What?" It was one of the humans with a voice that sounded like a person's—the small one, Reatur thought, though without several humans together it was harder to be sure.

He noticed that the afterimages were fading from the first two eyes that had been flashed and opened them again. Yes, they could see. He was relieved to find he was not blind for good through a third—no, half—of his field of vision. Blind as a human, he thought, and through his annoyance knew a moment's pity for the strange creatures.

"What is that thing?" he asked, walking toward the human

and pointing at whatever he was holding. The domain-master spoke slowly and repeated himself several times.

"Reatur?" The human put the question-ending on his name.

"Who else?" he said. For the first time, it occurred to him to wonder whether real people looked as strange to humans as humans did to real people. He pointed again and asked again, "What is that thing?"

The human—yes, he decided, it was the male called Sarah—finally understood. *"Camera,"* he said in his own language, then "picture-maker" in the Omalo tongue.

"Ah," Reatur said. He had no idea of how the humans' picture-making gadgets worked, but he admired what they did. Some of them would spit out pictures right away, pictures as marvelously detailed and accurate as the one of the strange thing the humans had shown him just after their house fell from the sky. Reatur had an image of himself, one of Ternat, and another of his castle; the humans, to his surprise, had not even charged him for them.

"Why the big light?" he asked.

Sarah tried to explain; Reatur gave credit where it was due. But he did not understand the explanation. For one thing, Sarah did not have enough words. For another, the domain-master suspected that some of the ideas were as strange as humans. As best he could gather, the picture-making thing needed a lot of light to see by. He supposed that made sense.

Sarah put the picture-maker into one of the pockets of the coverings humans wore. Reatur had only gradually realized those *were* coverings, not part of the humans' skins.

From a different pocket, Sarah drew out something else. Reatur heard a click. Light streamed out of the thing, not in a single blinding flash but steadily and at a lower, more comfortable level. *"Flashlight,"* Sarah said. Reatur tried to remember the word; his language had no equivalent for it.

Sarah shone the light at Reatur's feet, courteously keeping it out of his eyes. The light splashed over Biyal's body. "The budding female?" Sarah asked.

"Well, of course," Reatur said gruffly—humans had a gift for asking about the obvious.

"At the budding female I close look?"

It took several tries, backed by a good deal of gesturing, before Reatur figured out what Sarah meant. The domain-master hesitated. He had cleared the chamber in the mates' quarters by himself after Biyal died—he did not want other males to have anything to do with *his* mates, or even to venture into that part of the castle. But he had not kept the humans out of the mates' quarters. They were too odd to worry about their planting buds on his mates. And poor Biyal would never bud again, that was certain.

"Look if you care to," the domain-master said at last. "Yes," he added a moment later. Humans needed things kept simple.

He started back toward the castle. One of his eyes watched Sarah bend over Biyal's corpse. That peculiarly human motion still struck him as grotesque. Humans could not widen, though. He was sure of that. They did the best they could with the weird bodies they had.

As did everyone else, he thought. That reminded him of the watch he was still posting on Ervis Gorge. Nothing whatever had happened there since Fralk—on whose eyestalks the domain-master wished the purple rash—was urged to go back to his own side and stay there. Reatur wondered whether he was wasting his males' time by keeping them at the gorge. He decided to leave them in place a while longer. Up against a rogue like Fralk, fewest chances were best.

The male dropped the lamp at Fralk's feet; in fact, he almost dropped it on one of Fralk's feet. "What's all this about, Mountenc?" Fralk asked. He was both surprised and a little angry. As eldest of eldest, he was not often exposed to such rude behavior.

But Mountenc was angry, too. "This stinking thing didn't even live as long as a mate, Fralk," he snapped. "It doesn't light up anymore, and I want my eighteen stone blades back for it."

"I never said how long it would last, Mountenc," Fralk pointed out.

"Four nights isn't long enough," the other male retorted. "I kept it on all through the dark so I could see to work, and now look." He picked it up and used a fingerclaw to click the little switch that made the light come out. No light came. "It's dead," Mountenc said contemptuously, "and I want my blades back."

"First let me see if I can make it live again," Fralk said. He did not have the blades anymore. He had traded them for something else. At the moment, he could not remember what, but he had turned a profit.

From the way Mountenc was glaring at him with three eyes at once, he did not think the other male would care about that. "You'd better," Mountenc said.

"I will do what I can." Fralk was pleased to notice that none of his concern showed in his voice. He was a good deal less pleased when he remembered how many little lamps he had sold. If they all started dying, he was liable to end up dead himself.

By the time Fralk was done talking Mountenc around, though, the other male was halfway polite again. Of course, had someone given him the promises he had made Mountenc, he would have been happy, too. He wondered if he could make those promises good. Time to find out, he thought as he carried the defunct lamp over to the humans' tent.

Next to the tent stood the thing—Fralk thought of it as a land-boat—the humans used to travel about. It rolled on the round contraptions humans seemed to prefer to skids. Thinking about the flying boat that had almost fallen on him, Fralk reflected that humans not only seemed to like traveling, but also seemed very good at it.

That only made him wonder again why nobody had ever seen any of them before. Maybe they really did come from the Twin-star.

As the humans liked, he paused beside the tent and did not go straight in. "Hello!" he called, and then added the human word: *"Zdrast'ye!"* Nothing happened. He hailed again. Still nothing. He said something unhappy, not quite out loud. Sometimes the humans went wandering through Hogram's town on foot. He hoped they had not chosen today to do that. Today he really needed them.

He hailed again. Finally the entrance to the tent opened. Fralk was so relieved that he hardly minded the hot air that came blasting through the doorway. The human who looked out was still adjusting the outer skins he and his kind wore. *"Brrr!"* the human said, a word whose exact meaning eluded Fralk.

A moment later, another human appeared beside the first. This one was also playing with his outer skins and taking too long to do it for Fralk's taste. Having only two arms made humans clumsy, he thought with a touch of scorn.

"Fralk, yes?" the second human said. He was the only male with a voice like a person's, which made him easier for Fralk to name. He still found humans hard to tell apart by sight.

"*Da*, Katerina Fyodorovna." Fralk said the name carefully; he still stumbled when he used human speech. He had learned, though, that the second part of each human's name was a memory of his father. There, amid so much strangeness, was a custom that made perfect sense. Back to the business in his claws, Fralk thought. He asked, "Is Valery Aleksandrovich here?" Of all the humans, he could speak with that one best.

The male Katerina moved his head back and forth, which Fralk thought weird but had come to learn meant no. "Shota, me here," Katerina said. "Valery, Sergei—" The human groped for a word. "Gone."

"Gone looking, make pictures," Shota said.

"Da," Fralk said, to show he understood. The humans were as curious about Hogram's domain as Fralk was about them.

Shota said something in his own language, too fast and complex for Fralk to follow. He made Fralk more nervous than any other human. Maybe it was a holdover from their first wary meeting, when Fralk had feared the human's picture-making device was a weapon. Or maybe it was that Shota made the alarming yip Fralk had decided was human laughter more often than any of the others.

He was yipping now, as he reached out to touch Katerina in the area below the front of the other male's head, between the arms. Katerina knocked his hand away; the smaller male's face, always pink, turned a deeper shade of red. Humans' colors did not mean nearly so much as his own folk's, but the change, accompanied as it was by a hostile-looking gesture, made Fralk wonder if Katerina and Shota were about to fight.

But Shota said something else that made both humans yip. Katerina turned his head back toward Fralk, as Fralk might have turned a polite eyestalk on someone with whom he was talking. "You, ah, want what?" the human asked.

Fralk held up the lamp that had failed Mountenc. He clicked the little fingerclaw sticking up out of it that was supposed to make it light, then clicked it over and over, back and forth. "No light," he said. "Dead. Can you fix it, make it light again?"

Shota scrambled down from the tent. "Give to me," he said. Fralk put the lamp in his hand. The act made him notice the human's two extra fingers. They did not make up for his missing arms, Fralk thought.

Shota shook the lamp. Fralk had done that, too, trying to make it work again. He had heard nothing and asked the human if he did. *"Nyet,"* Shota said. He bared the grinders in his mouth. "Not hear is good. Not—" He made as if to throw the lamp on the ground.

"Broken," Fralk supplied. "If it is not broken, why does it stay dark?"

Shota called something to Katerina. Then he turned the lamp upside down, so the part that lit was on the bottom. He twisted the lamp in his hands; to Fralk's surprise, it came apart into two pieces.

Fralk extended an eyestalk to peer at what Shota was doing. The human was trying to pull out part of the lamp's guts and having trouble. Muttering, he put down the lamp and drew off the outer skins from his hands. *''Brrr!''* he said again. He picked up the lamp, moving quickly now, and pulled out two cylinders. Under those outer skins, Fralk saw, fascinated, his fingers had claws after all, though they were small and blunt.

Katerina had gone back into the tent while Shota worked with the lamp. Now the smaller male reappeared and tossed Shota a pair of cylinders identical, as far as Fralk could see, to the ones that had just come out.

Shota put in the new ones and put the outer skins back on his hands. This time he said, ''Ahh!'' He twisted the two pieces of the lamp together, and it was as if they had never been apart. He clicked the little fingerclaw. The lamp lit. He handed it back to Fralk.

''Thank you,'' Fralk said, relieved—Mountenc would be no trouble now.

Shota picked up the cylinders he had removed from the lamp. ''These dead,'' he said. ''Use much, they die, not give—'' He ran out of words halfway through his explanation. Fralk got the idea, though. Somehow, light was stored in the little cylinders, and they held only so much. Mountenc had used his lamp all the time, so it failed faster than any other.

''They will *all* do this?'' Fralk demanded in horror. The glow of the lamp he was holding caught one of his eyes. He hastily clicked the lamp off—why waste its precious life during the day?

''All,'' Shota told him.

He felt as tenuously supported as he had crossing the bridge back from the Omalo domains. He pointed to the cylinders Shota was still holding. ''You have more of those, I hope?''

Shota's yipping laughter had an odd quality to it, one Fralk had not heard before. It sounded somehow ominous. It was. ''We have,'' Shota said. ''What you pay?''

No wonder Shota made him nervous, Fralk thought as the bargaining began. No matter how peculiar the human looked, his stalkless eyes were as firmly on the main chance as Fralk's own, or even Hogram's. Fralk knew no higher praise.

* * *

The prints emerged from the developer, one after another. As each came out, Sarah Levitt pounced on it like a cat leaping onto a bird. She had been impatiently pacing ever since she put in the roll of film, three hours earlier. "Any mall back home has a shop that'll run prints out in an hour flat, while I'm spending half my life waiting here," she complained. "So much for high tech."

Emmett Bragg was the only other person awake inside *Athena*. "The machines in those shops are about the size of a pickup truck, too," he said. "They got this one small enough for us to take along. What difference does it make if it's not quite as fast?"

Another picture came out. Even the roller was too slow to suit Sarah. She tugged the print free. "What if you need a picture sooner than in three hours?" she said.

The question was rhetorical, but he answered it. "Then you ought to think to bring a Polaroid along."

She glared at him, thinking he was being sarcastic or patronizing or both at once. His face, though, was serious. "You mean it," she said, surprised.

"Well, sure." He looked at her across a mental gap perhaps as wide, some ways, as the one separating people from Minervans. "Get yourself good and ready beforehand, and the run you're making is a piece of cake."

"But—" Sarah gave up. Emmett was a pilot first and then an astronaut; of course his world revolved around checklists. He even had a point, she supposed. But medicine was less predictable than fighters or spacecraft; things happened all at once instead of sequentially, and so many variables were running around loose together and bouncing off each other.

"Never mind." Bragg came around to look over her shoulder. She heard him suck in a quick, sharp breath of air. All he said, though, was, "Not pretty."

"No." Sarah was almost disappointed that he had not reacted more strongly, before she remembered that he had been through Vietnam. If anything could give him what was close to a doctor's clinical detachment, that was probably it.

The pictures were anything but pretty. No matter how alien Biyal's body was, what had happened to it was grimly obvious, and the stark background of the field where Reatur had left it only made it more pitiful.

"This is how they get more Minervans?" Emmett asked.

Then, without waiting for an answer, he went on. "Not much in the way of obstetrics hereabouts, is there?"

"No," Sarah said again. Then her helpless fury burst out. "There's not one goddamn bloody bit of obstetrics here, and I don't know if there ever will be, or even can be. You see the big wounds?" Her finger hovered over them, first on one print, then on another.

"I see 'em," Bragg said.

"That's where each baby is attached to the female—attached by a big blood vessel. When the babies reach term, the skin over them splits and they let go—and the mother bleeds out, all over the floor." She had cleaned her boots several times. Biyal's blood was still in the crevices.

"Anything you could do to keep it from happening?"

Bragg, Sarah thought, saw straight through to essentials, as with, she reluctantly admitted to herself, his comeback about the Polaroid. Such automatic competence was—daunting. She answered the only way she could. "I don't know. I doubt it. I wish I could, but I don't know."

"You want the chance to try, don't you?"

Startled, she swung around. He was closer to her than she had thought, well inside her personal space when they were facing each other. "How could you tell?" she asked. She did not pull back right away.

"Way you talk." The crow's-feet at the corners of his eyes crinkled in amusement, but the eyes themselves were watchful as ever, a flyer's eyes or, Sarah thought, a marksman's. Being . . . targeted like that was faintly unnerving. But Bragg's voice was light. "You sound like a test pilot going into training with a new machine."

"I guess I do," she said, laughing. "Only with this one, I'm not only not sure whether it will fly, but whether it ought to fly."

The crow's-feet crinkled a different way. Sarah was not sure how it was different, but it was. "Why shouldn't it fly?" Bragg kept with her metaphor.

"Because it looks—" For a variety of reasons, Sarah did not feel like going on, but in the end she did. "It looks like Minervan females are just designed—evolved, whatever—to have one set of babies and then die. Pat's trying to find out if it works that way with the animals here, too, not just the people. And I think the females have those babies young, really young—none of them is much more than half as big as a male."

Bragg pursed his lips, sucked in air between them. "Doesn't leave a whole lot of room for women's lib here, does it?"

"It's not funny, Emmett," she said hotly.

"I never said it was."

It was not an apology, but it was close enough for Sarah to let herself sag wearily as she said, "Suppose I can save a few females while we're here. What happens then? Will they conceive again, and just die next time? Will they live and not conceive again? If they do that, can the Minervans handle the idea of adult females? I don't think the question even arises here."

"Is it your business to turn their whole society upside down?" Bragg asked. "That's what you'd be doing, sounds like."

"I know," she said unhappily. "But is it my business to watch people—intelligent creatures, anyway—die before they have to? And die like this?" She held up the pictures. As if to emphasize her words, another one came out of the developer and lay in its tray, mute evidence of horror.

"Maybe your business is just that. Minervans aren't people—aren't humans," Bragg corrected himself before Sarah could. "We get into enough trouble back home, trying to ram our ways of doing things down our neighbors' throats. Maybe you ought to just let these folks go to hell—or even heaven—their own way."

"Maybe I should." Regretfully, Sarah let it go at that. Bragg, as usual, was straightforward, logical, probably even sensible—and everything in her rebelled at what he was saying. If she ever thought she had a way to keep Minervan females from dying in childbirth, she would try it, and Minervan society would just have to take its lumps.

Bragg started for the galley. "I'm going to get something to munch on," he said. "Want to come along?"

"Why not? God knows when—or if—Irv's coming back tonight. He's slept in Reatur's castle a couple of times already this week. Even inside a sleeping bag—"

"That's a cold bed," Bragg finished for her.

She nodded. "And after looking at these pictures, I don't think I'll rest easy tonight, anyhow. I could use the company."

The pilot gave a thoughtful grunt at that.

In the galley, he chose a packet of smoked, salted almonds. Tearing open the aluminum foil, he said, "I don't suppose the Minervans have anything like beer." He sounded wistful rather than hopeful.

"You know perfectly well they don't," she said, rehydrating

a tube of apricots—all the food on *Athena* was in free-fall-safe containers. "If you ever head away from the ship, make sure you take rations along. The local water or ice ought to be all right, but don't try eating anything. You'd regret it."

"That's what you've been saying," he agreed, crunching.

"Believe it," she told him. "The more I find out about biochemistry here, the more toxic it looks."

"Funny," Bragg said. "Same basic chemicals, right?" At Sarah's nod, he went on, "So how come they didn't work out the same way they did back home?"

She held up a finger so he would wait while she swallowed. "Back home, life got started in the tropical seas. You could call the water here a lot of different things, but tropical's not any of them."

"Isn't that the sad and sorry truth?" Bragg's drawl thickened, reminding her of where he was from. A moment later, he was focused again. "Different conditions, you're saying?"

"Exactly. Back on Earth, everything is geared to functioning well at high temperatures. Even animals that live in weather not much better than Minerva's—polar bears and such—do it by using a lot of insulation to keep warm. But there's no such thing as warm weather on Minerva, and from the biochemistry there never has been. Instead, all the adaptations have been to meeting the cold on its own terms. Minervan tissues are full of every different kind of antifreeze you can think of. Not tasty."

"Like drinking your radiator, eh?" Bragg chuckled.

Sarah stayed serious. "Just exactly. The *Viking* results suggested that, but of course the biochemistry experiments were nowhere near done when—when Reatur smashed it."

"And now it's in his trophy room. That's pretty strange." Bragg shook his head.

"I know." Sarah nodded slowly. "I was in my senior year when *Viking* landed, and I was heartbroken when the transmissions stopped. I never thought then I'd meet the—person who stopped them."

"Something to that," he admitted.

"At the time," she recalled, "I wanted to kill him."

"You and NASA both," Bragg said. "The scientists, anyhow. I was just getting into the program then, and I think the administrators all wanted to give Reatur a big fat kiss, for guaranteeing them all the budget they wanted from then on. They saw farther down the road than the white-coat boys."

"That makes once," Sarah said tartly. Not being enamored

of the NASA bureaucracy, she added, "We could have got here three years faster if we'd just piled up all our paperwork into one stack and walked from Earth."

Bragg let out a loud bray of laughter, then half choked trying to swallow more. "Got to keep quiet," he reminded himself. "Everybody's asleep. Now that we've got a world making day and night for us again, no more sleeping by schedule—naturally, soon as I'd finally got used to it."

Sarah looked at her watch. "Half past two," she said. "I didn't know it was *that* late." She yawned, almost as if by reflex. "Even the extra forty minutes a day we get here won't help much. Let's go to bed."

"Best offer I've had today so far."

Sarah had been turning away. Now she glanced back at him sharply. His tone had been easy, but he was watching her, too. Marksman's eyes, she thought again, discomfited.

"To sleep," she said, ready to be really irritated if he made something of that. He didn't. But as she walked out of the galley, she still imagined she felt his gaze on her back. She did not turn around again; she was just as glad not to know for sure.

4

The sun skipped in and out from behind clouds. Ternat felt its warmth as he slowly walked south, back toward his father's castle from the domain of Dordal. Summer really was on its way, he thought. The warm weather fit in well with his sour mood.

Reatur had said Dordal was an idiot, the domain-master's eldest remembered. If anything, that had been generous of Reatur. Dordal cared not a runnerpest voiding for the threat from across the Ervis Gorge. His eyestalks had wiggled until Ternat thought—hoped—they would fall off. Reatur's eldest was not used to being laughed at. He did not care for it.

He did not care for anything about Dordal's domain. Its crops were scrubby, and of varieties he did not like. Of its meat animals, the massi were too fat and the eloca too thin. Half the herders chewed ompass root—good luck to them if those scrawny eloca ever got loose and started running all over the landscape.

Maybe ompass root was Dordal's problem, too, Ternat thought. His hands closed as he disagreed with himself: he would have smelled the fumes from the root. Dordal was a happy fool all by himself.

He had not even cared to learn about humans, though the bellow of their flying house had been heard in his domain. Some quiet questioning among the younger males in Dordal's castle had made that plain to Ternat. But Dordal dismissed the roar as "a freak storm" and could not imagine humans as anything but ugly people.

Ternat almost sympathized with that. Dordal was plenty ugly himself.

The sun came out again and stayed out. The weather got warmer and warmer—easily warm enough to melt ice, Ternat thought. Yes, it was shaping up to be a miserably hot year. The humans might enjoy it—they were and somehow stayed hotter than anything alive had a right to be—but the excess melt it would cause would only make trouble and work for people.

As if thinking of humans were enough to summon them into his presence, Ternat saw a couple of their traveling contraptions leaning against a large rock. Ternat envied them those gadgets. He wished he had one, but his legs were both too short and too many for the thing to do him any good. But the round legs the gadget had—and, come to think of it, the humans' flying house, too—looked to be better for travel than skids, at least when snow was not drifted deep.

Behind the boulder, Ternat saw a human's foot. To judge by the posture, the human was lying down. That might be interesting, he thought. Except when sleeping, humans were no fonder of being horizontal than people were. And humans, so far as Ternat knew, did not have the habit of sleeping at midday.

He stepped off the path so he could get a better view of what was going on back of the rock. It was not one human back there, he saw after a moment, it was two. Well, that made sense—one for each traveling contraption on the other side of the boulder. But they were lying together in such a tangle of arms and legs that he had to look with three eyes before he was sure.

Under their outer layers, he saw, humans had the same pinkish-tan skins they did on their faces—at least their legs, the uncovered parts, did. Ternat wondered what they were doing. Humans did a lot of strange things, but he had never seen them at anything so strange as this before.

They separated and got up off the square of woven stuff on which they had been lying. They quickly began putting on the outer layers for their legs. They were too engrossed in that to pay any attention to Ternat and soon had the task done.

Before they did, though, Ternat noticed they were different. The taller one had a dangling organ that reminded him a little of his own male parts, though those only came out when he was with a mate. He was sorry for the human for having only one, and thought it ludicrous for the thing to be sticking out there all the time.

Then he thought about the other human, the male *without* the organ. . . . He suddenly stood stock-still in the field as the pos-

sible meaning of that sank in. Given what he had watched, it
made only too much sense.

He hurried back to the path and started home as fast as he
could go. Reatur had to hear this news right away. Maybe he
would know what to do about it.

Pat Marquard put on her long johns as fast as she could; the
skin on her thighs and calves, wherever they had not pressed
directly against Frank's, was all over gooseflesh. She pulled her
pants over the thermal underwear and bent down to put her socks
and boots back on. That was when she saw the Minervan.
"We've been watched," she told Frank.

"Huh?" His head jerked up; he had been tying his boots,
too. "Oh, it's just a native," he said in relief. He grinned a lazy
grin at her. "Maybe he learned something."

"Maybe he did." She rolled up the blanket, shivering briefly
at the idea of fooling around without it on this planet full of
permafrost, then carried it around the rock and strapped it behind her bicycle seat.

She wondered if the Minervan would come over and try to
talk with them, but he seemed to have business of his own. With
a touch of regret, she let him go on. Still, she supposed Irv had
a point when he recommended against forcing contact on the
natives. Things could get nasty if *Athena*'s crew made themselves unwelcome.

"Shall we get going again?" Frank climbed onto his bicycle.
So did Pat. "Sure."

"Only way to keep warm is to keep moving," Frank said as
he began to pedal. He grinned again. "Well, almost the only
way."

"Uh-huh." Pat looked at the ground instead of at her husband. The alleged path they were riding on was rough enough
that he saw nothing out of the ordinary there. But while Frank
whistled cheerfully and his breath steamed out as if it were the
traditional after-sex cigarette smoke, Pat was anything but satisfied.

Frustration stretched her nerves taut. She had been so sure a
couple of miles' worth of isolation would let her find the release
she needed, but it had not worked out that way. Now she didn't
know what to do.

She knew exactly when things had begun to go wrong: aboard
Athena. She had always needed privacy to relax when she made
love, and a curtain spread in front of a cubicle was not enough.

Every noise from outside made her tense up, fearing—irration-ally, she knew, but no less powerfully on account of that—that she and Frank would be interrupted. After most of a year, failure became as ingrained as success had been before.

It wasn't, she told herself, that she didn't love Frank. She did; she was sure of that. But it had been a long time now since she had left clawmarks on his back. She wondered if he still could turn her on.

She also rather wished she hadn't thought about Irv just after yet another unsatisfactory time with Frank. From the noises she occasionally couldn't help noticing on *Athena*, Irv had had no trouble keeping Sarah happy. Sometimes she wondered if the secret was transferable.

Reatur felt his claws dig into the smooth ice of the floor, a mute sign of his disbelief. "You're sure?" he said for the third time.

"No, clanfather, I'm not *sure*," Ternat repeated patiently, "but it looked to me as if the two humans were mating, and one of them seemed to have male mating parts—or rather, a single male mating part. Does that not imply that the other human is a female?"

"I suppose so," Reatur said unwillingly. He still had trouble taking in what his eldest was telling him. "A female that acts like a male—by the gods, a female that has lived long enough to learn a male's wisdom. Even from people as strange as hu-mans are . . ." His voice trailed away.

"Why not just ask them?" Ternat said.

"Would they tell the truth? If I had that kind of female with me, would I admit it? It's as unnatural as—as—" Reatur stopped, at a loss for a comparison. He thought for a while, groping for a way to understand. "Maybe it means these females have never mated."

"Then what were the two humans doing behind the rock?" Ternat asked. "Clanfather, you know as well as I, when the urge comes on you to mate, you mate."

"And if you are a female, when you mate, you bud, and when you bud, you die. There is no other way. With us, with nosver, even with runnerpests it is so. How could it be different with humans?"

Ternat did not answer; he had no good reply to make. Reatur had no answers, either, only endless questions—and the same hopeless hope he always felt when he thought of the sorrow of the mates. What would Lamra be like, if somehow she could live on after the buds dropped from her? Reatur tried to imagine Lamra's wild and sunny nature transformed by, say, Ternat's years. He gave up; he could not make the mental leap.

Then he had another thought. As long as he was imagining Lamra surviving one budding, why not more than one? What would it be like, coupling with a mate who could appreciate the act with full wit, as well as skin? If the humans had that—

"They may be luckier than any people dreamed of being," he said softly.

"Clanfather?" Ternat did not follow him.

"Never mind." Reatur's breath hissed out under his arms. "I suppose you're right, eldest. I'll just have to ask them."

Ternat walking after him, Reatur began looking for a human. Usually he could not go down a hallway without stumbling over three of them; now that he wanted one, they were nowhere to be found. He finally saw one some ways off in the fields, pointing his picture-maker at a male pulling weeds between crop-plants. The subject seemed uninspiring to Reatur.

When the human heard the domain-master coming, he turned his head so his two poor trapped eyes would point the right way. The human hesitated before asking, "Reatur, yes?"

"Yes." Reatur was not offended; he had trouble telling humans apart. This was one of the three that rumbled. "Irv?" he guessed. His odds of being right were better than one in three. He was certain neither the rumbler called Emmett nor the one called Frank cared about weeds.

"Yes," Irv said, and Reatur felt pleased with himself.

The domain-master turned an extra eyestalk on the male who was weeding. "Why don't you go do that someplace else, Gurtz?" When Irv started to follow the male, Reatur muttered to himself. "You stay, Irv; I need to speak with you."

"Reatur?" The human plainly did not yet understand why the domain-master had come to talk with him.

"You did well to get Gurtz out of the way, clanfather," Ternat said. "The fewer who know of this, the better."

"Yes, wouldn't the gossip fly?" Reatur agreed. He gave his attention back to Irv, who was not following the conversation between the domain-master and his eldest. Reatur tried to find a way to get around to his question an eyestalk at a time but saw no way to do anything but ask it straight. "Irv, are you a male or a mate?"

Quick and unambiguous, the answer came back: "A male."
Reatur was surprised at how relieved he felt.

Still, finding out that one human was respectably male did
not mean they all were. The domain-master thought about the
two most often in company with Irv and picked one of their
names. "Is Sarah a male or a mate?"

The long pause before Irv answered told Reatur what he had
to know. He felt his arms droop. Irv must have realized there
was a problem, for even when he did reply at last, his voice was
much softer than Reatur was used to from him. "A mate," he
said.

"I was right, clanfather," Ternat said.

"So you were, eldest." Reatur's voice was as heavy as Ternat's. Intellectually imagining something was a long way from
having it confirmed, especially when it was something as hard
to believe as this. "Are any *other* humans mates?" the domain-
master asked Irv.

He had to try that one a couple of times before he was sure
Irv understood it. The answer he finally got rocked him from
mouth to feet. *Half* the humans were mates.

"Sarah and Pat *and* Louise?" Ternat echoed, as stunned as
Reatur.

"Do you use them?" the domain-master asked. That required
more explanations before Irv saw what he meant, and then even
more as the human tried to respond. Human ideas of society left
Reatur even more confused than he had been; he had not thought
that possible. He got the salient point, though. "You *do* mate
with them?"

"Yes," Irv said.

Reatur forgot his own earlier speculation. "How could you
bring them along with you, then, to die far from more of their
own kind?" he asked, appalled at the human's callousness.

Despite Irv's growing fluency with his language, Reatur took
a while to grasp that his wild guesses had been somewhere close
to right. From what the human said, his people's mates did not
necessarily bud when they coupled—"What's the point of coupling, then?" Ternat said; Reatur hushed him—and did not die
when they budded.

"How can that be?" the domain-master asked. "The
blood—"

"We made different, people and humans," Irv began.

"A good thing, too. I wouldn't want to look like that," Ternat said. Though he privately agreed, Reatur waved his eldest to silence again.

Luckily, the interruption had not thrown Irv far offstride. "Different inside, not just outside."

"Different *how*?" Reatur persisted. When buds fell from a mate, they left holes. Blood had to gush through holes, he thought. Maybe human mates did not drop six buds at a time. But even if—wildly unlikely notion—they only dropped one, that should be plenty.

"Ask Sarah how different," Irv said. "Sarah knows of bodies."

"All right, I'll do that." Humans' characters were still hard for Reatur to gauge, but Sarah struck him as being a very straightforward and competent male. . . . The domain-master flailed his arms—*not* a male! "Ask a mate?"

Irv spread his hand, a take-it-or-leave-it gesture humans used. "Sarah knows," he said. "Sarah knows of bodies, well and not well."

"A doctor?" Reatur said.

"Doctor." Irv repeated the word several times.

Reatur used the same trick when he was trying to remember something. He was glad to notice any point of similarity with humans, now that this gaping gorge of difference had opened up. The idea of learning from a mate still jolted him, so he asked, "Do any other humans know of bodies?"

"Pat does," Irv said after a moment's pause.

Wondering at his hesitation—didn't the fool human know what his friends were good for?—the domain-master said, "All right, I'll ask him." Then he stopped—from what Irv had said, Pat was no more male than Sarah. "I'll ask one of them," Reatur said lamely. One of these days, he added to himself.

"Irv, you should have spoken sooner of this—difference—between humans and people." Ternat sounded accusing. Reatur had trouble blaming him, but hoped Irv could not read his tone.

If the human did, he hid it well. "How?" he asked. "You thought us like you, yes?"

"Yes," Reatur said. "Of course," Ternat agreed.

"We thought you like us," Irv said. "Till Biyal, we thought you like us. After Biyal—" The human stopped.

Reatur wished humans really changed colors or did something he could gauge to show what they were feeling. The movements of their strangely placed mouths told a bit, but not enough, at least not for him. He would have given a lot right then to be inside Irv's head, to know which words the human was choosing and which he was casting aside.

Irv finally resumed, "After Biyal, we knew you not like us. We not know what you think when you know you not like us, so we not say. Now you know, now we talk. Yes, Ternat?"

"Yes," Reatur's eldest said reluctantly. The domain-master made sure he did not let his eyestalks wiggle. Irv had done a neat job of turning things around on Ternat. However weird humans were—and the more he learned of them, the weirder they got—they were not stupid. He would have to make sure he remembered that.

Ternat got the point, too. "From how far away do you come, to be so strange?" he asked.

"Very far away." It was all the humans ever said.

Now that Reatur was beginning to get a feel for both how odd and how close-mouthed they were, he wondered what surprises lurked behind those three self-evident words. "I believe it," he said, and for the moment let it go at that.

"Fralk, one of the humans is outside," a retainer said. "He wishes to speak with you."

"Do you know what he wants, Panjand?" Fralk asked.

"No, eldest of eldest," Panjand said stolidly.

Fralk suspected that the servant had not bothered to ask. He felt the muscles around his mouth tightening in annoyance. He did not have time for humans now, even if he was Hogram's liaison with them. The domain-master had given him enough other things to do to keep any three males busy.

"Will you see him, eldest of eldest, or shall I send him away?" Panjand asked.

"I'll see him," Fralk said mournfully. He put his pen beside the cured hide on which he had been writing and stepped away from the table. "Put a few more drops of *por*-juice into that bowl of isigot blood to keep it from clotting," he told Panjand. "I'll finish up these notes in a while, after I'm done with the human."

Panjand widened himself. "Yes, eldest of eldest."

Fralk, meanwhile, was gathering effusiveness around himself as if it were one of the outer skins humans wore. He opened the door Panjand had shut. *"Zdrast'ye,"* he said, and then peered with three eyes at the human standing in front of him. "Sergei Konstantinovich," he finished after a barely perceptible pause.

"Hello, Fralk," the human replied in the Skarmer tongue. "How are you?"

His accent, Fralk thought, was improving. "Well, thank you. What can I do for you today?" He discarded some of his expansive manner; Sergei was as businesslike as Hogram.

The human proved his instinct right, coming straight to the point. "You use axes, knives from us to fight, ah, Omalo across, ah, Jö—Ervis Gorge?"

"Well, of course," Fralk said. "I told, ah, Shota all about that."

"Not use for that," Sergei said.

"What?" Fralk said, though he understood the human perfectly well. "Why not? You traded them to us; they are ours now. What business do you have telling us what to do with them?"

Sergei hesitated, then said, "Humans—more humans—across Ervis Gorge."

Fralk felt his arms flap limply against his body as he took that news in. Humans were so strange that he had never imagined there being more of them. "How many more humans?" he got out at last, wondering if all the lands he knew were going to be overrun by the funny-looking creatures. It was not a pleasant idea; he would not wish a plague of humans even on the Omalo. On second thought, maybe he would.

"Six." Sergei held up fingers so Fralk could not misunderstand him.

"These humans are of your domain?"

"*Nyet,*" Sergei said, surprising Fralk.

"Of your clan, then? Of the same first bud, I mean."

"*Nyet,*" Sergei said again.

Exasperated, Fralk burst out, "Well, is your clan even friendly with theirs?"

"No," Sergei repeated after another pause.

"Then why in the name of the first Skarmer bud do you care what happens to them?" Fralk's satisfaction at losing his temper quickly dissipated in the effort he needed to get meaning across to the human.

Sergei replied as slowly, groping for words and concepts. "My domain, other humans' domain not fight now. We your friends. Other humans friends with people across gorge. You, they fight, maybe my domain, other humans' domain fight, too."

Fralk opened and closed his hands several times. He had not

thought about humans having politics of their own, either. He brightened. "How's this?" he said. "We won't harm these other humans at all; we'll just use your axes and hammers on the miserable Omalo."

"You get hammers, axes from us. What Omalo get from other humans?"

Fralk wished he were back inside, keeping records for a project that had nothing to do with humans—at least, he had thought it had nothing to do with humans. Humans had a gift for making difficulties all out of proportion to their numbers. "What *do* the Omalo get from these other humans?" he asked.

"Not know." Sergei spread his hands.

"Wonderful." Along with the advantage surprise would give the Skarmer, Fralk had hoped the males who crossed the gorge would carry with them the superior weapons he had obtained for them from the humans. That would make him a hero as well as the rich male he was becoming. But now . . . "Do humans have weapons stronger than axes and hammers?"

"Yes. Our—" Lacking the word in Fralk's language, Sergei perforce used one from his own. "—firearms stronger. Stronger a lot."

"Do these other humans also have firearms?" Fralk echoed the strange sound as well as he could.

"Yes," Sergei said. "Not as good as ours, but yes."

Fralk had a really appalling thought. "Would the other humans give firearms to the Omalo?"

"Not know," Sergei said. "Not think so."

That was something, anyway, Fralk thought. "Do they have hatchets and hammers? Would they give those to the Omalo?"

"Not know if have. If yes, they give, I think."

As Sergei did not have eyestalks, Fralk could not even vent his feelings by wishing the purple itch on them. His dream of a quick, easy conquest aided by marvelous new weapons he personally had helped obtain from the humans looked to be just that—a dream. He tried to find something to be optimistic about and finally did. "At least," he said, "the Omalo won't surprise us."

The reversal in the sentence left the human floundering, and Fralk was in no mood to help him along. Partially changing the subject, Sergei asked, "How you go across Ervis Gorge, fight Omalo?"

He could not have found a better question to restore Fralk's good humor. "I was just keeping track of the frames involved when you got here," he said. "We're making them faster than we thought we could, and we should have plenty when the time comes."

He repeated himself several times. "Frames?" Sergei said. He did not know the word, and context was not enough to give him its meaning. That made Fralk hope the Skarmer plan was something even these oh-so-clever humans had not thought of.

"Here, I'll show you," he said. "Come with me." He led Sergei toward a large shed not far from where they were standing. As they walked, Fralk remarked, "You know, of course, that as spring turns to summer, water flows through Ervis Gorge."

"*Da,*" was all Sergei said, disappointing Fralk, whose "of course" had been solely for effect. Then he reflected that humans, being so beastly hot themselves, would not find water as much a nuisance as people did. He had already noticed that they preferred it to ice. That, he thought, was their problem.

Inside the shed, half an eighteen of males—three crews of three—were busy using vines and dried massi eyestalks to lash curved pieces into frames that looked like bowls bigger across than a male was tall. "We'll stretch hides over them, and then—" He paused dramatically. "If we put them on water, they'll stay on the top of it, even with a couple of males inside. We call them 'boats.'" He used the borrowed Lanuam word as if it were part of the Skarmer tongue, hoping Sergei would think his people had had the idea for themselves.

"Boats," the human repeated. He was silent for some little while, looking at the frames. Then he asked, "In Ervis Gorge, ice, water, rocks all together, *da*?"

"Yes," Fralk agreed. And yes, he thought, humans plainly knew plenty about water.

"You use boats with ice, water, rocks all together? These boats?" Sergei pointed at the frames.

"Yes. I told you, they'll stay on top of the water."

"*Bozhemoi,*" Sergei said. "When ice, rocks, ah, touch boats, then what?"

Fralk had not thought about that. The Lanuam, from whom the Skarmer clans had bought the concept of boats, had never mentioned it. Maybe they would have if asked, but the Skarmer did not know the right questions. Having been on the other end of a few deals like that, Fralk admired the distant Lanuam and resolved to pay them back if he ever got the chance.

Now, though, he put the best appearance he could on things.

"Most will not be hit at all; others will endure some damage and keep on. We should not lose many."

"*Bozhemoi*," Sergei said again. It was another of those annoying human words with no clear meaning, but Fralk did not think the human seemed enthusiastic.

"Hurry up," Sarah said, hopping up and down. "I'm turning into an ice cube." She was only wearing shoes, shorts, a T-shirt, and a bicycle helmet; the temperature hovered right around freezing.

Irv shoved the wide stepladder next to *Damselfly*. As soon as it was in place, Sarah bounded to the top, hitting only every other rung. Irv climbed up beside her and helped her down into the cockpit. When she was safely onto the seat, he swung down the cockpit cover and latched it closed.

Sarah held a checklist in her hand and went through it item by item. "Just like Emmett," she said. Irv could hear her teeth chattering; *Damselfly*'s thin Mylar skin—glorified Saran wrap, Irv thought—did nothing to block sound.

He got off the ladder, carried it out of the way, and went to his station at *Damselfly*'s left wingtip. "Radio check," Sarah announced through the little set that hung on his belt.

"Reading you fine," he answered. "Do you read me?"

"Five by five. I'm going to charge up my battery now." She started pedaling furiously, powering a small generator. After a minute or two, she said, "Thank God—I'm starting to warm up."

Louise Bragg was standing by the other wingtip. "Battery holding its charge all right?" she asked.

Irv saw Sarah's head move as she checked the gauge. "Looks real good," she said. "I'm going to engage the prop now." The big airfoil started to spin. *Damselfly* rolled forward. Irv and Louise went with it to hold the wing level, first walking, then at a run.

"Airborne!" Sarah shouted, so loudly that Irv heard her both over the radio and straight from the cabin of the plane for which she was not only pilot but also engine. "That's always so smooth," she added a moment later, much more quietly. "The first time I did it, I didn't even realize I'd gotten into the air till my ground crew started cheering." Then she fell silent once more, concentrating on her pedaling.

Damselfly gained altitude and began a slow turn toward Reatur's castle. It was almost silent in the sky; only the clicking whir of the bicycle chain and the whoosh of air past the propeller revealed its presence, and they faded past notice by the time it had flown a couple of hundred yards.

"How's it handle?" Irv called when he saw his wife was having no trouble keeping the ultra-ultralight in the air.

"No problem," Sarah answered. "If anything, it's easier than flying it on Earth. The denser air's giving me more lift, just like they thought it would back home." Her voice confirmed her words; she did not sound as if she were straining.

The Minervans working in the fields had not paid *Damselfly* much attention while the humans brought its pieces out of *Athena* and put them together. The locals had no idea what it was for. The only flying thing they had ever seen was the spacecraft itself, and *Damselfly*, Irv thought, was about as much like *Athena* as a feather duster was like a hawk.

But when the Mylar and graphite-epoxy contraption got into the air, the Minervans stopped whatever they were doing. They let out piercing hoots of amazement and pointed with arms and eyestalks both. Several came rushing over to Irv and Louise, still pointing and shouting excited questions at the same time.

Louise turned to Irv in some alarm. "What *are* they saying?" she asked. She and Emmett spent more time on *Athena* and less with the Minervans than the other four Americans and had picked up less of the local language.

"I don't quite know myself," Irv said. Enough Minervans were clustered around him that much of what they were asking came through only as babel. He also saw that many more had come to him than to Louise. That made him give a mental sigh. Even exhilarated as they were, the locals remained nervous of a mature female.

As he listened, he finally began to catch on to what the Minervans were saying. About what he should have expected, he supposed: What is it? How does it work? Can I ride on it? Can I get one?

He had trouble staying polite as he answered the last question; his mental image of a Minervan on a bicycle seat pedaling like a madman made him want to giggle. But the natives kept after him. *Athena* and the capabilities it represented were beyond their comprehension, but *Damselfly* they could appreciate.

"Whew!" he said to Louise when the Minervans at last believed him when he insisted the ultra-ultralight could not carry passengers, was not made for their shape, and was the only one of its kind. "They never thought of flying, so of course it looks easy to them."

"I wonder what they'd think if we told them we'd been to the moon and back eight years before anybody flew a person-powered plane around a one-mile course." Louise was Sarah's backup on *Damselfly* and knew more about what had gone into its design than Irv did.

In any case, the anthropologist was more interested in the effect the plane had on the Minervans than in its technology. "If the next ship here brought a dozen *Damselflies* adapted for the natives—assuming you could—they wouldn't need any other trade goods like the ones we brought, and they'd come home showing a profit."

Louise let out a cynical snort that sounded very much like one of Emmett's. "That's as good a reason as any for NASA not to let 'em do it, and better than most."

"I suppose so." Irv looked north and east. *Damselfly*, cruising at not much more than a man's height off the ground, was almost right down on the horizon. Irv thumbed the radio switch. "How's it going, darling?"

"Important discovery—it is possible to sweat on Minerva. Who would have thunk it?" Irv could hear the effort in her words, and the way she spaced them so they would not interfere with her breathing.

"How's *Damselfly* going to do as a picture platform?" he asked.

Suddenly fatigue was not the only thing putting pauses between her words—exasperation was there, too. "I'm busier than hell in here, just trying to keep this beast flying—I haven't had a lot of time for pictures."

She had a point. By airliner standards, her controls were crude to the point of starkness: a stick, a radio switch, a prop control switch, a prop pitch gauge, an airspeed indicator, a battery charge gauge, and the camera button. But no airline pilot had to make his plane go by himself.

Still, Irv said, "On the return leg, why not see how much altitude you can gain without wearing yourself out too badly, and squeeze off a few shots. They're pictures we can't get any other way, you know—the main reason we brought *Damselfly* along."

"You mean it's not just a special exercise bike for me? Thanks for the news." Irv felt his ears grow hot under the flaps of his cap. But despite her sarcasm, Sarah pedaled harder, until she got the ultra-ultralight a good thirty yards off the ground. "Even with the battery and the denser air, this is plenty," she panted.

"All right," Irv said mildly.

Sarah was not quite appeased. "It had better be. Most crashes with this beast I could walk away from, but I'm up high enough now to break my neck." She clicked off. A few seconds later she came back on, sounding worn and sheepish at the same time. "The view from up here *is* spectacular. I can see all the way over to Jötun Canyon."

"Just looking ought to be plenty as far as that's concerned," Louise said sharply. "I wouldn't want to fly over it, not with the funny wind conditions it's bound to have. *Damselfly*'s not exactly built to handle gusts, you know."

"Seeing it and flying over it aren't the same thing. I'm going to let my altitude go now. I've shot a whole roll—that ought to keep you happy, Irv."

"So it should," he agreed, unembarrassed. Aerial photography had taught anthropologists and archaeologists a lot of things they had never noticed when they were stuck on the ground. Irv would have killed to get a Piper Cub onto *Athena*. That being in the dream category, he would cheerfully settle for whatever *Damselfly* could show him.

The ultra-ultralight slowly approached. The prop fell silent as Sarah stopped pedaling. *Damselfly* touched down as lightly as one of its namesakes.

Sarah reached up and popped the catch on the canopy, then opened it so vigorously that *Damselfly* shook. Irv trotted up with the special stepladder. He climbed to the top to help his wife emerge. The sight of her flushed sweaty skin—and of so much of it—forcibly reminded him how little he had seen of her lately, both in the figurative and literal senses of the word. He thought unkind thoughts about Minerva's climate.

Sarah had the weather on her mind, too, but in a different way. "For God's sake, get me some clothes," she said after much too brief an embrace. "If I let myself stiffen up, I'll be hobbling around for days." As if to underscore that, she started to shiver.

She jumped down from the ladder. Louise handed her the warm outerwear. She scrambled into it, while Irv wished the engineer had been a little less efficient. He could have done with another hug.

"And now, as medical officer, I wish I could prescribe a good hot shower for myself. Unfortunately, the closest I can come is to wipe myself down and bake under the heat lamp for a while. Have to do, I suppose." She started for *Athena*.

Irv and Louise knocked down *Damselfly* by themselves—Sarah, after all, had done plenty in flying it. They stored the pieces aboard *Athena*; neither of them even thought about leaving the fragile ultra-ultralight out were the elements could touch it. A hailstorm or even a windstorm would turn it to junk in a hurry.

As they were carrying the tail spar, to which *Damselfly*'s rudder and elevators were attached, Louise looked at her watch. "I think I'll stay aboard when we're done here. We ought to be getting today's transmission from Houston in about another twenty minutes."

"I guess I'll stay, too." Irv patted the pocket where he had the roll of film he had extracted from *Damselfly*'s camera. "I'll wait for this to run through the developer so I can see just what we've got."

Louise did not say anything, but before she turned away Irv saw her raise an eyebrow. He silently swore at the developer for being so slow that it made obvious his real reason for hanging around *Athena*: He had every intention of warming up Sarah a different way after she turned off the heat lamp.

That hopeful notion came to naught, anyhow. Some of the males in the fields must have told Reatur about *Damselfly*, for the chieftain walked up just as Irv was carrying the last piece of the plane, the propeller, to *Athena*.

Reatur was full of questions and had trouble following Irv's answers because he had not actually seen *Damselfly* up in the air. The only thing he had to compare to its flight was *Athena*'s thunderous arrival, and Irv had already thought once about how unlike were those two things covered under the umbrella of one word.

And so, fascinated and confused at the same time, Reatur kept trying to understand. He finally invited Irv to the castle to explain further. He was so polite about it that the anthropologist could not find any good way to say no. No doubt, Irv thought sourly as they walked along a path through the fields, Reatur thought he was doing him a favor.

By the time he got back to *Athena*, Sarah was asleep. Grumbling, he went back and fed the roll of film into the developer. Even as he did, though, he knew his mind was not on what the prints would show.

* * *

The three males stood at the base of *Tsiolkovsky*'s boarding ladder. Even to the inexperienced eyes of the two Russians aboard, they looked ill-kempt. "More seedy beggars," Oleg Lopatin said, curling his lip in distaste.

"Yes," Yuri Voroshilov said; from the chemist, it almost counted as a major speech. Lopatin would have wondered had much more come from him. If anyone could have stayed sane alone through a nearly three-year Minerva mission, Lopatin would have bet on Voroshilov. Assuming, the KGB man thought, that he was sane now, on which Lopatin reserved judgment. That Yuri was competent counted for more.

Beggars the Minervans were in the most literal sense of the word. They held out several arms apiece toward *Tsiolkovsky*. Lopatin clicked on the outside mike. He had not learned a lot of the local language, but he had heard that phrase too often to mistake it: "Give! Please give!"

Lopatin had no use for beggars. Had it been up to him, he would have sent them packing, and in a hurry, too. But the orders from Moscow were clear: do nothing to antagonize the natives. Lopatin obeyed orders.

All the same, he did not care for them. As he often did, he said, "Will you do the honors, Yuri Ivanovich?"

"Yes," Voroshilov said again. He got some trade goods out of a box by the inner airlock door, closed it after him, opened and closed the outer one, and started down the ladder. Lopatin trained a machine gun on the Minervans below. There had been no trouble with the locals, but he stayed ready for a first time.

The Minervans recoiled when they first saw Voroshilov—these newcomers might have heard about humans, an amused Lopatin thought, but they had never set eyes on one before. One male let out a contralto shriek that would have made any movie heroine proud.

"You want what?" the chemist asked when he was on the ground. The Minervans pulled back again at the sound of his deep voice.

Then one of them, visibly gathering his courage, stepped toward Voroshilov again. He repeated the sad chant all three males had been making: "Give! Please give!"

"Here." Voroshilov pulled out a pocket knife and briefly took off one glove so he could use his thumbnail to pull out a blade and show the male what the artifact was. The Minervan shrieked again, this time, if Lopatin was any judge, in delight.

Seeing their comrade rewarded, the other two males also came up to Voroshilov. He gave one of them another pocket knife, the other a chisel with a transparent gold plastic handle.

"Hot, yellow ice!" the Minervan exclaimed as he held the chisel up to one eyestalk so he could peer through it.

All three males made themselves short and fat to thank Voroshilov and were so happy they did not take fright when he bowed in return; Lopatin had seen other locals start running at what was to them a startling gesture.

As he always did, Voroshilov asked, "What you do with tools I give you?" And Oleg Lopatin, not for the first time, thought the chemist was much more animated dealing with the Minervans than he ever had been with his fellow humans. Voroshilov's pale, rather thin features lit up; real expression came into his voice.

The answer he got was the one he and Lopatin heard most of the time: "Take them to Hogram's town to get what we can for them."

"And after that?" Voroshilov persisted.

Again the reply was familiar. "We hope we will have enough then to pay Hogram the back rent on our plots, so we will not have to give them up and come to the town for good to try to make a living there."

"Good luck to you," Voroshilov said. Inside *Tsiolkovsky*, Lopatin sardonically echoed, "Good luck." The Minervan peasants would not earn as much as they thought for the trinkets Voroshilov had given them. Too many such goods from Earth were available around Hogram's castle; almost every day, the Russians there reported another drop in price.

Well, the bumpkins would find that out soon enough. He watched them trudge off toward the town. Each of them kept a couple of eyes trained on Voroshilov as he climbed up into *Tsiolkovsky*. The locals would have a story for the rest of their lives, Lopatin thought.

"What do you suppose they'll end up doing a few weeks from now?" he asked when his companion was back inside.

"Building boats," Voroshilov said promptly.

"I expect you're right," Lopatin agreed. "Building boats, earning whatever wages Fralk and Hogram choose to grant them, living wherever they can, with only their labor to sell."

"Proletarians," Voroshilov said.

"Exactly so. The revolution will come here one day, just as it has on Earth."

"Not now," Voroshilov said with what sounded like alarm.

Lopatin made a mental note of that tone, but only a small one, because Voroshilov was right. The Minervans here were just entering a capitalist economy, not coming to its conclusion. And from what Lopatin had gathered from the Americans' reports, the natives on the far side of Jötun Canyon were still frankly feudal.

Barring the genius of a Lenin, then, the time for the revolt of the proletariat was still far away. Lopatin had a very good opinion of himself, but he knew he was no Lenin.

"Back to work," Voroshilov said, and headed off for his lab.

A strange one, Lopatin thought as the chemist walked down the passageway. He had had the thought many times and still did not care for it. He wanted—he needed—people to be orderly and predictable. Anything he did not understand, he mistrusted.

Voroshilov, for instance, had gone far longer than any of the other men on *Tsiolkovsky* before even trying to approach Katerina. He had gone so long, in fact, that Lopatin began to wonder if he was a homosexual who had somehow escaped all the screening for that kind of criminal behavior. Lopatin would not have much minded if he was; it would have given him a hold on the quiet chemist. But it was not so. As far as the KGB man could tell, Voroshilov was just painfully shy.

He waited until clanks and clatters told him that Voroshilov was busy again, then called up a computer index to which no one else on *Tsiolkovsky* had access. In it were his files on the other five crewfolk. He recalled Voroshilov's. One of the documents was called "Poetry"—it was a transcription of the set of jottings Lopatin had found on one of his periodic searches through the ship. The scribbles themselves were back in their hiding place.

"Love songs," the KGB man muttered under his breath as he read them again. They were amazingly good, amazingly sensuous, and every one had Katerina's name in it. Just glancing at them made Lopatin wish she were there. She had not warmed much in his embrace during the brief time she let him share her cubicle, but he still savored the relief her body had brought.

Men were not like women, he thought thankfully, remembering the old joke about the fellow who came into a tavern complaining that the lovemaking he had just had was the worst he had ever known. When the man behind the bar asked him how he would describe it, he grinned and said, "Magnificent!"

Regretfully, Lopatin sent the poems back into the computer's memory. He also sent a sharp glance back toward where Voroshilov was still working. Nobody with that unprepossessing an exterior had any business having all those fine words running around loose in his head. Lopatin doubted everyone on principle but felt real suspicion of anyone who concealed himself the way the chemist did.

Tried to conceal himself, the KGB man amended. If he ever needed one, he had a handle on Voroshilov, all right. He smiled. Katerina was a very nicely shaped handle, now that he thought of it.

The ball, a hide cover over soft *teag*-fiber, flew past Lamra. She let out a frustrated squawk as she went after it. She had thought she had an arm in the right place to catch it, but somehow it got by her. It usually did.

She widened herself so she could pick up the ball. "Reatur always catches it," she said. "It's not fair."

"Throw it back to me," Peri said. When Lamra did not throw it back right away, the other mate's voice got louder. "Throw it back to me! Throw it back to me!" Lamra still did not throw it. Peri came over and took it away from her. "Mine!"

Lamra snatched it back. She used a couple of free hands to hit Peri. She was older and bigger than the other mate, but that did not stop Peri from hitting her, too, and poking her with a fingerclaw. She yelled and threw the ball at Peri as hard as she could. She missed. The ball bounced away.

Neither mate cared about it anymore anyhow. They were too busy fighting with each other. Other mates came running to watch and to add their shouts to Lamra's and Peri's.

Lamra had taken control of the fight and was just about to tie three of Peri's arms into a knot when the door to the outside world came open and Reatur walked in.

"What's going on here?" he asked. "What's this racket all about?"

"She took my ball away," Peri said, squirming away from Lamra and pointing at her with the arms that—too bad!—she hadn't got to knot up after all.

"Not your ball," Lamra said. She gathered herself to grab Peri again and really give her what for. Reatur turned an extra eyestalk her way and pointed at her with an arm that did not seem to have anything better to do. Regretfully, she subsided. She might have known he would notice.

"Back to what you were doing, the rest of you," Reatur told the crowd of mates around Peri and Lamra. They went, though almost all of them kept an eyestalk on what was going on. Even so, Lamra wished they would do what *she* told them to like that. Maybe being big like Reatur helped.

He had been talking to Peri. Filled with her own not quite happy thoughts, Lamra had paid no attention to whatever he was saying. She was a little surprised when Peri, after squeaking, "I will," hurried away. Several of the other mates were playing a game of tag. Peri joined them. In a moment, her trouble with Lamra forgotten, she was frisking about.

"Now you," Reatur said to Lamra. He had not forgotten, even if silly Peri had.

"It *wasn't* her ball," Lamra said.

"I know that," Reatur said. "You all play with everything here in the mates' chambers, so how could any of it belong especially to any one of you? That's not what I wanted to talk with you about, Lamra."

Then he did something Lamra had never seen him do with any other mate, though he had before with her, once or twice: he widened himself down very low, so that he was hardly taller than she. She still did not know what to make of that—she felt proud and nervous at the same time.

"You ought to know better than to squabble that way with Peri," he said.

"It's not fair," Lamra said. "She squabbled with me, too."

She saw Reatur's eyestalks start to wiggle, saw him make them stop. That was just one more thing she did not understand: Why would he want to make himself stop laughing? Laughing was fun.

"So she was," he said. "But she"—he lowered his voice a little, so the others could not hear—"is just an ordinary mate, and you, I think, are something more. So I expect more from you."

"Not fair," Lamra said again.

"Maybe not. Would you rather I expected less from you than you are able to give?"

"Yes. No. Wait." Lamra had to stop and work that one through. Reatur was talking to her as if she were another male. His words were as badly tangled as she had hoped to make Peri's arms. "No," she said at last.

"Good," Reatur said. "So you'll behave yourself, then?"

"Yes," Lamra said. Then she wailed, "I don't want to behave myself!" The world suddenly seemed a more complicated place than she wanted it to be.

"I know you don't," Reatur said gently. "Doing it anyway is the hard part. It's called being responsible."

"I don't want to be whatever you said—responsible. It's silly, like not laughing when you want to laugh." Lamra turned an eyestalk away from Reatur to show she was not happy with him. "And like widening yourself so you're so short and fat that you look like a toy nosver."

"Do I?" Reatur laughed then, so hard that Lamra doubted he could see straight. He also resumed his regular height. "Is this better?"

"Yes," Lamra said, though she could hear the doubt in her own voice.

"All right." Reatur hesitated. "How are the buds?"

Lamra looked down at herself. She was beginning to have a swelling above each foot, but the buds did not inconvenience her yet, and so she did not think about them very much. "They're just—there," she said, which seemed to satisfy Reatur. "How are Biyal's budlings?"

She saw that she had startled Reatur; his eyestalks drew in, then slowly extended themselves again. "One mate has died," he said. "The others seem to be holding their own. It won't be long before we bring them back to live in here. The male is doing well."

"I miss Biyal. She was fun to play with—not like Peri, who squawks all the time," Lamra added pointedly. She let air hiss out from her breathing-pores in quite a good imitation of Reatur sighing. "I suppose the new ones will be even more foolish."

"I suppose they will." Reatur turned an extra eye her way. "I've hardly ever heard a mate say she missed another one after that one—after that one budded," he said slowly. "You remember more than most, don't you?"

"How can I tell that?" Lamra asked. There Reatur went, confusing her again. "I only know what I remember, not what anyone else remembers."

"That's true." Reatur was trying not to laugh again, she saw. He stopped for a while, then went on in a musing tone. "What would you be like if you could hope for my years, or even Ternat's?"

"Don't be silly," she told him. "Who ever heard of an old mate?"

"Who indeed?" he said, and gave a sigh so much like hers that she could not help wiggling her eyestalks. He reached out and awkwardly patted her between her eyestalks and her arms.

"All I can tell you, Lamra, is that I hope the male you bear takes after you. Having such wits around to grow would be precious."

Lamra thought about it. She was not used to taking such a long view; being as they were, mates did not have occasion to. Finally she said, "You know, that would be nice, but I'd rather it was me."

Reatur looked at her with all six eyes at once for a moment, something he had never done before. "So would I, little one. So would I." Then he said something she did not understand at all. "I'm beginning to envy humans, curse me if I'm not."

He left the mates' chambers very quickly after that.

5

Several Minervans kept an eye, or two, or three, on Frank Marquard as he got ready to descend. The lead male of the group was the one called Enoph. "Why are you going down?" he asked for the third time as Marquard checked and rechecked the lashing of his line around the big boulder that would secure it. "Tell me again, in words I can understand."

"I try," the geologist said in halting Omalo. He knew he could not have explained even if he spoke the language fluently. The Minervans had not developed the concepts they needed to grasp what he was up to.

"You know I walk on path down this far, more than halfway down Jöt—" He caught himself; the human name for the canyon meant nothing to the locals. "Down Ervis Gorge."

"Not just on the path," Enoph said with the sinuous wriggle of his arms that Marquard mentally translated as a shudder. "Away from it, too. How do you dare go where you might fall? Especially since you have only two arms and two legs to hold on with."

"How I go? Carefully." Marquard sighed when Enoph only opened and closed a couple of his hands in agreement. So much for the old joke. "You see how I go. When not on path, always have rope—how you say?—tied to big rock. If fall, not fall far."

"Yes, I grasp that," Enoph said—a natural image for a six-armed folk to use. "You humans are clever with ropes. I suppose you have to be. But *why* do you do what you do?"

"To learn from rocks," Marquard said. That was as close as he had come to rendering *geology* into Minervan.

"A rock is a rock." Enoph had said that before. Now, though, he paused to think it over. "Maybe not," he amended. "Some rocks are harder than others, some better to chip at than others. Do you want to learn which ones are best for tools? I could show you that."

"No, not for tools. Want to see how rocks change in time. New rocks near top of Ervis Gorge, rocks older down low."

Enoph wiggled his eyestalks, which meant he was laughing at Frank. I do better as a comedian when I'm not trying, Marquard thought. "All rocks are as old as the world. How could one be older than another?" Enoph asked.

Marquard shook his head; like other Minervans who had spent a good deal of time with humans, Enoph understood the gesture. "Think of two *fossils* I find in rocks," the geologist said.

The key word was in English. Again, though, Enoph followed; the locals had not really started wondering about long-ago life preserved in rocks, but Maquard had shown them the couple of specimens he had discovered and had found giving them a new word easier than the elaborate circumlocution he would have needed to say the same thing in Minervan.

"I remember," Enoph said. "One looked just like the foot of a nosver turned to stone. How can a nosver turn to stone?"

That, Marquard thought, needed a longer and more complicated explanation than he could give. Fortunately, it also was not quite relevant. "Where that rock like nosver from?"

"Not far from the top of the gorge, as I recall," Enoph answered. "What of it?"

"Now think on other *fossil*."

"That weird creature?" Enoph made the shuddery gesture again. "It looked like an eloc, or rather a piece of an eloc, but hardly bigger than a runnerpest. Even new-budded eloca are three times that size."

"No animal like that now, yes?" Marquard asked. Enoph repeated his hand-closing gesture. The geologist went on. "Then that rock old, old, old, yes? No animal like that left now, yes? And that rock from where?"

Enoph pointed an eyestalk at a spot halfway down the side of the canyon. He suddenly turned four of his other eyes toward Marquard. The geologist smiled; no Minervan had ever shown him that much respect before. He also realized Enoph was no fool—he had not had to point out all the implications to the male. With data presented the right way, Enoph was plenty smart enough to work out implications for himself.

"You humans have the oddest notions," he said. "I see this

one is true, but who would have thought rocks could have ages? How does it help you to know this?''

The Minervan, Marquard thought unfairly, sounded like a congressman about to vote against a research appropriation. ''The more you know, the more you can find out,'' the geologist answered. ''If you know nothing, how find out anything? Know one thing: this big rock''—he pointed to the boulder to which he had lashed himself—''come down from up *there*.'' He pointed to a level not far from the one the older fossil had come from.

Minervans did not jump when they were surprised. If they had, Enoph would have. ''How can you know that? I helped move it—and a nasty job it was—to secure the bridge to the Skarmer side of the gorge.''

Getting the idea of ''bridge'' across took a good deal of gesturing and guessing, not least because there was no bridge for Enoph to point at. When Frank Marquard finally thought he understood, he asked the Minervan, ''Where bridge now? Not see.''

That got a response from several of the males who had come down, and not a polite one. They turned all their eyestalks away from the western side of the canyon and extended sharp finger-claws as far as they would go. They also turned the bright yellow that Marquard had learned to be the color of anger.

''The stupid Skarmer wanted to cross to this side of Ervis Gorge and take our land and our mates from us,'' Enoph said. ''Seeing them try with the rope bridge up would have been plenty funny. How they propose to cross the gorge without it I cannot say.''

''Anyone with the wit even of a mate would see it can't be done,'' another male said. There was loud agreement from his companions.

Marquard looked toward the western horizon, which was, in essence, the distance-blurred western wall of Jötun Canyon. He had not thought his Minervan vocabulary would need to include terms like ''invasion.'' He looked again. Like Enoph, he had no idea how the Skarmer would get across the canyon if the people on this side did not feel like letting them.

''They say they do this?'' he asked at last.

''The Skarmer *say* all manner of foolish things,'' Enoph said scornfully. ''I think that comes down to them from the first Skarmer bud. What they can *do* is something else again.''

''I hope you right,'' Marquard said. All the same, he remembered, and rather wished he hadn't, something he had read or heard so long before that he had forgotten just where: "Son, if a man comes up to you in a bar and wants to bet he can make the jack of spades leap out of the deck and spit apple cider in your ear, never bet with that man because, son, if you do, sure as hell you'll end up with an earful of cider."

He snorted, imagining the fun he would have translating that into Minervan. His breath steamed out. What he did say was, "You watch, ah, Skarmer side of gorge to know Skarmer not come?"

"Aye, we watch," Enoph said. "A waste of time, but we watch—the domain-master would have it so. Like you when you check your rope so carefully, he takes few chances."

"Thank you," Marquard said; being compared to Reatur had to be a compliment. The geologist gave the line another yank, though now he was convinced it would hold—if that boulder had supported a rope long enough to stretch across Jötun Canyon, his relatively tiny weight would not send it tumbling into the abyss.

He made the check just the same. It was, after all, his neck. Moving slowly and cautiously, he began to descend. The going was still a long way from extreme; he did not need to think to pick hand- and footholds. He thought about the Skarmer instead. Jötun Canyon struck him as a handy sort of thing to have between oneself and unfriendly neighbors. . . .

"At least," he muttered, "till they figure out how to shoot across it." He reminded himself to tell Irv about what Enoph had said—and Emmett Bragg, too, come to think of it. Assessing threats was part of Bragg's job.

As he lowered himself, he began concentrating more and more on his own job. The wall of Jötun Canyon was like an enormous geological layer cake, with him the tiniest of ants nibbling data from it.

In more literal terms, the canyon wall was sandstone alternating with conglomerate, with an occasional thin layer of igneous rock telling of a time of vulcanism. Frank felt like cheering every time he came across one of those. He collected igneous specimens with special care. Potassium-argon dating from them would give him absolute dates on which to hang the relative dates of the stratigraphy he was developing.

Thought about another way, the conglomerates might have been even more impressive than granite or basalt. The rocks accreted in the sandy matrix ranged up from pea-sized to bigger than a VW bus. When the glacier meltoff got rolling, it did not care what it moved. Anything in the way went.

For the moment, though, Marquard was scrambling over neither pragmatically valuable igneous rock nor awe-inspiring conglomerates. This layer was just rather weathered yellow-brown sandstone. He got out his geologist's hammer and took several small specimens.

He grinned wryly as he wrote up a data tag for each one. If he had taken all the specimens he wanted, *Athena* would have ended up too heavy to get them back to Earth.

His eyes flicked over an oddly shaped shadow, and he bent down for a closer look. Only remembering that he would alarm the Minervans above kept him from shouting out loud. Finding a fossil was always good for a rush.

The thing was not very big and was built on the same radial pattern dominant all over Minerva. Aside from that, it didn't look like anything with which Frank was familiar. No reason it should, he thought; it was a couple of hundred million years old if it was a day. Maybe Pat would have some idea of what it was related to.

He photographed the fossil in situ. Then, using hammer and chisel, he freed the stone in which it was embedded from the canyon wall. He was glad it was small. That way he could get it all out, which would make his wife happy.

He wondered what Pat would have done had he stumbled over the Minervan equivalent of, say, *Brachiosaurus*. He had a picture of her holding a gun on the rest of *Athena*'s crew and as many locals as possible until they dug out the whole specimen. When Pat set her mind on something, she generally got it.

She would have nothing to complain about this time, he thought as he wrapped the fossil in bubbled plastic and stuck it in the bag he carried on his belt just for such lucky finds. Minervan fossils, Frank thought fondly, were the most fun Pat had out of bed.

Tolmasov pulled off the headphones—both the static of the scrambled transmission and Lopatin's furious shouts were giving his ears a workout. "Calmly, Oleg Borisovich, calmly," he urged.

"The devil's grandmother take calmly," Lopatin yelled across the kilometers from *Tsiolkovsky*.

Tolmasov scowled. When a KGB man started calling on the devil and his relations, something really had gone wrong somewhere. The oath was a surer sign of trouble than Lopatin's using the scrambler, as a matter of fact: give a security man a scrambled circuit and of course he will use it.

"At least stop swearing long enough to tell me what you're swearing about," the pilot suggested.

"The Americans, those deceiving sons of—"

"What about them?" Tolmasov broke in sharply, though Lopatin seemed ready to go on in that vein for some time yet. "What about the Americans?" the colonel repeated, letting the snap of command enter his voice.

"Sergei Konstantinovich, the Americans deceitfully concealed the true location where their *Viking* came down. When *Athena* landed east of Jötun Canyon, it was no navigational error. They knew where their spacecraft was, and went there. All the data they published over the last decade and a half were false, and deliberately false at that."

Tolmasov rubbed his chin as he thought. "How can you be certain of this?" The whole thing struck him as a ploy more in character for the KGB than the Americans, who were usually too naive to come up with such ideas.

"We have people in NASA," Lopatin reminded him. Tolmasov would have been surprised if the Americans did not know that, too. As if reading his mind, Lopatin went on, "No, Sergei Konstantinovich, this is not disinformation fed our folk by the CIA. *Athena*'s crew has sent word back to Houston that they are in contact with the very male who wrecked the *Viking*. Do you think any navigational error would have been likely to put them so precisely on the spot?"

"*Nyet,*" Tolmasov said flatly. More to himself than to the KGB man, he mused, "How best to use the information?"

"Beat them over the heads with it," Lopatin answered at once. "The American hypocrites always embarrass us for not blabbing everything to the heavens as they do. Now we can pay them back, and let us see how they enjoy it."

"You know, Oleg Borisovich, I like that." Tolmasov could not keep the surprise from his voice; he was not used to liking Lopatin's suggestions. He let out an anticipatory laugh. "I will enjoy seeing the good Brigadier Bragg embarrassed. Till this moment, I had not thought such a thing possible."

What I really would enjoy, Tolmasov thought, is seeing Bragg's fighter in the center of my radar screen, and hearing the tone that tells me my missile has locked on to his tailpipe. He sighed. Even in a fantasy, it was all too easy to imagine Bragg somehow evading him. The man was good.

The colonel blinked. Lopatin had said something, and he had missed it. "I'm sorry, Oleg Borisovich. I was wool-gathering."

"I said, is Katerina Fyodorovna still occupied with her researches at the town? Perhaps she should return to *Tsiolkovsky* for a time, to perform data analysis and transmit some concrete results to Moscow."

"I will inquire, Oleg Borisovich," Tolmasov said blandly. "Out." He knew how delighted Katerina was with Lopatin.

When the rover came back, Tolmasov decided, he would send it off to *Tsiolkovsky* with Katerina aboard. She would want to examine Rustaveli and Bryusov before she left.

The colonel's mouth twitched wryly, and he sighed. Ever since the rover had left, he had had the only woman on this part of the planet all to himself—and made love with her exactly once. They were both too busy.

Sighing again, Tolmasov killed the scrambler circuit. He switched frequencies to the one the Soviets and Americans used to talk back and forth. He felt his blood heat. Dueling with Emmett Bragg brought its own excitement.

Reatur walked down the spiral ramp into the cellars. The flashlights he carried in two of his hands gave much more light than the ice globes full of glitterers set into the wall every so often. The domain-master was glad to be carrying the twin bright beams. More than once, he had almost stumbled off the edge of the ramp and reached the bottom faster than he wanted to.

Come to that, the glitterers were not shedding as much light as they should have. Reatur made a mental note to get after a couple of the younger males to feed them more often. Nothing, he thought resentfully, ever got done unless he turned an eye-stalk toward it himself.

The cellars might have been dim, but at least they were cool. Down half a male's height below the surface, there was always ice in the ground—never any risk of the cellar collapsing, as there was in very hot weather with the parts of the castle above-ground. If it weren't for the lighting problem, Reatur would have been just as happy living underground. He did not like summer.

"Never hurts to have something to complain about," he said aloud. "Especially something I can't help." He listened to his voice echoing back from the gloomy corridors.

There was no help for breaking out the stone tools, either, not any more. As the weather grew warm, small pieces of worked ice like hoe blades got soft and brittle and started to melt. So, unfortunately, did swordblades. Hardly anyone made war during high summer. Swinging weapons of stone and timber was usually reckoned more trouble than it was worth.

Usually. Reatur kept remembering Fralk's threats. Nobody could tell what the Skarmer would do. They were so sneaky, the domain-master thought, they likely could not even tell themselves. He paused. Did that mean they took themselves by surprise?

He chased the thought around his arms a couple of times, then gave it up as a bad job. The miserable Skarmer would do whatever they did, and he would deal with it. That was what a domain-master was for. A domain-master was also for making sure the crops stayed tended no matter what the Skarmer did. A fine thing it would be if those wretches stayed on their own side of Ervis Gorge and the domain went hungry because everyone had forgotten the crops from worry over them!

Reatur got to the threshold of the chamber where the stone farm tools had been stored after good weather had returned last fall. He shone one of the flashlights into the underground room.

The furious hoot he let out rang through the cellar. Turning the other flashlight on himself, he saw he was as yellow as the sun, and no wonder! He had every right to be furious. The tools, which should have been grouped in neat rows by type, were dumped in a higgledy-piggledy pile.

The domain-master stormed up the ramp. Males who spied his yellow color got out of his path as fast as they could. He let them go until he saw Ternat. Almost literally by main force, he took his eldest back down to the cellar with him.

"This was your job!" the domain-master shouted. "Look at the mess you made of it! Did you let a herd of massi run through here, or what? Curse it, Lamra could have done better than this—eighteen times better! How do you propose to run this domain one day if you can't do the simplest things properly?" He turned the second flashlight on his eldest, to see how he was taking it.

Ternat's eyestalks drooped with shame, but he was as yellow as Reatur. "I'm going to tear an arm off Gurtz, or maybe two, that worthless mate-budling of a nosver. He said he would see it was taken care of, and sounded as though he knew how to do it. After a while, none of the stone tools were left above ground, so I assumed he'd dealt with things."

As Ternat's fury grew, Reatur's abated. He let air hiss out through his breathing-pores. "So that's how it was, then?"

"By the first Omalo bud, yes, clanfather. That Gurtz! I'll melt his—"

"Yes, do, but he's taught you a lesson, too, hasn't he, eldest?" Reatur watched Ternat's eyestalks lengthen and shrink in surprise and confusion. "Simple enough—if you give a male something to do, always check to make sure he's done it. You may sleep less on account of it, but you'll sleep better."

Ternat thought that over. He slowly began to regain his usual color. "I think you've found truth here, clanfather. Yes, I will remember. And now," he added grimly, "I'll go and deal with Gurtz."

"Don't leave him too sore to work," was all Reatur said. "After all, having made this mess, who better than he to set it right again? And I will want it set right again, and soon. If we lose any time cultivating the crops because of Gurtz's blundering, what you do to him won't be enough. I'll settle the slacker myself, even if he is a bud I planted."

"I'll tell him you said so."

"Yes, do."

Reatur and Ternat went up the ramp together, the domain-master lighting the way. While his eldest hurried off to deal with the luckless Gurtz, Reatur went to check on how the infant male budded from Biyal was doing.

"He will be a fine one, clanfather," said the budling-keeper, a male named Sittep. "He is the youngest here, of course, but already tries to take food away from males a quarter of a season older than he is."

"Bring him out. Let me turn three eyes on him."

Sittep returned with the young male a few moments later. Wriggling in his grasp, it was blue with fear. It tried to bite him, then voided on the two hands that were holding it. "A spirited budling," Sittep said. His eyestalks gave the slow wiggle of resigned amusement.

"Yes," Reatur said, admiring the budling-keeper's patience. He stepped closer to give the budling the careful examination he had promised. It lashed out with the three sharp fingerclaws of one tiny hand. The domain-master jerked an eyestalk back just in time. "He moves quickly enough, that's certain. You said he's been eating well?"

"Yes, clanfather—nothing shy about him at all, as you've seen. Usually, with the very small ones, I have to make sure they get their fair share, but this one has no troubles there. He's fast, he's strong—''

"Good. We'll set him to running down vermin in the halls," Reatur said. Sittep's eyestalks started to quiver again, then stopped, as if he were not quite sure the domain-master was joking. "Never mind," Reatur told him. "Seeing the new budling reminds me life goes on, that's all. With the humans' being here tying everyone's eyestalks in knots, sometimes that's hard to remember.''

"I understand, clanfather. The combination of the humans and the Skarmer would be plenty to make anyone worry," Sittep said sympathetically.

"Aye, sometimes it all seems too much—'' Reatur broke off, embarrassed to have shown his mind so clearly to one of his males. Not even Ternat should have to listen to him maundering on so, let alone the budling-keeper, whose biggest responsibility was making sure his charges did not kill one another before they understood that they were not supposed to.

Just then, the budling did managed to break loose from Sittep. It scuttled around like a berserk runnerpest until the budling-keeper and Reatur managed to catch it again. In that undignified process, it clawed Reatur twice and bit him once.

"With your permission, clanfather, I'll put him back now," Sittep said, holding the squirming, squalling budling a good deal tighter than he had a moment before.

"Go ahead." Reatur was still working the hand the budling had bitten, trying to squeeze out the pain. "You'd think the idiot little thing would know who'd planted its bud," he grumbled. "Or at least that you and I were the same sort of creature it was, not a couple of clemor out to run it down and eat it.''

"It's still very young," the budling-keeper reminded him.

"I know, I know." All the same, Reatur thought as Sittep returned the budling to its chamber, the foolish creature should have had more sense—but then, Biyal had never had much sense, even for a mate. Somehow Reatur was sure the budlings from Lamra, male and mates, would behave better.

He could only see if he was right, though, after Lamra was dead. He hated the idea of that, more than he had for any other mate he had known. Air hissed out through his breathing-pores. Even without the humans, he would have had plenty to keep his eyestalks all knotted up.

* * *

"The boats are coming along excellently, clanfather," Fralk told Hogram. "We have plenty of workers to put frames together and stretch hides over them. As you foretold, the prospect of work has drawn males from many straggling farms." A little flattery never hurt, Fralk thought, especially when what he was saying also happened to be true.

Hogram, though, had been hearing—and discounting—flattery longer than Fralk had been alive. "By the time Ervis Gorge fills, I presume we will have made enough boats to send across as many males as we have planned."

"Yes," Fralk said confidently. Again, he was telling the truth—no point to lying about something Hogram could so easily check, and something where failure would make itself so obvious come the day.

"Good." Hogram's voice was dry. Fralk had to remind himself that the domain-master was smart enough to think along with him. After a pause perhaps intended to let the younger male remember just that, Hogram went on, "Will the cursed things actually stay on top of the water once our males are in them?"

"*Float*, you mean?" Fralk brought out the Lanuam technical term as if it belonged in his mouth; he could see he had impressed his overlord. He beckoned with the arm opposite Hogram and called, "Panjand, Iverc! Bring up the basin and model. I'm ready to show them to the domain-master now."

The two males slowly came up from the back of Hogram's reception-hall. They carried the heavy stone basin between them, holding on with three arms apiece. One of Iverc's hands slipped. The basin tilted until he could regain his grip. Water sloshed over the edge.

"Ah," Hogram said, extending another eyestalk toward the advancing males. "I'd wondered why they weren't using a vessel made of ice. Now I see." His eyestalks wiggled. "Put water in ice and you won't keep either one long."

"No," Fralk agreed, as respectfully as if Hogram had said something clever rather than coming out with a cliché. "Set it down here," the younger male added when Panjand and Iverc brought the big stone bowl up to him.

The two males widened themselves to do as he asked and stayed in the posture of respect until a wave from Hogram released them. In one of his free hands, Panjand was carrying a small boat. He passed it to Fralk.

Fralk gently set it on the water. "You see, clanfather, it does *float*."

"So it does, by itself," Hogram said. "But will it bear weight and still stay on top there?"

The domain-master might reject the fancy foreign word with which Fralk enjoyed showing off, but he knew what questions to ask. "Iverc," Fralk said.

The male handed him the stickwork cage he had been holding in the hand away from Hogram's eyes. A half-tame runnerpest scurried about inside. Fralk undid the lashings that held the cage closed. He reached in and picked up the runnerpest. Its tiny arms flailed at him, but it did not really try to claw.

"The runnerpest's weight, clanfather, is about the same in proportion to this small boat's capacity as that of a load of our males will be to a full-sized boat," Fralk said. He set the little animal down in the boat. The unfamiliar sensation of moving on water made the runnerpest chitter with terror but also made it freeze in place where Fralk had put it.

Hogram peered at the laden boat with three eyes, turning another on Fralk. "Very interesting, eldest of eldest," he said at last. "You seem to have most of the answers we need." Coming from Hogram, that was highest praise.

The runnerpest, of course, chose that exact moment to try running away instead of holding still. The boat overbalanced; water began pouring in. There was a fancy foreign word for what happened when something that had been *floating* abruptly ceased to do so. Fralk could not have thought of it to save his eyestalks. He stared in numb dismay as the runnerpest, all its appendages writhing frantically, went down through the water to the bottom of the stone bowl.

As befitted his years, Hogram kept his self-possession. He pulled the runnerpest out of the basin and set it on the floor. It scuttled off with the speed that had given its kind their name. Fralk watched it go, wondering if his hopes were fleeing with it.

"I presume our males will be instructed not to leap over the walls of their boats while crossing Ervis Gorge," Hogram said drily.

"What? Yes, clanfather. Certainly, clanfather!" Fralk realized he was babbling and did not care. The domain-master's sarcasm was a small enough price to pay for a botched demonstration; Hogram could have canceled the whole boat-building effort or put another male in charge. In his relief, Fralk missed something Hogram had said. He contritely widened himself. "I'm sorry?"

"I was wondering, eldest of eldest, if the humans know anything about these *boats*. They're such hot creatures that tricks with water should come as naturally to them as those with ice do to us."

"They have said one or two things, clanfather," Fralk answered cautiously, "but as I am still only a budling in such matters myself, I am not certain how much help they can be. I also have not shown them the fullness of my ignorance, lest they demand more for what they know."

"Good enough," Hogram said, and Fralk had to fight to keep from changing color in relief—he had dreaded that question and been sure Hogram would ask it. The domain-master went on. "I was wise, it seems, to set you over both the building of the boats and dealing with the humans, if the two enterprises have the links they appear to."

"No male of your clan has ever doubted your wisdom," Fralk said. That was true enough and politer than saying that no male— himself very much included—expected Hogram to go so much as a fingerclaw's width against his own advantage.

"Keep at it, then, eldest of eldest," the domain-master said. "Be sure I shall be watching with six eyes what you accomplish."

"The notice you grant me is more than I deserve." Fralk widened himself. He had already suspected that some of the males who helped build boats also passed word on to Hogram. Had he been domain-master, he would have kept an eyestalk or two on that project himself. As he had thought a moment before, Hogram was too clever not to protect his interest so.

After a few more polite exchanges, Fralk took his leave. A little while later, he unrolled a hide in front of one of the leading town merchants. Small red rectangles, each decorated with a white cross, spilled out.

"And what are these?" asked the trader, whose name was Cutur.

"Something new from the humans," Fralk answered. "Look—an eighteen of tools in one—a knifeblade, a rasper, an awl . . ." He used a fingerclaw to pull each tiny claw out of the case as he named it. "And they are all of this hard shiny stone the humans use, see, not of ice, so they're good winter and summer, but so small and light that no one will mind using them."

"Interesting—some, anyway." Cutur never sounded more bored than at the start of a dicker.

This time, though, Fralk had the edge. He had gotten the humans to promise not to give out the little red-cased tools through any other male. A similar promise from him to Cutur made the price the merchant paid hefty enough to suit him.

Of course, a good part of that price would go back to the humans, in exchange for the little cylinders that kept some of their gadgets alive. Hogram would get a fair chunk himself, as was the domain-master's right. Even Fralk, though, had little about which to complain over what was left. Before long, he thought, he would be the richest male who was not a domain-master throughout all the Skarmer lands.

The humans, taken as a group, would not be much poorer, although Fralk was convinced he was cheating them outrageously. Their trade goods were not only unlike any that had ever come into the Skarmer domains but did things Fralk had never imagined tools doing. They could have demanded eighteen times as much for them as they got.

But as long as they stayed satisfied with perfectly ordinary local products in exchange for their unique ones, Fralk was not about to argue with them. No one held a knife to their eyestalks to make them deal as they did. And no one, Fralk thought, had to hold a knife to *his* eyestalks to make him turn a profit. None of the males sprung from Hogram's buds was that kind of fool.

Irv was at the control board when the ship-to-ship light went on. He picked up the mike. "*Athena* here, Levitt speaking," he said in fairly good Russian. "Go ahead, *Tsiolkovsky.*"

"Thank you so much, Irving Samuelovich. Colonel Tolmasov here. Be so good as to fetch Brigadier Bragg, if you please. What I have to say must be discussed at the command level."

"Hold, please." Frowning a little, Levitt cut the mike. Tolmasov's English always sounded starchy, but this was worse than usual. Irv hit the intercom switch; Bragg, he knew, was in his cabin, going over computer printouts. When the pilot answered, Levitt said, "Tolmasov's calling—says he won't talk with anyone but you. Something's hit the fan, sounds like."

"Doesn't it just?" As usual, Bragg sounded calm, unhurried. Irv was reasonably sure that behind his cool facade he had the same worries and fears as any other man, but if so, he did a hell of a job of hiding them. "Be right there," Bragg finished. "Out."

Levitt opened the channel to *Tsiolkovsky* again. Tolmasov replied at once. "Sergei Konstantinovich, here is my commander," the anthropologist said as Bragg came in and sat down beside him.

"What do you have to say to me that you cannot tell my crew?" the pilot demanded. The blunt question sounded even ruder in Russian than it would have in English.

"Brigadier Bragg, I am calling to convey to you a formal protest over your concealment of the true landing site of the *Viking*, and over your cynical exploitation of this concealed knowledge to contact the natives who encountered that spacecraft after it touched down."

"Protest all you like, Sergei Konstantinovich," Bragg said. "We got new landing coordinates just a little before we set down—we had to recompute our burn to get down where the boys in Houston told us to."

"The new coordinates were contained in the coded message you received?"

"You know better than to expect an answer to a question like that."

"Perhaps I do." Tolmasov's chuckle fell into place as if it had been included in stage directions. He went on reprovingly. "The cultured thing, Brigadier Bragg, would have been to share your new information with us. Your failure to do so naturally makes us doubt your cooperative spirit."

"The cultured thing, Sergei Konstantinovich, would have been to tell us the Minervans on your side of Jötun Canyon were thinking about mounting an invasion of this side." Bragg's voice went hard. "Since you didn't bother doing that, I don't see how you have any cause for complaint."

Silence stretched.

"The natives here are not under our control, Brigadier Bragg," Tolmasov said finally. "Whatever they intend, they had it in mind long before our arrival."

"I never said they didn't. I only said it was uncultured not to warn us about it, which it is. Bragg out." The mission commander broke the connection. He leaned back in his chair, pleased with himself.

Irv Levitt did not blame him. "That hit Tolmasov where he lived. Call a Russian uncultured and then take away his chance to say anything back—"

"Mm-hmm." Bragg steepled his fingertips. "Have to remember to thank Frank for picking up on that—it let me embarrass Tolmasov instead of the other way around. He ought to be about ready to chew nails." The pilot blinked. "You know

what, Irv? I wish I had a cigarette. I quit fifteen years ago, but
the urge still comes back sometimes. Sneaks up on me, I guess.''

Irv had a tough time imagining anything sneaking up on Emmett Bragg. Picturing him through a haze of tobacco smoke was
much easier. No wonder, Levitt thought with one of those odd
bursts of insight that are at once crazy and illuminating—Bragg
looked like nothing so much as the original Marlboro Man.

The mission commander got up and stretched. ''That was
fun, but I'm going back to work now.''

''Off to paint a hammer and sickle under the window?'' Irv
asked innocently.

Bragg snorted. ''You know, I just might. Only trouble is,
Sergei's got hisself—*him*self—a Yankee star or two under his.
Just stayin' even with that one is nothing to be ashamed of.''
He turned serious. ''Them and us, we've been saying that about
each other since the end of the Second World War now, and
each usin' the other to push himself along. And here we both
are on Minerva. Not too shabby, is it?''

He was gone before Irv came up with an answer. Even after
a year, Bragg had depths that could take him by surprise.

Lamra scratched herself in four places at once. The skin that
stretched over her growing buds itched. Sarah pointed a picture-
maker at her. It clicked. ''Give me a picture of me, please?''
Lamra asked. She held out the two hands that were not busy.

''Not that kind of picture-maker,'' Sarah said after Lamra
had repeated herself two or three times.

Embarrassed, Lamra pushed in her eyestalks. ''That's right.
I forgot. The one that lets you give pictures right away voids
them out of its bottom. This is the other kind, the one that holds
them in.''

''Yes, Lamra.'' Pat stooped beside her. That made the mate
nervous, the same way she had felt funny when Reatur widened
himself to her. The human went on. ''Other mates not see that.
Some males not see that.''

''I have eyes. Eyes are for seeing with.'' Lamra shut all of
them at once. Sure enough, the world went away. She opened
them and it came back. Both of Sarah's eyes were pointed at
her. ''How can you stand only seeing half of things?''

Sarah's body made the jerky motion that meant the human
was not sure what to say. Finally Sarah answered, ''Humans
like this. No humans different—humans not think what different
like.''

"How sad," Lamra said.

The place where Sarah's arms and body were joined jerked again. "Some ways you people not think what different like, too."

Lamra turned a third eyestalk toward the humans—this was the kind of talk she loved, and she got it too seldom. None of the other mates cared about it; even Reatur did not talk that way with her every time he visited the mates' chambers. It was as if he had to remind himself to take her seriously, while Sarah always seemed to.

"What could be different about us?" Lamra asked. "We're only people, after all. People are just people, aren't they?" Sarah did not say anything. "Tell me what's different about us," Lamra persisted. "Tell me. Tell me!" In her eagerness to find out what Sarah was talking about, she hopped up and down.

"How you different?" Sarah said at last. Something had changed in the human's voice. Lamra could hear that, but she did not know enough of humans to be sure what the change meant. Sarah hesitated again, then went on. "Lamra, you know what happens after—after you bud?"

"After I bud, I'm over, of course," Lamra answered. "Who ever heard of an old mate?"

"Humans not like that. Not male, me—mate." Sarah pointed at himself—no, herself, Lamra thought through roaring confusion. "I old—old like any other human. Mates—human mates—who, uh, bud not die then. Can live on."

"Live on?" From her tone, Lamra might have been talking about one of the three moons coming down from the sky and dancing in the fields. She did not so much disbelieve Sarah as find her words beyond comprehension. "Live on?" she repeated. "Who ever heard of an old mate?"

The proverb helped anchor her to the familiar, the here and now. She had never needed such an anchor before—this was *much* stranger than Reatur's turning all his eyes on her.

"Who ever heard of humans?" Sarah asked. Lamra had no answer to that. The human—the human *mate!*—continued. "Because a thing *is*, does that mean it *must be*?" He—no, she—said that several different ways, working hard to get the meaning across to Lamra.

Even so, it was a struggle. "Too hard," Lamra complained. She hadn't liked it when Reatur asked that sort of question, either.

"All right. Question not so hard: You want to have buds, live on after?''

Sarah asked it as if it could only have one possible answer. Lamra did not see it so. "What would I do?" she wailed. "Who ever heard of an old mate?" This time the saying truly reflected how perplexed she was.

"*Not* want to live on?" Sarah pressed. "Want to die like Biyal, put blood over whole floor?''

Lamra had never really thought about not dying until the human raised the question in her mind. Now that she turned a couple of eyestalks on it, the prospect of spilling her blood out all over the floor did seem unpleasant if another choice was available. "Will you make my buds go away?" she asked. "I don't think I want you to do that."

"Not know how," Sarah said.

"What *will* you do, then?''

Sarah muttered something to himself—no, herself; Lamra would be a long time getting used to that—in her own language, then dipped her head to the mate in the human motion that meant the same as widening herself. After a moment, the human started talking people talk again. "You know right question to ask."

Sarah sounded like Reatur, Lamra thought. The mate realized that was true in a couple of ways—Sarah's voice was like a male's. How could she be a mate? That whole tangle of eyestalks would just have to keep. "You didn't answer me," Lamra said accusingly.

"Not know good answer." Sarah's sigh was just like a person's. "Try to stop blood when buds fall from you. Not know how now. Not even know if able. Try, if you want.''

"I don't know, I don't know, I don't know." Lamra again thought how much Sarah sounded like a male, both in the timbre of her voice and in the complex way her mind worked. That thought helped the mate find a reply at last. "Ask Reatur," she said. "If Reatur says it's all right, then it's all right with me, too.''

"Your body," Sarah said. "Your life."

"Ask Reatur."

Sarah threw her hands in the air. Lamra had never seen a human do that and did not know what it meant. All Sarah said, though, was, "All right. Ask Reatur. Ask Reatur now." She stood up and started out of the mates' chambers.

Lamra watched her go. She scratched the itchy skin over her buds again. The notion of not ending when the buds dropped off was still a long way from real to her. For that matter, the time when the buds would drop still seemed a very long way off. To a mate, anything further away than tomorrow seemed a long way off.

Morna came rushing in. Lamra was so lost in her own thoughts that the other mate managed to grab two of her arms and almost pull her over. That roused Lamra. She squealed, straightened up, and tugged back. Morna jerked free. She ran away, squealing herself. Eyestalks wiggling happily, Lamra dashed after her.

The rover purred along until the right front wheel hit a big rock hidden by a snowdrift. The tough little vehicle climbed over the stone but came down with a jolt that rattled its two riders—it did not have much in the way of springs or padding for the seats. Every possible gram of weight had been left off.

Shota Rustaveli's teeth came together with a click that effectively served as a period to the song he had been singing. He clutched at his kidneys with a theatrical groan. "So this is what it's like to serve in the tank corps," he said.

Valery Bryusov did not reply for a moment; he was busy wrestling the rover back on course. "I would not mind having a few tons of steel around me to smooth out the ride," he said as the machine finally straightened out.

"Nor would I." Rustaveli shivered. "A few tons of steel would also enclose a space which could be heated," the Georgian went on wistfully. Only a windscreen and a roll cage separated him from the cold all around; not enough, he thought, but again it saved weight. He did not think well of saving weight, not after nine days in the chilly, drafty rover.

Snow spattered off the windscreen. Some blew over and spattered off Rustaveli's face. He swore and wiped it away. It was blowing on Bryusov, too, but the Russian paid it no mind. Like everyone aboard *Tsiolkovsky* but the Georgian, he seemed perfectly comfortable on Minerva and wore his coat and fur hat as if he had thrown them on only as an afterthought.

"I want something warm," Rustaveli said. "A woman, by choice."

"Sorry I can't oblige you there," Bryusov grunted. "Will you settle for some tea?" Without waiting for an answer, he pulled to a stop so Rustaveli could pour from the vacuum flask without spilling tea all over himself.

The Georgian drank quickly; had he hesitated, he would have been taking iced tea by the time he got to the bottom of his glass. He savored the warmth. "Not a woman," he said, "but it will have to do."

"I wouldn't mind a glass myself," Bryusov said. "I could use a break."

Rustaveli felt his cheeks grow hot—*not* the kind of warmth he had been looking for. "I'm sorry, Valery Aleksandrovich. That was thoughtless of me." He poured for the linguist. Baiting Bryusov was enjoyable when he did it on purpose; being accidentally rude was something else again.

Despite the snow flurries, the day did seem less grimly chill without the wind of the rover's motion. Rustaveli looked around. "Good enough for some pictures," he decided, and reached for the camera beside him.

Through the spattering snow, the countryside was much more rock-ribbed than it was around *Tsiolkovsky*'s landing site. Of course, by now the ship was 120 kilometers to the southwest; Jötun Canyon lay only a few kilometers eastward. If the land hereabouts was rock-ribbed, Rustaveli thought, the canyon made a gash big enough for a heart transplant.

Something moved that was not snow. Rustaveli and Bryusov saw it at the same time. The linguist grabbed for binoculars, Rustaveli for a long lens for his Nikon. "Not a Minervan," Bryusov said after a moment. "Not one of their domestic animals, either, or not one we've seen before."

"No." Rustaveli watched the animal through the camera's viewfinder. "It doesn't move like a domestic animal." The more the Georgian studied the beast, the greater the unease that flowered in him. He held the camera in one hand while making sure with the other that he knew where the Kalashnikov was.

The Minervan animal did not move like anything domesticated. It moved like a tiger, as nearly as could a creature built on this planet's lines. Like all Minervan beasts the Soviets knew about, it was radially symmetrical, with six legs, six arms, and six eyestalks above them.

But where Minervans ambled and their domestic animals plodded, this creature stalked. Its legs were long and graceful, its arms, by contrast, relatively short but thick with muscle and appended with talons that put Minervans' fingerclaws to shame. Even its eyestalks had a purposeful motion different from anything Rustaveli had seen before. Somehow they reminded him of so many poisonous snakes.

Three of those eyestalks fixed on the rover. "It's spotted us,"

Bryusov said, dismay in his voice. A moment later, he sounded unhappier yet. "It's coming this way."

"I noticed that myself, thank you." Rustaveli was pleased he was able to make light banter when he would sooner have jumped off the rover and fled. That was what his body was screaming he ought to do, though his brain had a nasty suspicion the animal would be faster than he was. Instead of running, he set down the Nikon and picked up the assault rifle.

The Minervan animal drew closer. Even when less than a hundred meters away, it was not easy to see; its mottling of brown and dirty white made it blend into the background the same way a tiger's stripes camouflage it in tall grass. The parallel, Rustaveli thought, was probably no coincidence.

The Georgian's head swiveled as the beast prowled around the rover, peering at it—and its occupants—from all sides. "Maybe we ought to get moving again," Bryusov said nervously.

"I have a feeling the beast can go faster than twenty kilometers an hour, and I know quite well the rover can't," Rustaveli said. "Or were you planning to outmaneuver the thing?"

Bryusov did not bother answering that. With their six equally spaced legs, Minervans were more agile than Earthly beasts or machines. The linguist slipped out of his safety harness and stood up so he could take a picture of the creature without also including a view of the back of Rustaveli's head.

Maybe the motion set the beast off. Things happened too quickly for Rustaveli to be certain afterward of cause and effect. He was sure that Bryusov had not got all the way to his feet when the Minervan animal let out a shriek—an unearthly shriek, he would think later and then reject the word; how else was a Minervan animal supposed to sound?—and sprang at the rover.

Reflex screamed *attack*. The Kalashnikov was hammering against Rustaveli's shoulder before he realized he had raised it. Hot brass cartridge cases spit backward. The assault rifle's staccato bark drowned the squall of the Minervan beast.

That squall cut off abruptly, as, a moment later, did the AK-74. Rustaveli grabbed for another magazine and slapped it into place. He did not fire again, though—no need. He was sure he had missed as often as he had hit, but even part of the clip of high-velocity 5.45mm bullets had been plenty to knock down the Minervan creature. It was still twitching and thrashing, but it was not going anywhere, not anymore.

Bryusov sat down with a thump that made the rover shake.

Then he half rose again and used a gloved hand to brush spent cartridges off the seat. He cut in power to the wheels; the rover silently rolled toward the dying animal. "Let's see what we have," the linguist said.

"We have at least one person, Valery Aleksandrovich, who is glad these beasts don't hunt in packs."

Bryusov thought about that and gave a shiver that had nothing to do with the weather. "Make that two, Shota Mikheilovich. My old grandmother always used to go on about the wolves that would come out of the deep woods to raid the farms around her village when she was a girl. The only wolves I've ever seen are the ones in the Moscow Zoo, and that suits me just fine."

"Me, too." For once, Rustaveli agreed completely with his companion.

The Minervan animal had fallen over, giving the two humans a good view of the mouth in the center of its circle of eyestalks. The needlelike teeth inside were plenty to cancel any lingering doubts about its nature.

One of the beast's arms lashed out and smacked against the side of the rover, hard enough for the two riders to feel the jolt. Rustaveli swore and put a couple more bullets into it, carefully aimed to pierce the nerve centers Minervan creatures had under their eyestalks. The big carnivore convulsed one last time and lay still.

Bryusov took more photos. Rustaveli got down from the rover and used a gloved hand to dig through snow till he found a few pebbles. He tossed one at the beast. When it did not stir, he moved closer and threw another pebble, hard this time. Only then was he satisfied that the beast was dead.

Its claws were too big to fit into a specimen bottle. He took one anyway. If all else failed, he thought, he could have it mounted on a chain and wear it around his neck. He took other, more conventional specimens, too; Katerina would never have forgiven him for failing there. The stink of alien body fluids made him cough.

The dead Minervan beast still had one twitch left. Rustaveli gave a backward leap any Russian folk-dancer would have been proud of. He came down next to his Kalashnikov and had it pointed at the carnivore in essentially the same instant. The beast was inert again. He shook his head in self-reproach. "Jumpy," he muttered.

"In the most literal sense of the word," Bryusov said admiringly. "Had you thought about the Olympics?" The Georgian really looked for the first time at the distance he had put between himself and the animal. He whistled softly. "Talents you had not dreamed of?" Bryusov asked.

Rustaveli was not one to stay shaken for long. Grinning, he switched to English. "I've always been good at the broad jump—ask Katerina."

"Why? What does she know about your ath—" Bryusov made a sour face as he finally caught on.

"Yes, she was once one of my chief athletic supporters," Rustaveli went on blithely, still in English. This time Bryusov did not respond at all. Calls himself a linguist, Rustaveli thought scornfully—he's only a dictionary that walks like a man. Sighing, the Georgian went back to hacking bits off the animal he had killed. When he was sure he had enough to keep Katerina happy, he got up. "Let's go back, Valery Aleksandrovich. So long as we don't exactly retrace our way, every kilometer we cover is a new one."

"True enough." Bryusov pulled his fur cap down a little farther on his forehead; it was starting to snow harder. "I won't be sorry to get back to our comrades."

"I won't be sorry to get back to heating." Rustaveli knew he was repeating himself and did not care. He climbed onto the rover and buckled on his shoulder belt. The machine glided away, leaving the dead beast to whatever passed for scavengers on Minerva.

The snow began falling heavily—thick, wet flakes that clung to the rover's windscreen and made Bryusov slow down. "Springtime on Minerva," the linguist grunted.

"Yes," Rustaveli agreed, as sardonically. "The southern latitude equivalent to Havana, Katerina said, and at a season much like May. I wonder how our ally Comrade Castro would enjoy the weather—about as much as I do, I daresay."

Bryusov slowed still more. "I don't like this at all. I can't see what I'm doing."

"If it gets worse, we can stop and put tent fabric over the rover's frame till it blows itself out. I hate to do that, though, when we're on the way back, no matter how much I'd like to be warm."

"I feel the same way. Besides, the heater uses a lot of energy, and the solar panels aren't putting out much in this weather. Even so, though, we may have to if—" The linguist never got his "if" out. The rover's front wheels went into an enormous hole filled with drifted snow. The rover was not supposed to flip over, no matter what happened. It flipped over anyhow.

Bryusov and Rustaveli shouted as the world turned upside down. Both shouts cut off abruptly. The Georgian had the wind jerked from him as his shoulder harness brought him up short. The linguist was less fortunate. He had not bothered to strap himself in after standing up to photograph the Minervan carnivore. His head smacked a bar of the rover's roll cage.

When he could breathe again, Rustaveli made several choice comments in his own language. After a moment, he noticed that Bryusov was not answering—the linguist lay unmoving in the snow. Rustaveli wished he had not wasted his curses before.

He reached out to kill power to the wheels. Then, holding on to the frame of the rover with one hand, he unbuckled his safety belt with the other. Olga Korbut, he thought, would have spun around in midair to land gracefully. He was happy enough not to have dislocated his shoulder.

Bryusov was breathing. Rustaveli muttered silent thanks for that. The linguist remained unconscious, though, with blood on his face and the side of his head. None of the cautious things Rustaveli did to try rousing him had any effect.

The Georgian tried the radio and got only static for an answer. That sent panic shooting through him. He certainly wasn't getting any incoming signal. If he wasn't getting out, either, the rest of the crew would not even know that Bryusov and he were in trouble until they missed their next scheduled call—and even then, what could they do? Assuming they could find the rover at all, they were several days' forced march from it. And Bryusov might not have several days.

Knowing that he had to think straight for his companion's sake helped bring Rustaveli out of his fright. He scrambled out of the rover. Turning it back over, unfortunately, proved more than a one-person job. Another design flaw, he thought, and immediately filed the idea away—no time to worry about it now. The radio was the pressing concern.

The most obvious reason for its failure was damage from the accident. Rustaveli could do nothing about that. But, he reasoned, crash damage should have silenced the radio, not left it flatulent. "The antenna!" he said out loud. It would hardly do much good, buried in a snowdrift.

He had to bend a kink in the springy wire to make it go up past the body of the rover. Even then, it was less than half as tall as it should have been. That was the best he could do, though.

He crawled back under the rover's chassis and tried the radio again. "Rustaveli calling, Rustaveli calling. Do you read? Emergency. Do you read?" The repetition was very much like prayer.

"Shota! What's wrong?" Katerina Zakharova's voice sounded as if she were talking from behind a waterfall, but it was the most welcome thing Rustaveli had ever heard.

"Katya!" he exclaimed, then went on more calmly. "We've had an accident—this damned buggy overturned. Valery's hurt."

"Hurt? How? How badly?" Even through the roaring static, the Georgian could hear Katerina turning into Dr. Zakharova.

"How badly I don't know," he told her. "He's unconscious—hit his head. This was fifteen minutes ago, maybe more, and he hasn't come to yet. I haven't tried moving him—"

"Good," she broke in. "Don't, not unless you have to."

"I know that. I also didn't much fancy the idea of undressing him to check for anything else wrong, not while it's snowing." As it always did, his wry sense of humor reasserted itself. "So much for springtime in Havana."

"Rustaveli." That was Colonel Tolmasov, doing his best to mask the concern in his voice. "Give me your exact position."

The panel connected to the gyrocompass was hard to read upside down, but Rustaveli managed. "Distance 112.7 kilometers, bearing 63°."

There was silence for a moment from the radio; Rustaveli could picture Tolmasov drawing a line on a map. "Near Jötun Canyon," the colonel said at last.

"*Da*, Sergei Konstantinovich." Somehow, Rustaveli managed a chuckle. "A good deal closer to the Americans than to you, as a matter of fact. Only one tiny obstacle in the way." He laughed again—only a gorge that dwarfed anything Earth knew!

Tolmasov was businesslike as usual. "Can you right your vehicle?"

"Not by myself. I've tried. If Valery comes around—" As if on cue, Bryusov moved and groaned. "Rustaveli out," Shota said. He bent by his companion. "Valery! Are you all right? Do you know who I am?"

"Head—" Bryusov muttered. He started to lift his left hand to his head, then stopped with another, louder groan. Under the blood that splashed it, his face was gray.

Katerina and Tolmasov were both screaming at Rustaveli on the radio. He ignored them until Bryusov drifted away from consciousness again. This time, though, the linguist seemed less deeply out. He was also, Rustaveli saw with much relief, able to move his legs and right arm, although he whimpered whenever his left arm so much as twitched. The Georgian relayed the news.

"No broken back or neck, then," Katerina said. "That's something."

"Exactly what I was thinking. But that arm . . . and he has no idea of where he is or what he's doing. He took a nasty shot in the head."

"Do you think he can hold out until Dr. Zakharova and I can reach you?" Tolmasov asked, still sounding very official.

"Comrade Colonel, I do not know," Rustaveli said with equal formality. "What choice has he, however?"

"I am coming to that." Now something was in Tolmasov's voice: distaste. Whatever he was about to say, Rustaveli thought, he was not happy about it. Then Tolmasov went on, and the Georgian understood why. "Shota Mikheilovich, you were facetious when you said the Americans were nearer to you than we are, but you were also right. They have some sort of very light aircraft with them. If I ask, they may be able to cross the gorge and treat Valery. If I ask. Do you want me to ask?"

Rustaveli knew the colonel wanted to hear a no. Tolmasov had been ready to bite nails in half when the Americans proved as able as he to throw around charges of deception. Begging help from them had to be the last thing he wanted to do. Or almost the last thing—he couldn't be eager to have Bryusov die, either. To say nothing of the linguist himself, news of a death on Minerva would hurt the Soviet space program the same way one would damage the Americans' effort.

It all came down to how badly Bryusov was hurt. If he just had a knock on the head and, say, a broken wrist, Rustaveli knew enough first aid to patch him up. If, on the other hand, he had managed to do something nasty like rupturing his spleen, the Georgian would never know it till too late.

"You'd better call *Athena*," he said.

There was a long silence from Tolmasov, followed by an even longer sigh. "Damnation. Very well."

Rustaveli could tell he had just lost points with the colonel. "Sergei Konstantinovich, think of it this way: if Valery dies after we summon the American doctor, of if the doctor refuses to come and he dies, whose fault is that? Not ours, certainly. But if we do not call—"

"A point," Tolmasov admitted after another pause. He was sounding official again, which Rustaveli took as a good sign. "I will call the Americans."

6

"How do I know what would happen if a mate survived budding?"* Reatur demanded. "They come to ripeness, they mate, and then they die. Always. That is what it is to be a mate."

"But what if one does—*did*—live?" Sarah Levitt persisted. "If mates grow up, too, what they like then?" She wished her grammar were better and her vocabulary bigger. She needed to be persuasive. "What—how much—of lives you waste when mates not live, die young?"

Reatur did not just order her to shut up and go away, as a medieval English baron might have dealt with someone proposing revolutionary social change. Sarah had to give him that much. *Baron* was about as close as anyone had come to translating the Minervan word that literally meant "domain-master," but Sarah knew it lacked meanings that were there in the Minervan and added connotations missing from it. And Reatur's domain was a long, long way from medieval England.

The domain-master turned a third eyestalk her way. He began to sing something, or perhaps to declaim. Since he had no music to accompany the words, Sarah was not sure which; whichever it was, he used his arms to help her follow the rhythm of his words. The meaning was something else again. With an obviously memorized piece like this one, Reatur could not pause and explain himself as he went along. Sarah gathered it was a sad—song?—but that was about all.

Eventually Reatur realized she could not fully understand. He broke off and started speaking simply again. "It is about a domain-master who has had three of his mates bud all on the same day, and about his sorrow as he gives the last of them to the scavengers. Every male who has brought a mate to budding knows this sorrow. How could we not? We are not beasts, and mates are not beasts.''

"No, but mates not people, not now—die too soon. Let mates be people, too. I try to let Lamra live after budding, let her be person, let her grow to be person. Yes?" Sarah watched Reatur intently. She wanted nothing in the world—nothing in two worlds—more than the chance to try to save Lamra. She could feel her face twisting into a frown of concentration as she cast about for the words to make him see things her way. At last she found the very phrase she needed.

The radio on her belt squawked.

She jumped. That perfect phrase vanished from her head. Reatur was startled, too, startled enough to jerk in his eyestalks.

"You read me, Sarah?" Emmett Bragg asked from the tinny little speaker. "Acknowledge, please."

"I'm here, Emmett—at the castle, talking with Reatur."

"Come back to the ship, please, right away." Even with the "please," it was an order.

"Five minutes?" she pleaded. Maybe those right words would come back.

"This second," Emmett said flatly. "Emergency."

"On my way." Sarah's hands folded into fists. Wearing gloves, she did not even get the painful release of nails biting flesh. She turned back to Reatur. "Must go now. Talk more of Lamra later, yes?"

"I suppose we may," Reatur said.

Sarah had to be content with that. "Damn, damn, damn," she muttered under her breath as she trotted down the hallway toward her bicycle. The timing could not have been worse. Reatur had been weakening. She was sure of it.

She leapt onto the bicycle and worked out some of her frustration by fairly flying back to the ship. She braked so violently that she almost went headfirst over the handlebars. If this wasn't a genuine life or death emergency, she thought, she was going to peel some paint off the corridor walls.

But it was. She could see that on Emmett Bragg's face. Then she hesitated. Emmett was in the control room, and so was Irv— she breathed silent thanks that the emergency had nothing to do with him—and so were Louise and Frank and Pat. Nobody looked damaged, though everyone was as somber as Emmett.

Somber, to Sarah's way of thinking, did not constitute an

emergency. She set hands on hips. "What the hell's going on?" she snapped. "Where's the beef?"

"Hon, it's on the other side of Jötun Canyon," Irv said.

She stared at him.

"The Russian rover's had an accident," Emmett said. "One of their people is down and out—head and arm injuries at the very least, maybe more."

"What's that got to do with me?" she demanded. "They have a doctor of their own."

"Who is at the moment almost seventy miles from the rover, and stuck on foot without it," Bragg said. "Whereas we have bikes to get to the edge of the canyon fast, and *Damselfly* to get over it—the rover's only a mile or so away from the far edge of the canyon." He held up a map with a red dot felt-tipped in to show the location. "This mess happened an hour ago, tops. You could be there before sunset, but their doc is three days away."

"Get *Damselfly* over Jötun Canyon?" Sarah said faintly. "Any kind of nasty wind and I could be several miles straight down, too."

Bragg nodded. "I know that. I told Tolmasov I wouldn't give you any orders, and I'm not. But he asked for our help, and if there is any, you're it. You're the doctor, and you're the pilot here, too. It's up to you, Sarah. No hard feelings if you say no."

"Except to the hurt Russian," she pointed out. "If he lives to have them."

"There is that," Bragg said.

"Sarah—" Irv began, and then shut up. She knew a moment's gratitude that he recognized the decision was not his to make.

"Let me see the map," she said. Emmett Bragg passed it to her. She studied it. "How wide is the canyon right here? It seems to be one of the narrower stretches. Is it less than ten miles? It looks like it."

Bragg took the map back. He pulled a clear plastic ruler from one of his coverall pockets and applied it to the image of the gap and then to the scale of miles at the bottom left-hand corner of the sheet. "Good eyeballing," he said. "It's just under nine, as a matter of fact."

"Bryan Allen flew *Gossamer Albatross* across the English Channel. That's twice as far and then some, and I've got a better plane than the *Albatross* ever dreamed of being," Sarah said. "I'm going."

"If the *Gossamer Albatross* came apart, all what's-his-name would have got was wet," Irv said. "If something goes wrong with *Damselfly*, or if you get the winds you know perfectly well you could—''

Sarah did not want to think about that. Jötun Canyon was deep enough that, if the worst did happen, she would have plenty of time to reflect on her folly as she fell. "Irv, if you were hurt on this side of the canyon and the Russians had a plane, I hope they'd try to help.''

Frank Marquard had been quiet till now. "How high are the canyon walls on either side, relative to each other?" he asked abruptly. "If the land west of the canyon is a quarter-mile higher than it is on this side, you won't be able to climb up to it. If it's a quarter-mile lower, you'll never get back.''

Everyone crowded around to peer at the map, either upside down or over Emmett Bragg's shoulder. "Seems all right," Sarah said after a long, hard look. "Call Tolmasov, Emmett. Tell him I'm on my way. Find out what first-aid supplies their rover has, too. I'll save weight with my kit that way, because I won't carry anything they already have.''

"Right.'' Bragg turned to his wife and Irv. "Y'all heard the lady. Break out the pieces of *Damselfly* and get 'em onto the towing carts. Pulling 'em to the edge of the canyon, I expect you'll be working near as hard as Sarah will going over.'' Louise simply nodded and left. Irv followed a moment later, shaking his head and muttering under his breath.

There's nothing I can do about it, Sarah wanted to call after him. But he knew that as well as she did. Knowing and accepting were two different things—all she needed to do was think of Lamra to see the truth there.

"I'll get my bike, too," Pat Marquard said.

"What for?" Sarah, Emmett, and Frank all spoke together.

"So you can ride behind me," Pat said to Sarah, as if the two men were not there. "You should be fresh when you get into *Damselfly*, not worn out from spending half a day pedaling.''

That made such plain good sense that Sarah could only nod her thanks and hug Pat, who returned the embrace. Emmett Bragg lifted the radio microphone. "*Athena* calling Soviet expedition.''

The reply was immediate. "Tolmasov here. Go ahead, old man.''

"Sergei Konstantinovich, our doctor will try, repeat try, to fly *Damselfly* across Jötun Canyon to help your injured crewman.''

"Thank you very much, Brigadier Bragg. We are in your debt."

"You don't thank me, you thank the lady, and I just may call in that debt one day, if I see a way to do it."

"Er, yes." Tolmasov sounded wary again, Sarah thought, frowning. Emmett never let up; he saw everything as a confrontation.

As if to belie that, the mission commander went on, "For now, though, we only need to know what your rover has in the way of medical gear, so we can avoid duplication."

With *Athena*'s computers, any of the Americans could have called up the answer to that as fast as he typed in the question. Tolmasov's promised "One moment, please," stretched to several minutes. At least he had what Sarah needed when he finally did come back on the air. That, she supposed, counted for something.

Mist and distance shrouded the land on the western side of Jötun Canyon. Sarah did stretching exercises to work out the kinks of a morning and early afternoon spent riding behind Pat Marquard. After a moment, Sarah turned her back on the canyon. She did not want to think about it before she had to.

Instead, she watched her husband and Louise Bragg reassemble *Damselfly*. Irv was whistling something as he made sure every wingnut was tight. Sarah took longer than she should have to recognize "Santa Claus Is Coming to Town." She started to let out a snort, then stopped abruptly. If using a silly song helped remind him to be careful, that was all right with her.

"Ready when you are," Louise said a little later. Pat, who had been reduced to a spectator once they got to the edge of the canyon, made herself useful by carrying the special wide stepladder to *Damselfly*.

"Let's do it." Sarah got out of her jacket and insulated pants and immediately started to shiver. Jogging over to *Damselfly* did nothing to warm her up.

Irv waited at the top of the stepladder to help her down into the ultra-ultralight. When she was seated, he handed her the clear plastic bag in which she had put her supplies—it was a pound or more lighter than her regular medical bag. She secured it to a spar behind her with duct tape.

"Be careful," Irv said. "I love you."

"I know. I love you, too." She strapped the biking helmet under her chin. When she was done, she reached up to touch his cheek. "This is what you get for marrying a doctor. I'll be all right."

"You I wouldn't worry about. But this damn contraption isn't made for the kind of air you may get over the canyon."

She shrugged. "People aren't made for banging their heads, either." Checking to be sure the prop was not engaged, she started pedaling furiously to charge the battery—and to stop her teeth from chattering. She hardly noticed Irv lowering the canopy over her and dogging it in place.

"Radio check," Louise said. "Testing, one, two, three."

"Read you five by five," Sarah answered. "How do you read me?"

They went through the rest of the preflight checklist, making sure all the controls worked. Sarah watched the charge gauge climb. By the time the battery was all the way up, she was no longer freezing. She glanced to either side. Irv and Louise were standing by at *Damselfly*'s wingtips. She waved to show them she was ready. When they waved back, she flicked the propeller-control switch. The big airfoil, taller than she was, began to spin.

Damselfly rolled bumpily forward, the two wingpersons—a word Sarah formed and rejected in the same instant—running alongside to hold it level. "Airborne!" Irv yelled as the ultra-ultralight lifted off the ground.

"Roger," Sarah said, to let him and Louise know she knew. As always, *Damselfly* was painfully slow gaining altitude. Even so, after less than a minute the ground dropped away as if the plane had a rocket in its tail. "Watch that first step," she murmured to herself as she peered down and down and down into Jötun Canyon. "It's a mother."

"Say again, *Damselfly*?" Louise requested.

"Never mind," Sarah said, embarrassed. Then she gave all her attention back to pedaling and to watching the little compass Irv had glued to the control stick. The far wall of the canyon was too far away to give her any landmarks toward which to steer and the sun was invisible through thick gray clouds. She laughed a little; *Damselfly* had not been designed for instrument flight.

Some of the clouds were underneath her. Jötun Canyon was plenty big enough to have weather of its own. Sarah was just glad the clouds didn't altogether block the western wall from view. Seeing it loom out of the fog too late to dodge was the stuff of nightmares.

"Everything all right, hon?" Irv sounded as if he expected her to go spiraling down into the canyon any second now.

"No problems," she answered, taking her left hand off the stick to flick on the radio's send switch. "I'm even getting warm. Exercise and all that." Keeping *Damselfly* in the air was hard work, closer to running than to bicycling on the ground. "I should be across in less than half an hour. Off I go, into the wild gray yonder—"

"Oh, shut up," Irv said. Chuckling, Sarah switched off. Her husband would be too busy fuming to worry about her for a while. She pedaled on. The breeze from the fresh air tube began to feel delicious, not icy.

Looking down between her busy feet, Sarah saw she was above the deepest part of the Jötun Canyon. Something moving down there caught her eye. She could not tell what sort of beast it was, any more than a jetliner passenger can name the makes of cars he sees from 30,000 feet. Just with level flight between the canyon's walls, she was half that high over the bottom herself.

She wondered what lived down there. Whatever it was, it was not a full-time resident, not unless it nailed itself to the biggest rock it could find when the yearly floods came through. Maybe not then, either.

Then all such mental busywork blew away with the gusting tailwind that swept *Damselfly* along with it and threatened to make the ultra-ultralight stall. Sarah gasped, pedaled harder, and hit the prop control switch to make the propeller grab more air. A moment later, she also turned on the plane's little electric motor to add its power to hers.

For a few queasy seconds, she thought none of that would do any good. Gusts were the worst problem with human-powered aircraft; one of five miles an hour gave *Damselfly* as much of a jolt as a 30-mph gust did to a Cessna. The flimsy little craft did not want to answer its controls. From the way the spars creaked, Sarah wondered if it was going to break up in midair. "Don't you dare, you bastard," she said fiercely, as if that would do any good at all.

Damselfly held together. Sarah brought the plane's nose down. Her legs were blurs on the pedals. She never knew whether her efforts saved her or the gust simply subsided. What she did know was that all the sweat on her body had turned cold.

When she was sure the ultra-ultralight—and her voice—were in full control again, she thumbed the radio's send switch. "Hello back there," she said. "Before, I was worrying about whether the Russians would have blankets and such for me. Now all I care about is a change of underwear." She was surprised at how easily she could joke about what had just happened. No one, she thought, really believes in the possibility of her own death.

While Irv and Louise exclaimed tinnily through *Damselfly's* speaker, Sarah shook her head, annoyed at herself. Philosophizing after the fact was all very well, but the cold sweat still coated her and her joke had almost been no joke at all, but literally true. She had believed in death, all right.

The western edge of Jötun Canyon grew closer. Sarah resisted the temptation to put on another mad burst of effort so she could reach it fifteen seconds before she would have otherwise. As in distance running, staying within herself counted. She could feel how much the one emergency had taken out of her.

At last she had land under her once more at a distance to be measured in feet rather than miles. She hit the radio switch again. The Russians could not reply on the frequency *Damselfly* used, but they were supposed to be listening. "*Damselfly* calling the Soviet rover," she said in slow, careful Russian. "I am on your side of the canyon. Please send up a flare to show me your location." She repeated herself several times.

All the while, she was scanning the horizon. If her navigation had been good, the flare would rise straight ahead of her. No sign of it there. No sign of it anywhere, in fact. What was— Sarah frowned, groping for the name—Rustaveli's problem?

There! The brilliant crimson spark hung in the air. It was north of where she had expected it; the gust over the canyon must have thrown her off worse than she'd thought. She twisted the control stick, working first ailerons and then rudder to go into the long, slow turn that was the best *Damselfly* could do.

The flare slowly sank while she approached. Now she eyed the ground instead of the sky. Motion drew her gaze. That was no Minervan down there, that was a man! "Soviet rover, I have you visually," she said triumphantly. "Coming in to land."

Rustaveli waved her on.

"—*Snap, crackle, pop*—really bad," came out of the radio. Irv didn't think it was haunted by Rice Krispies. What he did think was than no one had planned for *Damselfly* to be on the ground ten miles from the nearest receiver. The transmitter was not made to carry that far. No wonder the signal had static in it.

"Say again, Sarah," he urged.

More Kellogg's noises, then, ''—not really bad,'' she said. ''Broken ulna, concussion, nasty cut, maybe''—static again— ''cracked ribs. But no sign of internal bleeding. He'll get—'' Sarah's voice vanished once more.

''Say again,'' Irv repeated, and kept on repeating it until the static cleared.

''He'll get better,'' Sarah said, almost as clearly as if she were standing beside him with Louise and Pat. Grinning, Louise clasped her gloved hands over her head, as if to say, ''The winnah, and still champion . . .''

Nodding, Irv asked the question that was even more important to him. ''And how are you, hon?''

''Tired. Otherwise okay,'' she answered. ''I won't try to come back today. I need the rest, and it's too close to sunset to make me want to risk any funny winds the change from day to night might bring on over the canyon. Once was too f—'' The signal broke up again, but Irv had no trouble filling in the participial phrase he had not actually heard.

''Concur,'' Louise said, over and over till Sarah acknowledged. ''Wait at least till midmorning; let the air settle as much as it's going to.''

''Will you be warm enough tonight?'' Irv worried. Even when Minervan days got above freezing, nights stayed in the teens or colder.

''Plenty, thank you, Grandmother,'' Sarah answered, which made Pat giggle and Irv's ears turn hot under the flaps of his cap. ''You can all be jealous of me, too, because I'm eating something that doesn't come off our ration list. The Russians have this very nice little smoked lamb sausage called, ah—''

''*Damlama khasip,*'' an accented male voice supplied: Shota Rustaveli.

''Nobody wants to hear about it,'' Irv said. He *was* jealous, and so were Pat and Louise, if the lean and hungry looks on their faces meant anything. The food they had with them, which they would have eaten without much thinking about it, suddenly seemed too dull for words. Smoked lamb sausage . . . Irv felt his mouth watering.

Pat touched his arm and held out her hand for the radio. When he gave it to her, she said, ''Sarah, I'll bet they're as sick of that as we are of freeze-dried waffles.''

''You are only too right,'' Rustaveli said. Under the rueful amusement in his voice, the Russian—no, Georgian—sounded perfectly serious. ''A pity we have no better way to meet than this *Damselfly* of yours. Who knows what I might do for a freeze-dried waffle?"

Louise Bragg grabbed the radio. "Sarah, did you check that one for brain damage, too?" The humans on both sides of Jötun Canyon laughed together.

"People, I think the best thing we all could do now is rest," Sarah said. "We've had a long day, and another one is coming up tomorrow." She switched from pragmatic physician to wife, but only for a moment. "Love you, Irv. Out."

"Love you, too. Out." Irv fired up the portable stove to melt snow and then boil water for the dinner packs he, Pat, and Louise had brought along. The chicken à la king, he knew, wasn't really bad. But that was the trouble—he *knew* it. *Damlama khasip*—such an exotic name. What would it taste like? He was intrigued enough to wonder out loud.

"Like making love with a stranger after being married for years," Pat suggested. She dug a spoon into her own food, tasted it, and sadly shook her head. "Married to somebody boring," she amended. No one argued with her.

It was nearly dark by the time they were done.

"We'd better keep watch through the night," Irv said, "or your husband, Louise, who I hope is not boring"—she stuck out her tongue at him—"will have our hides when we get back to *Athena*."

He tore three scraps of paper off a notebook page, kept one, and handed the others to the women. "Write a number between one and ten," he said, "and then show it." He scrawled a 5 himself. Louise revealed an 8, Pat a 2. "All right, I'm odd man out; I'll stay awake a while. Who shall I roust when I sack out?"

Pat and Louise looked at each other. After a few seconds, Pat said, "I'll take the middle watch."

"If you're silly enough to volunteer, I'm silly enough to let you," Louise said at once. "I hate sleeping in shifts." Yawning, she unrolled her sleeping bag. "And I am beat." She climbed in and zipped the bag up so little more than her nose showed. "G'night."

Pat got into her sleeping bag, too. "I'll wake you about ten, Minervan Standard Wristwatch Time," Irv said. She nodded. Louise was already breathing slowly and regularly.

Irv walked around, wishing for a big blazing campfire; as night fell, the horizon seemed to close in on him, until the unknown lay hardly farther away than his outstretched fingertips. City boys like me don't really realize how dark night can be without street lights and such, he thought. It took a distinct effort of will not to turn on his flashlight and wave it about, just for the sake of something to see.

Stars would have helped, at least to ease his mind, but the clouds wrapped them away in cotton wool. Once, for a moment, he saw a wan smudge of light in the sky—one of the three little Minervan moons, though without a set of tables he had no idea which. Thicker clouds soon drifted over it and made it disappear.

That left Irv his ears and nose, left him a wolf pacing a prairie not his own. He was not evolved to know which little innocuous night noises were not innocuous after all, which of the scents on the chilly breeze would have sent any sensible Minervan beast running for its life. The local odors reminded him of nothing so much as how an organic chemistry lab smelled from a good way down the hall.

Something crunched behind him. He whirled, one hand grabbing for the flashlight, the other for the .45 on his belt. "It's only me," Pat said softly. "I can't sleep."

"Jesus." Irv felt himself getting angry. He knew it was his adrenaline all dressed up with no place to go, but knowing that did not make the anger any less real. "Good thing you didn't try sneaking up on Emmett like that," he said, inhibited in volume because he did not want to wake Louise. "He'd've handed you your head instead of going into palpitations like me." His heart was still thumping in his chest.

"Sorry." Pat made her whisper sound contrite. She stepped closer to him. "I just figured I'd wander over and keep you company for a while, that's all. If you want, I'll go away again."

"No, never mind. Now that you're here, I'm glad you're here—but damn, Pat!" They both laughed. Remembering his earlier thought, Irv went on, "We'll have to keep it down so we don't bother Louise."

"Sure, but I don't think it'll be a problem. She sleeps like a stone—must be a clear conscience or something." Was that bitterness there? Hard to be sure, with only a whisper to go on. Hard to imagine anyone having anything against Louise, too.

Irv's brain finally paid attention to what his nose had been telling him. He scratched his head. Odds were, knowing him, that he had just missed it before, but still . . . "Did you have perfume on while we were biking up?" The sweet muskiness cut through the strange Minervan odors and struck deep into his senses.

"No," she said.

He scratched his head again. "Don't tell me you put it on just for me. I'm flattered, but—"

Pat interrupted him, but not with words. Her mouth was soft against his and clung with something close to desperation when he started to pull away. She was almost as tall as he and just about as strong. "I've wanted to do that for a long time," she murmured.

"Have you?" Irv said, amazed. Even through his protective clothing and hers, he could feel her breasts press against him; his gloved hand found itself at the curve of her waist. "You've done a good job of hiding it, then."

"I've done a good job of hiding lots of things. The worst part is, Frank doesn't even notice." Her low-voiced laugh had knives in it. "And don't tell me you've been getting all you want from Sarah, either. There isn't enough privacy on *Athena* to let you get away with a lie. There isn't enough privacy on *Athena* for anything." She made it into a curse.

What she said was true enough, he thought dizzily as Pat kissed him again. No privacy . . . He knew, for instance, that she had a tiny brown mole just under her right nipple, that the hair between her legs was a couple of shades darker than the tarnished gold curls of her head. Till this moment, he had not spent much time thinking about any of that, but he knew.

He also knew that Sarah had told him no more times lately than he had been happy with. It was hard to think of Sarah right now, with Pat's tongue, agile as a serpent's, toying with his, trailing warmly over his cheek and sneaking under the flap of his cap to tease his ear.

He felt his body respond. So did Pat. Her hand pressed him through his trousers. For a moment, his hands pressed, too; the firm flesh of her buttocks yielded beneath his fingers. She arched her back, thrusting her hips against him.

At last their mouths separated. The chill of the long breath of air Irv gulped in helped him bring his body partly back under the control of his will. Trying to make light of what was happening, he said shakily, "God, Pat, if I were twenty-one again I'd haul your pants down and screw you right here, even if we both froze our asses off."

"Do it," she said. "I want you to." She was still rubbing him, stroking him, trying to goad him to action.

"Pat, this is foolish," he said as gently as he could, reaching down to take her hand away and suppressing a spasm of regret

almost before he knew it was there. "I'm not twenty-one anymore; I don't let my cock do all my thinking for me. You're not
twenty-one, either. Don't you think we're too far from home to
do anything that would hurt any of us?"

"I hurt now," Pat retorted. "You would, too, if you'd been
faking it all the way out from Earth orbit. And the only way
Sarah'd be hurt is if she found out."

"She would. I'm a lousy liar about that kind of thing." Not,
Irv thought, that I've ever had much to lie about. His one brush
with infidelity had come at a drunken party a few years back.
He and a girl—God, he'd forgotten her name—were fooling
around in a walk-in closet when he passed out between second
and third base.

He had always reckoned the next day's killer hangover pun-
ishment to fit the crime. He had not been seriously tempted to
wander since. Come to think of it, he had not been seriously
drunk since, either.

"You don't want me." Pat's voice was flat, despairing.

"You know better than that—you damn well ought to."
Though subsiding, Irv still stirred at the memory of her touch.
"But what I want and what I'm going to do are two different
things. Pat, jumping on you is tempting as hell, but it's just more
trouble than it's worth—for me, for Sarah, for Frank, and for
you. For Louise, too, if she happens to get up to pee at the
wrong moment."

"She won't," Pat said, but Irv saw her sag.

He nodded slowly to himself. If privacy was her hang-up,
reminding her she didn't have it seemed like a good idea—
assuming, of course, that he really didn't feel like getting
laid. Well, that was the assumption he had made, and he still
thought it was the right one. "Pat, if what you need is being
alone, you should have had a good time on the collecting trips
you took with Frank."

"I hoped that, too," she said bleakly. "Didn't work, not for
me, anyway. Frank, now—Frank had lots of fun. It's easy for a
man—you get your jollies every time."

"Frank doesn't know you don't?" he asked. She shook her
head. "Maybe you ought to let him know." Maybe I ought to
shut up, too, he thought. A marriage counselor I'm not.

"How am I supposed to do that?" she demanded, setting her
hands on her hips. " 'Gosh, I'm so sorry, honey, but for the last
year you haven't turned me on at all'?" Her voice was a dangerous parody of sweetness.

Irv winced. *Definitely I ought to shut up,* he thought. "There are probably better ways," he said carefully.

To his surprise, she started to laugh, and even sounded as though she meant it. "Do you know, Irv, you may be too sensible for your own good. It's hard to be sensible when you're horny."

"Tell me about it," he said. "It's hard to be sensible when a fine-looking wench tries to kick your feet out from under you, too."

"Hmm. I didn't think of that. You suppose it would have worked?" Pat leaned toward him. "No, don't run away," she said when he started to pull back. "Now the only question is, should I kiss you or punch your lights out?" She ended up doing a little of both, pecking his cheek and tromping on his foot hard enough to hurt. "There. That'll keep you guessing. Now, what time has it gotten to be?"

He blinked at the change of subject, then pulled back his sleeve so he could check his watch. "A little before nine."

"Go to sleep," she told him. "I'm too wound up to sleep now, so I may as well start my stretch early."

"Are you sure?"

"Yes. Go on, will you? I'll be fine."

"Okay. Thanks." Irv took a couple of steps, then looked back doubtfully. Pat sent him on with an impatient wave. He got out of his shoes, climbed quickly into his sleeping bag, and zipped it up. Sleep took a while coming, though.

Louise lay a few feet away. From the way she was snoring, she was out like a light. Irv suspected that he could have led a brass band past her without waking her up, let alone playing slap and tickle with Pat. Suddenly he wanted her more than he had when she was in his arms.

He shook his head. Turning down a woman who offered herself like that was not one of the easier things he had done. He laughed at himself. "It's not as if I've had a lot of practice," he said under his breath.

"What's that?" Pat asked.

"Nothing. Just brain-fuzz." He rolled over and eventually went to sleep.

"Adin, dva, tri!" Rustaveli shouted. At "three," he and the American doctor pushed on the rover with all their might. She was even smaller than Katerina, but determination and no little strength made up for her lack of size. Grunting and swearing,

she and Rustaveli fought the rover's weight until it overbalanced and flipped back onto its wheels. It jounced a couple of times, then sat still.

"Well done!" Valery Bryusov cheered from a few meters away. His left arm was splinted and in a sling rigged from a piece of blanket. He made a rueful gesture with his good hand. "I wish I could have helped."

"Never mind, Valery Aleksandrovich." Rustaveli sprang onto the rover and tried the motor. The vehicle rolled ahead. He stopped it and grinned. "Thanks to Sarah, ah, Davidovna, you are fixed, now it is fixed, and we will be going back to our comrades."

"Carefully, I hope," Sarah said. She picked up the blankets she used to supplement the flimsy costume that was all she wore inside her pedal-powered plane and started to redrape them.

Bryusov stepped forward to help her, but Rustaveli beat him there. After so long with just Katerina to think about, he was astonished at how much the mere sight of a different woman excited him. But when his hands "accidentally" started to slide down from her shoulders, the flinty look she gave him stopped him in his tracks. "Excuse me," he muttered, surprised at how embarrassed he was.

"All right, then," she said. But her voice did not imply that it was all right; her voice warned him not to try it again. This, he thought, could be one seriously stubborn woman. Maybe he should be just as well pleased not to be spending three years of his life in close company with her. Nevertheless—

"Sarah Davidovna, we are in your debt," he said.

"I especially," Bryusov agreed. "The more so as you had to make a journey dangerous to yourself to help me, and our nations are not the best of friends."

Under the awkward blankets, she shrugged. "There aren't any nations here, just people—and not very many of us. Compared to anyone or anything else on Minerva, we're all closer than brothers. If we don't help each other, who will?"

"You are right," Rustaveli said, though he knew Oleg Lopatin would have hurt himself laughing at such a notion—and perhaps Colonel Tolmasov, too. For that matter, he doubted that all the Americans on Minerva were as altruistic as this Dr. Levitt; otherwise, for instance, Tolmasov would have been happier dealing with Emmett Bragg.

While Rustaveli was working through that chain of thought,

Bryusov asked what the Georgian should have. "How may we help you now, Sarah Davidovna?"

"*You*, Valery Aleksandrovich, can help best by staying out of the way and not risking any further harm to yourself," she said firmly. "Shota Mikheilovich, if you would, you could help me swing *Damselfly* around so that it faces back toward Jötun Canyon once more. That will save me the trouble of flying around in a long, slow semicircle before I can head back to my own people."

So much for the brotherhood of all men on Minerva, Rustaveli thought. Still, the request was entirely reasonable. "Show me what to do."

He walked over to the ultra-ultralight with her. "Very simple," she said. "You take one wingtip, I'll take the other. Then we walk around till the plane points the way we want it to. Just be careful not to poke your fingers through the plastic skin."

"*Da,*" he said absently. He was amazed at how easily the plane moved. "This, ah, *Damselfly* cannot weigh even as much as I do."

"Not even close," the American doctor agreed. The aircraft soon pointed east, but she still looked discontented. Rustaveli understood why when she said, as much to herself as to him, "Now how am I supposed to get into the blasted thing?"

He saw the problem at once. The canopy opened at the top, and there was no way to clamber up without tearing the plastic film of the fuselage to ribbons. He rubbed his chin; whiskers rasped under his gloves as he thought. Finally he snapped his fingers, or tried to—the gloves effectively muffled the noise. "Suppose I drive the rover alongside your plane here? You could climb on top of the roll cage, and I will help you down onto the seat inside the plane."

After his try at feeling her up, he wondered if she would hesitate. She didn't, not even for a second. "Fine," she said. "Let's do it."

The rover purred up to *Damselfly*. Rustaveli turned off the engine and set the brakes on all four wheels. Then he scrambled up onto the top of the machine. Sarah Levitt came swarming after him. "You do that very well," he said.

"I haven't been on a jungle gym since I was nine years old, but it's not the sort of thing you forget." Sarah undid the canopy and sat on the metal bars of the roll cage with her feet dangling down into—what would one call it? The pilot's compartment?

The engine room? Wondering that, Rustaveli was almost caught by surprise when the American doctor said, "Lower me."

Rustaveli hooked his feet at the corners of intersecting bars and took a firm grip on Sarah Levitt's waist. He was glad she was a small woman; it made her weight easier to control as she slid into *Damselfly*. Although his arms traveled up her torso as she descended, he took no undue liberties.

"Thank you," she said, in a way that thanked him for that as well as for his help.

He backed the rover out of the way and walked around to the other side of *Damselfly* so he could close the canopy. When it was latched, he asked, "Now what?"

"No need to shout," she said. "The skin is too thin to cut down on sound." She was already pedaling hard, though the propeller had not yet begun to spin. Her legs did not slow down as she went on, "Go to the end of one wing and run along with me, holding it level, when I start to taxi."

He sprang to attention, and snapped off a salute sharper than any Tolmasov would ever wring from him. "I am yours to command."

Under her white plastic helmet, the American doctor's eyes twinkled. "You are a very silly man, Shota Mikheilovich. How did you manage to sneak past all the selection boards?"

He winked at her. "Simple. I did not tell them." He was whistling as he walked out to the wingtip.

The big propeller, tall as he was, revolved slowly at first, then faster and faster. "Now!" Sarah Levitt shouted. *Damselfly* rolled forward, startlingly fast; Rustaveli was into a trot almost at once. Then he was running, and running for all he was worth. For a moment, it seemed to him that he was the one on the point of becoming airborne.

Then *Damselfly's* wheels lifted clear of the ground. The plane was going faster than the Georgian could match. He pulled to a stop and stood panting, his breath a cloud of fog around his head. The American doctor briefly took one hand off the control stick to wave to him and Bryusov.

They both waved back. The linguist walked up to Rustaveli as *Damselfly* skimmed eastward, toward Jötun Canyon. "I'm sorry you will have to do all the driving as we return to our comrades," Bryusov said.

Rustaveli was still watching the ultra-ultralight diminish in the distance. *"Nichevo,"* he said. "It doesn't matter. At least I won't have to pedal home."

* * *

"There!" Louise Bragg shouted. She slapped Irv on the back.

He staggered, straightened and followed her pointing finger with his eyes. At first he could make out nothing through the mist, but then he, too, spied the moving speck. He held the radio to his mouth. "Honey—uh, *Damselfly*—we have you visually."

"Good. I don't see you yet. Now shut up and let me work." Sarah's voice came in panting gasps.

Irv picked up the video camera and kicked in the zoom lens. *Damselfly* seemed to leap toward him, though it was still well out over Jötun Canyon. No gusts, not now, he thought—as close to a prayer as a secular man would let himself come.

Beside him, he heard Pat saying, "Come on, dammit, come on," over and over to herself. He nodded, which made the image he was taping jump. Somehow, the way Pat was pulling for Sarah made him easier about what had happened—and what had almost happened—the night before.

Then he could hear the prop's whoosh and the rattle of the bicycle chain that fed the power of Sarah's legs to the ultra-ultralight. She was above level ground now, on this side of the canyon. Irv switched off the camcorder and set it down so he could jump and yell.

"*Damselfly* has landed," Sarah said, touching down only a few feet from where she had taken off. Her ribs were heaving with exhaustion; she sat slumped over the control stick.

She managed a tired wave for Irv as he set the wide stepladder beside *Damselfly*. He undid the latches to the canopy, flung it open, and leaned over to help her climb out.

"Thanks," she said when she stood beside him. "All I can say is, the next time the Russians want my services, they can jolly well come see me."

He sadly shook his head. "I knew it had to happen—all that exercise has made your brain atrophy."

"Not to the point where I can't feel cold." She poked him in the ribs with an elbow. "Help me into my gear, will you?"

He did, saying, "I'm glad you're back."

"You and me both," she agreed feelingly. "There were a few seconds on the way over when I doubted—but let's not talk about that. I don't even want to think about it."

"Neither do I. Why don't you just relax and let Louise and me knock down *Damselfly* so we can take it back to *Athena*?"

"If I sit still too soon, I'll stiffen up." Sarah walked around while Irv and Louise attacked the ultra-ultralight with wrenches. Pat fell into step beside her. Irv felt a nervous twinge whenever they happened to look his way. Stupid, he told himself—nothing happened.

The only time Sarah said anything even remotely sexual on the way back, though, was just after she emerged from behind a boulder where she had gone to answer a call of nature. "I *have* stiffened up," she grumbled, then she grinned wryly at Irv. "Better not ask me to get on top anytime in the next few days."

"Damn, just when I was hoping to break out the trampoline," he said, so innocently that she almost forgot to glare.

They got back to *Athena* a little before sunset. Emmett Bragg took the 8-mm cassette from the video camera as if it were worth its weight in diamonds and handed it to his wife. "We transmit this first thing tomorrow," he told her.

"Why?" she demanded. "It'll tie up the link. Wouldn't you rather send data than pretty pictures?"

"Most of the time, sure. With this, I'd sooner be on the network news. And we will, too—tape of the American doctor flying back after saving the Russians' bacon? They'll show that all over the world. When you think about what it'll do for our program, the data can wait."

They all looked at each other. No one argued with him.

Reatur had grown used to having humans around. He did not realize it—he would have indignantly denied it—until four of the six strange creatures went away on their traveling contraptions and the other two stayed close by the building that had fallen from the sky. Without their poking their stalkless eyes into every corner of his domain and throwing questions at him like snowballs, he found himself bored.

Now they were back, and Sarah, just as though he—*she*, curse it—had never been away, was pestering him about Lamra. He did not want to think about Lamra right now. To keep from having to do so, he changed the subject. "Why did the four of you leave so suddenly the other day?"

"To help a hurt human."

"Ah," Reatur said. Then he brought himself up short. "Wait. Four of you went away. None of you was hurt, am I right?" At Sarah's head-wag, he went on, "The two who stayed were not hurt, either, true?" Again the human wagged her head. "That accounts for all the humans there are, doesn't it?" he asked. "So where did the hurt one come from?"

"He from domain called *Russia*," Sarah replied, which told Reatur nothing. "Not same domain as ours. He hurt on far side of Ervis Gorge."

More humans? More *domains* of humans? The idea disconcerted Reatur as badly as it had Fralk. The domain-master started to ask about it, then stopped. Something else Sarah had said was of more immediate concern to him. "You went *across* Ervis Gorge?" he asked, hoping he had misunderstood. But Sarah was moving her head up and down once more. "How?" Reatur asked faintly.

"In small machine that goes through air." Sarah spread her single pair of arms to mimic wings and moved her two legs as she did when she was inside the contraption.

Reatur felt brief relief, then had another unsettling thought. "These other humans from the other domain"—he did not try to pronounce it—"do they also have one of these machines for moving through the air?"

"No." Sarah's answer was quick and positive.

"Then they couldn't give one to the Skarmer?" The idea of humans dropping out of the sky was quite bad enough. Thinking of armed westerners crossing Ervis Gorge through the air was simply horrifying.

But Sarah said "No" again. Reatur turned an eyestalk on himself. Good—he had not been alarmed enough to turn blue. Showing fear to any human would have been embarrassing; showing fear to a human mate did not bear thinking about. Mates had enough trouble in their poor short lives that they should never be burdened with a male's concerns, as well. Intellectually, Reatur knew the three human mates were not like those of his kind. Emotionally, that still had not sunk in.

Sarah helped drive the point home, though. "About Lamra—" she resumed, more stubborn than any of Reatur's males would have been when the domain-master was so plainly unwilling to discuss the matter.

"We will talk about Lamra another time, not now," Reatur declared.

That should have settled the matter, but Sarah rudely refused to let it stay settled. "What you do now instead? What more important than Lamra? You not talk of Lamra, Lamra die. What more important than Lamra not dying?"

He had to think for a moment to come up with an answer, but at last he did. "I am going to check with the watchers I have placed at the edges of Ervis Gorge. If the Skarmer somehow manage to root themselves on this side, Lamra will not be the only one who dies." He started to leave.

"You run from me," Sarah said. Reatur watched himself start to go yellow. That it was partly true only made him angrier. The human went on. "How Skarmer—how *anyone*—cross Ervis Gorge?"

"How should I know?" Reatur yelled, so loud that Sarah stepped back a pace and a male stuck an eyestalk around a corner to make sure everything was all right. The domain-master was a person who, if poked by one fingerclaw, hit back with three. He kept right on shouting. "Until you told me, Sarah, I didn't think anyone could cross it through the air. For all I know, the sneaky westerners may come by way of water when the gorge fills up." That was the most ridiculous thing he could think of, but he was cursed if he would admit it. "Since I don't know *what* they'll do, I have to point my eyestalks every which way at once, don't I?"

"Yes," the human mate conceded reluctantly. Reatur had not intimidated her, though, for she continued. "We talk of Lamra later, yes?"

"Later, yes. Not now." This time, when the domain-master walked past Sarah, she let him go.

But her voice pursued him. "Maybe Skarmer does—*do*—use water. Humans go by water sometimes."

Reatur kept walking. His color slowly faded. He decided he preferred being bored to being harassed. He had grown so used to being harassed by humans that it had taken some time without them to remind him how things had been not so very long ago.

A drop of water hit him in an eye as he walked out of his castle. Summer was close now; everything was starting to melt. Dealing with humans gave the domain-master the same feeling as that splash. They melted all his certainties just as the summer sun worked on his home.

The males working in the fields, he saw, were not working very hard. He started to shout at them, then decided he would be wasting his temper. Stone tools made everyone slow. At least the males were accomplishing more with those than they would have with ice, which grew more frangible day by day.

Some of the males were working in the very shadow of *Athena*, and not turning so much as a single eyestalk toward the huge, strange structure. They were used to humans, too. Reatur wondered if that was good or bad. Good, he supposed: nothing at all would have gotten done if everyone was still as bemused as at first. But finding a human as normal as an eloc did not seem right, either.

Having just had that thought, Reatur had to wiggle his eye-stalks at himself when he passed the human called Frank, who was on his way back from Ervis Gorge, without even stopping to chat. And this Frank had shown Enoph that rocks, of all the crazy ideas, had ages just like people! That was a notion deserving of days of talk, but Reatur had other things on his mind at the moment. Frank, after all, would be here tomorrow, and the day after, too.

Reatur had watchers posted along the entire stretch of Ervis Gorge that marked the western frontier of his domain, but most of them clustered close to the castle. That was where most of his people lived and also where the bridge across the gorge had been.

Ternat was one of the watchers. He carried three javelins, as if he expected a horde of Skarmer males to come roaring across the gorge at any moment. He widened himself when he saw Reatur approaching.

"Never mind that, eldest," Reatur said impatiently, and Ternat resumed his normal height. "I'm glad to see you so alert."

"One day the domain will be mine, clanfather, unless the Skarmer steal it from me. I do not intend to let them."

"Well said. I came to ask you to spread word to your fellow watchers: use one eyestalk to look at the sky from time to time."

"The sky, clanfather? No one can go through the sky. No one save humans, I mean," Ternat amended, as he would not have before *Athena* came down.

"Aye, humans," Reatur said—no escaping the creatures, not anymore. "I learn there are humans on the western side of Ervis Gorge, too, humans of a different clan from the ones here. Who knows what treacherous tricks they may have taught the Skarmer?"

"The Skarmer need no one to teach them treachery," Ternat said. "But—more humans?"

"I don't like the thought any better than you, eldest, but pulling in my eyestalks won't make it go away. So—look to the sky."

Ternat let the air sigh out through his breathing-pores. "The sky, clanfather." He sounded as happy as Reatur felt.

The two males bored in on Fralk. Each of them carried two spears and two light spears, as did he. Each watched him with three eyestalks and used a fourth to see what the other was doing. The smooth way they moved together told of how often they had done this before—to them, Fralk was just another victim to be dispatched.

He sprang at one of the males, hoping to put him out of action and make the fight even. But, though he shifted his own spears to the hands near the male he had chosen, that warrior blocked his blows with almost bored ease. And Fralk, who needed a shield of his own to protect himself against that male's counterthrusts, had but a single shield to withstand the onslaught of the fellow's comrade.

That sort of fight could not last long. Fralk knew a brief moment of triumph when he managed to deflect a couple of thrusts from the second male, but all too soon one got home. Fralk let out a high-pitched squeal of pain.

"Eldest of eldest, you are as dead as a strip of sun-dried massi meat," declared the drill-leader, a skinny, cynical male named Juksal. "Or you would be, if we were fighting with spears with real points. And the rest of you," he called to the crowd of males watching the fight. "What does this teach you?"

"Not to get caught between two males," his audience chorused.

Juksal feigned deafness. "Did I hear some runnerpests chirping? I asked, what does this teach you?"

"Not to get caught between two males!" This time it was a shout.

"All right," Juksal said grudgingly. "You budlings know what to say, anyhow. Do you know what to do so that won't happen?"

"Form circle!" the males shouted.

Fralk yelled with the rest, but all the while was thinking that what he really wanted to do was kill the accursed drill-leader. Any other time, any other place, Juksal would have widened himself the instant he saw Fralk and stayed widened till the younger male was gone. Not, Fralk added to himself, that Juksal frequented places where he would be likely to see him.

But here on this practice field, because he had managed to live through a few brawls, Juksal had clanfather's authority over the group of males in which Fralk found himself. He used it, too, and seemed to take special delight in making Fralk the object of his lessons. Fralk ached after every one of them.

He knew he had to learn to fight. As the male in charge of the boats, he would be going across in one of the very first ones. He did not think the Omalo on the other side of the gorge would

greet him with hoots of delight. He even realized that being
singled out this way by Juksal might earn him his comrades'
sympathy and make them more inclined to protect him than if
they thought of him as a pampered noble. Maybe Juksal thought
he was doing him a favor.

Maybe, in fact, Juksal *was* doing him a favor. That did not
make him hurt any less, or like the drill leader any more.

"All right," Juksal suddenly screamed. "You've just spotted
eighteen eighteens of Omalo, all running toward you! Don't just
talk about your stinking circle—make it, or you're dead males.
Now, now, now!"

Predictably, a good deal of waste motion and rushing to and
fro followed. The band of males got into their double ring a lot
faster than they had the first time they tried it, though. Then
Juksal had been screaming that they should have brought along
a tray of relishes so the Omalo would have something to eat
them with. Now all he did was turn yellow. Since he seemed to
be yellow about half the time, Fralk doubted he was very angry.

"All right." The drill-leader swept out an arm. "They're *that*
way, and there aren't as many of them as you thought at first.
Matter of fact, there's more of you. Go poke holes in 'em."

A few of Fralk's companions were veterans of border clashes
with other Skarmer clans—the two who had set on him were of
that sort. More, like he, had never seen action. They shook
themselves out into a crescent-shaped skirmish line and rushed
in the direction Juksal had shown.

"Yell, curse it!" the drill-leader shouted at his warriors.
"Make 'em want to void right where they're standing!"

Fralk yelled as loud as he could, feeling foolish all the while.
Soldiers were necessary things for a clan to have, but as eldest
of eldest he had never expected to be one himself. But then, he
had never expected Hogram to conceive of planting a new
Skarmer subclan east of Ervis Gorge.

Every time he was tempted to imagine himself wilier than the
clanfather, he broke a mental fingerclaw on the hard ice of that
fact. The Great Gorges had been barriers between great clans
as long as there had been great clans. Thinking of one as anything else required a leap of imagination beside which Fralk's
own schemes were as so many tiny runnerpest budlings.

"Come back, the lot of you," Juksal called, breaking into
the younger male's musings. The band reversed itself. "All right,
enough for the day. Fling your spears at the targets and then

knock off." As if suddenly remembering to be harsh, the drill-
leader added, "Try to scare 'em if you can't hit 'em!"

Neither of Fralk's casts hit the leaf-stuffed massi-hide target.
Neither missed by much, though. He consoled himself with the
thought that if the target had been a male caught in a volley,
maybe he would have dodged someone else's spear and been
brought down by one of these.

He was also glad none of the humans had been watching.
They did watch the Skarmer males drill fairly often; the sound
of their picture-makers clicking away had become a familiar part
of the exercises. At first Fralk thought they were filled with awe
at the might and savagery of the Skarmer forces.

Most of the males still thought that. Juksal certainly did;
whenever a human came around, he urged his warriors to show
the strange creatures how fierce they were.

But Fralk, unlike his fellows, had learned to read expressions
on the humans' strange, boringly colored features. When the
corners of their odd mouths curved up, they were amused. Fralk
did not know why the Skarmer drills amused them, but he was
sure they did.

Well, he thought, still feeling the ache under one arm, he'd
like to see how a human would fare, attacked by four spears at
once. Attack a human on the side where he had no eyes and he
was yours—he wouldn't even know he was in trouble until he
was dead.

Fralk stopped. A couple of human concepts he had been having trouble with suddenly made sense. *Right* and *left* had given
him no problems; they were just opposites of one another, what
he thought of as *three arms apart*. But *behind* . . . behind was
the direction where humans had no eyes, the hidden direction.
Made as they were, poor strange creatures, no wonder they
needed a special word for it.

Behind . . . it even had a weird kind of logic to it, or at least
economy, which to Fralk's mercantile mind was about the same
thing. Like those of any reasonable language, Skarmer prepo-
sitions classified objects through their relative distance outward
from oneself. Sometimes that led to clumsy ways of thinking
and of speaking: Juksal, for instance, was *closer-to-Fralk* than
the male named Ising, but *farther-from-Fralk* than the one called
Kattom.

How much easier to say—and to think—that Juksal was *behind* Kattom. And how much easier to wish the miserable drill-

leader were *behind* Ising, and *behind* a good many more males as well, so he could neither see nor bother Fralk anymore.

Fralk knew what wishes were worth. If wishes were all that mattered, every starving tenant-farmer would become a clan-father overnight. Most times, Fralk knew that too well to need to remind himself of it.

But wishing Juksal would disappear was too pleasant a thought to slap down. Fralk's eyestalks quivered with guilty pleasure as he walked back toward Hogram's town.

7

Reatur had left a piece of hide with some writing on it in the mates' quarters. It had been there a few days. Most of the mates paid no attention to it. A couple scribbled on the blank parts. Then Lamra rescued it. She could not read, not really, but she did know that the written signs had sounds that went with them and knew what some of those were.

If you made one sound, and then the next one right after it—why, you'd just said *ice*! That was what those two signs had to mean! Ice! Lamra was so excited at her discovery that she stared at the hide with all six eyes at once, paying no attention to anything going on around her. She might have heard the door to the mates' chambers opening, but if she did, she ignored that, too.

She was taken by surprise, then, when Reatur asked from right beside her, "What do you have there?"

Three eyestalks jerked up from the hide. Not only was Reatur standing there, but Sarah the human, as well. How had they managed to sneak up on her? Well, no matter. She was glad they were here, Reatur especially. "Look!" Lamra said, pointing to the signs she knew. "This means 'ice,' doesn't it?" None of the mates cared about anything like that.

Reatur bent an eyestalk down to see what she was talking about. "Why, yes, it does," he said slowly. "How did you know that?" He kept one eyestalk on the word she had figured out and moved another around so he could see what was going on; the remaining four peered straight at Lamra.

"If you say the sounds of these two signs together, they make the word," she explained. Reatur did not answer. He just kept looking at her with those four intent eyestalks. She began to worry. "Am I in trouble?" she asked. She had never heard of mates knowing what writing meant. Maybe they weren't supposed to.

After a long pause that made Lamra worry even more, Reatur said, "No, you're not in trouble." She watched herself go from alarmed blue to the green of relief and happiness.

"What?" Sarah asked. The talk had passed her by.

"I know what these two signs say," Lamra told the human proudly, showing which ones with a fingerclaw. She pronounced them separately, then together. " 'Ice!' Do you understand?"

"Yes. Understand," Sarah said. She beat her two hands together, again and again. The noise startled Lamra, who pulled her eyestalks in halfway. "No, no," Sarah said quickly. "With humans, noise means, 'good for you.' "

Humans were very strange, Lamra thought, not for the first time: trust them to scare someone when all they meant was "good for you." The mate let her eyestalks come out again, though.

She watched Sarah turn her head so her eyes pointed at Reatur. "You see?" the human said. If a person had been talking, Lamra would have thought that was triumph in her voice.

Maybe it was. Reatur's grunt lay between annoyance and resignation. "I told you once already, did I not?" he said sharply. The human bent her head down—a person would have widened himself instead.

"You see about what, Reatur?" Lamra asked.

"About you," the domain-master said. Seeing that Lamra did not follow him, he went on. "The human will try to see that you don't die when your time comes to bud."

"Oh," Lamra said, and then, louder, "Oh!" She still did not know what to think about that and was surprised that Reatur would even let Sarah try. "Are you sure?" she asked him.

"No," he said. "I don't know if I should be doing this at all. I don't know if Sarah can keep you alive. But I do know I don't want you to die. If it turns out you don't have to, good. If not— the sorrow of the mates."

If Reatur thought things might turn out all right, Lamra was willing to accept that. The same curiosity that had helped her begin to figure out written signs made her turn a couple of eyestalks on Sarah and ask, "How will you go about keeping my blood inside me? It comes out very quickly." She had never watched a budding; Reatur didn't let mates do that. But once or twice she had seen the chamber afterward, before it was cleaned, and she had picked up ideas from overheard snatches of talk. She more or less knew what happened in there.

Sarah turned her head back to Lamra. "Not know. Try to find out." Then the human's head swung toward Reatur again. "Mate knows good questions to ask, yes?"

"That she does," the domain-master said. "She always has, ever since she learned what words are for. It's one of the reasons I would like to see her stay alive."

"I wish the two of you wouldn't talk about me like that, as if I weren't there," Lamra said indignantly.

Reatur and the human both stood quite still for a moment. Then Sarah started making the odd noise humans used instead of honest, eyestalk-wriggling laughter, while Reatur widened himself as if he were a mate and Lamra the domain-master. "I humbly crave your pardon, clanf—ah, clan*mother*," he said.

"Don't you make jokes at me." Now Lamra really was angry, angry enough to turn yellow.

Reatur's voice changed. "I'm sorry, little one. I didn't mean to tease."

"Well, all right." Of their own accord, Lamra's eyestalks started to twitch. Imagine her telling off the domain-master! Better yet, imagine her getting away with it! She remembered that Sarah had not answered her question. She asked it a new way. "If you don't know how to keep me from ending yet, how will you find out?"

"Good question again," Sarah said.

Lamra felt herself yellowing up once more—she wanted an answer that was an answer, not just words that sounded nice but didn't tell her anything. Finally she got one.

"Try with animals budding," the human said. "See if animal mates live after what I do. If yes, I do with you. If no, I do new thing with another animal mate, see if live after *that*."

Lamra thought it over. "That sounds like it might work," she admitted. "What if none of the animal mates lives, though?"

Sarah opened her mouth, then closed it again without saying anything.

"Then you won't, either, Lamra," Reatur said.

"That's what I thought. That's what's supposed to happen, though, so I don't need to worry about it, do I?"

"Of course not," he answered at once. "I'll do all the worrying. That's one of the things a domain-master is supposed to do. I worry so other people don't have to."

"All right," Lamra said, relieved. "I'm not much good at worrying—you need to think about one thing for a long time to do it right, and I have trouble with that. There are so many interesting things to think about that sticking to just one is hard."

"All mates like this?" Sarah asked Reatur, again as though Lamra were somewhere else.

"No," was all he answered.

"Then I see why you want this one to save."

"Yes," Reatur said.

The way they talked made Lamra feel foolish. She was just herself and could not imagine being any different from what she was. Her only perception that she was in any way remarkable was that she found other mates boring some of the time. And since they often did not seem to know what to make of her, either, that worked both ways.

"Sarah, if you do find out how to keep me from ending when my buds drop, will it be something only humans can do, or will Reatur be able to do the same thing with other mates later on?"

"Other mates?" Reatur exclaimed. "I hadn't even begun to think about that." He started to turn blue, which startled Lamra—what had frightened him?—until he went on, "If all our mates and all their budlings and all *their* mate budlings lived to grow up, how would we feed them all? This domain just raises enough for the folk it has now."

He and Lamra both turned anxious extra eyestalks toward Sarah. All the human—the human *mate*, Lamra reminded herself; somehow humans dealt with the problem that worried the domain-master—said, though, was, "Not know."

"Fair enough," Reatur said. "Worry about one thing at a time. If Lamra lives after budding, then we will see what to do next."

"Yes," Sarah said. "Good sense."

Lamra had not thought so far ahead when she asked her question, but she recognized the trouble once Reatur showed her it was there. "If this harms the domain, clanfather, you don't have to let Sarah do it." The sacrifice seemed small to her. She had been going to end when her buds dropped, and the time that might come after still did not feel as though it belonged to her.

Sarah started to say something, then stopped with her mouth half open. As was fitting, she looked toward Reatur—the choice was his.

"I don't suppose one full-grown mate will eat up all the spare food in the domain," he said. "Go on, Sarah; I said yes before and I say yes again. No matter what happens later, Lamra is worth it.''

Lamra widened herself to the domain-master. She had done that countless times before, but only because she had been taught to. For the first time it was the gesture of conscious respect and gratitude it was meant to be—now she understood why she did it.

Sarah bent from the middle toward Lamra—the human gesture that meant the same as widening. ''I try hard to save you,'' she said.

''Thank you.'' Still strongly feeling the ceremony inherent in the gesture, Lamra widened herself in return. Sarah bent again. They could have gone on saluting each other for some time, but Reatur chose that moment to leave, and Sarah walked away with him.

The mates' chambers were always boisterous, with mates chasing one another and yelling at one another all through the day. To Lamra, the place seemed empty without Reatur and Sarah. She did not feel like playing with her friends. Even if she had, the growing buds were starting to make her too slow to keep up.

Another mate came up to her. Peri was left out of games a lot, too, as she was also growing buds. ''What did the domain-master and the—the funny thing want with you?'' she asked, awe in her voice. Why did Reatur keep spending time with a mere mate, especially one with whom he had already mated?

''Reatur and the *human*,'' Lamra said, flaunting her superior knowledge, ''are working on ways to keep mates alive after budding.''

''You're teasing me,'' Peri said shrilly. ''Nobody can do that.''

''I'm not, either. They are so.''

''Don't be silly,'' Peri said. ''You can't fool me, Lamra, not this time. Who ever heard of an old mate?''

Something moved, down in the bottom of Jötun Canyon. The motion was tiny, but anything visible at all from down there had to be good-sized. Shota Rustaveli swung up binoculars for a closer look. Having the depths of the canyon suddenly seem to jump seven times closer always unnerved him; it was as if he were flinging himself down into the abyss.

''What is it?'' asked Yuri Voroshilov, who did not have field glasses with him.

''Yuri Ivanovich, I don't know.'' Rustaveli could feel his forehead crinkle in a puzzled frown. "I can't figure it out. Maybe it was just the sun, flashing off water down there."

"*Bozhemoi*," Voroshilov said softly.

Rustaveli did not follow him for a moment. Then the biologist echoed that "My God" himself. Yesterday the bottom of the canyon had been dry. If it had water in it today, it would have more tomorrow, and as for the day after that . . . "Forty days and forty nights and then some," he said.

"*Da.*" Voroshilov laughed softly. "Strange, is it not, how after three generations of a godless society, we still have the biblical images in the back of our minds, ready to call up when we need them?"

"Ask the devil's mother why that's so," Rustaveli suggested. They both laughed then.

"Such impudence." If Oleg Lopatin had said that, Rustaveli would have bridled. Voroshilov only sounded amused. Then, sighing, the chemist grew more serious. "The flood is upon us, Shota Mikheilovich, in more ways than one."

"Eh? What's that?" Rustaveli's mind was elsewhere. He wanted to get down to the water. There might be—there likely were—plants and animals down in the canyon that stayed dormant until the yearly floods came and then burst into feverish activity. Plenty of Earthly creatures did things like that, but who could guess what variations on the theme Minerva might offer? No one could guess—that was why they were here, to find out.

But Voroshilov was thinking along very different lines. "We will have trouble, for one thing, if Lopatin does not leave Katerina alone. I know, because I will cause it."

That got Rustaveli's attention. His head snapped toward Voroshilov. The chemist was such a quiet fellow that he even announced insurrection as if it were no more important than a glass of tea. He meant what he said, though. The Georgian could see that.

"Slowly, my friend, slowly," Rustaveli urged, wondering how—or whether—to head off Voroshilov. He had no use for Lopatin, but still . . . "The *chekist* is also a man, Yuri Ivanovich," he said carefully. "I suppose he has the right to try his luck with her."

"This I know," Voroshilov said heavily. "To approach her is one thing. But he has *hit* her, Shota Mikheilovich; I have seen the marks. That is something else again. That I will not stand, even if he has made her too afraid to speak up for herself."

Rustaveli scowled. Unfortunately, that sounded all too much

like Lopatin. And Katerina had been down to *Tsiolkovsky* lately; she and Voroshilov had just come back to the environs of Hogram's town. The chemist probably knew whereof he spoke.

"What will you do?" Rustaveli asked.

"Give him a taste of his own when he rotates up here next week. I was hoping you would join me—on the left, of course."

"A black-market beating, eh?" Though not a native Russian-speaker, Rustaveli understood the slang expression; everyone who lived in the Soviet Union dealt on the left, some more often, some less. Had the Georgian caught Lopatin cuffing Katerina around, he was sure he would cheerfully have pummeled him. Doing it in cold blood, planning it well in advance, was not the same thing. "Lopatin is a pig, *da*, but should we not see first if Tolmasov can bring him to heel?"

"A pig and a snake both," Voroshilov growled. "Not only does he abuse Katya, he paws through my cabin and types my poems into his computer file for evidence. Evidence of what I do not know—perhaps only that, no matter how I try, I am no Akhmatova or Yevtushenko." The chemist's broad, fair face darkened with anger. His gloved hands folded into fists; had Lopatin been there at that moment, he would have had a bad time of it.

Rustaveli knew that the *chekist* snooped. Anything he wanted to keep to himself, he wrote in Georgian—let Lopatin make what he could of *that*! But then, snooping was part of Lopatin's job. "Let us talk to Tolmasov," Rustaveli repeated.

Voroshilov gave him a sour look. "You southerners are supposed to be men of spirit. So much for folk legends."

"You Russians are supposed to be steady and unflappable," Rustaveli retorted; he did not add "and boring," as he might have. "If we go home, we will be heroes, so nothing may happen to us, but what of our families? I, for one, do not care to have the KGB know I assaulted one of theirs. Or do you think we could disguise ourselves as Minervan hooligans?"

He had hoped to make the chemist laugh, but Voroshilov was still scowling. They walked on a while in silence. Finally Voroshilov grunted, "Very well, we will speak with Tolmasov. Once."

As always, Rustaveli rejoiced at the warmth inside the tent. As always, his *valenki* squelched on mud; keeping the tent heated to a temperature humans found bearable meant that the frozen ground underfoot thawed out.

By luck, Tolmasov was there and Katerina was not. The colonel glanced up from the report he was writing. He set aside his pen at once. "Why the long faces, comrades?" he asked. Rustaveli nodded to himself; he might have known Tolmasov would notice something was wrong.

Voroshilov did the talking. He was more fluent than Rustaveli expected, more fluent, in fact, than the Georgian had ever heard him—just as he had been all day, come to that. Anger lent him words he could not normally command.

Tolmasov held his face impassive as he listened. Finally he said. "I have seen the mark you mean, I think: the bruise that runs close by her left breast and along her ribs?"

"*Da*, Sergei Konstantinovich, that is the one," Voroshilov nodded.

"Katerina said it came from a fall." Tolmasov's features clouded. "If that is not so—"

"Yes, what then?" Rustaveli deliberately made his tone mocking. "What do you dare to do to a man with such, ah, influence?" The only way he saw to make Tolmasov take real action was to suggest he could not.

"I command here, not Lopatin." The pilot's words might have been graven in stone. Rustaveli made sure he did not smile. "I shall inquire further of Dr. Zakharova, and shall take whatever action I find appropriate," the colonel went on. "Thank you for bringing this matter to my attention." He turned his eyes back to the report, in its way a dismissal as formal as were his last couple of sentences, spoken for the record.

"He will do nothing," Voroshilov predicted as soon as they were far enough from the tent to speak without Tolmasov's hearing.

Rustaveli shook his head. "Tolmasov disdains to use his strength against the weak, but I should not care to be in his way after having done so myself." He rubbed his gloved hands in anticipation of Lopatin's comeuppance.

But the comeuppance did not come. Rustaveli waited for Tolmasov to travel down to *Tsiolkovsky*, for Lopatin to be peremptorily summoned to the tent, for orders or warnings to come from Earth. Nothing happened. Day followed day, busily, yes, but otherwise routinely.

Voroshilov waited, too, with growing unhappiness. He was always quiet. Now he turned downright taciturn—dangerously so, if Rustaveli was any judge. He tried to draw out the chemist and failed. Voroshilov answered only in grunts. Those were more than he gave either Tolmasov or Katerina, but they were not enough.

Fearing a brewing explosion under that silent mask, Rustaveli finally did what he had told himself not to: he talked with Katerina about the trouble. "Yuri worries about you," he said as they walked through the marketplace of Hogram's town.

"Why?" she asked. "I am a grown woman, Shota Mikheilovich, and quite able to care for myself."

That gave the Georgian the opening he had hoped for. "Can you?" he countered quietly. "What of your ribs?"

She stopped so suddenly that a Minervan behind her had to swerve to keep from running into her. The male angrily waved arms and eyestalks as he went past. Katerina paid no attention. "Not you, too!" she said. "Sergei was after me about that last week. They're almost healed—why make a fuss now?"

"Because I worry about you, too, Katya."

Her eyes, challenging a moment before, softened. "Sweet of you, Shota, but truly, no need. I'm hardly even sore anymore."

"A bruise is a bruise," Rustaveli shrugged. "Where it comes from is something else again."

"Sergei went on the same way." Katerina tossed her head. "It came from my own clumsiness, nowhere else—I tripped over my own feet and fell against the edge of a lab table. Lucky I didn't break a rib."

If she was dissembling, Rustaveli thought, she had talent to go on stage. "I begin to think I have made a fool of myself," he said slowly. He grinned. "Not for the first time, I fear."

He did not win an answering smile from Katerina. "Will you please talk sense?" she snapped. "Did you think we would go through the whole mission without accidents? Even if you did, hasn't Valery's arm taught you better?"

"Without accidents, of course not. Without other things—"

"What other things?" She was starting to sound angry.

Tolmasov, Rustaveli realized, must have been so circumspect that Katerina had no idea what he was driving at. That made sense, in case Voroshilov's accusation happened to be wrong. Rustaveli had not thought it was; it fit too well with what he knew—well, what he thought he knew—of Lopatin.

The Georgian sighed. He wished he had been more discreet himself. Actually, he wished he had kept his mouth shut. But since he hadn't, he had to ask it straight out: "Then the *chekist* truly did not hit you?"

Her eyes widened—suddenly, he saw, all the roundabout

questions fit together. "Oleg? No. He is . . ." Her grimace made her lack of enthusiasm plain, but she went on. "In his own way, he has discipline, too, Shota Mikheilovich. What he might like to do, I would sooner not think. But he values the mission, and holds himself in; one can tell such things." She spoke calmly, dispassionately, then grew more urgent. "I value the mission, too; I want no trouble rising over me. Do you understand, Shota?"

"Da," Rustaveli said, a little regretfully. "But you'd better let Yuri know. He is not thinking kindly thoughts of Oleg Borisovich Lopatin."

"Yuri? He is so quiet, one never knows what he thinks. If he were to let loose of his temper—and isn't Lopatin due up here tonight? Yuri!" she said again, in an entirely different tone of voice. *"Bozhemoi!"* She turned and ran in the direction of the tent as if she had forgotten Rustaveli was beside her.

And so, he thought as he watched her sidestep Minervans, she likely had. He supposed he should have felt virtuous, having saved the mission from what might well have been serious trouble. He did not feel virtuous. He was thinking of his grandfather instead. The old bandit was dead now, but he would have boxed Rustaveli's ears if he ever found out his grandson had saved a KGB man a beating.

The Georgian laughed and swatted himself lightly on the earflaps of his cap. Penance paid, he followed Katerina back toward the tent.

The noise was so loud, it did not let Frank Marquard think. A few days before, he had looked down into Jötun Canyon, observed the flood, taken some pictures, and gone back to *Athena* conscious of nothing more than a job well done. Now he was a half a mile from the edge of the canyon, but the roar and boom coming up out of it were enough to stun. And the flood was just beginning.

He lifted the flaps of his cap and stuck in earplugs. They helped, but only somewhat. As at a rock concert, he still felt the noise through his feet, through his skin, and through his soft palate when he opened his mouth to breathe.

And with the earplugs in place, he could not talk to Enoph. He took them out and tried to yell above drumroll and thunder. "How you stand noise?"

The Minervan spoke through the din rather than over it, not raising his voice but talking more slowly so each word came out distinctly. "It happens every year," he said. "We can get used to it or we can go mad. Getting used to it is easier."

"I suppose so." Frank tried speaking as Enoph had and found to his surprise that it worked. He had heard stories of men talking in normal tones under factory racket but had never believed them. Now he did.

The vibration of the ground grew more severe as he got closer and closer to the edge of the canyon, until it was like walking during a moderate earthquake. Being a Los Angeles native, Frank had done that more times than he cared to remember. Here, though, the shaking went on and on. He consoled himself by thinking that anything that could have shaken loose would have done so millions of years before. That reassured the rational part of him; the rest still wanted to find a doorway to stand in.

He crawled the last few feet to the edge of the canyon, not wanting to be pitched over it if a slab of ice or a boulder happened to smash into the side especially hard. As he looked down, though, awe cast away fear.

The mist above the waters was thick and sparkling, like a sun-dappled fogbank viewed from above. That was exactly what it was, Frank realized. It would have concealed a great deal on Earth but it could not hide the Minervan floods.

Water thundered, roared, bellowed, cast itself upward off obstacles or off itself, and flung iceberg fragments and great stones into the air with mindless abandon. Frank squeezed off several pictures, knowing none of them could convey the sheer scale of what he was seeing. It was like watching gray whales mate in deep water. He had done that once, off the California coast.

He stuck an infrared filter on his lens. After that, the color values on his shots went south, but they did a better job of piercing the mist to show the watery fury that rampaged beneath.

"It grows steadier later in the season," Enoph said. "More of the gorge is filled, and a more regular flow replaces this first rush of water."

Marquard nodded; that was as computer models had predicted. The models had even warned of the mist above the water. What they had not done, could not do, was prepare him for the wonder the spectacle brought.

"Flood ever rise to top of canyon, spill out?" he asked. The computer had said that might happen, if everything went exactly right—exactly wrong, he supposed, from the Minervans' point of view.

Enoph turned blue with fear at the very idea. "You humans have terrible thoughts! What would be left of a domain?" Not much, Frank thought, not when the main local building stone was ice. For Enoph's sake, he was glad the simulation had been on the extravagant side.

The geologist took two more pictures, which finished off the roll. He decided against reloading; better to wait a couple of days and come back. That would tell him something about how fast the water was rising in the canyon.

He walked back toward *Athena*. He wanted to feed the roll into the developer now, so that he could see how it came out. When he got back to the ship, he found one roll processing and another in the IN bin with a Post-it note from Sarah attached: "Bump yours ahead of this and you die!" Knowing Sarah, she meant it. Frank sighed and stuck his film behind the other waiting roll.

He heard his wife's voice from the front cabin. No one else seemed to be aboard. Even Emmett and Louise, who hardly ever went away, were off doing something or other with Reatur; he had seen them by the castle. Frank grinned to himself. Such chances were not to be wasted. He walked forward, whistling to let Pat know he was coming.

She turned around in her seat, waved so he could tell she saw him, then went back to speaking Russian. "I had hoped the creature lived on your side of the canyon, too, Shota Mikheilovich, or had relatives there, but if not, not. *Athena* out."

Rustaveli also signed off. With a discontented grunt, Pat complained to her husband. "He doesn't have any idea about what's related to what. He's just thinking in terms of this species or that, not genera or families or orders. He'll end up hauling all his data home so the bigwigs in Moscow can try to make sense of it. Why'd he bother to come?"

"He doesn't have the computers we do," Frank answered. He scratched his head, trying to remember what she had told him a couple of days before. Succeeding made him smile. "If he'd found that little burrowing thing, he'd never have guessed it was related to the one the Minervans call a runnerpest. They don't look anything alike."

Pat smiled, too. "Oh, you were listening after all. You're right. That burrower is so adapted to underground life that without computer extrapolation of what its ancestors used to look like there'd be no telling which order it belonged to."

"Mm-hmm." Frank paused a moment. "Quiet in here."

"It is, isn't it?" Pat's gaze swung back to him. "Is that a hint?"

"More than a hint, you might say. Call it an invitation."

Something passed over Pat's face and was gone before Frank was sure he had seen it. Then her eyes went to the floppy she had been using while she talked with her Russian opposite number. Finally, though, she shrugged and said, "Why not?" Not the most enthusiastic response in the world, Frank thought, but it would do. He slipped his arm around her waist as she got up. They walked back to their cubicle.

Afterward, he leaned up on his elbow in the narrow bottom bunk. Pat lay beside him, not moving, not talking, looking up at the foam rubber mattress pad over their heads. "All right?" he asked, more hesitantly than he had expected.

"I guess I'm just tired," she said, shrugging again. Bare as she was, that should have been enchanting. Somehow it was not. She'd said that more than once lately, times when she'd been less responsive than he had hoped. And she still did not look at him.

He thought for a while. Over the years, he had grown used to pleasing Pat and pleasing himself thereby. He took things as he found them, but this failure was something he would sooner not find again. "Anything I can do to help?" he said hesitantly.

Now her eyes turned his way. "This is the first time you've offered that," she said. Curiosity mingled with—accusation?—in her voice.

"Didn't think I needed to before."

"Hmm." She was studying him as dispassionately as if he were one of her specimens. "Well, maybe." Her tone was judicious, too.

"Is that 'well maybe I didn't think so' or 'well maybe I can'?" He pantomimed the confusion he was feeling.

She laughed. Now the jiggles that produced excited Frank. He could not have said why, unless it was relief at no longer being studied like a runnerpest. "Well, maybe"—she paused wickedly—"a little of both." Her hand took his and guided it.

"Better?" he asked some time later. She bit him on the arm. It wasn't the answer he had looked for, but he did not complain.

Fralk and Hogram let thunder wash over them as they watched the flood. A boulder the size of Hogram's castle slammed into the side of Ervis Gorge. The ground quivered like the skin of a massi with an itch. "You propose to send our boat through *that*?'' the domain-master demanded, stabbing a fingerclaw at the chaos far below.

Invading the Omalo lands wasn't *my* idea, Fralk wanted to say. He had too much sense to yield to temptation. Hogram appreciated frankness, but he did not appreciate males showing how clever they were at his expense.

"The flood is still new, clanfather," the younger male said carefully, "and is sweeping along the debris that has accumulated in the gorge since last summer. It will grow calmer."

"It had better," Hogram snapped. He turned an eyestalk from the flood to Fralk. "How would that runnerpest in the toy boat you showed me have fared if you dropped half my roof on it, eh? That's what the trash in the water will be doing to the boats trying to go across, isn't it?"

"I suppose there may be a few accidents."

"Accidents?" Hogram echoed. "Is that all you can say? Accidents? Can you be sure any of these *boats*"—the way he stressed the word emphasized that it was foreign—"will get across Ervis Gorge at all? Or will the folk far north of here, picking corpses from the gorge after the flood subsides, be surprised at how many foolish males got themselves killed in the water?"

Anger burst inside Fralk. "Clanfather, are you pulling in your eyestalks? If so, tell me plainly, so I can free the males who are building boats for more productive duty. I also suggest that you release your males from weapons training, if you do not intend to use us as warriors."

After being so blunt, Fralk wondered whether Hogram would turn all eyestalks toward or away from him. How many males, he thought, could claim total rejection by their own domain-master and his Omalo counterpart? It was not a distinction Fralk craved.

But Hogram, with the perspective age brings, was not infuriated by the younger male's presumption. If he was amused, he was too canny to let his eyestalks show it. "We must press on," he said. "Think of the profit wasted if we let that labor go for naught. But I still turn blue whenever I think of trusting myself to one of the contraptions those males are building."

You won't be in one of them, Fralk thought. But that was not something even he dared say aloud. Instead he answered, "Clanfather, we will succeed. The Skarmer will be the only great clan to straddle a floodgorge. One day, our domains will fill the eastern lands."

Hogram's eyestalks quivered now. "May you prove right. That day, however, is not one I will live to see, nor you, either. Worry about planting our first bud, not the ones that may spring from it."

"As you say, clanfather." No denying that Hogram made sense. But Fralk's ambition ran further than he would admit to anyone, especially to the domain-master, whose position only made his already suspicious nature more so. If Fralk established a new domain on the far side of Ervis Gorge, and if his descendants kept pushing back the Omalo and setting up new domains of their own, might they not eventually prefer to style themselves after their first domain-master?

Great clan Fralk. The young male had repeated that to himself often enough, when he was sure no other male could hear. He liked the sound of it.

"Hello, *Athena*. Houston here." Irv Levitt thumbed on the recorder. The mission controller back home would not pause for acknowledgment, not with back-and-forth transmission time near twenty minutes. Irv was about to go on about his business—most of what Houston had to say was Emmett Bragg's problem, not his—when the controller, as if reading his mind, continued. "We have some new instructions for you, Irv." His voice came in scratchy across the millions of miles but was perfectly understandable.

Now that the mission controller—his name was Jesse Dozier—was talking to him, Irv said, "Me? What's up?" just as if the man could hear him. Catching himself, the anthropologist laughed at his own foolishness.

He had only talked over a sentence or so, and that not directly relevant to him, or so he thought. "—continued excellent response to the assistance you folks gave the Soviets, both here and in the States and from around the world," Dozier was saying. "Interest in the Minerva mission hasn't been so high—or so favorable—since just after *Athena* touched down. The polls are running strongly for continued contact and exploration."

Polls . . . Irv felt his mouth twist. He half wished polling had never been invented. These days, no politicians dared moved half an inch past what their polls told them. They followed so closely that most of them had forgotten how to lead.

Again Dozier's words ran parallel to his thoughts. "We're preparing to have the new appropriation submitted while things look so good. And to help nail it down, we'd like to be able to show Congress another major success. That's where you come in, Irv."

Levitt blinked. "Me?"

Dozier, of course, took no notice. Irv shut up and listened. "From the data you folks and *Tsiolkovsky* have sent back, it seems likely that the two groups in whose lands you find yourselves will soon be at war. We want you to arrange a radio hookup with the Soviets, so that the leader on your side of Jötun Canyon can confer with the ruler on the western side. Think what a feather in your caps it will be if you can mediate a dispute between rival factions of an alien species.

"Louise"—the mission controller changed the subject—"we have some new subroutines to speed up your number-crunching. First—"

"Dozier, you are stoned out of your gourd," Irv said. Now he didn't care if he missed some of the feed from Houston. He wished he hadn't heard any of what Dozier had just finished saying. What did they think back home, that Reatur and the domain-master across the canyon were a couple of Third World dictators, to be brought into line by threatening to cut off their weapons shipments?

"Sounds like it," Emmett Bragg said when Irv, throwing his hands in the air for extra emphasis, shouted that question at him.

"But we don't have anything like that kind of leverage on them," Irv said, still loudly. "Tolmasov had it right—they were going to fight whether we were here or not. The other fellows want to cross, Reatur doesn't want to let them. Where's the room for discussion?"

"Good question." Bragg laughed two syllables of a humorless laugh. "Maybe, if we're real lucky, the Russians won't cooperate. That'd get us off the hook."

"Maybe." Irv was as skeptical of that as Emmett sounded. The Russians spent even more time beating their breasts about how peace-loving they were than the United States did. They would have to link—Hogram? Irv wasn't sure he remembered the western chieftain's name—up with Reatur, assuming Reatur was willing to talk. . . . "Do you suppose Houston would let me beg off if I told them the domain-master would feed me to the crows for bringing up the idea at all?"

"You could try, I suppose, but I don't think it'll fly. Trouble is, Houston already knows Reatur's got an open mind, because if he didn't, he'd never have gone along with your wife's trying to save that female. If he's game for that, chances are he'd be willing to talk peace, too.''

"You have this disgusting habit of being right.'' Irv sighed. "Of course, just because he'll talk doesn't mean he'll agree to anything. I wouldn't, in his shoes.''

"Neither would I, not that he wears shoes. And somehow I don't think the art of negotiation's come as far here as it has back home. Which is to say that Reatur's more likely to call the westerner every name in the book than talk turkey with him.'' Bragg grinned crookedly. "Which is what you said a while ago.''

"You know it, I know it, the Russians here know it, I'm sure the Minervans know it, too. What do you think the odds are of convincing Houston?''

"Slim, Irv, slim. After all, they have the experts there. Just ask 'em.''

"Thanks a lot.''

"Valery Aleksandrovich, do you seriously believe Hogram will make peace with the clans east of Jötun Canyon?'' Oleg Lopatin demanded. "He has been preparing for war since we landed, and for some time before that.''

"You are right, Oleg Borisovich,'' Valery Bryusov agreed. The linguist did not like admitting Lopatin was right about anything. He consoled himself by mentally sneering at the way the KGB man pronounced Hogram's name: he said it as if it started with a *G*, as most Russians did with foreign words that began with the sound of rough breathing. "Still,'' Bryusov went on, "we must make the effort. Moscow would not be pleased if we let the Americans brand us as warmongers.''

"No,'' Lopatin growled, dragging out the word as if it pained him. "But Moscow will not be pleased if we forfeit the position of trust we have earned here, either. And asking Hogram to do something he manifestly does not wish to do may well bring that fate down on our heads.''

"You are right,'' Bryusov said again. This second admission hurt twice as much as the first one had. Bryusov scratched at his arm. His fingers clicked on the plaster of his cast. He knew it was there, but reflex made him scratch every so often anyhow. Both long-unwashed skin and healing bone itched ferociously.

"Now I wish I were up at the tent by Hogram's town instead of here on *Tsiolkovsky*,'' Lopatin grumbled. "We must tread carefully, subtly.''

"Colonel Tolmasov will do well.'' Bryusov slightly stressed

the pilot's rank to remind the *chekist* who was in charge. All Lopatin knew of subtlety, the linguist thought, was how to knock on a door at midnight. "Sergei will make Hogram understand that the request to confer with the eastern chieftain comes from our own domain-masters," he continued, "and as dutiful males we have no choice but to convey it to him."

"I suppose so," Lopatin said in a tone that supposed anything but. "Negotiations have their uses, like any other tool. But once these fail—and fail they will, quite without help from us—we must be prepared to extend our full support to Hogram and his males."

Bryusov frowned, wondering if he had heard the KGB man correctly. He saw he had. Coughing, he reminded Lopatin, "Oleg Borisovich, these are capitalists about whom you speak in such glowing terms. Alien capitalists, *da*, but capitalists even so." Had it been the end of the sixteenth century rather than the end of the twentieth, he would have been accusing Lopatin of devil-worship.

But the *chekist* was no mean Marxist-Leninist theologian himself. "There is nothing wrong with capitalism as it emerges, Valery Aleksandrovich, only when in its decadence it stands in the way of the arrival of true socialism, as it does on Earth. Here on Minerva, capitalism is the progressive ideology and economic structure. To the east of the canyon, the domains are feudal in organization, is it not so?"

"Bozhemoi." Bryusov was not used to eyeing the KGB man with respect; carefully veiled contempt was what he usually felt for him. But he had to confess, "That is a very pretty argument, Oleg Borisovich."

"Yes, I know," Lopatin said complacently.

A clever *chekist* is still a *chekist*, Bryusov reminded himself.

"Interesting also, I think," Lopatin went on, "how here as well as on Earth the Americans find themselves aligned with the forces of reaction while we stand with those of progress."

"Most interesting," the linguist agreed. The more he thought through the implications of what Lopatin had said, the less he liked them. He held up his healing arm. "Don't forget how the Americans helped us—helped *me*—at great risk to themselves. Here on Minerva, if nowhere else, we truly have a classless society of humans."

"Of humans, perhaps," Lopatin said, as if making a great concession, "but not of intelligent beings. And what we do here

will also be closely observed by people's movements all over
the world back home.''

"And by the Americans and their friends." Now Bryusov
was genuinely alarmed. Bringing quarrels from Earth to Minerva was bad enough, but letting a Minervan quarrel create
trouble on Earth struck him as worse.

"Moscow will instruct us as to our proper course," Lopatin
said.

He sounded as if he were trying to reassure the linguist, but
Bryusov remained unassured. The *apparatchiks* back home were
as rigid as Lopatin. "I would sooner let us make our decisions
on the spot," Bryusov said. "Surely we have a better feel for
the Minervans than do men who have never seen one."

"Even the Americans, with their prattling of liberty, are not
so foolish as that," Lopatin said. "When Houston gives an order—as it did about these talks—the crew of *Athena* simply
obeys."

"Oleg Borisovich, this is the first time I have ever heard you
argue that we can do no better than imitating the Americans,"
Bryusov answered mildly. He cherished the glower the *chekist*
gave him.

Reatur glowered at the box Irv held in one of his large, strange
hands. The domain-master had come to accept and eventually
to ignore such boxes in humans' hands, even when the voices
of other humans came out of them. He had never imagined a
person's voice might also travel in such fashion—especially not
if the person was a Skarmer. "He won't be able to see as well
as hear, will he?" Reatur asked for the third time.

"No," Irv answered. "*You* see into Skarmer lands?"

"No," Reatur admitted unhappily. "Let me listen to his lies,
then, and have done, so I can go on working to keep my domain
safe from his greed."

When humans sighed, the domain-master thought, they
sounded eerily like people. Irv pressed the box here and there
and then spoke into it. A rumbling voice—a human male's
voice—replied at once. It belonged to neither Emmett nor Frank;
Reatur recognized the way they sounded. So there truly were
more humans than he had seen. . . . Despite everything the
weird creatures had said, he had wondered.

Irv brought him out of his eyestalk-twiddling by handing him
the box. "Talk into it," the human said. "Hogram hears you."

"So, Skarmer, what have we to say to each other?" Reatur demanded in trade talk.

"How should I know?" Hogram used the same clipped, simplified speech. He sounded old, Reatur thought. The Omalo domain-master had known that; it had to be so, if Hogram's eldest of eldest was a male who could be entrusted with responsibility. But hearing Hogram's voice made the knowledge real in a way it had not been before.

"Why are you talking to me, then?" Reatur said.

"Because the"—Hogram used a word Reatur did not know—"asked me to."

"The who?"

"The two-legged, two-armed creatures who make strange things like the box we are using to talk now. That's what they call themselves in their own language."

"Oh. The ones here call themselves 'humans,' and so we use that name for them, too."

"Call them whatever you like. They are strange enough and strong enough that I do not care to tell them no without some truly pressing reason—nor do you, I notice."

"Never mind what I do," Reatur snapped. "The humans here say that if we talk, perhaps we can find a way not to fight. Stay on your side of Ervis Gorge and you will prove them right."

"If I could, I would. But we have too many males, too many mates for our land to feed. If you peaceably yield your domain, perhaps we can work out a fate for your males less drastic than the one Fralk first proposed to you. Some of your budlings might be allowed to live on, to plant buds themselves and to work with us toward building a new land."

"What do you mean, work with you?" Reatur did not trust the sound of that smooth-sounding phrase. "As what?"

"You know that many of us are traders rather than farmers or herders," Hogram said. "We could, I suppose, use some males whose talents lie in those directions."

Rage ripped through Reatur. "Use them as slaves, you mean, without even right of appeal to clanfather. For they'd not be of the same clan as your precious young Fralk, now, would they? You Skarmer aren't traders, Hogram, you're cheats and thieves."

He was deliberately insulting, trying to infuriate Hogram as he had been infuriated. The Skarmer domain-master, though, seemed armored against insult. "In your obstinacy, Omalo, you have made me become more generous. Cherish that; not many may boast of it."

"Imagine my delight." Reatur made his voice as hot with scorn as the melt-water that brawled through Ervis Gorge. "Save such praise for dealings with your fellow Skarmer, who can properly appreciate it." He shortened his eyestalks in surprise as he thought of something new. "Why even think of crossing the gorge, Hogram? Why not seize the domains of your neighbors, if you need land so badly? Surely that would be simpler for you."

"I wish you had been budded a fool; my life would be easier." This time Hogram sounded as though he really was giving a compliment, not sardonic as he had been before. "In truth, though, all the Skarmer domains hereabouts find themselves in the same straits as do I: too many folk, not enough food. My domain might be bigger were I to conquer them, but no better off."

That made sense to Reatur. He almost wished it had not; he had not expected to be able to see out of Hogram's eyestalks. Thinking of the Skarmer domain-master as a male with problems of his own was less comfortable than simply thinking of him as the enemy. It could be useful, though, if it gave him clues about how Hogram would plot.

As if changing the subject, Reatur asked, "Do your humans come in two kinds, one with a deep rumbling voice and the other that sounds like a person?"

Hogram, Reatur thought, was sharp or at least suspicious. The Skarmer domain-master's voice turned cautious at once as he answered, "Yes, they do. What of it?"

The reply was innocuous enough, but Reatur felt like hooting with glee. Instead, as casually as before, he asked, "Have they told you that the ones who sound like people are mates, and the others males?"

By Hogram's response, he already knew that the humans on the Skarmer side of the gorge had not. And if Hogram suddenly learned something as unsettling as that, it might help drive him apart from his humans. Reatur was convinced that such a rift would prove useful; he still wasn't sure what powers humans had, but keeping those powers estranged from the Skarmer had to be a good idea.

"I know what you are thinking: you want to make me fear the—" Hogram used his own word for humans. Yes, he was sharp. "But who ever heard of an old mate?" So the Skarmer had that cliche, too, did they? "I waggle my eyestalks at you and your deception both," Hogram finished.

Reatur would have thought it funny, too, had he not known the truth. He thought of Lamra for a moment, but made himself dismiss her from his mind; Hogram demanded all his attention. "If you think I am lying, ask your humans for yourself."

"Bluff all you like, Reatur. I will ask them, and afterward know you for the liar you are. That will be remembered, when we cross to the east side of the gorge."

"Do you think your boasts make me blue with fright? If you are foolish enough to come, we will be ready for you. But"— Reatur remembered—"the humans asked us to talk so we would not fight, not so we would quarrel more with words. Can we find a way to keep you on your side of the gorge where you belong, and to keep our domains at peace?"

"There is no way to keep us on this side of the gorge alone," Hogram declared. "As for peace, I have offered to let males of yours survive. If you do not resist us, obviously, more will live. We would not be deliberately harsh."

"You offer less than I and mine have already. You know I will not accept." As he sparred, Reatur had been thinking of what he could propose to Hogram. Now he set it forth. "If we knew you were not planning to invade, we might rebuild the bridge across the gorge. Then, in years when we had good crops, we could trade our surplus to you rather than to one of our Omalo neighbors who was less lucky. That would let you support more people on your domain."

"How many more? How often do you have that kind of good year? If it were more than one year in three, I would be surprised—and try to buy your secret from you. Is it?"

"No," Reatur said after thinking over and rejecting a lie. Melting the truth a little might save him trouble now but would earn more later.

"You bargain strangely, Omalo, but I accept your word. Well, then: if in one of those rare good years you do sell us food, how much do you suppose we could haul over the bridge? Enough for a few eighteens of males, perhaps, but not much more. That does not suffice."

Reatur let the air hiss out through his breathing-pores. "Which leaves us where we began."

"So it does." Hogram also sighed. "For a moment there I had hope, but you are right. I could wish you sprang from a Skarmer bud, Reatur, but that is not so. As is, since you will not give us what we need, we shall take it from you."

"You may try, Hogram, but you will fail."

"If a Skarmer wants a thing, Omalo, be assured he will have it, and pay less than the former owner would like. Reatur, I want your domain, and I tell you you will not keep it. The day your eyestalks turn away from our direction, we will come."

"You lie. Past that, I have nothing more to say to you."

"Nor I to you," Hogram said. "Our actions will speak."

Reatur sighed again. For the first time since he and Hogram had confronted each other with their voices, he paid attention to the human who had made the confrontation possible. "Take your box away, Irv," he said, suddenly so weary his arms and eyestalks felt like drooping. "We are finished."

The human touched a button; the box, which had been letting out a quiet hiss, became completely silent. "You, Hogram make peace?" Irv asked. "Not follow all words—you, Hogram not use same words you, me use."

"Trade talk has Omalo words, Skarmer words, and words from other great clans all mixed together; males from different great clans use it when neither speaks the other's language," Reatur explained. He was glad to blather on about trade talk. While he was doing that, he would not have to think about everything Hogram had said.

"Lingua franca," Irv muttered. Then, as if noticing that meant nothing to Reatur, he did some explaining himself. "Humans with words not same do same thing sometimes."

"Ah," Reatur said politely. Interesting how, every once in a while, humans acted very much like people.

But no male of his domain would have been so rude as to ask again, as Irv did, "You, Hogram make peace?"

"No," Reatur said. "I didn't think we would, I told you we wouldn't, and yet, curse it, you kept at me, making me waste time I could have spent helping my domain get ready for whatever the miserable Skarmer have in their sneaking minds."

Irv spread his hands in the human gesture that meant it wasn't his fault. "My domain-masters tell me what to do. I must go in direction they point. Your males do that for you." Then Irv bent at the middle and stayed bent. Had he been a person, Reatur realized, he would have been widening himself in apology.

The domain-master gestured for him to resume his usual height. Irv did—yes, apology was what he had meant. "You are right—you should obey your domain-masters," Reatur conceded, although the plural puzzled him. "This time, though, they were wrong. Hogram and I had nothing to say to each other, not about peace."

Irv spread his hands once more. Reatur hardly noticed. He was thinking about Hogram now, like it or not, and about how confident the Skarmer had sounded. If Hogram's males could not cross Ervis Gorge, he had no business sounding like that. But how could they, with the yearly flood rising day by day? Reatur could hear the waters booming and could feel their pounding through his feet. He turned his mental eyestalks in all directions but could not see how the Skarmer might best the flood.

But Hogram could. Reatur was sure of that. It frightened him.

8

The female eloc saw Sarah coming. Of course it did, she thought in some annoyance—with eyes that looked every which way at once, Minervan creatures were next to impossible to sneak up on. The eloc had seen Sarah before. It did its best to run away.

Its best was not good enough. It was so very gravid that it could scarcely waddle to the far end of its little pen. She hurried after it. It was right on the point of dropping its buds, and she wanted to see what she could do to keep it from bleeding to death immediately afterward.

The female eloc, unfortunately, knew nothing about that. As far as it was concerned, Sarah was weird, probably a predator, and certainly dangerous. It made a brief rush at her, trying to stick her with one of the horns that projected out from its body below each arm.

She skipped backward faster than the eloc could come after her. The horns were not very long, anyhow; the Minervans, who had to herd eloca, had sensibly bred them so they were less formidably equipped than their wild relatives.

"It's all right," Sarah crooned, as if to a spooked horse back on Earth. Maybe that had some effect; maybe the eloc decided that making the little charge satisfied its honor. At any rate, it stood quiet and let her come up to it, though the four eyes it kept turned her way showed that it still did not trust her.

She crooned some more. She needed the beast relaxed; it was not much shorter than she and a lot thicker. And this was a female, an animal sure to die young. Male eloca were the size of a cow, even if they looked more like what would happen if a squid seduced the Jolly Green Giant's hockey puck.

The female flinched from Sarah's hand. Although she wore gloves, her flesh was warm enough to disturb the Minervan animal. She moved slowly and carefully. At last the eloc let her stroke and prod the tight-stretched skin over one of its buds.

Was that the beginning of a split, or was she only feeling what she wished she would? She stooped to take a good look. Sure enough, the female's skin had begun to crack.

"All right," Sarah breathed. She had been irrationally certain that the eloc would drop its budlings when she was sound asleep or, worse, when she was just on her way back from *Athena* for another peek at it. Maybe luck was with her after all.

As poor Biyal had, the female eloc grew calm as the budding process advanced—almost, Sarah thought, as if it knew it would soon have nothing more to worry about. She hoped to change that.

All the same, she doubted she would succeed, not with this first try. Surely some Minervan somewhere would have thought of—would have tried—packing the cavities from which the budlings dropped to keep the inevitable flood of blood from following. But if so, Reatur was ignorant of it. Did that mean the effort had earlier been discarded as useless, or that Minervans could not see what seemed obvious to her? Before long, she would find out.

The budding proceeded much as Biyal's had. It seemed uneventful; all that happened was that the split over each bud steadily grew wider and longer. Knowing how it would end, Sarah was not lulled as she had been before. She used the time she had before the crisis to prepare for it.

From her backpack she drew out six gauze pads, each stuffed into one of her socks. Her last couple of pairs would just have to do till she got home. She slapped a strip of duct tape onto each sock, to hold it in place on the eloc's hide. As she set each makeshift bandage on the ground, she shook her head in wry amusement. These were not the instruments she was used to working with.

"I never thought I'd be a vet, either," she said out loud. The eloc steadied at the sound of her voice. She suddenly realized that sounding like a male Minervan had its advantages: the eloc had the habit of obeying voices much like hers. She laughed at herself. She also was not used to feeling macho.

She could see the budlings' feet now. They wiggled and

thrashed, though the baby eloca were still attached to the female. The budlings were the size of terriers. Sarah hoped they would not get in her way when she tried to work on the female. Why, she wondered, did she think of these things too late to do anything about them?

Then such bits of irrelevance vanished from her mind. The budlings grew to be entirely visible; she could see how they were joined to the female's circulatory system by their mouths.

They dropped off, all of them at once.

Sarah never noticed whether they got in her way or not; she was too busy with the female. As Biyal had, it simply stood, bleeding its life away. It did not try to gore her or strike at her when she began slapping her bandage packs over its spurting wounds.

Streams of its cold blood drenched her parka and trousers. She ignored that, too. Two bandages were in place now, the hemorrhaging from those orifices reduced to a trickle. She shoved a third plug into place, pressing hard on the duct tape so that it would cling to the eloc's skin. She grabbed for the fourth bandage.

About then she noticed how limp the eloc's arms and eyestalks had gone. She also noticed that the stream of blood from the fourth orifice was less than it had been from the first three. Even as she watched, the flow grew slower still and then stopped. The female eloc was dead.

"Oh, hell," Sarah said, surprised at how disappointed she was. She had not expected to succeed with this first try, but her hopes had risen when she saw that her bandages seemed to do some good. The eloc, though, lost enough blood through the orifices she had not plugged to kill it before she could get to them.

Two things occurred to her. One was the most ancient medical joke around: The operation was a success but the patient died. The joke was old, of course, exactly because it was rooted in human fallibility. Ever since the first medicine man, every doctor in the world had seen his best fall short of being good enough.

Her second thought sounded frivolous but wasn't: What would the little Dutch boy have done if he had had to stick his finger into six holes in the dike at once? "He'd've got help or drowned," she answered herself out loud.

Only then did she realize what a mess she was. She might have been working in an alien abattoir, for the eloc's blood dripped from her hands and arms and was splashed over the rest of her clothes. The fabrics were all supposed to repel moisture, but they hadn't been designed for a workout like this. Neither had *Athena*'s laundry facilities.

She picked up the socks and gauze packs that were still clean. After taking a step away from the female eloc, she went back to salvage the three she had used. The gauze would never be the same, but her gore-soaked socks might come clean. And even if they didn't, she could use them again the next time she tried to save an animal. Nothing from Earth was automatically disposable on Minerva.

The eloca budlings scattered as Sarah walked toward the gate of the pen. She did not look like any Minervan creature that ate eloca, but she was bigger than they were, and that was plenty to set off the alarms evolution had built into them.

A couple of budlings got out before she could slam the gate shut. A Minervan caught one of them after a brief chase and shouted for other males farther away to run down the other. While they were pursuing it, the first Minervan, still holding the squawking eloc budling, said to Sarah, "You shouldn't have let them get loose like that. They might have been lost for good."

"Sorry." She studied the local. One reason she found Minervans harder to tell apart than humans was that they did not always keep the same side of their bodies to her. Still, this one both looked and sounded familiar. "Sorry, Ternat."

"Never mind now; just remember for next time." Reatur's eldest, Sarah thought, seemed a good deal like the domain-master. He turned a couple of eyestalks toward the dead female eloc. "You didn't have much luck there."

"No, not much," she admitted.

"Reatur wants you to succeed." That sounded like an accusation, but was Ternat condemning her for failure or Reatur for hoping for something else?

She answered carefully. "This first try. Here learn some, try again. Maybe learn enough so Lamra lives. Try."

"What if you cannot learn enough before Lamra's budlings drop?"

"Then I fail. Not say to Reatur I do, only I try." Make something of it if you're going to, she added, but only to herself.

But Ternat's reply was mild. "That makes me think you are honest. People who give wild promises generally cannot live up to them. I suppose it must be the same with you humans." He turned an eyestalk toward the newly budded eloc he was holding. "I will take this one to the herd, so it can get used to being among its own kind. If I delay too long, the foolish thing will grow up thinking it is a person, and fall easy prey to wild animals because it will stray too far from the big males who could protect it."

Sarah's gloves left unpleasant smears on the notebook she pulled from a pocket. Ignoring them, she scrawled, "Imprinting—tell Pat" on the first blank page she found. Humans knew so little about Minerva that even casual conversation like this gave important new data.

Ternat was already moving away. "What you do with dead eloc mate?" she called after him.

"Thank you for reminding me," he said without stopping. "I'll make sure someone sees to the butchering."

It was, she reminded herself, only a domestic animal. She knew the Minervans did not treat their own mates so. All the same, she had a vision of bright, funny little Lamra hacked apart by stone knives and served up with the local equivalent of Brussels sprouts. It made her more determined than ever to save the mate.

Sighing, she walked back toward *Athena*. She wished for a shower even more than she did after a turn in *Damselfly*. Wishing, however, kept failing to equip the spacecraft with the requisite plumbing.

She stripped off her outer clothing just inside the air lock and walked down the hall to the lavatory and mini washer-dryer in her long johns. Minervan body fluids smelled stronger and nastier in *Athena*'s heated air than they had outside, where the mercury reached an all-time—since the landing, anyway—high of 46°.

Emmett Bragg stuck his head out of his cubicle to see who was going by. His eyes flicked to the parka and pants slung on Sarah's arm. "No luck, eh?" he asked, adding, "You're dripping on the floor."

"I know, and on my sleeve, too. One more thing to wash. No, no luck, Emmett. The damned female bled right on out on me. I might as well not have been there. How do you plug six holes at once with just two hands?"

"Three times two is—" He let the words hang in the air.

"—too much manpower to commit," she finished for him. Then she stopped. Emmett did not say things by accident. "Or is it? Would you let me train a couple of people—Irv and Pat, I guess, because they know most about the Minervans—to be ready to try to save Lamra, all at once? It'd take a lot of time, to practice with me on animals, time they may not have because they'll be busy with other things.''

"Have 'em make the time. Can you think of anything more important we're doing here, for us or the Minervans?''

"No, but I know I'm not objective about it. Thanks for seeing things the same way.'' She leaned forward and kissed him on the cheek.

For a moment, the look he gave her made her feel more naked under her long johns than she had during any of the who-knew-how-many times before when he'd happened to see her wearing a lot less. She also realized she didn't dislike the feeling. She rather wished Irv looked at her that way more often.

Telling herself it would be purely in the nature of an experiment, she thought about kissing Emmett again and making a proper job of it this time. Just then, though, from behind the privacy curtain Louise called, "Come on, Emmett, get back here and help me make sense of this latest weirdness from Houston.''

"Be right with you—have to make sure the decks get swabbed, though,'' he said.

Sarah snapped off a parody of a salute and made a face at him as he disappeared. "Aye, aye, Captain Bligh.'' Saved by the bell, she thought as he went back to the rear of *Athena*.

She sternly told herself not to wonder whether she had been saved or thwarted.

As if to put that question to rest, she waylaid Irv when he got back to the ship, all but dragging him to their cubicle. She had no complaints once they were there; even if Irv took her for granted out of bed, she liked what he did in it. Finding that that was still so relieved her more than a little.

"Well,'' he said as she slid off him, "what brought that on?''

"What do you mean?'' she asked, hoping her guilty start did not show.

Evidently it didn't. "You've been too busy to be interested almost since we landed,'' Irv said, "and now you go and rape me. Don't get me wrong—I kind of like it. I've missed you, if you know what I mean.''

"Mm-hmm,'' she said, wondering who had been taking whom for granted. "I do know. I'm sorry. It's just that—''

"—we're busy all the damned time. Yeah. I know.'' He poked her in the ribs.

She yelped. "What was that for?''

"For not answering my question.''

"Oh." She tried to keep things light. "Does it really matter where you get your appetite, so long as you eat at home?"

When Irv didn't answer right away, she was afraid she had made things worse instead of better. She could not tell what was going on behind his eyes. That worried her, too; back on Earth she'd never had trouble reading him. When had she stopped being able to, and why hadn't she noticed?

Then his face took on an expression she recognized: mischief. He rearranged her on the mattress pad. "Best idea you've had in a while," he said. Of themselves, her fingers tightened on the back of his head.

Tolmasov took a skipping half step to stay up with Fralk. Comfortable Minervan walking pace was a little faster than what was comfortable for him. "You building all boats you need?" he asked.

"*Da*, Sergei Konstantinovich, we will have enough," Fralk answered.

His Russian was better than Tolmasov's command of the local language. Knowing he needed the practice, the pilot tried to get his thoughts across in the Skarmer tongue anyway. "You having all males you need to go in boats?"

"*Da*," Fralk said again. His three-armed wave encompassed the camp growing outside Hogram's town. He and the human were a couple of kilometers away, walking and talking as Tolmasov might have with a friend back on Earth.

Something made a noise in the bushes off to one side of the path. Things had been making noises in the bushes all along; by now the Russian paid no attention to them. Fralk also had ignored them—till now. Now he turned blue and started moving away from the bushes that hid whatever was making the noise.

Tolmasov backed off, too. "What is that?" he asked, pointing to the animal he faintly glimpsed through foliage.

"A krong," Fralk said; it was not a word Tolmasov had heard before. "I did not know they came so close to the town anymore," the Minervan went on. "With luck, it will have just fed and not be interested in eating anything else."

When the pilot heard that, he unslung his Kalashnikov and clicked the change lever down from safe to full automatic. Whatever a krong was, it didn't sound like a household pet.

The beast emerged from the undergrowth. Tolmasov was surprised to discover that he recognized it. He doubted there could be many kinds of brown and white, long-legged, big-clawed large predators in the Minervan ecology. This had to be the same sort of animal as the one that had attacked Valery and Shota in the rover.

Fralk was getting bluer and bluer. Tolmasov did not blame him. Had he been facing this monster unarmed, he would have been frightened, too. Even with a rifle in his hands, he wished for zoo bars between the krong and him.

The animal let out a low, growling squall, almost what the pilot would have expected from an angry leopard. The krong did not charge at once, though. It slowly sidled forward. It kept more eyestalks on Tolmasov than on Fralk. Minervans it knew; he was an unknown quantity.

Its cry rose to a shriek. Even if Tolmasov did not, Fralk knew what that meant. "Run!" he shouted. "Here it comes!"

The krong's first bound showed it was faster than a Minervan. It went straight after Fralk. Either it had decided Tolmasov was not dangerous or it hoped to deal with him after it had slain the more familiar prey.

The bark of the AK-74 rose above the krong's screams. As the first bullets slammed into it, the animal changed direction with the agility of most Minervan beasts. It rushed at its new tormentor. Tolmasov fired in short bursts, watched blood and tissue spray from the wounds he made. He was wishing for something heavier than a Kalashnikov—say, an anti-tank missile—when, less than five meters from him, the krong went down at last.

Fralk had stopped fleeing as soon as he saw the krong was no longer after him. Now he slowly came back toward Tolmasov and the dead beast. His eyestalks kept shifting from it to the Russian and back again, as if he could not choose which was more important to look at. He was still bright blue.

"More krongii around?" Tolmasov demanded. He was trying to figure out how many rounds were left in his magazine and swearing at himself for not carrying a spare.

But Fralk answered, "No. They hunt alone." He spoke his own language; he was still too rattled to use Russian. Several of his eyes went toward the krong again. "You killed it." Green began to take the place of blue on his skin.

"Da," Tolmasov said shakily. He was doing his best not to think about how close the krong had come to making it mutual. Big game hunting, which he had always slighted, suddenly looked a lot more like work.

"You killed it," Fralk repeated. Now his eyestalks turned

toward the pilot—or rather, Tolmasov saw in a moment, toward his Kalashnikov. The Minervan said, still in his own speech, "You spoke of this weapon before. I am sorry, but I have forgotten its name."

"Firearm," Tolmasov supplied automatically. "Rifle, to be exact."

"Rifle. Spasebo." Fralk was pretty much himself again, if he could remember to say thank you in Russian. He went on in that language. "What we have to give you so you give us rifle? You say once firearms more strong than ax, hammer. Now see much more strong. What we give, to get rifle?"

Damnation, Tolmasov thought. So far as he knew, none of the Russians had ever fired a shot where the locals could hear it—Shota and Valery met their krong away from what passed for civilization here. But now Fralk knew what bullets could do. . . . Sure enough, he was staring with four eyes at the chewed-up carcass by his feet. "What we give, to get rifle?" he said again.

"Fralk, I am sorry, but I do not think we can sell you a rifle," Tolmasov said.

"Why? Only want to use rifle on Omalo. Fill Omalo full of holes, like krong here full of holes."

Tolmasov sighed. "Fralk, I told you before that there are other humans on the Omalo side of the canyon. If you used a rifle to fight the Omalo, you might also hurt or kill one of these other humans. That could bring their domain and ours to war, and in our homelands we have weapons much, much worse than rifles." We've used some of them on each other, too, he thought, and as much by luck as anything else, not the worst ones.

"What if other humans give Omalo rifles, fill us full of holes?" the Minervan asked. "You leave us so we not fight back?"

The pilot frowned. "I will find out," he promised. Fralk had asked before whether the Americans would give firearms to the Minervans east of Jötun Canyon. That had been before he knew what bullets could do, though. Now he was really worried. Tolmasov still could not imagine Emmett Bragg being so stupid as to arm the natives with weapons dangerous to humans, but he could not overlook the possibility, either. Helping the Skarmer would not look good back on Earth, but neither would standing idly by while they got slaughtered.

Tolmasov felt the wish that came over every commander now and then, the wish to be safely back in the ranks again, with nothing to worry about and nothing to do but what somebody else told him to do. As every commander must, he strangled that wish in its cradle.

He would have had scant time to indulge it in any case, for Fralk was going on in a mixture of Russian and the Skarmer tongue. "We will give you whatever you want if you give us one of these rifles to take across the gorge and use against the Omalo. Anything! No price could be too great!" The Minervan abruptly stopped, realizing no sensible merchant said things like that.

"Fralk, if I gave a rifle to your people, I would not only have to worry about your hurting the humans east of the canyon; I would also fear for the safety of my own crew here." Tolmasov spoke first in Russian, then as best he could in Fralk's language—he needed the Minervan to understand.

"*Nyet*, Sergei Konstantinovich, *nyet*," Fralk said urgently. "Never hurt you—you our friends. Give you—" He used a Skarmer word the pilot could not follow; Tolmasov raised a hand to show that. "Males you keep so you hurt them if we do any bad thing to you," Fralk explained.

"Ah. Hostages." Tolmasov gave him the Russian word.

"Hostages," Fralk repeated. "Thank you. Yes, I am sure Hogram would agree to give you *hostages*"—he politely dropped the human term into a sentence in his own tongue—"so you could trust us with one of your rifles."

Tolmasov knew he ought to say no and walk away. What the Minervans did to each other was their business. If humans meddled in it, only trouble would result. But he didn't know what the Americans had done on their side of Jötun Canyon, and Fralk was so eager. He would have been, too, in the Minervan's place.

The pilot decided to temporize. "I talk with my domain-masters," he said. "If they say yes, then we trade rifle. If no, we cannot." He was confident even the blockheads back in Moscow had better sense than to authorize letting the natives get their three-fingered hands on an AK-74.

From the way Fralk's appendages were quivering, he was confident Tolmasov had in effect just said yes. "Thank you, Sergei Konstantinovich! We would have beaten the Omalo anyhow. Now we will surely smash them—they will widen themselves before us forevermore."

"Hmm," was all Tolmasov said. Fralk made a more enthusiastic would-be conqueror than he quite liked. Maybe changing the subject would calm the Minervan down. Tolmasov pointed at the krong's carcass. "We leave this here?"

"Yes, I suppose so—the meat is vile," Fralk answered. "Long

ago there was a bounty on their claws, but since none has been seen this near town in a good many years, I suppose that offer has melted." He did not want to talk about the krong. He wanted to talk about Tolmasov's rifle. "From how far away can it kill?"

"Farther than you can throw a stone," the pilot answered. He did not want to tell Fralk the Kalashnikov was accurate out to three or four hundred meters and could kill from a kilometer away if a round happened to hit.

What he did say was plenty. "Wonderful!" Fralk exclaimed. "Wonderful!" Tolmasov had never heard a Minervan burbling before. "Hogram will be as excited as I am at the prospect of doing away with the wretched Omalo while at the same time keeping our males safe."

"Remember what I say," Tolmasov warned him. "My domain-masters may not let us sell you rifle. They say no, we not sell." He started walking away from the dead krong, back toward Hogram's town. Maybe if Fralk could not see the beast anymore, he would stop being so heated—not really the right word to apply to a Minervan, the pilot thought—about what the Kalashnikov could do.

No such luck. The Minervan went right on babbling until Tolmasov rudely left him outside the humans' tent and went in alone. Oleg Lopatin looked up from the radio handset he was checking. "I've seen you looking happier, Sergei Konstantinovich," he said.

Tolmasov was so frazzled, he did not even mind unburdening himself to the KGB man. "I almost wish I'd let the miserable creature eat us," he finished. "That might have ended up doing the mission less harm than letting the locals find out about firearms."

"Possibly not, Comrade Colonel," Lopatin said. Tolmasov grew alert; Lopatin only used formal address when he had something on his mind. "Would it not accord well with Marxist-Leninist principles to render fraternal assistance to this advanced society in its struggle against the oppressive feudal aristocrats on the eastern side of Jötun Canyon? The dialectic of history supports the Skarmer; how can we not do the same?"

"Two good reasons: This is Minerva, not Earth; and there are people on the other side of the canyon. I have more loyalty to my own kind than I do to dialectical materialism." The moment the words were out of his mouth, Tolmasov knew he had said too much. And words were never unsayable, not to a *chekist*.

But Lopatin's response was mild. "Marxist-Leninist princi-

ples hold universally, Sergei Konstantinovich. You know that as
well as I. Tell me, what had you planned to do about Fralk's
request?"

"Nothing," Tolmasov answered honestly. "Or rather, say I
had consulted with Moscow and they told me he could not have
his rifle. A little discreet checking with Bragg will let me make
sure he isn't giving the Omalo firearms."

"Yes, by all means check with Bragg," Lopatin said. "But
perhaps you also really should ask Moscow about this question.
Then there can be no room for misunderstanding. This is only
a suggestion, of course."

But it wasn't only a suggestion, as Tolmasov knew. That was
what he got for leaving himself open to the KGB man. "Let me
talk with Bragg first," the pilot said, dickering now. "If I have
his clear assurance that he is not giving guns to the locals, a
decision from Moscow is unnecessary. Otherwise—"

"Good enough," Lopatin said, to Tolmasov's surprise and
relief. "Call now, why don't you? Even I will admit, Sergei
Konstantinovich, that our colleagues back on Earth are not always as timely as they might be. The longer the opportunity we
give them, the better."

He said that with the air of a man making a great concession,
perhaps so he could act as if he were repaying Tolmasov for his
slip of a few minutes before. But the pilot, like most men on the
frontier, already had a low opinion of the alleged experts back
home. Not only were they slow in making up their minds, they
were sadly disconnected from the reality he was living. That
scheme for peace talks between Hogram and the eastern chieftain, for instance . . . Tolmasov could have told them—did tell
them—it was a waste of time. They had forced him to go ahead
with it anyway and proven him right.

So who knew what Moscow would instruct now? They might
well order him to let the Minervans have an AK-74. That would
leave the whole expedition vulnerable in a way it had not been
before. As a soldier, he hated the idea of making himself more
vulnerable.

Well, odds were Bragg would bail him out, he thought as he
went over to the radio. The American mission commander was
an enemy, but never a stupid one. He had to have better sense
than to go arming the natives. Tolmasov turned a dial to get the
frequency he needed. "Soviet Minerva base calling *Athena*,"
he said in English.

The answer came promptly enough, in Russian. "*Athena* here,

Sergei Konstantinovich." A woman's voice, more heavily accented than his when speaking her language. "Pat Marquard here."

"Hello, Patricia Grigorovna. I need to ask a question of Brigadier Bragg, if I may."

"Wait, please," she said. He did, but not long. Bragg came on the other end of the hookup.

"Hello, Sergei Konstantinovich. Not your usual time for a call. What's up?"

The shrill American flavor he gave his words and the lazy way he drawled them out should have made him sound like a fool when he spoke Russian. Tolmasov wished they did. Unfortunately, he could not imagine Bragg sounding like a fool no matter what language he used.

Swallowing a sigh, the colonel got on with it. "I was, ah, wondering, Brigadier, whether you've traded any firearms to the Minervans on your side of Jötun Canyon." Only the faint pop of static came from the circuit. "Brigadier Bragg?" Tolmasov said at last.

"I'm here," Bragg answered at once. "Why do you want to know?" Hard suspicion filled his voice.

Because if you haven't gone and done something idiotic, then there's no chance I'll have to, either, Tolmasov wanted to say. He could not, not with a Soviet tape recorder and an American one preserving his every word. "I was curious about how they've adapted to them," he replied instead. "Not what the natives are used to at all, don't you know?"

"No, I don't," Bragg said flatly. "I don't believe you, either, Sergei Konstantinovich. You sound more like someone sniffing around to find out what his little friends will be up against if they manage to get across the canyon. And that, Comrade Colonel"—the contempt with which he loaded Tolmasov's rank was stinging—"is exactly none of your damned business. *Athena* out."

Tolmasov found himself staring in numb dismay at a silent microphone. He made himself look up from it and saw Oleg Lopatin aiming his best I-told-you-so smirk at him. "Moscow," the KGB man said.

"Moscow," Tolmasov echoed dully.

"You should have seen it, clanfather!" Fralk exulted. "The krong was nearly on me, but then the *rifle*"—he pronounced the human word with care—"roared louder than half an eighteen of krongii and put holes in it. It turned on Sergei, but he made the rifle roar again and again, till the krong fell over, dead.''

"A krong, so close to town?" Hogram's fingers opened and closed in distress. "I'll send out some males, to make sure none of its mates can drop her buds anywhere near here. I thought we'd hunted them out long ago. I'm glad you weren't hurt, eldest of eldest.''

Not an eighteenth so glad as I am, Fralk thought. But it was not like Hogram to miss the main point so completely. "Aye, send out the hunters, clanfather," Fralk said, "but get one of those rifles for us, no matter what it costs. If it fills a krong full of holes, think what it would do to the Omalo.''

"Hmm. I suppose so, yes. The humans *are* careful with them, aren't they? They never left one lying around so we could, ah, borrow it to see how it works. That always made me think the things were valuable.''

"Valuable?" The younger male was still so excited, he could hardly contain himself. "Clanfather, listen to me: Sergei said that if his own domain-masters refused his permission, he could not yield one to us no matter what we paid for it.''

"*Did* he?"

That piqued Hogram's interest, Fralk thought. "He did. He also said the humans on the other side of Ervis Gorge may have these firearms for the Omalo.''

"Did he?" Now Hogram was roused all right, Fralk thought. "And these humans—our humans—would refuse them to us?''

"No matter what we paid," Fralk agreed.

"The humans take our goods, aye, but I have not seen them go wild over anything, nor use it as we use the tools and trinkets we get from them," Hogram said. "That says to me they are what they claim, explorers seeing the kinds of things we have rather than merchants in the same sense as ourselves.''

Fralk had not worked that through for himself, but it made sense. Hogram's gift for pointing an eyestalk toward such subtle points had helped lift his clan to the status it enjoyed among the Skarmer these days. "If they do not truly need anything we have, it weakens us," Fralk remarked. "How can we make them reach out with the arm that is turned in the direction best for us?''

"They have only two arms apiece, but they turn them every which way," Hogram said. "Were they not so strange in seeming, I would take them for spies. If I were to order them to stay in their own tent and their sky-boat until they do as we desire,

I think that might persuade them to obey. After all, eldest of eldest, what good are explorers who are not allowed to explore?''

"None." Quite without calculation, Fralk widened himself before Hogram. The domain-master's gift for subterfuge had not diminished as his years grew long. It grew with them instead, until even creatures as weird as the humans held few mysteries for him. Fralk was used to believing his own machinations hidden from Hogram. Suddenly he suspected that what he had imagined to be a wall of solid earth was in fact but a thin pane of clear ice.

A motion of Hogram's arms recalled the younger male to himself. "You said our humans will be talking with those on the other side of Ervis Gorge, and with their own domain-masters?"

"Yes, clanfather." Fralk slowly resumed his usual height.

"That will take some time. Let's give them, oh, half an eighteen of days. If after that time they still refuse to sell us one of these whatever-they-call-thems, we will find out how they enjoy exploring the hot, muddy inside of that gaudy orange tent—the cursed thing reminds me of the color a presap mate takes on when it's ripe for budding.''

"It *is* ugly, isn't it?'' Fralk's eyestalks quivered a little.

"Hideous is a better word." Hogram changed the subject. "The boats are now ready, I take it?''

"Yes, clanfather." Fralk never would have come where Hogram's eyestalks could spy him were that not so. "We have the boats, we have the males to fill them. Now we are only waiting for the waters to grow calmer. As you yourself said, we do not want accidents while we are crossing the gorge." He knew there would be accidents anyway; if they waited for the waters in Ervis Gorge to be completely calm, they would wait until the flood had drained away.

The odor of resignation Hogram exuded said he knew the same thing. The domain-master asked a different question. "How will our males react to being in these boats on the water? They will never have done anything like that before. If they are all blue with fright when they get across, they will prove nothing but prey for the Omalo.''

"Clanfather, I think I am more afraid of Juksal than I could be of any water," Fralk blurted. This time Hogram's eyestalks wiggled, and not a little. "Laugh all you like," the younger male went on, "but I don't think I'm the only male who feels that way.''

"Good." Hogram *was* still laughing. "It's good to know our veteran warriors can inspire fright. If they do the same to Reatur's males as to our own, we will surely triumph." The domain-master paused; his eyestalks stopped moving. "Reatur . . . he worries me."

"He is able, clanfather," Fralk said, remembering that Reatur had scared him a good deal more than Juksal ever managed to do. "But he is not as able as you."

"Hmm. Well, maybe." Hogram's skin turned a deeper green; Fralk's flattery had pleased him. Flattered or not, though, he was still Hogram. "Let me point out to you, eldest of eldest, that I will not be east of Ervis Gorge meeting Reatur. You will."

Fralk knew that was true. He would just as soon not have been reminded of it, though.

"They did what?" Reatur shouted. All the males who could hear him—which meant a lot of males—turned a couple of extra eyestalks in his direction. That shout meant trouble. What kind they would find out later, but the trouble was already here.

"They ran a whole herd of massi back into Dordal's domain, clanfather," the male named Garro repeated.

The domain-master did not need to look down at himself to know he was turning yellow. "Dordal has gone mad if he thinks he can get away with that," he said furiously. "He knows we outweigh him two to one. And he's a lazy piece of runnerpest voiding to begin with. What stirred his eyestalks up all of a sudden, to let him think he can go raiding without our tying them in knots for him? I'll take a band of warriors that will—"

Garro interrupted to answer Reatur's rhetorical question. "A couple of his males were wiggling their eyestalks and jeering that we couldn't do anything about it because we were too busy worrying about imaginary dangers from across Ervis Gorge."

"Ervis—" Reatur felt his breathing-pores tightening up, as if they were trying to keep out a bad smell. Unfortunately, he knew the threat from west of the gorge was not imaginary. That limited what he could do. His first angry vision of arming all the males in the domain and leading them up to smash Dordal's castle melted like ice in a hot summer.

His skin went back to its usual green as calculation ousted rage. "I can't let him keep those massi," he said slowly. "If I do, his males will steal more. Not only that, Grebur will think he can nibble at my domain, too. Between them, curse it, they could prove more trouble than the Skarmer."

"Could and probably will, clanfather," Garro agreed. "I still don't see how anyone can cross Ervis Gorge when it's full of water."

"Neither do I, but Hogram does," Reatur said. "The humans' magic or machine or whatever it was let me talk with him, don't forget. He thinks he can cross. If he didn't, why would he try to turn my domain topsy-turvy?"

"Who can tell why a Skarmer does anything?" Garro said scornfully.

"Hogram is sly, but not stupid," Reatur said. "I wish he were." The domain-master paused a while in thought and then gave his orders. "Find Ternat. Tell him to march eight—no, nine—eighteens of males into Dordal's domain. They are to take more animals than were stolen from us, and to bring them back to our land. Tell him to move fast, too; no one knows when the Skarmer are coming, and to beat them back we may need every male we can find."

Garro repeated the orders until Reatur was satisfied he had them all. Then the younger male hurried away. Reatur watched him go. He wished Dordal's eldest would overthrow him, not the sort of thing a domain-master often wished even on an enemy—such wishes had a way of coming back to bite the male who made them.

Reatur abruptly repented of his wish, not because he feared overthrow—Ternat was the best eldest a domain-master could hope for—but because Dordal's replacement might prove competent. Having a competent domain-master on his northern border was not something Reatur needed.

Having an incompetent one there was quite bad enough.

What he really ought to do one of these years, he told himself, was topple Dordal and install a loyal male of his own budding—someone like Enoph, say—as domain-master up there. That would solve the problem once for all, or at least until Enoph's eldest succeeded him, which presumably would be Ternat's problem and not Reatur's.

And if I set Enoph in Dordal's place, Reatur asked himself, how is that any different from Hogram's wanting to put Fralk in mine? For one thing, he thought, Enoph and Dordal were both from the first Omalo bud, not foreigners like the Skarmer. For another, Reatur would be doing the overthrowing, not having it done to him.

He doubted whether Dordal would appreciate that part of the argument. Too bad for Dordal, one of these years.

His plans for doing unpleasant things to his neighbor melted as he saw a male hurrying toward him in a way that could only mean something else had gone wrong. He wanted to turn all six of his eyestalks away from the male, to pretend the fellow did not exist. That, sadly, was not what being domain-master was about. "What is it, Apbajur?" he asked, letting the air sigh through his breathing-pores.

"We're beginning to get enough melting on the northern walls of the castle to be a nuisance, clanfather," Apbajur told him.

Reatur sighed again. That was a nuisance every summer, and in a hot one—as this one was looking to be—a major nuisance. "We'll just have to start spreading dirt, I suppose," the domain-master said. A good layer of dirt on the roof and walls helped shield the ice beneath from the heat of the sun.

"I thought so, too, clanfather," Apbajur said. He was a master water-molder and ice-carver, and had a good feel for such matters. "But I wanted to get your permission before I started pulling males from the fields for the work."

"You'd best do it," Reatur said, though he felt like cursing instead. First, males to watch Ervis Gorge for the Skarmer, then more to deal with Dordal, and now this. The crops would suffer because of it. Of course, they would suffer a good deal more if the Skarmer invasion succeeded or if Dordal's males kept raiding, and Reatur did not want to live in a castle falling down around him.

Taken by itself, any one thing was always easy to justify. Weighing that one thing against all the others going on at the same time, though, was not so simple.

Two males came rushing toward Reatur from different directions. One was shouting, "Clanfather, the eloca are—!"

At the same time, the other cried, "Clanfather, the nosver have got into the—!"

Reatur felt like pulling in all his eyestalks and pretending to be a stump. He might have done so, had he thought Onditi and Venots—or even one of them—would let him get away with it. Sadly, he knew better.

"One at a time, please," he said wearily. Onditi had got to him before Venots, so the domain-master pointed to him first. "What have the cursed, miserable, stupid eloca gone and done now?"

* * *

"Are you sure you should have brushed Tolmasov off that

way?'' Irv asked Emmett Bragg after listening to the tape of the conversation between the two pilots.

Bragg bristled. "Damn straight I'm sure." When he swore, Irv knew, he was both angry and in earnest. "Long as the Russians keep to their side of Jötun Canyon, none o' their business what we do over here. Besides, if they even think we've given guns to the Minervans here, maybe they'll get serious about keeping Hogram's gang on their own side where they belong."

"Or maybe they'll give them guns, too, to keep things balanced," Irv pointed out.

"Hadn't thought of that." Bragg frowned, but his face cleared after a moment. "I don't believe it. Tolmasov's not that dumb. No matter what he thinks of us, no way he'd let the natives have the drop on him. I wouldn't, not in his long johns."

"I suppose not," Irv said. "If we started shooting at each other here, it could even touch off a war back home."

"Yeah." Bragg nodded. "Like I said, Tolmasov's not that dumb. But he's no friend of ours, either—good for his digestion to get stirred up every once in a while. Let him stew."

"All right, Emmett." Somewhat reassured, Irv went back to work. He had spoken his piece, and Emmett hadn't gone along. Fair enough. Bragg's judgment had been good so far, he told himself. Likely it was this time, too. He didn't necessarily trust the Russians that far himself, either.

Tolmasov listened to the tape from Earth once more. He shook his head. He wasn't used to getting orders this simple. " 'Use your own best judgment regarding firearms for the Minervans,' " he repeated. "Who would have thought Moscow could be so generous?"

"And what is your best judgment, O mighty boyar?" Shota Rustaveli asked.

"If I were a boyar, my best judgment would be to clip the tongue of such an impudent subject," Tolmasov retorted, but he could not help smiling. Rustaveli reveled in being impossible. More seriously, the pilot went on, "My best judgment is to be very sorry that I have to tell Fralk my domain-masters will not let us sell them any Kalashnikovs."

Rustaveli wore gloves, even inside the tent. He clapped just the same. "That is an excellent best judgment to have, I think."

"*Da,*" Katerina said, looking up from a microscope.

Oleg Lopatin did not say anything. His wide shoulders jerked in a shrug. Tolmasov did not think Lopatin was pleased. He did not much care. If the KGB man knew what was good for him, he would follow orders. To give Lopatin his due, something the pilot did only reluctantly, he had been obeying Tolmasov with military exactness. Let him keep right on doing it, Tolmasov thought as he went out to find Fralk.

As he explained himself, he watched the Minervan turn yellow. He had seen them do that among themselves, but rarely at him: humans and Minervans tried to stay on best behavior around each other. He knew it was not a good sign.

"Your domain-masters do not understand that we need these rifles," Fralk said. "They are far away. You are here. Let us buy a rifle, and the success we have with it will float above their orders as ice floats on water."

"I am sorry." Tolmasov spread his hands. "Even though they are far, I cannot disobey my domain-masters any more than you can Hogram."

"Cannot?" Fralk said, now resembling nothing so much as an outraged banana with a great many arms. "Will not, I think, comes nearer the truth." An outraged sarcastic banana, Tolmasov thought. He shook his head to try to drive away the mental image—this was what he got for spending so much time with Rustaveli.

The real problem was that Fralk had it right. Tolmasov did not like lying to the Minervan. He did not hesitate, either. "Do you go against Hogram's wishes as soon as he cannot see you? My domain-masters would punish my disobedience when we got home."

"This is your final word?" Fralk demanded.

"I am sorry, but it is."

"You will be sorrier." Had Fralk been a human, he would have turned on his heel and stomped off. Instead he averted all his eyestalks from Tolmasov as he left. That got the same message across, the pilot thought glumly.

He walked through one of the market areas that ringed Hogram's town. If he shut his eyes, the racket there reminded him of the little stalls in Smolensk—and every other Russian town—where farm women sold city housewives the beets and chickens they raised on their private plots of land. Minervan males' high voices only made the resemblance closer.

Two males came up to Tolmasov, one on either side. One carried a spear, the other a Soviet-made hatchet. "Please go back to your cloth house now, human," the male with the spear said. It did not sound like a request.

"Why?" Tolmasov asked. Doubting whether either male spoke any Russian past the word *human*, he went on in their language. "Many times I, people like me come here. Not do harm, not bother Hogram's males. Just look. Why not look now?"

"Because Fralk demands it, in Hogram's name," that male replied. He lifted the spear to block the pilot's path. "Go back to your cloth house now."

"I go," Tolmasov said, thinking Fralk had wasted no time in starting his petty revenge.

When he got back to the tent, he found the revenge was not petty. More armed males surrounded the orange nylon bubble. One of them was laying down the law to Oleg Lopatin—the Minervans had never heard of the KGB. Lucky them, Tolmasov thought.

Then he got close enough to hear what the Minervan was saying, and things abruptly stopped being even a little bit funny. "You strange creatures have interesting devices, and for their sake we have let you do and go as you would," the male told Lopatin. "Now you will not share one of these devices with us, so why should we keep extending to you the privileges you earned only with good behavior?"

He sounded like a soldier repeating a memorized message. Tolmasov suspected that was partly because Lopatin's grasp of the Skarmer language was still weak, and he would not have understood everything on the first try.

"Only want to go out, look," Lopatin protested.

"You strange creatures have interesting devices—" The male went through his routine again. As far as Tolmasov could tell, he used just the same words he had before. Someone had given him those words. Hogram or Fralk, the pilot thought, disquieted. They were ready for us to say no.

Shedding his own escort, he strode over to the male who was keeping Lopatin just outside the tent. Lopatin actually gave him a grateful look, something he had never before earned from the *chekist*. The Minervan, of course, used a spare eyestalk to see Tolmasov coming—no chance of taking a native by surprise, as he might have a human guard.

"What you do here?" Tolmasov asked in his sternest tones. When the male started to go into his routine once more, the pilot cut him off. "I hear this before. What you do with us humans?"

The Minervan had more than one groove to his record after

all. "From now on, you stay here inside this ugly house. You do not go out for any reason. If you do not do what we want, the domain-master says, we will not let you do what you want. He is a trader, not a giver."

"We only do what our domain-masters order," Tolmasov said.

"And I only do what my domain-master orders of me," the male retorted.

Tolmasov tried a new tack. "We show we Hogram's friends many times, many ways. Why so angry now, at one small thing?"

In warmer weather, he would have been sweating. This— house arrest—would wreck the mission's ability to gather data. He had the bad feeling Hogram knew that. Being manipulated by the natives was not something the pilot had anticipated; their technology was too primitive to let him think of them as equals. But that did not, worse luck, mean they were stupid.

For that matter, they knew more about humans than Tolmasov had suspected. "One small thing, is it?" the male said. "Then why did you conceal the fact that one of you is, of all the disgusting notions, a grown-up mate? Did you know it would only make us reckon you more monstrous than we do already?"

"Not hide," Tolmasov insisted. He shared an appalled glance with Lopatin. They had known about Minervan females' short lives for some time now and had slowly gotten used to the idea. This was not Earth. Expecting everything to work the same way would have been foolish. So, evidently, would have been expecting the Minervans to understand that. Tolmasov fell back on the only answer that might do some good. "No one ask us."

"Ah, and so you said nothing. A merchant's reply, we call that," the male said. Relief flowed through Tolmasov; he had helped himself rather than hurt. But the male went on, "If you are merchants, too, you will see that we do what we must to make you deal as we want. When you do, all your privileges will be restored. Till then, you stay in here. Now go in."

"How long we stay?" Tolmasov asked.

"Till you show us what we need to know. I told you that. How long it is depends on you."

"Cannot do what you want," the pilot said.

"Then you'll stay in there a long time," the male answered.

"We don't have the food to withstand a long siege," Lopatin said, in Russian.

"We don't have anything to withstand a long siege," Tolmasov answered in the same language. That was—what was the fine American phrase?—a self-evident truth.

"Go in now," the Minervan male said, in no mood to let the two humans chatter away in a speech he could not follow. At his gesture, his followers raised their weapons. Short of opening fire, Tolmasov and Lopatin had no choice but to obey.

Inside the tent, Shota Rustaveli and Katerina had been listening to everything that was going on. Rustaveli greeted Lopatin with an ironic bow. "Good day, Oleg Borisovich, and welcome to the Gulag."

"That's enough from you, you Georgian—" Lopatin growled before Tolmasov followed him in.

"That's enough from both of you," the pilot said sharply. "I cannot command us to like one another, but we *will* treat each other with respect, all the more so in this tight space. Think of it as spaceship discipline if you must."

Everyone nodded. Then Katerina said, "Think of it as living in a two-room apartment with four generations of your family." This time everyone laughed.

"Da," Tolmasov said. He had lived like that himself. Everyone had lived that way in Smolensk when he was small, in one of the Stalin-Gothic apartment blocks that had gone up like ugly toadstools after the Great Patriotic War. Afterward, he had never thought those memories would be funny. Now he was grateful to Katerina for using them to break the tension of the moment.

"The resemblance will grow even closer when the chemical toilet clogs up," Rustaveli said. He sounded sardonic as usual, but he looked serious. He was right, too. After a few days—a week, at most—with four people in permanent residence, the tent would be a decidedly unpleasant place to live.

"The heater will need another charge of gas before long, too," Katerina said. "And the stove. Afterward, we'll have no way to make tea, or to make our concentrates into hot food. Come to that, we may not even have water."

Tolmasov grimaced. Maybe the Minervans would let them go out to gather ice and snow, maybe not. If not, the siege would end in a hurry.

"If the natives want our Kalashnikovs so badly, maybe we should give them a good taste," Lopatin said. Then, before anyone could shout at him, he shook his head. "No, it would not do. Like it or not, we live in the age of media. Regardless of what a few well-placed bullets might accomplish here, they would do more damage back on Earth."

"Imperialism *is* easier when word of what it takes to build an empire never leaks out," Rustaveli said. "Georgia has learned that all too well, from underneath." For a moment, the brooding expression in his dark, hooded eyes, the way the shadows sat on his narrow cheeks, made him seem almost as alien to the three Great Russians in the tent with him as did the Minervans outside.

A real fight might have sprung from his words. Maybe he intended that. Just then, though, a Minervan called, "Sergei Konstantinovich, come out, please. Come alone." He spoke Russian.

"Fralk," Tolmasov mouthed silently. Not seeing what other choice he had, he went. *"Zdrast'ye,"* he said somberly. "What do you aim to do with us?"

"Do with you?" Fralk returned to his own language. He sounded altogether innocent, a good enough reason, Tolmasov thought, to suspect he wasn't. "Nothing at all. We will merely keep you here and at your sky-boat."

His pause, again, was perfectly—too perfectly—contrived. "The machine that goes back and forth between here and your sky-boat may continue to do so . . . provided it goes by the same route it always uses. Other than that, you humans may not leave the sky-boat, either. Males are on the way to enforce Hogram's command there."

"Thank you for letting us eat and stay warm, at any rate." Tolmasov did his best to stay polite. He was seething inside. Sure enough, the locals had spotted the humans' weakness. Being on Minerva without exploring was like sharing a bed with a beautiful—and expensive, oh so expensive!—trollop without making love.

"We have no wish to harm you humans in any way," Fralk assured him. "As you know, I owe you my life. But Hogram, wanting many other males to be preserved thanks to your rifle, can no longer cooperate with you when you do not cooperate with us."

"You should write for *Pravda*," Tolmasov muttered, which meant nothing to Fralk. But the Minervan was doing a good job of reproducing the more-in-sorrow-than-in-anger, it's-for-your-own-good tone the paper often took. The pilot went on. "My domain-masters—"

"Are far away," Fralk interrupted. "Hogram is here, and so are you. You would do well to remember it."

Tolmasov waved at the spear-carrying males. "Hard to forget."

"Think of them as being here to protect you, if you like," Fralk said.

Tolmasov did not know how to say "hypocrite" in the Skarmer tongue, and Fralk did not understand the Russian word. The conversation, accordingly, lagged. Tolmasov went back into the tent. Fralk's voice pursued him. "Think on what you do, Sergei Konstantinovich."

"Bah!" The pilot flung himself into the chair in front of the radio. He worked off some of his fury by profanely embellishing the warning he sent to Bryusov and Voroshilov in *Tsiolkovsky*.

After the sparks stopped shooting from Tolmasov's mouth, the two men on the ship did not reply for some little while. At last, timidly, Valery Bryusov asked, "Do I understand that you want us to obey the Minervan males when they arrive?"

"Yes, curse it," the pilot growled. "If they keep letting the rover travel back and forth, I don't see what else we can do. We cannot fight them unless they attack us first—as Oleg Borisovich has said, public opinion back home would never support it. We will just have to see just who can be more stubborn, us or the Minervans."

Over the next ten days, Tolmasov developed a rankling hatred for the color orange. He had never been fond of Oleg Lopatin; although the KGB man did his best to be self-effacing—something he could not have found easy—Tolmasov began to despise him in earnest. Shota Rustaveli's jokes wore very thin, Even Katerina started getting on the pilot's nerves. And he was grimly certain everyone crowded into the tent with him was sick of him, too.

Then Voroshilov called from *Tsiolkovsky*. "Moscow wonders why we aren't sending them data based on new journeys, just analysis of what we'd done a while ago."

"Screw Moscow, Yuri Ivanovich," Tolmasov said. No one had said anything to Moscow about their confinement, hoping the standoff would resolve itself before they had to.

"Thank you, no," the chemist answered. "What, though, do you propose to tell them back home? I cannot see us avoiding the issue any longer."

Tolmasov sighed. "I fear we will have to tell them the truth." Voroshilov was a quiet, patient man. When he started chiding—however gently—the pilot knew he could not sit on his hands any longer.

The message that came back to *Tsiolkovsky* was circumspect but not ambiguous: "Use whatever means necessary to stay on good terms with the natives and continue your scheduled program of exploration."

"Which of us becomes drill-master?" Shota Rustaveli asked when Bryusov relayed the word from Earth.

That, Tolmasov thought gloomily, about summed things up.

Fralk watched with five eyes as the human opened a catch and clicked a curved brown box into place on the bottom of the rifle. "This holds bullets," Oleg said.

"Bullets," Fralk repeated—so many new words to learn! All of them were necessarily in the human language, too; his own lacked the concepts for easy translation. "Bullets, bullets, bullets."

"*Da. Khorosho*—good. The bullets come out of the muzzle when you pull the trigger."

"Muzzle. Trigger." Fralk said the words while Oleg, holding the rifle in one many-fingered hand, pointed out the parts with the other.

The human held out the rifle. "Go ahead. Pull the trigger."

"What?" Fralk watched himself turn blue with alarm. "You said, uh, bullets, would come out!" He had seen what bullets had done to the krong. He didn't know how to make them go where he wanted and didn't want them to do that to Oleg or him.

"Go ahead. Pull," Oleg insisted.

Hesitantly, Fralk reached out with a fingerclaw. The trigger was hard as stone but smooth as ice. He pulled. Nothing happened. "No bullets," he said, relieved.

"No, no bullets," Oleg agreed. He took back the rifle, then touched part of it above and to one side of the trigger. Fralk had not realized it was a separate piece, but the front end of it, the end toward the muzzle, moved. "This is the change lever," Oleg said.

"Change lever," Fralk repeated dutifully.

"*Da*. When the front of the change lever is here, at the top, you cannot pull the trigger. Always carry the rifle with the change lever like that, so it does not shoot by accident."

"At the top," Fralk echoed. The idea of a rifle that could shoot by accident tempted him to turn blue again. A spear or an ax did what it did because some male made it work. If no one was around, it would just lie there. The rifle sounded as though it had a mind of its own. Fralk wondered if he could trust it away from its human masters.

Oleg did not give him time to dwell on that. He moved the change lever. "With it here, in the center position, the rifle will shoot many bullets, one after the other." He moved it again. "With it here, at the bottom, the rifle will shoot one bullet at a time."

"Why the choice?" Fralk asked.

"If enemy is close, you use up fewer bullets and save them for other foes."

"Oh," Fralk said. That made sense, of a sort. So many things to think about . . .

9

The wind howled out of the south, blowing the snow it carried along almost horizontally. Reatur stood in the middle of his field with all his arms happily stretched out. "A spell of decent weather at last," he said. "I was sick of all that heat."

"All *what* heat?" the human beside him muttered. Louise was bundled in even more false skins than humans usually wore; she—Reatur hardly had to remind himself of that anymore, something he could not have imagined a few eighteens of days ago—even had a covering for her eyes, transparent as ice but harder to melt.

The domain-master gestured expansively. "We often get a few stretches of nice southerly breeze," he said. "I'm particularly glad to have this one, because it will help keep the castle walls solid."

" 'Nice southerly breeze,' " Louise echoed. Then she sighed, a sound that, when human mates made it, was eerily like the one people used in the same situation. "Glad cold good for something."

"It's not cold," Reatur protested, only to have Louise sigh again. One thing about which people and humans would never agree was what constituted good weather.

"Never mind," Louise said—she realized that, too. "Much ice melting at edge of land where all ice—makes storms come, blow even here."

Reatur started to answer but stopped. Not for the first time, one of the ideas a human casually tossed out made him look at the world in a different way. It had never occurred to him that what happened in one place could affect weather somewhere else.

"Is the weather across Ervis Gorge the same as it is here?" he asked after a moment's thought.

"Not much different. Why?"

"The one bad thing about snow is that it makes things far away harder to see. If it's snowing on the Skarmer side of the gorge, they made decide to hit us now because the males I have watching won't know they're coming till too late."

Louise's wrappings made trying to read her expression, always a tricky business with humans, a waste of time now. But when she said, "One more thing to worry about," Reatur's eyestalks could not help twitching. No matter how strange they looked, in some ways humans thought very much like domainmasters.

As if thinking about humans had conjured up more of them, three came into sight trudging along the new path that led from the castle to their flying house. Or perhaps, Reatur thought on seeing Irv, Pat, and Sarah together, it was Louise's mention of one more thing to worry about that made them appear when they did.

The newcomers had their heads down. They were talking among themselves in their own language. They all jerked in surprise when Reatur called, "Any luck?"

They turned toward him. He saw how splattered with eloc's blood they were; the wind brought its sharp scent to him, budding and death intermingled in the odor. With that smell so thick, he hardly needed to hear Sarah's glum reply. "Not much."

"Some," Pat corrected. "Budding far along when we get to eloc's pen. Not have much time to get ready. Do better next try."

The humans had been saying that since Sarah's first go at saving an eloc mate. They had yet to keep one alive, Reatur thought gloomily. As if picking his thought from the air like a snowflake, Sarah said, "Not enough luck, not yet. If eloc was Lamra, Lamra dead now."

"How much longer till Lamra buds?" Irv asked. By dint of endless work, he was starting to speak the Omalo language quite well.

After a moment's thought, Reatur answered, "An eighteen of days, an eighteen and a half at the outside." When the humans first put forth the idea of saving Lamra, he had been of two minds about wishing them success. Now, though hope of that success looked as far away as ever, he knew how downcast he would be if they failed. That made no sense to him, but he was getting used to common sense collapsing whenever humans touched it.

What Pat touched was the gore-splashed front of her false skins. "Go get clean," she said to Reatur, and started to walk on toward the flying house. Then she added, "Wish I had hot water," which left him almost as confused as when he had realized how his feelings about Lamra's survival had changed.

One of water's few virtues, to Reatur's way of thinking, was being better for washing than ice or snow. But *hot* water? Hot water was a weapon of war, good for shooting at a foe from a distance or undermining the thick hard ice of his walls. Did Pat mean she was going to wash herself in it? The domain-master knew humans loved heat, but that was taking things altogether too far.

He never thought to wonder how Pat felt about his living in a castle made mostly of ice.

The boats bumped down the path toward Jötun Canyon. The path, meant only for occasional travelers, was not nearly wide enough to accommodate so much traffic. Minervans and their beasts of burden slogged eastward, using the roadway more as a sign of the direction in which they should go than as a means of travel in itself.

Oleg Lopatin marched along with them. He was whistling cheerfully, something which, had they heard it, would have filled the rest of the crew of *Tsiolkovsky* with disbelief. But, he thought, he had every reason to be happy.

For one thing, he was doing conspicuously less than the warriors all around him. True, his AK-74 was slung over his shoulder and he had a heavy pack on his back, but he was not hauling boats on ropes like the Minervans. Nothing satisfies the soul like watching others work harder than oneself.

For another, he was doing, actually doing, something every Soviet officer dreamed of and planned for. He was marching to war against the Americans, in a place where they had no nuclear weapons to make life difficult.

So, he whistled.

Fralk turned an eyestalk toward him. "How do you make that peculiar noise, Oleg Borisovich?" the Minervan asked in good Russian.

"You just pucker your lips and—" Lopatin began in the same

language. Then he remembered who—and what—he was talking to. "Never mind," he said lamely, switching to the Skarmer tongue. "Your mouth, mine not same."

Fralk sighed. "No, I suppose not." Even so, a minute or so later he sent air hissing up and out through his mouth. It did not sound like whistling; it sounded like a steam valve with a leak, Lopatin thought. The sight of Fralk's breath smoking out would have completed the illusion, but Fralk's breath did not smoke. It was too cold.

The KGB man found another reason to be glad he was marching—he stayed warmer this way.

He passed Minervans practicing their paddling on boats set down by the side of the road. They were none too efficient at best; when they turned three or four eyestalks—and their concentration—on the human instead of their job, they grew positively ragged. Unlike Lopatin, they would not freeze in moments if their coracles flipped them into the icy water now rushing through Jötun Canyon. Also unlike him, though, none of them could swim a stroke.

He expected a good many to drown on the way across. That was too bad, but it could not be helped. Fralk and Hogram, he knew, felt the same way, or they never would have tried crossing the canyon in the first place. And Fralk was also forethoughtful enough to have got the best paddlers in the whole force for his boat.

Had Fralk not come up with that idea for himself, Lopatin would have suggested it. He was going into that coracle, too. But Fralk was no one's fool. When it came to self-interest, Minervans and humans thought very much alike.

The roar of the torrent in Jötun Canyon had filled Lopatin's ears all day. He was starting to screen it out, as he did the city noise of Moscow. Now he let himself hear it again. The irregular grind of ice on ice that was part of the racket made him frown. Even the best paddlers might not save him.

That thought came back to haunt him as he peered down from the rim of the canyon and saw through swirling snow the cakes of ice flowing by. He wondered whether Fralk was also full of second thoughts.

More likely, the Minervan was too busy to have time for them. Gangs of males had been laboring to smooth and widen the path down to the water since before the flood began. Even so, it was none too smooth and none too wide. It was also steep and icy. Getting warriors down to where they could cross the stream was no easy job. Getting the boats down there was worse. Lopatin was glad all that was Fralk's problem, not his.

To give him his due, Fralk was as ready as anyone trying something for the first time could be. The changeovers of the rope crews had been planned with almost balletic precision. Moving the boats along was not the problem it had been on the trek from Hogram's town. Keeping them from taking off on their own and sliding into the water without any warriors in them, however, presented problems of its own.

Though his own engineering talents were electronic rather than mechanical, Lopatin admired the solution Fralk and his comrades had come up with. At the top of the canyon, most of the boat-pullers abruptly turned into boat-holders, moving behind their burdens to control them and stop them from running away.

The KGB man clicked off several pictures, fast as the auto-winder would let him. He wished he had *Tsiolkovsky*'s video camera with him, but understood why Tolmasov had said no. Both in the water and across it, he was going into real, serious danger—taking the precious camera along would have risked it as well.

But the stills he was getting could only suggest the smooth discipline of the maneuvers the warriors were carrying out. Ballet was not quite the right comparison after all, Lopatin decided after watching for a few minutes. The groups of males working together reminded him more of public Komsomol displays of mass exercises.

One of Fralk's constantly twisting eyestalks happened to light on Lopatin. "Oleg Borisovich, you should be on your way down, not gawking up here," the Minervan scolded.

The Russian felt his face grow hot, snow flurries or no. "You are right, eldest of eldest," he said formally. "I apologize." Hoping the spiked soles of his boots would hold, he started down the slope.

"Careful, there," he heard Fralk yell behind him. "No, no, no, don't foul the ropes, you spawn of a spavined eloc. Come around *this* way. There—better, isn't it?" The general as traffic cop, Lopatin thought, smiling.

In spite of wearing spikes, he soon came to envy the Minervan males their six legs. They could slip the claws on their toes into the tiniest cracks in the roadway to anchor themselves. And even if they fell, they had six arms with which to reach out and grab something. Don't fall, he told himself grimly, and tramped on.

Fralk hurried past him. Instead of shouting at males getting ready to maneuver boats down the path, now the Minervan was shouting at the males who were starting to put boats into the water. "No, you idiot! Keep the rope attached! Keep it—"

Too late. The boat was already sliding downstream. The warriors who had let it get away stared at it with a couple of eyestalks and apprehensively back at Fralk with the rest. He screamed abuse at them. Lopatin chuckled. He did not understand even half of what Fralk was yelling, but anyone who had ever soldiered recognized the tone.

One of the males past whom Lopatin was marching wiggled his eyestalks at the human. Even in an alien species, Lopatin could tell this was a veteran: his spears and shields were old and battered, not shiny new ones like those most of the warriors carried, and pale scars seamed his hide.

"Taught that little budling everything he knows about fighting, I did: me, Juksal," the male said. "Even sounds like a warrior now, doesn't he?"

"Yes, and a leader of warriors," Lopatin agreed.

"Taught him everything he knows about fighting," Juksal repeated. The Minervan boasted like a veteran, too, the KGB man thought. Lopatin had listened to more stories about the Great Patriotic War than he ever wanted to remember. Almost all of them, a security man's automatic cynicism told him, were lies.

He was drawing near the boats at the makeshift landing when he happened to recall a piece of a war story he had thought long forgotten. The fellow who told it was a Stalingrad survivor and had the campaign ribbon to prove it. "The worst of the worst times," he had said, "was when the Germans had us pinned back against the Volga and the drift ice on the river made it damn near impossible to get supplies across to us."

Loptin looked at the chunks of ice floating by, looked at the coracle to which he was about to entrust his precious, irreplaceable neck. He wished—oh, how he wished!—he had never remembered that story.

Emmet Bragg frowned as he examined the latest photo from one of the weather and mapping satellites *Athena* had left in orbit around Minerva. Emmet had a whole spectrum of frowns, Irv thought—this one went with real live serious problems. "What's hit the fan?" Irv asked.

"I'm not quite sure," Emmett answered; the frown changed

shape, to reflect his uncertainty. "Here, see what you make of this." He leaned over to show Irv the picture, pointing with a ballpoint pen at the part that was troubling him.

"This dark line here?" Irv asked.

Emmet nodded. "That's the one. Nothing like it on any earlier pictures o' that area. That's the country just west of Jötun Canyon from here, you know."

"I recognized it." Irv peered at the picture. Now he was frowning, too. "What do you suppose this is?"

"A lousy picture, for one thing, through scattered clouds and without enough resolution. I wish we had a Defense Department special instead of these miserable terrain-mappers—that'd tell us what was what."

"Back when we set out, who'd have thought we'd need to be able to kibitz at card games from space?" Irv asked reasonably.

"Nobody, worse luck," Emmett answered. "But I wish somebody had, because one of the things that line could be is the Skarmer army headed out to do its thing."

Irv felt his frown deepen till it matched the one Emmet was wearing. "Yeah, it could, couldn't it? They could be doing something else just as easily, too, though, or it might not be Minervans at all."

"I know, I know, I know." Bragg looked unhappy. "A spy bird would tell us, one way or the other. As is, all I can do is guess, and I hate that." The mission commander sat brooding for a minute or so, then snatched at the radio set.

"Who are you calling?" Irv asked.

"Frank," Emmett said. He spoke into the microphone: "Frank? You there? Answer, please."

A moment later, Frank Marquard did. "Your humble canyon-crawler is here, humbly crawling his canyon. Found another fossil about twenty minutes ago, too. What's up, Emmett?"

"I don't know for sure, but I think maybe the Skarmer are coming. If they are, they'll be heading up our side of Jötun Canyon. I don't think you want to be there when they do."

"Are you certain they're coming?" Frank asked. "I'm further north than I've been before, and I've found some interesting strata here, things that don't poke through down by *Athena*. I don't want to leave if I don't have to."

"I'm not sure," Bragg said, looking as though the admission pained him. He always looked that way when certainty eluded him, Irv thought.

"Then I'm not leaving," Frank said.

Bragg made a fist, pounded it against his knee. He glanced over toward Irv. Order him back, the anthropologist thought. But before he could speak, Bragg turned back to the microphone. "You be alert out there, you hear me?" he said.

"Sure I will," Frank said. "We need more lerts."

"Not a good time for jokes," Bragg said with a snort. "I mean it. *Athena* out." He was shaking his head as he put down the mike. "Lerts."

"If it's not right there in front of him, Frank doesn't worry about it," Irv said. He thought of Pat's bitter words the night after Sarah had flown across Jötun Canyon. He had done his best to avoid thinking of that night ever since or thinking of Pat in anything but a purely professional way. Most of the time, that worked pretty well. For a moment, though, even his skin remembered how she had felt in his arms.

"Yeah, I know," Emmett said, bringing Irv back to the here-and-now. "But I can't make him come in just on account of my vapors. He's got his job to do, down there in the canyon."

"I suppose so," Irv said. He sounded halfhearted, even to himself.

Bragg looked at him. "You, too, huh?"

"Yeah. Logically, though, you're right. Don't misunderstand me, Emmett." Walking in front of a train was surer trouble than getting on Emmett Bragg's bad side. Offhand, Irv could not think of much else.

"Yeah, logically." Bragg grunted. "Then why don't I like it?"

The KGB studied Disneyland because visiting Soviet dignitaries liked to go there. One of the attractions, Lopatin had learned from a friend, was something called "Mr. Toad's Wild Ride." Never having read *The Wind in the Willows*, Lopatin did not know much about this Mr. Toad, but he was sure the ride he was taking was wild enough to horrify any amphibian ever hatched.

The coracle tossed in the surge like a toy boat in a bathtub with a rambunctious three-year-old. All the Minervans in it were blue with fright. Could Lopatin have changed color, he would have been blue, too. He wondered if Tolmasov had let him go along in the hope he would drown, and thought of ways he could get revenge even on a Hero of the Soviet Union when he got back to Earth.

If he got back to Earth. At the moment, he would not have

given a counterfeit kopeck for his chances of making it to the far side of Jötun Canyon, let alone home again. Two boulders of ice had already missed the boat by a lot less than he cared to think about; he had fended off another one, fortunately smaller, with a pole.

And his coracle was luckier than many. One of the chunks of iceberg that just missed it smashed a boat a little further downstream. Minervans splashed into the water as the coracle instantly turned to kindling. A couple of warriors managed to hang on to floating debris; the rest simply disappeared.

Even if he managed to grab something, Lopatin knew, he would quickly perish; this temporary river was frigid as the waters around Vladivostok in December. There, at least, the Minervans had the advantage on him. To them, any liquid water was warm. They might drown, but they would not freeze. A dubious distinction, he thought.

The spray blowing in his face had already left his nose numb. And when he bent down to scoop water from the bottom of the coracle, the cold bit into his fingers through the heavy gloves he was wearing. His feet had also started to freeze.

Lopatin was bending to bail again when Fralk screamed, "Paddle! Paddle hard for your lives!" The KGB man jerked erect. A veritable ice mountain was bearing down on the boat.

"Mother of God!" Lopatin shouted. He had called on the devil's relatives often enough in his career, but could not remember the last time he had named any of the Deity's. Luckily the Minervans, unlike his comrades, would not notice.

He grabbed a paddle from one of the males, jammed it into the water again and again. He did not know whether he was a better paddler than the warrior but could not bear to depend only on the efforts of others for his survival. Slowly, so slowly, the coracle moved ahead. The blue-white slab of ice, sailing along as majestically as a dowager queen, took no notice of the artificial insect in its path.

The Minervan whose paddle Lopatin had taken let out a shrill scream of terror and leapt overboard. The rest of the locals, along with the KGB man, dug in even harder. Lopatin refused to look up; he would risk nothing that might distract him from his desperate rhythm.

Were they gaining? He almost tried not to believe it, for fear of slacking. But surely that mass of ice was not headed straight at the coracle anymore. Surely . . . The wave the ice mountain pushed ahead of itself lifted up the boat's stern; Lopatin tried to tell himself he was imagining the wind of its passage.

Then it *was* past and some other boat's problem. Heart pounding, Lopatin rested for a moment. A few more like that, he thought shakily, and the whole fleet would be someone else's problem—probably the Virgin's, in whose existence he did not believe. After angrily telling himself that, he wondered whether Minervans had souls.

"Is water like this all the time?" Fralk asked. If he did have a soul, he had been nearly frightened out of it; the blue of his skin was the next thing to purple.

"I hope not," Lopatin answered, no sailor himself. In the aftermath of shared fright, he felt closer to the Minervan than he ever had, even during weapons training. Which reminded him: the only way Fralk would ever get his hands on the Kalashnikov was from Lopatin's dead body.

That didn't necessarily mean he would not get off a few shots of his own, though, when the time came.

The eastern wall of Jötun Canyon filled more and more of the sky ahead. Fralk saw it, too, and began to drift back toward his usual green. "We are doing it, Oleg Borisovich," he said. Lopatin did not think he was reading surprise into the Minervan's voice.

Nevertheless, he answered, "*Da*, Fralk, we *are* doing it." That was no small feat, either, not when the Skarmer were inventing watergoing technology from scratch. He peered upstream, downstream. The water was still full of boats, in spite of the dreadful swath that enormous hunk of ice had cut through them. "So are most of the rest."

Able to look in both directions at the same time, Fralk had already decided the same thing. "Enough of us will get across to fight well," he said, "if we can assemble quickly once we're there."

Lopatin nodded. After a while, the coracle was close enough to the eastern shore for him to look for landing sites. "There!" he said, pointing. "Steer that way. Looks like good, sheltered anchorage." He spoke the Skarmer tongue so the paddlers could understand him, but the key word, as happened so often, came out in Russian.

"Like a good what, Oleg Borisovich?" Fralk asked. "Tell me what that means."

"A good place to put up a boat," Lopatin answered. He

pointed again. "That piece of rock that juts out into the water shields the part behind it from the worst flow of the stream."

"Oh." Fralk did a token job of widening himself. "A good thought. It never would have occurred to me that something like that could make a difference. I'm glad you've come along."

That, Lopatin decided, made one of them. A problem with new technology, human or Minervan, was that it didn't have all the answers, not least because the people putting it together hadn't asked all the right questions. Fralk would have been perfectly happy to land any old place on the eastern shore; he hadn't refined his goals enough to see one place as better than another. That would be fine—until he needed his boat to get back to the other side and discovered it wasn't where he'd left it anymore.

The KGB man's mental grumbling did not keep him from helping to guide the coracle into the anchorage he had spotted. Fralk climbed out of the boat and tied it to a boulder. "I am back, Omalo, as I said I would be," he declared. The rest of the males in the coracle waved their arms and hooted.

Lopatin did not join the celebration, though he was as relieved as any of the Minervans to have made it to the other side. He was also a thoroughly practical man. Instead of wasting time cheering, he scrambled after Fralk out onto dry land.

A few hundred meters away, Juksal was already heading up-slope. Like Lopatin, he saw no point in staying in his boat an instant longer than he had to. He felt the same way about Ervis Gorge as a whole. The Omalo could do all sorts of hideous things to the Skarmer if they kept them trapped down here. Getting the warriors up to the flatlands was what needed doing, the veteran thought.

Warriors! Juksal's hands tightened around the spears he was carrying till his fingerclaws bit into the shafts. Calling a bunch of peasants and clerks warriors didn't make them such, nor did giving them spears. Just getting them to stay in their groups and do as they were told would be a fair-sized miracle.

Juksal wished he knew more about the Omalo. If they all got their eyestalks pointing the right way fast enough, the Skarmer might be in for a very unpleasant time. But who would believe anyone could cross a Great Gorge in the middle of the summer flood? A year ago, Juksal would not have believed it himself. With luck, the Omalo would not believe it, either, not until too late.

A spatter of snow blew past the warrior. He hoped for more.

It would help hide the boats—and the Skarmer males as they climbed the side of Ervis Gorge. Unless the Omalo were complete idiots, they would have watchers out. No one ever lived to be old by assuming his enemies were idiots. Juksal was no idiot.

As if thinking of watchers had made them spring into being, something moved far above him. Swearing to himself, he dove behind a rock. He stuck a cautious eyestalk around it to make sure of what he had just glimpsed. With luck, it would be an animal, not a male.

Now the snow hindered him. He could not tell what the thing up ahead was. He swore again, then paused to take stock of things.

"If I have trouble seeing it, it'll have trouble seeing me, too," he whispered. And he carried two spears long and sharp enough to make even a krong think twice.

Keeping himself widened as if before Hogram, Juksal dashed for the cover of another boulder. Again he poked an eyestalk around it and again found himself able to see little. If that was a male up there, though, he had not raised the alarm. More likely a beast, Juksal decided.

Then, through the muttering of the wind, he heard a sound that came from no beast: the *pound-pound-pound* of a hammer on stone. That was a male, then, and by the racket he was making, he had no idea Juksal was anywhere close.

The warrior scuttled forward, quiet as a zosid sneaking up on a runnerpest.

Shota Rustaveli looked nervously back over his shoulder as he stepped into *Tsiolkovsky*'s control room. He could have had a dozen legitimate reasons for coming forward, and in any case Yuri Voroshilov was, as usual, preoccupied in his lab at the other end of the spacecraft. Rustaveli was nervous anyhow.

"And I'm not even a soldier," he murmured to himself, surprised at the way his heart was pounding. The murmur was in Georgian, so that even if someone had been standing right beside him, it would have been only a meaningless noise. Can't be too careful, he thought—soldier or no, the idea of disobeying orders was seriously scary.

He glanced around again. Still no sign of Yuri. Of course not, he told himself angrily. He walked over to the radio, turned it on, found the frequency he needed.

"Hello, *Athena*. *Tsiolkovsky* calling." He held the mike close to his lips, spoke very softly. "Hello, *Athena*—"

"*Athena* here: Louise Bragg." The reply was likewise a whisper, for Rustaveli had turned the volume control down as far as he could and still hear. The tape would still be there to damn him later, but that was later. Now . . . now curiosity rode Louise's voice: "Your call is unscheduled, *Tsiolkovsky*. What's going on?"

"The Skarmer fleet is crossing Jötun Canyon, that's what, and Oleg Lopatin with them. He has his friend Kalashnikov along, as I suggest you remember when you go to tell him hello. That's all. *Tsiolkovsky* out."

He reached out to switch off the set. His hand stopped, just above the switch. The dials had already gone dark by themselves. His jaw clenched until his teeth ground against one another. Of all the times for a malfunction—

Then he heard footsteps coming up the passageway. Voroshilov paused at the entrance to the control room. He was shaking his head. "That was stupid, Shota Mikheilovich," he said. "Stupid."

"What was?" If Rustaveli could brazen it out, he would. "This damned radio seems to have gone out on us. I was just checking it."

"By calling the Americans." Voroshilov was not asking a question.

Rustaveli sagged. "I should have known the timing of the breakdown was too good."

"Yes, you should have," Voroshilov agreed. "I hope I managed to kill the circuit before you blabbed too much, but I'm not certain. You did surprise me, Shota."

"I'm so glad," Rustaveli muttered. Then, one by one, the implications of what had happened began to sink in. "You were monitoring me," he said slowly. With a dignity curious for one admitting such a thing, Voroshilov nodded. "Which means"— Rustaveli went on; he had not really needed the nod—"you're KGB."

Voroshilov nodded again. "But you will not mention that to anyone else, Shota Mikheilovich. Not to anyone. It is not relevant. I would do this no matter what I was, if I came by and found you at the radio."

"Why? You hate Lopatin," Rustaveli blurted. He wondered how that was possible if they were both KGB. He also wondered if it was even true or just a cover the two snoops used.

"Lopatin is a pig," Voroshilov said flatly. That answered that, Rustaveli thought, or at least proved Yuri an actor as well as a chemist and a spy. After a moment, picking his words carefully, Voroshilov went on. "But he is also following the orders he received both from Colonel Tolmasov and from the *rodina*, the motherland. You have no business meddling with his mission."

"No? What if he or his pet Minervan starts shooting at the Americans? Yuri Ivanovich, one of them risked her neck to fly the canyon and help Valery. Shall I repay that by not even warning them danger is coming their way?"

Voroshilov frowned. He still looked, as he always had, quiet, studious, a little boyish. And underneath it he was a *chekist*, Rustaveli thought. He swore to himself never to judge by appearances again.

"He may be *going* into danger, too," the chemist answered. "Bragg would not tell Sergei Konstantinovich whether he was giving firearms to the Minervans on the far side of Jötun Canyon. Had we been sure he isn't, maybe Lopatin could have stayed here. As it is, no."

"Would Katya have wanted you to cut me off?" Before this moment, Rustaveli would never have imagined KGB men susceptible to appeals to their feelings. He could not imagine a *chekist* going home to a wife he loved, to children perhaps, and plopping down in a chair to complain about the hard day he'd had.

But Yuri was different. Damn it, he had lived almost inside Yuri's socks for a lot more than a year now. Maybe he was a *chekist*, but he was not a bad fellow. And Rustaveli would have bet anything anyone cared to name that he did love Katerina.

"I don't know," he said now. He was troubled; Rustaveli could see that. But then he nodded toward the silent radio. "Too late to worry about it at the moment, though." He walked back toward his laboratory—and presumably, Rustaveli thought, toward his microphones and secret switches.

"Shit!" the Georgian said. He slammed a fist against the back of a chair. The thing was padded and did not hurt. "Shit!" he said again.

Chip, chip, chip. Frank Marquard went down on his knees so he could use his geologist's hammer with greater precision. He had not seen a conglomerate quite this fine-grained before. Anything new and interesting deserved to be a specimen.

Even through padding, his knees began to freeze. He sighed. He was so sick of being cold. As a lifelong inhabitant of Los

Angeles, he had had no practice living in a refrigerator. He remembered somebody on the selection panel asking about that and remembered answering that it would not bother him. He had known he was lying even then. Luckily, the people on the panel had not.

Pat was as Californian as he, but the cold didn't bother her as much. Or if it did, Frank thought, frowning, she didn't let on. Not so long ago, that would not have occurred to him. Now he wasn't so sure what Pat could hold back. He hoped—he thought—he was warming her up again, in a very different sense of the word, but he wasn't sure.

As he usually did, he tried to make the best of that. He supposed it was all to the good that he wasn't taking her for granted anymore. Boredom lay down that road.

Out of the corner of his eye, he saw something move. He looked up. Where had the Minervan come from? "What do you here, male of Reatur's clan?" he asked in the Omalo tongue.

The male did not answer. It came closer. How, Frank wondered, had it got below him without his noticing? Then he saw the spears in the Minervan's hands.

"Frank!" Louise shouted over and over in *Athena*'s control room. "Are you there? Come in, Frank!"

"Bozhemoi," Oleg Lopatin said softly when he saw the stained spears Juksal was displaying.

The warrior was proud of himself. "He had a little hammer with him, but he hardly even got it up before I struck him." He raised the hand on the far side of his body, showed the Russian the geologist's tool he had taken from the man he'd slain.

"Bozhemoi," Lopatin said again. The idea of going to war had been attractive in the abstract. Having a fellow human killed by a Minervan, though, was not really what he had had in mind, no matter how socially advanced the Skarmer were.

"Don't let your eyestalks droop, Oleg Borisovich," Fralk said. "You've told us how the humans on this side of the gorge are enemies to your great clan."

"Yes, but—" Sudden ghastly consequences flowered in Lopatin's mind. The Americans would assume he had killed their comrade. With the situation reversed, he would have jumped to the same conclusion. When a man with a rifle was around, who would think twice about natives and their spears?

Scowling, he thought furiously. Though the habit of secrecy

was deeply grained into him, he decided it could not serve him here. He would have to let *Tsiolkovsky* know what had happened, and that he had had nothing to do with it. He could not guess how far that would go toward mollifying the Americans, but nothing, now, could be worse than silence.

He thumbed the ON switch of his radio, brought it to his lips. "Calling *Tsiolkovsky*, calling—" he began. Then he noticed the SEND light had not gone on. When he switched to RECEIVE, no carrier wave hum, no static, came from the speaker.

Hopelessly, he peeled off the back of the set. Water gleamed on the integrated circuits inside. He had tried to keep the radio dry crossing Jötun Canyon, but its case was not waterproof. Who would have thought, on frozen Minerva, it would have to be? He dried the works as best he could, tried again to send. The radio was still dead.

Of course, it had taken a good many bangs, too, as he scrambled up toward the top of the canyon. Without tools he did not have, he could not tell what was wrong with the cursed gadget if nothing obvious like a loose wire leapt out at him. He could not fix anything more complicated than a loose wire, either.

And this, he asked himself bitterly, makes you a modern electronic engineer? The trouble was, it did. But that, at the moment, was the least of the trouble he was in, and he knew it.

Emmett Bragg would be wild when he found out about his countryman's death. And even Tolmasov was leery of Bragg.

"You *get* him on the radio and you find *out* what the hell he's playing at, do you hear me, Sergei Konstantinovich?" Bragg sounded like an angry tiger, Tolmasov thought. He did not blame his American opposite number, either.

"I am calling, Brigadier Bragg, calling repeatedly, I assure you. But he does not reply."

"Neither does Frank Marquard. What does that say to you?"

"Nothing I like," Tolmasov admitted.

"Me either," Bragg growled. "Near as I can see, it says your man's gone rogue on this side of the canyon. I don't like that, Sergei Konstantinovich, not one little bit. You better believe I'll do anything I need to, to protect the rest of my crew. Anything. Don't say you weren't warned."

"I understand." If Tolmasov could have got Lopatin in his sights, he might have dealt with him himself.

"You'd better. Bragg out."

Silence crashed down in the tent outside Hogram's town. Tolmasov sat staring at the radio for a minute or two before he got up. The mission had gone so well for so long, but when it decided to come apart, it didn't fool around. Someone on *Tsiolkovsky*—Rustaveli or Voroshilov, that had to be—calling the Americans, and whoever had not called cutting him off in midsentence. The pilot did not know whether to be angrier at caller or cutter.

And Lopatin! Tolmasov still did not know what to make of that. He did not want to think even a *chekist* could go out of control the moment he got off on his own, but he did not know what else to think, either. The fool's stubborn refusal to start or accept communication did not speak well of him.

The pilot turned to Valery Bryusov and Katerina, who had listened to his exchange with Bragg with as much shock and dismay as he had felt. "Comments?" he asked. Maybe, just maybe, one of them had seen something he had missed.

"Sergei, we have a major problem," Katerina said. Bryusov nodded solemnly. So, after a moment, did Tolmasov. The only trouble was, he already knew that.

Irv peered down into Jötun Canyon. He'd had the weight of a pistol on his hip before, but now he really felt it. The idea of using the gun on a Minervan horrified him. The idea of using it against an AK-74 horrified him, too, for a different reason—he was glad he had made a will before leaving Earth.

By rights, he thought, trying to blend into the bushes, this was Emmett Bragg's job. Emmett was a soldier, not an anthropologist playing pretend. But Emmett was also the pilot—the number one pilot and, if the worst *had* happened to Frank, the only pilot. He was not expendable as a scout.

The Minervans down in the canyon did not look any different from Reatur's males. Irv knew, though, that none of Reatur's males were there. These had to be the enemy, then—the Skarmer, the Russians called them.

And Oleg Lopatin. Without the frantic call from *Tsiolkovsky*, Irv would not have known which Russian accompanied the Skarmer over Jötun Canyon, but a human being's jointed, jerky motions were instantly recognizable against a backdrop of waving Minervan arms and tentacles. For one giddy moment, Irv hoped the human down there was Frank, but the Americans did not wear fur hats.

How had the Skarmer crossed, anyhow? Irv let his binoculars sweep past the knot of natives to water's edge. At first, the round bowl-shapes he saw there meant nothing to him. Then he realized they had to be boats. They looked dreadfully small and flimsy to stack against the current in the canyon, let alone the drift ice there.

Maybe, he thought, the Skarmer had not known the risk they were taking when they set out. Being too ignorant to worry about trouble had fueled a lot of human enterprises, too. Too bad this one was aimed in his direction.

Some of the Skarmer began moving upslope. Seen through lenses, the motion was magnified, menacing. Irv scuttled backward even while the rational part of his mind insisted he was in no danger. That did not stop his retreat. It did make him keep the binoculars trained as he backed away.

The tight knot of Minervans he had been watching broke up in the advance. He saw what they had been gathered around: Frank Marquard's crumpled corpse. The sight came as no surprise, but it was like a kick in the belly all the same.

Irv scrambled onto his bike and raced back toward *Athena*.

Ternat wished Dordal had been budded as a mate, so he—no, she, he would have been; this was almost as complicated as remembering half the humans were mates—could have died young, while budding six offspring as idiotic as himself. Reatur's eldest refused to perform the mental gymnastics he knew he needed to make the last arm of that sentence point in the same direction as the rest.

"Is this still our domain, eldest, or is it Dordal's?" one of the males with him asked.

Ternat considered. He had come this way earlier in the year, trying to convince Dordal that the Skarmer threat was real. All he had succeeded in doing was convincing Dordal that Reatur thought it was real, and so could be raided with impunity. "Still ours, Phelig," he answered, hoping he would make a better war-leader than he had an envoy.

The male's eyestalks drooped in disappointment. "Then we have to leave that fence alone?"

"I'm afraid so." Ternat had had an eye or three on the enclosure, too, until he decided where they were. "Don't worry. It won't be long."

That proved even truer than he had expected. The sun was falling west through clouds toward Ervis Gorge when the war band came upon a pen that had been thrown down. Snow had fallen since then, to cover any tracks, but Ternat still caught the rancid stink of massi voidings. He did not have to see to follow the trail. It led north. "Anything from here on, we can take back with us. Either Dordal's males stole it from us, or we'll steal it from them," Ternat shouted. His comrades cheered.

No formal post marked the border between Reatur's domain and Dordal's. On either side of the border that was not marked, though, males knew who their clanfather was. The ones on Dordal's side knew to run away when a large band of strangers came up from the south.

The scent trail grew stronger. Ternat began to wonder if he and his males were walking into a trap. He doubted whether Dordal had the wit to set one, but one of the northern domain-master's bright young males—say, a male much like Ternat—might.

Sure enough, not long after the idea crossed Ternat's mind, a male pointed casually toward a large boulder off to the side of the path. Just as casually, Reatur's eldest turned an eyestalk in that direction. Someone was peeking out at them.

"Let's go on a little ways and then rush back," Ternat said after a moment's thought. "That way we'll stand between the spy and his friends, so he won't be able to run to them."

As if unaware, the males ambled past the boulder. Ternat swung an arm down. Shrieking, brandishing their spears, the raiding party reversed themselves and ran to catch the male who had been watching them.

"Take him alive!" Ternat yelled. "We need answers."

Had the spying male fled, he would not have got far, not with nine eighteens of warriors after him. But he did not flee. Indeed, Ternat wondered if he could flee. Even after he widened himself in submission, he was one of the thinnest males Reatur's eldest had ever seen, and one of the filthiest as well.

He was not blue with fear under his dirt, though, and Ternat understood why a moment later, when he cried out, "Hurrah! You've come to get the beasts back!"

Anticlimax, Ternat thought. Having been all keyed up to fight or pursue, here he was, greeted as a savior. Lowering his spears—surely there could be no harm in one starveling male— he said, " 'Back'? You're one of Reatur's herders?"

"That I am—Elanti the massi-herder, at your service. I'm glad you fellows came at last. I was getting right hungry, skulking around here so's I could keep one eyestalk on the animals."

"I believe that," Ternat said. "Phelig, give him something to eat." While Elanti fed with every sign of ecstasy, Ternat quietly asked the warriors, "Does anyone know if he's truly ours?"

Eyestalks writhed as the males stared at Elanti and at one another. A male named Ollect, whom Fralk knew to be from the northern part of the domain, said, "He's ours, eldest. He's been herding massi up here near the border for a long time." A couple of other males spoke up in agreement.

Elanti stopped gobbling for a moment and said reproachfully, "Eldest, eh? Reatur'd know who I was without asking."

That, Ternat thought, was probably true. "The domain-master knows all sorts of things I must learn one day," he answered.

"Hmm. Not stuck up about it, anyway." Elanti popped yet another chunk of dried meat into his mouth. When it was gone, he said, "Dordal's thieves have my massi—well, suppose you'd say Reatur's massi, but I'm the one herds 'em—in a little valley not far from here, along with some herds of their own. They've also got males posted on both sides of the trail there, so's they can jump on anybody coming straight up to take them home again."

"Sounds like the cursed robbers," Ternat said, forgetting he had been thinking it would take someone much like him to set an ambush.

"There's more," Elanti said. "I've had a lot of eyestalks on the land hereabouts lately, and a bit before then, too." Ternat suspected he meant he had done some smuggling over the border; he turned all his eyes away from Elanti for a moment to show he did not care. The herder sounded relieved as he went on, "Happens I know a way that gets you round the far side of one of those bands. You hit 'em from a direction they're not expecting, nip in and grab the beasts, then deal with the other band—"

"Yes," Ternat said slowly, liking the scheme. "If you're right, Elanti, the clanfather will make you rich for this." And if you're wrong, he did not add, you'll never betray anyone else again. The herder ought to be able to figure that out for himself.

Evidently he could. "Don't much care about being rich," he answered. "Getting my massi back, that's the important thing, them and maybe a few of Dordal's better ones to pay me back for the trouble I've had. Maybe even more than a few."

"You'll get them," Ternat promised, carefully not wiggling his eyestalks at the greed in Elanti's voice. After all this was over, he told himself, detailing someone to watch the herder for a while would be a good idea. Elanti might have more stashed away somewhere than Reatur did under the clan castle.

But all that was for later. Now he and the war band followed Elanti away from the plain, inviting trail of the massi toward the other path the herder said he had found.

Lamra looked down at herself, all around. Half the time, she thought the six big bulges that almost hid her feet looked ridiculous. The other half of the time, she hardly noticed them. They had been part of her so long that she was used to them.

She tried to remember what she had looked like before the budlings began to grow. Like any other mate, she supposed. It was hard to believe that. When she stopped peering at herself, she could see several nearby. It was even harder to imagine she would ever look so straight-up-and-down again. The humans kept saying she might, but then humans were pretty hard to imagine, too.

She had trouble playing now, she who had once been among the swiftest and most agile mates. Because she had grown so clumsy and slow, the others hardly tried to include her in their games anymore.

She wondered if the idea that she would probably not be around much longer also made them want to stay away from her. She doubted it. Few mates could think far enough ahead to conceive of death as anything but a word. She had trouble doing so herself. She was not aware of a time when she had not been, so would she not always be?

But she knew that, no matter how things seemed, the reality was that Reatur, unchanged so far as she could tell in the time she had been alive, had been about the same long before that. And she knew mates, many mates, had ended in the time since she had started paying attention to the world around her. She could die, too.

She looked at the piece of cured hide she held in one hand and at the marks written on it. Reatur knew she had this piece and did not mind. More of the marks were beginning to make sense to her. Each one she learned made the rest easier to understand. If she lived, one day she would be able to read.

The door to the mates' chambers opened. Reatur came through. He looked tired, Lamra thought—his eyestalks, even his arms, drooped. He had not come to see the mates so often lately as before, and when he did, he was always tired.

The mates swarmed around him. He had kind words for all

of them, as he usually did: praise for Peri's scribbles—which, Lamra thought, did not look a thing like real writing—an eyestalk wiggle of glee when some other mate in the crowd—Lamra could not see who—threw a ball that actually went in his direction.

Lamra tried to wait for him to notice her. She was at the edge of the group because she could not move quickly anymore, and a lot of mates had dashed by to be with the domain-master. That made her angry, and she was not very patient, anyhow. When she could not wait any longer, she shouted "Reatur!" as loud as she could.

Two of his eyestalks looked in her direction. "Your turn will come, little one," he said, and went on with what he was doing. The promise kept her quiet a while longer. Then she shouted for him again.

"Soon," Reatur said, more sharply this time. Lamra shifted from foot to foot to foot to foot to foot to foot. Finally, when the domain-master had talked with or cuddled the rest of the mates, he turned his eyestalks toward her again. "Now, little one, come with me and we will talk."

He led her off to one of the smaller chambers. The other mates dispersed. At first they had resented the special attention Reatur gave Lamra, but now they were used to it. They quickly got used to things that had once been strange—humans, for instance. Lamra was much like her companions in that respect.

"Well, little one," Reatur said, "what have you been doing since I saw you last?"

She waved her piece of hide. "I've learned a lot more marks. Look, this says, 'that was the year so much ice melted that the roof'—did something. I don't know what this part means." She pointed at the words that had defeated her.

He turned an eyestalk toward it. " 'Fell in,' " he told her. "That's very good, Lamra. You've been working hard."

"So have you," she retorted, "or you'd have come around more often to see me."

Air hissed out of his breathing-pores. "You're right—I have and I would. It's—" He paused, as if wondering whether to go on, but at last he did. "—it's been difficult."

Lamra responded more to his tone than to his words. "Why are you sad, Reatur?"

"Among other reasons, because the humans still haven't had any luck with mates from the herds, and your budding time draws near," he said. "I never wanted you to die, Lamra, but finding hope that you might not and then seeing it fade is hard."

"I don't want to die, either, Reatur. Maybe I won't, still. But if I do, well—"

"Don't say it," the domain-master said, and so Lamra did not repeat the old saying about old mates. After a moment, the domain-master went on, "Aside from that, Dordal's males have stolen some of our massi, the Skarmer have crossed Ervis Gorge in things the humans call 'boats,' and they or another, different kind of human killed one of the ones we know. And aside from *that*, everything is fine."

Lamra did not always recognize sarcasm. It escaped her this time. Even had she caught it, she would have paid it no mind, not when it came along with Reatur's other news. A human dead! She had not even been sure humans could die. "Which one is dead?" she asked anxiously; three of the strange creatures had become closer friends of hers than anybody save Reatur.

"The one called **Frank**," he answered. Lamra knew relief—she had hardly even seen that one.

Still, she said, "How sad for the humans. There were so few of them even before."

Reatur angrily jerked his arms. He started to turn yellow. "It will be sad for us if we can't push the cursed Skarmer back down the gorge. If this domain gets a new master, a Skarmer master, your budlings will never live to grow up. And you—if you do live but we lose, what would a Skarmer chieftain make of you? Nothing good, I tell you that."

Lamra tried to keep herself from turning blue. She hadn't thought about any of the things Reatur had said, and they all sounded terrifying. "We have to win, then," she said at last. "We will. We have you, and the Skarmer don't." Even as she said that, she saw herself greening up again. Reatur, she was convinced, could handle anything.

"I wish it were that simple." The domain-master sighed. "I came to see you to get away from my worries, and here I've given them to you instead. You're brave for not fussing about them."

He widened himself to her, then left before she could figure out how to respond. The boom of the door closing after him sounded very final.

Pat Marquard stumbled as she walked toward the latest penned eloc mate on the point of budding. "Careful," Irv said. He had said it several times already—wherever her eyes were focused, it was not on the ground under her feet.

"Sorry," she answered. Her voice sounded far away. She did not look at him.

Sarah said gently, "It's all right if you want to go back to the ship, Pat." Irv nodded.

Thinking about how to reply brought Pat back toward the here-and-now. She shook her head. "If I don't have anything to do, I'll go even crazier than I am now. I'd rather try to work than just sit and brood."

Sarah glanced toward Irv. He nodded again—he would have said the same thing. His wife shrugged. They walked on. Irv wondered how much they were going to accomplish. For one thing, they hadn't kept a mate alive yet. For another, if the invaders from the west won, the future for which they were trying to save Lamra would prove depressingly short.

Irv also thought about Oleg Lopatin. Tolmasov sounded as anxious to be rid of him as was everyone on *Athena*. He must have flipped out, Irv thought for the umpty-umpth time. That was very bad, especially if some of the Russians had been worried enough about him to try to warn the American ship. And especially since he had his rifle with him.

Irv did not want to go up against a Kalashnikov, not even with six pistols—no, five now. "How are we going to fight back?" he asked Sarah—quietly, so Pat would not notice. Sarah only shook her head. Irv wondered whether that meant she didn't know or she didn't want to think about it now. Probably both.

The eloc mate in the pen was used enough to humans that it did not try to attack or waddle away as the three of them came up. It only turned one extra eyestalk in their direction.

"Now we wait," Sarah said grimly. By the look of things, Irv thought, they would not have to wait long. The eloc mate bulged like a fat lady trying to explode out of a spandex suit. Irv had learned, though, that as with pregnant women, appearances could be deceiving. Once they had spent three cold days waiting for a mate to drop her budlings, only to come back the next morning to find the small eloca scampering about the pen and the mate dead.

Waiting had been easier then, before—before Frank died, Irv told himself firmly. He did not *know* Oleg Lopatin had killed him. It was, however, a lot likelier than anything else he could think of.

And no matter how Frank had died, he was dead now, and

Pat no longer the bantering companion she had been. She kept pacing back and forth in the pen with that distant look in her eyes. Sometimes she answered when Irv or Sarah spoke to her, sometimes she didn't. The other two couldn't just talk with each other, either, not with her there. Time stretched endlessly.

After what seemed like six weeks but was in fact two and a half hours, Sarah, who had been peering and poking at the eloc mate so often it wasn't even resentful anymore, abruptly stood up straight. "The skin is starting to split. Let's get ready."

Irv squatted next to the eloc mate, two arms around it on Sarah's left. Pat came more slowly and squatted with two arms around the eloc on Sarah's right, so the three humans were equally spaced around it.

"We'll try it a little differently this time," Sarah said, reminding them of what they were about. "Instead of just trying to bandage those bleeders, we're going to shut 'em off. Here."

She passed two large surgical clamps to Irv, two more to Pat. "As soon as the budlings drop off, clamp the protruding blood vessel stumps. You'll need both hands for the job, so don't try to do 'em both at once. Do one, then the other, quick as you can without making a mistake. The way the blood comes gushing out, a whole lot of fumbling and you'll be too late to do much good."

Remembering how Biyal had bled out, remembering how he had watched several eloc and massi mates pour their blood onto the ground—and onto him—Irv knew his wife was right. He opened and closed a clamp several times.

The eloc grew placid—resigned was the other word that crossed Irv's mind, though he knew that was anthropomorphizing—as the budding process went on. The split in the skin above each bud grew longer and longer. Soon Irv saw the wet legs and bottoms of the two budlings in front of him. The legs were already wiggling, as if the newborn eloc were preparing to hit the ground running.

"Soon, now," Sarah breathed. Irv glanced over at her for a split second, suppressing a grin—she was nervously opening and closing a clamp, too. Veterinary OB was not what she had studied in med school. She did not notice him. "Soon," she said again.

Irv saw she was right. Now just about all of each budling was visible; he could see the blood vessels between their eyestalks that connected them to the mate, could see the much bigger vessels around which their mouths were sealed. The big ones were the ones he had to worry about. The bleeding from the others could be handled. Sarah thought so, anyhow, and Irv had nothing but respect for his wife's judgment.

As it had before, the moment came without warning. One instant, the budlings were still attached to the mate. The next, they were at Irv's feet, doing their best to get in his way. The mate's blood fountained out.

Irv had practiced what he was going to do countless times back on *Athena*. Grabbing and clamping a piece of rubber tube, though, was not nearly enough like reaching for a blood vessel when spurting gore not only made it hard for him to see what he was doing but also froze his fingers as it splashed over and between them.

The last time he had done such blind groping, he thought, he had been fifteen and had gotten slapped for it. He let out a grunt of triumph as his left hand closed round the big, soft, pulsing vessel. He squeezed, hard. The flow slowed. He slapped on the clamp.

He felt like shouting—the vessel was sealed. But no time for shouts. How much blood had the mate already lost where the other budling had dropped free? Too much? Only one way to find out. He leaned, grabbed, and after a few desperate fumbling seconds, clamped.

Then he had a chance to look up. Sarah had finished her part of the task just seconds before him. That made him feel proud— he was very much an amateur at this sort of thing. But then, with Minervans, so was everyone.

Seeing him finished, Sarah said, "Nice and quick. Good. We just may get a live mama out of this yet." She raised her voice a little. "How you doing, Pat?"

Again, hesitation. Then Pat answered, "I've got the first one just about clamped. I'll go to the other as fast as I can."

"Oh, hell!" Sarah exclaimed. She scrambled over to Pat's side. "Give me that!" Irv went around the eloc mate to see if he could do anything to help. His face fell when he saw the size of the pool of blood under the vessel Sarah was finally clamping. He could not imagine how any animal, Earthly or Minervan, could lose so much and live.

And sure enough, the eloc mate was sagging, its arms and eyestalks going limp in a pattern he had seen too many times before. Sarah recognized that, too. She looked at the eloc—the dead eloc—and at the clamp in her hand. She threw the clamp down, hard, on the frozen ground. It bounced away.

"I'm sorry," Pat said miserably. "I just can't—"

"I know," Sarah said. "Nothing to be done about it." But she could not help adding, "I really had hopes for this, though. Now we may not get another chance to test it before—before the real thing. Having a success behind us would have been nice. Oh, well."

She looked around to see where the clamp had gone, walked over to it, picked it up. Irv undid the five they had managed to place on the eloc mate. Only a few more drops of blood dribbled out as he freed each one; the mate was empty. He said, "We might as well head back to *Athena*."

Head down, Pat walked a few paces apart from her two companions. Sarah said, low-voiced, "Maybe I should show a Minervan what to do. A male would probably be more reliable than Pat is right now. I don't blame her, but—"

"I know." Irv thought about it. After a few seconds, he shook his head. "Not a good idea," he said as quietly as Sarah. "As far as I can tell, none of the males but Reatur and maybe Ternat would react well to the idea of helping mates survive. Too far outside their mental horizons. If he didn't think Lamra was special, I doubt Reatur would let us go on, either. And right now Ternat isn't here, and Reatur—"

"Has problems of his own," Sarah finished for him. She sighed. "Don't we all?"

10

Minervan summer days were not bad, not for someone used to Moscow weather as Oleg Lopatin was. Minervan nights were something else again, almost always ten below Celsius or worse. Every night reminded Lopatin of his military snow-survival course.

That he was in the middle of an armed camp now only brought the memory into sharper focus. Fralk's forces, battered and scattered by the crossing of Jötun Canyon, were back together now, as much as they ever would be. The Omalo had not struck at them. Tomorrow, with luck, the Skarmer would be out of the immense canyon altogether and up onto flat ground.

Lopatin did not plan to be with them.

Helping the Skarmer win the war against their neighbors to the east, maybe squeezing off half a clip at any Americans foolish enough to try to help the feudal Omalo resist the ineluctable logic of the historical dialectic . . . all that would be wonderful, so long as he did it step by step, in contact with *Tsiolkovsky*. Then he would be not only one of the instruments through which the dialectic unfolded but also carrying out Soviet policy, as defined before he headed east with Fralk's army.

Losing his radio changed everything.

Any Soviet officer who took matters into his own hands asked for trouble and usually got it. If he showed hostility toward *Athena*'s crew *without being hooked into the chain of command that could authorize such behavior,* he knew exactly what would happen. The Americans would scream bloody murder. They were probably screaming bloody murder already about Frank Marquard.

Moscow would say, would have to say, that Lopatin had been sent across Jötun Canyon purely as an observer. All the blame would land right on his shoulders. He could see it coming, just as he had seen that mountain of ice bearing down on his coracle.

As he had done in the coracle, he intended to get away now.

He only saw one course that might let that happen, and he hated it. But if he yielded himself up to the Americans, and told them how Marquard had died, he might put out for his own benefit the line he expected from Moscow. As far as his actions went, all he needed to do was tell the truth. Unfortunately, though, as a KGB man he knew for how little the truth often counted.

The Skarmer slept all around him. In an Earthly camp, fires would have lit his way—and let sentries see him. The Minervans had no fires; they liked the weather fine. Lopatin knew they had set sentries. With luck, he could evade them in the dark.

He slid out of his sleeping bag, quietly rolled it up, and stuffed in into his pack. He slung his rifle over his shoulder. He wanted to carry it, but knew he might need both hands free. Shooting his way to freedom would surely fail anyhow; even if it didn't, it would wreck the Soviet mission. But he missed the comfort of having the Kalashnikov ready to fire.

He slipped through the slumbering natives. Going in the right direction was easy, even in the darkness: any way uphill was right.

He wondered how he would ever get back across Jötun Canyon to return to *Tsiolkovsky*—after abandoning the Skarmer here, he would not be popular among them. Perhaps it would not matter. With Marquard dead, the Americans would have the supplies to let him fly home aboard *Athena*.

Home? No, to fly back to Earth. He doubted he could ever go home again. Times had changed since the Great Patriotic War, when so many Soviet soldiers earned time in the Gulag merely for seeing what western Europe was like. They had not changed so much, however, that a KGB man could expect to be greeted with open arms after being debriefed by the CIA, as Lopatin knew he would be.

He wanted to laugh. He wanted to cry. He wanted to swear. He was a good Party man and a loyal Soviet citizen, and he knew he would have to defect. Very slowly, he kept creeping out of the Skarmer camp.

Finally, after what seemed forever, the Skarmer began to thin out. Lopatin no longer had to pay attention to his every footstep for fear of falling over a native. He could move faster now.

The wind picked up. Clouds scudded by. One of the Minervan moons—Lopatin had no idea which one—shone through a break in the cover overhead. Far fainter than Earthly moonlight, it was better than the near-blackness he had known before. He picked up the pace again.

The moonlight also let a Skarmer sentry spot motion he might otherwise have missed. "Halt!" the male called. "Who goes?" Lopatin froze. Too late—the sentry had already picked up the alien quality of the way he moved. "The human! The human is running away!" the Minervan screamed.

That did it, Lopatin thought, hearing hubbub break out behind him as the outcry jerked warriors from sleep. "This way! This way!" the sentry shouted.

Swearing now in good earnest, the KGB man ran *that* way. Don't panic, he told himself. The terrain gave him plenty of cover. He dashed from boulder to boulder, keeping low, trying not to give that cursed sentry another glimpse of him. The Minervan moon stayed visible. Where moments before he had been glad to see it, now he wished it into the hottest pits of hell.

He scuttled over to yet another rock and paused, listening. Most of what he heard from the camp was chaos, but not all. Some males were moving purposefully after him, calling as they came. He shivered in his latest hiding place. Not even his darkest nightmares included pursuit by a pack of screaming maenads.

They were getting closer, too, terrifyingly fast. That alarmed him in a way different from their banshee cries—he had swerved away from his earlier direction of travel, away from where the sentry spied him. Yet the Minervans somehow still tracked him.

He found out how a moment later, when the warriors drew close enough for him to make sense of some of their shouts. "No, fool," one male yelled to another, "the scent trail leads this way!"

Scent! Lopatin was up and running again in an instant. Hiding would do him no good if the Minervans did not need to see him to find him. The KGB had cooked up a dozen stenches to throw dogs off the track. They would have been of more use to Lopatin had they been on the same planet as he was.

He was tempted to turn around and fire a couple of clips into the warriors behind him. That would drive them off, he knew. What he did not know was what would happen to his crewmates if—no, when—someone from here got back across Jötun Canyon with word that he had opened fire.

And so he hesitated and suffered the usual fate of those who hesitate. A Minervan sprang out from in back of a rock. Either Fralk had shouted orders at the beginning of the chase or the warrior was uncommonly wise about firearms: the first thing he did was smash the rifle out of Lopatin's hand with a spear. It clattered to the ground and rolled away. Lopatin dove after it. The Minervan jumped on him.

The spear had fallen, too. Even so, it was not much of a fight. Lopatin got in a kick that made the warrior wail, but the Minervan's fingerclaws stabbed through clothes to pierce the KGB man's flesh. One scored his cheek and missed his eye by only a couple of centimeters.

By then, other males were rushing up. "Human, we all have spears!" one shouted. "We will use them if you do not yield."

Lopatin went limp. The male he had been wrestling with cautiously disengaged. "Good idea," he said when he was convinced the fight was gone from his foe. "You almost kicked my insides out—those cursed funny big legs you humans have." He sounded more professionally interested than angry; after a moment, Lopatin recognized Juksal's voice.

"Here is his strange weapon," a male said from a few meters away.

"Good," Juksal said. "Hang on to that. We need it. We need it more than we need him. Without their fancy tools, these humans aren't so dangerous." If any Minervan had the right to say that, Lopatin thought dully, Juksal did. He wished none of them had the right.

Wishing did not help. Prodding him along with spears, the warriors led him back toward the camp. They met Fralk before they got there. "Oleg Borisovich, have you gone mad?" the Minervan demanded. Hearing the question in Russian only made Lopatin feel worse.

"*Nyet,*" was all he said.

"Then *what*?" Excited or upset people waved their arms in the air. So did excited or upset Minervans. Having three times as many arms as a human being, Fralk looked three times as excited or upset. He sounded that way, too.

"Politics. Human politics. I am sorry, Fralk, but I cannot help you anymore against the Omalo or the Americans."

The KGB man expected Fralk to get even more upset, perhaps to threaten all sorts of torture: he would have, standing where

Fralk was. Instead, the Minervan wiggled his eyestalks with a peculiar rhythm Lopatin had not seen before.

He said just what Juksal had. "Oleg Borisovich, it no longer matters whether or not you help us. We have your rifle, we have your bullets. We do not need you."

He was still speaking Russian. For the benefit of the warriors standing around, he translated his words into the Skarmer tongue. They all wiggled their eyestalks that same strange way.

So now, Lopatin thought, I know how Minervans laugh a nasty laugh. It was one bit of knowledge he would just as soon have been without.

Reatur had never seen more than half an eighteen of Skarmer at one time before. If he never saw even another one again, that would suit him fine. Altogether too many of them were coming up to the rim of Ervis Gorge now, straight at him.

He peered down at them. The gorge's slope grew shallower at the top; the warriors were approaching almost as quickly as if they had been on flat ground. But the ground was not flat. As soon as the Skarmer drew a little nearer, they would find out why he had let them come so close to getting out of the gorge before he dealt with them.

Which one was Fralk? The domain-master wanted to smash him personally. But, he decided reluctantly, he could not let the Skarmer get close enough for him to tell them apart. They were still well out of spear range, especially uphill. That was fine with Reatur. He did not need spears to smash them.

"Ready, warriors?" he called. Up and down his line, males shouted and waved their arms to show they were. "Then shove!" the domain-master yelled.

The Omalo had spent the last few days dragging as many large stones as they could to the edge of Ervis Gorge. Now, by ones, twos, threes, sixes, they stood behind the stones. At Reatur's command, they strained against them, pushed them down into the gorge.

The slope *was* shallow. Some of the boulders just skidded briefly. Others turned over once or twice, then fetched up against rocks sticking up from the ground and stopped. But still others picked up speed, crashed into the ranks of the Skarmer.

The Omalo shouted again, watching row upon row of their enemies go down in writhing heaps. "Don't just stand there!" Reatur shouted. "More stones!"

But as the males swarmed back to the next piles of stones,

something dreadful happened. It was so far outside the domain-master's experience that at first he did not fully grasp it. He saw flashes of light coming from a male in the front rank of the Skarmer, heard a loud, barking roar unlike anything he had known before. Something went *craaack* past an arm. And somewhere not far away, males, Reatur's males, were falling down and screaming.

He and his warriors, all of whom were seeing and hearing the same things, took a long, terrible moment to understand that all those strange, terrible things were eyestalks of the same beast. For Reatur, the realization came when he saw a human near the male from whom the flashes of light and the terrible noise were coming.

He had never seen the humans he knew using anything like this—weapon, he supposed it was—but it was too strange to have come from his own people, or even from the Skarmer. Compared to humans, he thought, surprised at himself, the Skarmer were closest kin. If humans had weapons, they would be strange, too.

Strange and deadly. A male not two steps from Reatur was on the ground, thrashing. The domain-master saw that he had a hole in him, the sort a spear might give, between two of his arms. As Reatur watched, the male voided bloodily and stopped moving.

Craaack! Another—whatever it was—whizzed by Reatur. He heard a wet slapping noise. A male behind him started to shriek. It all happened in the same instant. The domain-master pointed to the Skarmer with the weapon. "Get him!" he shouted. "Get him!"

More stones rumbled down. One just missed the human, another would have smashed the male with the weapon had it not kicked up and flown over his eyestalks. The Skarmer kept right on wielding it, though, and Reatur's males kept going down.

"More stones!" Reatur yelled. "More! More!"

His males heaved against a few more boulders. Others, though, stayed where they were, for the Omalo who should have pushed them into Ervis Gorge were running back toward Reatur's castle. In a way, the domain-master did not blame them. He wanted to run away, too, especially since a male died or was horribly wounded almost every time the strange weapon flashed and barked.

And now the rest of the Skarmer, encouraged both because of their foes' dismay and because they were no longer being pelted so heavily, reached the rim of the gorge. They were eager; Reatur's males, even the ones who had not fled, were wavering.

Off to one side, the Skarmer who had already gained the flatlands were starting to swing round to cut Reatur's males off from the way back. If they could manage that, they could surround and destroy them at their leisure, even without their cursed weapon. With it . . . Reatur did not like to think about what would happen with it.

"Back!" he shouted, hating himself for it but seeing no better course. He quickly added another command he hoped his males would obey: "Keep your order as you go!"

Most of them did. And, to his relief, the Skarmer let them escape. Why not, the domain-master thought bitterly. They'd already done what they needed to do. Reatur tried to stay optimistic. He thought about how much his avalanche had battered the invaders.

Enoph tramped by. He said just what Reatur was thinking: "We hurt them."

"Aye." The domain-master sighed; he could not afford the luxury of wishful thinking, not now. "But they hurt us worse. They beat us, Enoph, and right now I have no idea how to keep them from beating us again."

"What are we going to *do*?" Sarah hated having to rely on Emmett Bragg. Making a career soldier mission commander had always struck her as part and parcel of the Washington mindset about extraterrestrial intelligence, which, she was convinced, had been formed by too many bad science fiction movies—aliens had to be enemies, therefore had to be fought, therefore a soldier should be in charge. Simple. Simpleminded, too.

But now the crew of *Athena* found itself in the middle of a war. The aliens weren't all enemies; some of them had become good friends. They were better friends, certainly, than Oleg Lopatin ever would be, and Oleg Lopatin's AK-74 had killed and maimed more of them than she liked to think about.

Her medical training had not prepared her for war wounds. They were as ghastly on Minervans as on people, not just for themselves but because they were deliberately inflicted.

So she turned to Emmett. Having him in charge suddenly looked like a good idea after all. The trouble was, instead of instantly coming up with an answer that would solve their problems, he only scowled and said, "What are we going to do? I

don't see too much we can do, right now. Maybe the best thing
to hope for is that old Oleg didn't bring that many spare clips
for his rifle."

Sarah felt her lips tighten. That wasn't what she wanted to
hear. She said, "In your cubicle—"

He grinned at her, put her off-stride. "What do you know
about that? Haven't hardly coaxed you in there."

"*Will* you shut up?" The heat of her fury amazed her. Picking
her words carefully, saying them even more carefully, she went
on, "In your cubicle, there is a cabinet you keep locked. I
thought that perhaps—"

"—I had an Armalite stashed away there—a rifle," he
emended quickly, seeing that she did not follow. She gave him
reluctant credit for being all business once more. "Or maybe a
crate of grenades. Trouble is, I don't."

Sarah set hands on hips. "Well, what the hell do you keep in
there, then?" She was furious at him all over again, this time
for having her hopes dashed.

"This and that," he said. She thought that meant he wasn't
going to tell her, but he did, a little. "Some real special codes,
for one thing, the kind you hope you never have to use—I mean,
there's a lot worse things could go wrong than one crazy Russian."

"Like for instance?" Sarah asked, genuinely curious.

"Like the whole crew of *Tsiolkovsky* attackin' us on purpose—when we set out, remember, we didn't know how far
apart we'd be from them. Or like the natives bein' high-tech
after all, just without radio on account of they're telepaths or
some stupid thing, and overrunnin' *Athena*. They'd have to be
ready back home then, in case we had somethin' happen out of
Invaders from Minerva."

In spite of herself, Sarah giggled. "Stupid damn movie," she
said, having watched it on TV at least two dozen times since
she was a kid. A late-fifties low-budget sci-fi classic turkey, it
featured "Minervans"—who looked nothing like real Minervans—remarkable chiefly because the zippers in their costumes
were visible in several scenes. Every so often, coming up with
something silly like that, Emmett could surprise her and remind
her that he was human, too.

"Isn't it?" he said now, quietly laughing himself. "I'll tell
you what I wish I had in there, and it's got nothin' to do with
guns and such." He waited for Sarah to raise an eyebrow, then
went on, "I wish I had a couple o' bottles o' good sippin'

whiskey put away, for celebrating gettin' down here, gettin' back home . . .'' He paused, studied her in that way she found alarming and attractive at the same time. ''Maybe sharin' a little, now and again.''

''Hmm,'' was all she said. She was damned if she would encourage him.

''Doesn't matter anyhow,'' he said when he decided that was the only response he'd get. ''NASA doesn't understand that sippin' whiskey is for *sippin'*, if you know what I mean. When I put the idea to 'em, they just reckoned I wanted to get lit.''

''When you what?'' There was about as much likelihood of NASA bureaucrats okaying a couple of fifths of Jim Beam, she thought, as there was of dying of heatstroke on Minerva. My God, the manifest might leak out one day, and then somebody could kiss a career good-bye.

If anybody could see that, it was Emmett. He had boundless contempt for all bureaucracies save the military. For all Sarah knew, he had asked about the bourbon just to give the three-piece-suit boys fits. That was his style.

She expected him to chuckle and own up to twisting NASA's tail just for the fun of it. Instead, she saw with a thrill of alarm that he had what she thought of as his sniper's face back on— behind his eyes, he was taking dead aim at something. After a moment, she realized it wasn't her.

Or was it? ''Get lit,'' he said dreamily. ''That just might work.'' Now he was focused on her, sharply.

''What might work?'' she demanded. ''I hate it when people think through things and then leave out all the interesting parts when they start talking. It's like—'' She started to say ''sex without foreplay,'' but decided that might not be a good idea. ''I hate it,'' she finished.

Bragg nodded. ''Can't say I blame you.'' He spent the next several minutes explaining.

By the time he was done, Sarah wished she hadn't asked. She knew that was stupid. As soon as Emmett got this brainstorm, he would have come to her with it. The real trouble was, it made too much sense for her to tell him he was crazy.

But when he said, ''You know, I'm jealous as hell,'' she had all she could do not to reach up and bust him right in his grinning chops. She probably would have, had it not been so obvious that he meant it.

* * *

Fralk watched the latest raiding party come in from the north. They were leading enough massi and eloca to keep the Skarmer army fed for a couple of days. "We'll squeeze the Omalo domain until Reatur's eyes pop off their stalks," Fralk declared grandly.

His warriors cheered as the beasts, complaining every step of the way, passed through the gaps in the barricade of frozen snow. Other males, high-ranking by virtue of their closeness to Hogram—but none so close as Fralk!—spoke up in loud and prompt agreement.

Then someone said, "May the domain come down with the purple itch. When are we going to take out the cursed Omalo army?"

Sudden silence fell. The officers edged away from the male who had spoken, as if they wanted to show they had nothing to do with his words. It was Juksal, Fralk saw. What rank he had sprang only from his ability to fight and fight and fight and stay alive. Still, he had a great deal of that ability—and he had kept the human from escaping. Thus Fralk spoke firmly but politely: "By plundering the domain, Juksal, we also weaken the army, you know."

Juksal grunted. "Beat the army and the domain is ours. No matter what we do to the domain, the Omalo army can take it back if they beat us. We should have crushed them just as soon as we fought our way out of the gorge."

"Do you recall the state we were in when we made it out of the gorge?" Fralk asked indignantly. "Those accursed boulders almost wrecked us altogether, in spite of the rifle." He pulled in arms and eyestalks at the memory.

"The Omalo were worse," Juksal retorted. "Otherwise they wouldn't have run from us. We should have chased 'em and slaughtered 'em instead of letting 'em get away to have another chance at us."

"All in good time." Fralk saw his skin begin to take on the yellow tint of anger. With an effort of will, he made himself turn green again. He would *not* let Juksal make him angry. Now that the warrior was under his command instead of the other way around—that ghastly, endless series of drills with spears and shields!—he could listen or ignore, as he pleased. And now he was pleased to ignore. "In a few more days, when we are fed, rested, and otherwise recovered from the ordeal just past, we will sally forth and put an end to the Omalo once and for all."

Juksal had the stubborn rudeness Fralk would have expected

from someone who could find nothing better than fighting withwhich to make his way through life. "The Omalo will be feeding and resting and recovering, too, eldest of eldest." In his
mouth, Fralk's title was a reproach.

When Fralk started to turn yellow this time, he did nothing
to try to hide his feelings. "Yes, Juksal, I am eldest of eldest,"
he said proudly. "I am also commander of this army. Remember
that, please. Moreover, as commander I have just won a victory.
Remember that, too."

"You may have won it," Juksal said, "but you don't know
what to do with it."

"Warrior Juksal, you are dismissed," Fralk shouted. He was
yellow as the sun now.

Juksal widened himself, a salute as sardonic as his use of
Fralk's title. Still widened, the veteran waddled away. But he
could not resist having the last word. "There's humans here,
too, remember," he shouted back. "What if they have rifles,
too? What then, *commander*?" Resuming his full height, he
tramped off.

What then? Fralk did not like to think about that. But Lopatin
had said the humans over here probably did not have rifles. The
human Juksal had killed certainly was without one, or the warrior never would have gotten close enough to use a spear. Still,
Fralk trusted Lopatin's word much less than he had before the
human tried to escape. And *probably* was a far more reassuring
word on the other side of Ervis Gorge than here. Here, being
wrong would kill a lot of males.

All the more reason, then, for proceeding slowly and carefully, Fralk thought. Otherwise, he might run the army into a
krong's nest before he found out the beast was there. He remembered how Tolmasov's rifle had riddled the krong back on the
west side of Ervis Gorge. What would have happened, though,
had the krong had a rifle, too?

"Hit them *now*!" Ternat shouted. His males cried "Reatur!"
and rushed through the brush toward Dordal's waiting warriors.
They yelled back. The snorts and whistles of the massi Ternat's
band had already freed only added to the din.

This time, Ternat thought as he drew near the enemy, his
warriors lacked the advantage of surprise. They had just finished
smashing one half of Dordal's would-be ambush and sent the
survivors fleeing to warn the other half. Ternat wished Dordal's
warriors were like humans, blind to half the world around them.

Were that so, none of the first batch of males might have escaped.

As it was, Reatur's eldest was happy enough with himself. Because people were as they were, surprise attacks were hard to pull off. But Dordal's males had been surprised, sure enough, when the war band came crashing through the undergrowth at them. A good three out of every eighteen had turned blue and thrown down their spears; Ternat's warriors had some of them back with the massi. Even the ones who hadn't turned craven also had not fought well, most of them.

Then Ternat had no more time for reflection. Spears were flying, out toward his males and from them back at Dordal's. This second band was larger than the one his warriors had already smashed and better situated, too, with several large boulders giving Dordal's males almost the protection of a wall. If they stayed back there, they would have an edge.

Some did. More did not. As was true of the band Ternat led, most of Dordal's warriors were young males with more temper than sense. They charged to do battle with their southern neighbors.

Along with Reatur's name, the war band also shouted, "Thieves!" Dordal's males screamed insults back at them.

"Why aren't you hiding in the chambers under your castle, waiting for the Skarmer?" one of them yelled.

Ternat froze and almost took a spear in the gut because of it. But he had heard that voice before. "That's Dordal himself!" he cried. "Get him and we bring a lot more than massi home!"

The warriors surged forward. Now fewer spears were in the air, and more clutched tight between males' fingerclaws. One of Dordal's warriors thrust at Ternat. He turned the stroke aside with his shield, tilting it upward as he had been drilled. He thrust back, low. The male managed to get a shield down to block that spear but left himself open for Ternat's other one. He wailed as Reatur's eldest drove it home and bled like a mate when Ternat pulled it free.

Ternat and another warrior engaged one of Dordal's males from three arms apart. The beset male was good, but not good enough to resist for long two foes attacking from opposite directions. He went down, briefly yammering.

A rock grazed Ternat, just below one arm. He swore, twisted an eyestalk so he could look down at himself. He wasn't bleeding or swelling up too badly. He decided he would live.

He looked around for another male to take on. There weren't

any, not close. The bravado that had fed that first rush from Dordal's warriors faded as they found Ternat's war band meant business—and had more males than their own force. Even the chance to gain glory by excelling where the domain-master could see them was not enough. The northern males gave ground.

"This is harder work than stealing massi that can't fight back, isn't it?" Ternat shouted.

Dordal's males were less interested in returning taunts now, more concerned with finding safety behind their heap of boulders. For a moment they made a stand there, but the rocks proved an insufficient barricade. One of Ternat's males—Phelig, he saw it was—killed a warrior in the gap between two stones and then took control of it for himself. His fellows swarmed after him into the breach.

Then Ternat's warriors forced their way through another opening. That proved too much for their foes. Some surrendered, others fled. Dordal was one of those who tried to run. When three of Ternat's males dragged him to the ground, the last fight went out of his warriors.

"Get their spears and other weapons, and see to the wounded," Ternat said. As his warriors began to obey, he walked slowly over to Dordal. That bruise he had taken started to hurt. He had forgotten all about it till now.

As Reatur's eldest had remembered, Dordal was a large, imposing-looking male, very much the opposite of Elanti the massi-herder: even standing tall, he was so well fed he looked widened. His eyestalks, however, were at the moment drooping dispiritedly. He raised one eye a little to see who was coming up. He did not widen himself, though Ternat saw that he recognized him.

"Domain-master, you made a mistake," he said, giving Dordal the courtesy of a title he knew his captive might not enjoy much longer.

"What are you doing here, Ternat?" Dordal's voice was still proud but confused—he hadn't changed much since the embassy, Ternat thought.

"I would think that was obvious, domain-master—we are taking back what is ours. If you hadn't crossed the border, we wouldn't have come. Since you did—" Reatur's eldest let Dordal draw his own conclusions.

Those, as was characteristic of the northern domain-master, were bizarre. "I think you were lying about the Skarmer this

whole time, to lure me into raiding you without enough males."
Dordal sounded thoroughly indignant.

Ternat thought Dordal was a fool, but then he had thought
that for a long while. "I'm afraid your greed made you stretch
your eyestalks further than your arms would reach," he said.

Dordal started to turn yellow. Ternat's eyestalks twitched.
Dordal quickly greened up again. Even he was not so stupid as
to show his captor he was angry. "What will you do with me?"
he asked.

"Take the lot of you back to our domain, I suppose," Ternat
said. He hadn't thought much about that; he hadn't expected to
win such a complete victory. "Reatur will decide in the end. If
I had to guess, I'd say he's likely to let you go back home after
your eldest pays enough ransom to remind you not to trifle with
us again."

He waited for Dordal's reaction. It did not disappoint him.
This time Dordal turned yellow in earnest. "My eldest!" he
shouted. "Grevil won't pay a strip of dried meat for me! Let
that grabby budling loose among my treasures and mates and
he'll want to keep everything for himself."

Maybe Dordal did have some sense: that confirmed Ternat's
impression of the northern domain-master's eldest. It also confirmed that Grevil was his father's budling. Dordal, Ternat was
certain, would have done exactly the same thing in Grevil's place.

"Well, we'll just let Reatur sort that out," Ternat said. "Perhaps if Grevil doesn't grant you the respect and obedience a
clanfather deserves, Reatur will send some males north to help
you reclaim your domain—after the Skarmer are settled, of
course."

"I don't care a three-day-old massi voiding about the
Skarmer," Dordal howled. "And if I get my domain back with
help from Reatur's males, there will be cords running from his
arms to mine forever after."

"Yes, there will, won't there?" Ternat agreed cheerfully.
"Maybe you should have thought about that before you decided
to go massi-raiding. As it is, you'll have some lovely three-day-
old voidings to look at as we travel back to my clanfather's
domain."

Dordal twisted all his eyestalks away from Ternat. Reatur's
eldest did not care how petulant Dordal felt. While the northern
domain-master was not looking, he walked away. Dordal started
to talk again. He abruptly fell silent when he turned one eyestalk
back and noticed that no one was listening to him.

Ternat didn't care about that, either. He was shouting to his own warriors now, getting them back into some kind of order so they could lead their prisoners and the recaptured beasts home without half escaping in the process. Ternat did not have three eighteens of plans for overthrowing his clanfather. His time would come one day. Until then, he was content to wait.

And that, he supposed, only went to show that *he* was Reatur's budling. "Good enough," he said out loud.

Sergei Tolmasov watched Rustaveli lean back in his chair. As usual, the Georgian was wearing a mischievous expression. He said, "I doubt much work is getting done aboard *Tsiolkovsky* at the moment—not much that involves the brain, anyway, unless Yuri is reading Katya some of his poetry." He had just brought the rover back to Hogram's town after Katerina drove it down to the ship.

"Not much work getting done here, either," Tolmasov said, not rising to the bait.

"You, my friend, are entirely too serious, as I've said at least a hundred times."

"At least," Tolmasov agreed. Rustaveli snorted.

"That does not mean he is wrong, Shota Mikheilovich," Valery Bryusov put in. He often had trouble recognizing a joke.

"No, it doesn't," the pilot said, "because there *isn't* much getting done here." He had never imagined he could become irrelevant during the Minerva mission, but he had. He didn't like it one bit.

Damn Oleg Lopatin! *Athena* was screaming at Washington and, almost incidentally now, at Tolmasov; Washington was screaming at Moscow; and Moscow, not incidentally at all, was screaming at Tolmasov. He could not even blame any of them— had he been any place in the loop but where he was, he would have been screaming, too. But he had no one to scream at, not when Lopatin wouldn't use his cursed radio.

He couldn't even ask Hogram to send on a written message. For one thing, the local domain-master was barely in communication with his army on the far side of Jötun Canyon. Crossing that stream was almost as hard for the Minervans as getting to Minerva had been for the Soviet Union and United States.

For another, problems between people meant nothing to Hogram. Because Hogram had talked with the Omalo domain-master on the radio, he had to acknowledge there were more humans than the ones he had met. But he simply did not believe in a whole planet full of them, all at each other's throats because one man had gone berserk. Given what Hogram knew, Tolmasov wouldn't have believed it, either. Unfortunately, it was true.

And so the crew of *Tsiolkovsky* went through the motions of doing more research: Bryusov comparing country and town dialects, Rustaveli working on his rocks, Katerina and Voroshilov joining together on a biochemical study. None of it seemed to mean much now.

"Yuri isn't sorry Lopatin's gone and got himself in this mess," Rustaveli observed.

"Then why did he cut you off when you called the Americans?" Tolmasov answered his own question. "Because his head might roll, too, I suppose, if anyone back home"—as polite a euphemism as he had ever come up with for the KGB—"thought he'd overhead you and done nothing. But I daresay you're right, because of Katya if for no other reason."

"There are others," Rustaveli said slowly. The pilot glanced over at him—he rarely sounded so serious. Seeing he had Tolmasov's attention, the geologist went on, "Yuri complained that Lopatin snooped through the poems he wrote for her and stored them in his secret computer file. Evidence, I imagine, but only a *chekist* could say of what."

"I'd hate a man for that, too," Tolmasov said.

"And I," Bryusov agreed, though Tolmasov had trouble imagining Bryusov worked up enough about anything to hate the man who did it. Maybe if an academician from Arkhmolinsk stole something from one of his papers and published it first: anyone would be furious over that kind of pilfering.

Then the full meaning of Rustaveli's words got through to the pilot. "Wait a minute," he said. "How does Yuri know they're in Lopatin's secure file?"

"How else?" Rustaveli put a flippant shrug in his voice. "He read them."

"That's impossible." Tolmasov had tried to access Lopatin's secure file, tried and failed. If the pilot of a mission was not trusted with the passwords he needed to get into a KGB man's files, what were the odds a chemist would be? There was no way . . . no, there was one.

Rustaveli was waiting when Tolmasov looked up. The Geor-

gian nodded. "That's right," he said. "But you will notice I
have not told you any such thing."

"Like that, eh? No, of course, you haven't, Shota Mikheilovich. But Yuri! Who ever would have thought that about Yuri?"

"Shota hasn't what?" Bryusov asked. "Who would have
thought what about Yuri?" The linguist sounded as confused as
if his companions had started speaking Navajo.

"Never mind, Valery Aleksandrovich. Nothing important,"
Tolmasov said kindly. Some people, he thought, were really too
innocent to be running around loose.

His feeling of smug superiority lasted not quite two minutes.
Then he remembered he had thought the same thing about Yuri
Voroshilov. He shook his head. Sometimes you just couldn't
tell.

"Are you all right, Reatur?" Lamra asked when the domain-
master finally got around to paying attention to her. There,
though, she had little to complain about: he hurried through his
hellos to the rest of the mates so he could spend uninterrupted
time with her.

If he had looked tired before, now he looked tired and battered. One of his arms jerked when he sighed, a wince that
showed he had been hurt. "I've been better, little one," he
answered. "The domain has been better, come to that. The
Skarmer beat us, beat us badly."

She saw herself start to turn blue and tried to stop but couldn't.
"What will we do?" she said.

" 'We'?" Reatur asked gently. "Lamra, right now there
isn't much you can do. I wish there were. As for me, I am
going to fight them again. Maybe here, closer to the castle,
closer to where most of my males live, they will make a better
showing."

"What if they don't?"

The domain-master pulled in arms and eyestalks, released
them: a shrug. "Then we won't have to fight a third time, that's
certain. Do you understand what I mean?"

Lamra thought about it. "We'll have lost?" She didn't want
to say that; she didn't even want to think it.

But Reatur seemed to approve. "That's right," he said. "Your
thoughts should always be thin, clear ice, Lamra, so you can
use them to see through to what's there, no matter what it is. If
you don't think clearly, it's like trying to look through muddy
ice."

"Oh," Lamra said. She wanted to show Reatur she could use what he was telling her. "Then are you going to show me why you haven't opened one of your hands since you came into the mates' chambers? Do you have something in there? Is it for me?"

His eyestalks wiggled—slowly, but they wiggled. "Thin, clear ice indeed, little one. Yes, I have something for you in that hand." He turned so it was in front of her.

She held out a hand of her own. He gave her the present. She peered down at it with three eyestalks at once. "It's a runnerpest!" she exclaimed. "A little runnerpest, carved all out of wood. It's wonderful, Reatur. Thank you." She felt proud for remembering to say that. "Where did you get it? Did you carve it yourself?"

"Yes," he said. He hesitated, as if unsure whether to go on, but after a moment he did. "I wanted you to have something to remember me by, even if—the worst happens."

"I'll keep it always," Lamra promised. Then, wanting him to know she was still thinking clearly, she amended, "For as long as I have, anyhow."

"For you, that's always," Reatur said firmly.

"I suppose so." Lamra kept looking at the little runnerpest. "I'm going to poke this around a corner and scare Peri silly with it. Not that she isn't silly already, that is." No matter how hard she worked at it, staying serious was never easy.

This time, Reatur's laugh was unrestrained. "I'm glad I came to see you, little one. One way or another, you always make me feel better." He turned an eyestalk down toward her bulges. "Do you want to hear something foolish, Lamra?"

"I don't think you can be foolish, clanfather," she declared.

"That only shows how young and foolish you are still," Reatur said. "I was just thinking it's a shame you're carrying budlings. I'd like to plant them on you now."

"That *is* foolish," Lamra agreed. Once Reatur had succeeded in planting budlings on her, her interest in mating, once so intense, disappeared. She did her best to think like a male. Altogether unsure how well she was succeeding, she said, "There are lots of other mates here."

"I know," Reatur said. "It wouldn't be the same, somehow. Planting buds on you now would be like, like"—the domain-master sounded like someone groping after an idea—"like mating with a friend." He stopped in surprise. "That must be what the humans do, with their mates who live as long as males. It would be comforting, I think, especially in bad times."

"I suppose so," Lamra said indifferently. But the notion Reatur had presented was so strange, she couldn't help thinking about it. "If the humans keep me alive after my budlings drop, will I want to mate with you again?"

That seemed to surprise Reatur all over again. "I truly don't know, Lamra. If we're all very, very lucky, maybe we'll find out."

"Sometimes you just can't tell, Pat." Irv felt like an idiot the moment the words were out of his mouth, but he was lucky—Pat wasn't listening to him. She was off in that disconnected place where she had spent so much time since Frank hadn't answered his last radio call.

His wife glanced toward him and Pat, toward *Athena*, toward Reatur's castle. "I don't think that eloc mate is ever going to drop its budlings," Sarah said. They had checked the mate five times in the last two days. It looked ready, but it wasn't doing anything. "I'm going over to the castle to examine Lamra again," Sarah went on. "I just keep hoping she can hang on until we know we have some real chance of doing her some good."

Irv shrugged. "I think I'll head back to the ship. I'm hungry."

"Okay."

Sarah and Irv both paused, waiting for Pat to decide what she was going to do. She paused, too, as if rerunning a tape of the last few seconds in her head so that she could catch up with what was going on. Then she said, "I guess I'll go back to the ship, too."

"Make sure she eats something," Sarah told Irv. He thought about asking her whether she was speaking as doctor or Jewish mother, but keeping his mouth shut seemed smarter. A nod couldn't land him in trouble, but his big mouth had, many times already.

Sarah headed for the castle, pausing once to wave before she trudged on again. "Come on," Irv said to Pat. Again there was that delayed response, but less this time than before. She followed him to *Athena*.

Emmett Bragg met them just inside the airlock. " 'Bout time somebody showed up here," he grumbled. His pistol was belted on; Irv would have bet he had been pacing the corridor. "Don't want to leave the ship empty, and I need to go out and scout the route the Skarmer'll be using when they finally decide to get moving again. Won't be long now, I suspect.''

"Where's Louise?" Irv asked.

Bragg's eyes flicked to Pat. "She's—out," he said. Irv thought unkind thoughts about his mouth as he remembered Louise was out because she was doing some seismographic work that would—should—have been Frank's. Pat, luckily, didn't make the connection.

"Don't get too close to the Skarmer—or to Oleg Lopatin," Irv said. "Don't forget you're our ride home."

Emmett grimaced. "Don't remind me. I know I have to be a good boy, but I don't have to like it." He hurried out through the airlock, not bothering to hide his impatience to be gone. Things had been dull for him since *Athena* landed, Irv thought; Air Force pilots were adrenaline junkies from the word go. Well, Emmett had his fix now.

Irv turned back to Pat. "Let's see what we can find to eat."

"All right," she said indifferently.

The freeze-dried beef stew, Irv thought after he poured hot water into the package, tasted almost like what mother used to make, but not quite. He'd been eating it for so long that he had trouble defining the difference, but he knew it was there. Real food was one of the things he looked forward to about going home.

He rinsed the plastic tray, tossed it in the trash. Pat had only pushed her food around; hardly any of it was gone. "Come on. Eat," Irv said. He felt as if he were coaxing a reluctant toddler.

Pat took a couple of forkfuls, then put the package of stew down. "I don't feel much like eating. I don't feel much like anything." She would not look at Irv; she kept her eyes on her hands in her lap.

"You really should, Pat. We need you—" He hesitated. "—as strong as you can be." He hated himself for that little pause. Even more than the polite words it had been intended to replace, it called attention to what had happened.

Pat didn't answer. For a moment, Irv thought she was disconnected from the here-and-now again. Then he saw her shoulders shaking, saw two tears splash onto the backs of her wrists before she jerked up her arms to cover her face.

She hadn't cried before, not when Irv was there to see it and not, so far as he knew, any other time, either. "That's right," he urged, standing next to her. "It'll help you feel better. It's all right."

"It's not—all right." A gasped, hitching breath broke the sentence in half. "It's never going to be all right."

What do I say to that, Irv wondered, especially when it's true. Except for two of his grandparents, he had never lost anyone he loved. He knew how lucky he was. Because he was so lucky, he did not know firsthand how Pat felt, but he knew it was bad— worse now, he supposed, because she was letting what she had blocked away come out.

He bent down on one knee and put an awkward arm around her. She started to shake him off, then twisted in the chair until her head found the hollow of his shoulder. His other arm wrapped around her. Her tears were hot on the side of his neck. He held her while she cried herself out.

She looked ghastly when she finally raised her head—all the more so in the harsh blue-white glow of the fluorescent tube in the ceiling. Her blotched, wet-streaked face reminded Irv again of the toddler he had thought about a few minutes before. But the feel of her against him was like no toddler's.

He shook his head at the distracting thought and reached out and snagged a paper towel off the tabletop. "Here," he said. "Blow."

Pat did, noisily, and dabbed at her eyes. "Thank you," she said, and then again, in a different tone of voice, "Thank you."

"It's all right."

He was still holding her with one arm. When he started to pull back, she clung to him. "Don't let go, not yet, please," she said. "I wasn't, haven't been able to feel anything since—" Irv thought she was going to let that hang, but she made herself go on. "—since Frank got killed. It's like most of me's been stuck inside a glass specimen jar. I see things, hear things, but they don't connect, they just bounce off the glass. This—I really know you're here with me."

"Okay." That was one way of dealing with shock, Irv knew. If nothing got through the glass, nothing could hurt.

"Give me that paper towel again, would you?" Pat wiped at her face, crumpled the towel, and threw it away. "I must look like hell."

"Frankly, yes."

She let out a strangled snort that might have been—Irv hoped it was—the first laugh from her since her husband died. "You always say the sweetest things, Irv."

"I try."

He kept his tone deliberately light, but Pat's reply was serious. "I know. Thanks one more time." She held on to him, too, as if afraid to stop. "So good to feel something, anything, again."

"Good. That's good, Pat." Irv's brain was handling mixed signals. Consciously, he was glad he was able to do as a friend should, able to help Pat begin to accept her loss. Through his hands, through his skin, he picked up another message. He was very much aware that for some time he had been holding a woman in his arms.

More than anything else, he was annoyed with his physical response to that. *Not* the time or place, he thought. For a crazy moment, he felt seventeen again, walking from class to class with his books held awkwardly in front of him to hide an incongruous erection.

The Pat leaned close and kissed him on the cheek. It was not meant to be a passionate kiss; thinking back later, Irv was sure of that. Nor was the one he intended to give back. But instead of her cheek, his mouth found hers. With a sound half sigh, half groan, she clutched him to her.

There must have been some time in the minutes that followed when their lips were separated long enough for Irv to say *no* or *stop* or something of the sort. Afterward, that seemed logically certain, but he never could figure out when it might have been. Even when they were helping each other pull off boots and trousers, their mouths stayed glued together, and his still covered hers and helped quiet her moan soon after. A moment later, he made noises of his own and was similarly muffled.

Coming back to himself was nothing like the afterglow he cherished. It felt more like breaking a fever: what had just ended seemed strange and unreal, as if it had happened to someone else. But Pat's smooth thighs still gripped him; he still looked into her face from only a couple of inches away.

I'm sorry, was the first thing that occurred to him to say. That, he knew, was wrong. He levered himself with his arms and pushed off against the floor so he sat back on his knees. "I think we've been stupid," he said slowly.

Pat sat up, too, and reached for her pants. "You're probably right," she said as she started to put them on. "This isn't like the last time I—wanted you, though. I didn't expect it to happen. I didn't even particularly want it to happen. It just did."

"Yeah," Irv said. He started getting dressed, too. "I know." And what the hell am I going to do about it, he wondered. At the moment, he had no idea. "I didn't expect it to happen, either. I was just trying to comfort you, any way I could—" He pulled on socks. One didn't fit. It was Pat's. He tossed it to her.

She was nodding. "—and God knows I was looking for comfort, any place I could find it. You want to call it shared battle fatigue or something, and let it go at that?"

"That might be the best thing to do." That way, Irv thought, we can pretend—*I* can pretend—it never happened at all. He wished it never had happened at all. Wishing did just as much good as usual.

"Okay," Pat said. "I know what you were trying to do. Maybe you even did it. I guess I have to make myself go on, figure out how to go on, without Frank." She stood up. "Right now, I'm going off to the john for a minute." Irv winced. Pat saw it. "All right," she said, "I won't talk about it anymore. But this once, happening like it did, wasn't the same as it would have been a lot of other ways."

"Yeah," Irv said. He watched Pat walk out, then climbed into a chair. What she said was true. It even helped. Trouble was, it didn't help enough.

He got up, looked at himself in the glass of the microwave's door. It wasn't much of a mirror, but he doubted he could look at himself in much of a mirror. "Stupid," he told his reflection. It didn't argue with him.

He heard the airlock doors open, first the outer, then the inner. "Anybody home?" Sarah called. Irv was not an adrenaline junkie. The sound of his wife's voice almost made him jump out of his skin. "Anybody home?" Sarah said again.

"Back here," he answered. His voice, he thought, came out as a hoarse croak. He discovered another reason why he hadn't cheated on Sarah before: he didn't seem to be very good at it.

Sarah came walking down the passageway. "What took you so long?" she asked, sticking her head into the galley.

"Sorry."

She shrugged, took off her gloves, rubbed her hands together. "I'm going to make myself some coffee. Want any?"

Maybe he was only imagining how he sounded; Sarah didn't seem to notice anything wrong. "Sure," he said. "Thanks."

Sarah put two cups of water in the microwave. Pat came

in. Sarah glanced up. Irv waited for the world to fall to pieces. Sarah said, "Hi. I'm making coffee. Shall I put another cup in for you?"

"Would you?" Pat said. "I could use some."

"Sure." Sarah filled a third cup. The microwave started its soft whir. Over it, Sarah said to Pat, "You sound a little better."

Pat nodded. "I think maybe I am, finally. I've got to—we all have to—get on with things, no matter what's happened. I'm sorry I've been so useless. I just . . . needed some time, I guess."

"Of course you did," Sarah said. The microwave chimed. She got out the boiling water, poured in instant coffee, passed around the cups. "Here you go, folks, caffeinated mud. Real coffee is another thing I'll want lots of when we get home."

"Amen," Irv agreed. "Could be worse, though—don't the Russians have instant tea?" The idea of that drew groans from everyone.

"How's Lamra?" Pat asked.

"You *are* better," Sarah said, sounding pleased. "That's the first time in a good long while you've cared about what's going on. As for Lamra, she's very much herself, only more so, if you know what I mean. She has this new wooden toy runnerpest—maybe Reatur made it for her; I don't know—that she carries around everywhere. Won't let go of it for hell. She doesn't try to mother it, though, the way a little girl would with a doll. Not much call for learning to be a mommy on Minerva." That comment extinguished smiles from the faces of Pat and Irv.

"Not much longer now," Irv said.

"No—we have to keep those clamps and bandage packs handy," Sarah said. "We may need 'em any time. I just hope they'll do some good."

"We give it our best shot. That's all we can do. Having Pat"—he did not look at her and picked his words carefully—"feeling more like herself can't do anything but help."

"I hope so," Pat said.

"Irv's right. We might make this work yet." Sarah looked happier at the prospect than she had for a while herself.

Irv finished his coffee. Relief almost drowned guilt: evidently he didn't have a large scarlet *A* tattooed on his forehead after all. He couldn't forget those few incandescent minutes with Pat, but maybe, just maybe, he could convince himself they didn't matter very much.

And maybe he couldn't, too. While Sarah slept quietly beside him, her warm breath sometimes tickling his ear, he lay awake himself most of the night. "A conscience is a useless piece of baggage," he whispered. His, however, wasn't listening. For that matter, not even the rest of him believed it.

11

"They're coming!" It was anything but the best news in the world, Reatur thought as he heard the messenger's shout. That he had been expecting it did not make it any easier to take.

His males heard it, too. Some peered over the barricade of ice and snow on which they had been working frantically for the last few days. The Skarmer were not yet in sight. Reatur was glad the weather was staying right around the place where ice melted, so he and the males could work with both snow and water to create a sturdy barrier against the invaders. Had it been too hot to keep snow on the ground, they would have had to try to build the rampart of earth, which would have taken impossibly long.

The domain-master poked an eyestalk over the barrier himself, turned another on Emmett beside him. "Soon we will see them," Reatur said. "And then—"

The human jerked the places where his arms met his body in his kind's gesture of uncertainty. "And then we do what we do," he said. He had less of the Omalo tongue than the other humans.

"You *will* use your noise-weapon, too?" Reatur asked worriedly. It did not look like much; Emmett's big hand almost swallowed it. But the human had demonstrated it once, with lots of Reatur's warriors to see and hear. The roar, the flash had been much like the ones that worked such ruin on them at the edge of Ervis Gorge. "The males will be braver, knowing we can match the Skarmer."

"*Not* match," Emmett said sharply but quietly so the warriors close by would not hear. "Skarmer weapon shoot more, shoot farther."

"Yes, I know that. You explained it before." Reatur spoke as softly as the human. "But my males do not, so they will be braver. And the Skarmer do not, so they may take fright when you thunder at them."

"Good plan," Emmett agreed. That pleased Reatur; no matter how weird humans were, this one seemed to know a good deal about fighting. Now he was talking into the box that carried voices. Reatur wished he understood what Emmett was saying; he had only learned a few words of human speech. Now he had to ask, "Is all well, back beyond the castle?"

"All well," Emmett said. "They wait."

"So do we," Reatur said. Most times, he would sooner have acted than paused here to let the Skarmer descend on him. But if he attacked them in the open, he would be like a fat massi coming up to a male, too stupid to know it was about to be speared. The noise-weapon made that certain. Thus he waited, on ground of his own choosing.

His warriors' babble changed tone. The eyestalk that was looking northwest over the barrier told him why. The males emerging from in back of some gentle high ground could only be the enemy.

Some of them stopped short when they saw the obstacle the Omalo had thrown up in their path. The Skarmer could not go around it: it stretched from one patch of woods to another. If they wanted to fight Reatur's warriors, they would have to come straight at them.

More and more Skarmer came out. They began to deploy, forming into fighting clusters. The Omalo yelled abuse at them, though they did not understand the local tongue and were still too far away to hear much anyhow.

"Fralk has a funny way of arranging his warriors," Reatur said, poking up another couple of eyestalks so he could take in the whole picture at once. "Why that gap in the center? More of his males should be there, to meet us where we are strongest. But there are only an eighteen or so."

With one of the eyes that wasn't looking out at the Skarmer army, the domain-master saw Emmett looking over the rampart, too. The human had a gadget over his own eyes—not the noise-weapon, but something else. "Help me see farther," Emmett explained, lowering the device. "I see human there in center."

Always deep and, to Reatur, fierce-sounding, his voice was frighteningly grim now.

"A human." After a moment's thought, the domain-master realized what that meant. "Oh. That is where the noise-weapon will be."

"Yes."

"And he doesn't have his own males there so he won't hit them with the stones or whatever it is that the noise-weapon spits."

"Yes," Emmett said again. He made his mouth twist into the shape humans used to show amusement. Now he had his weapon again. "We give Fralk new thing to think about, yes?"

"Yes." The word felt good to Reatur. Fralk had been pulling him around by the eyestalks ever since the Skarmer forced their way out of Ervis Gorge. He had been reacting to what his enemy did. Let Fralk react for a change. "Go ahead, Emmett."

The human aimed the noise-weapon over the rampart, made it roar. Having it go off next to Reatur was like taking up residence in the middle of a thunderstorm. The domain-master did not care. "See how you like it coming your way, Fralk!" he yelled.

A flash, a boom—Fralk froze in horror. Turning four eyestalks toward Oleg, he screamed, *"You told me they didn't have rifles!"* He was too shaken to bother with the human language.

Oleg followed the Skarmer speech. "Not a rifle," he answered in the same language. He also followed Fralk, literally: a guard jerked him along by a cord tied around him between his arms and head.

"What do you mean, not a rifle?" Fralk shouted, still frantic. Flash, boom—another shot punctuated his words. With the couple of eyes that weren't on the human, he saw his males begin to waver. They hadn't expected the Omalo to have a weapon to match theirs.

"Not a rifle," Oleg repeated. "That is *pistol*"—a human word Fralk hadn't heard before, but one Oleg went on to explain—"like rifle, but not as good. Not shoot so far, not shoot so fast. Not hurt us where we are here."

"Oh." That made Fralk feel a little better, but not much. Flash, boom—his warriors were definitely having second thoughts now. *They* didn't know the *pistol* was too far away for its bullets to reach them. Fralk thought furiously. "Can I kill whoever has the *pistol* from here?" he asked.

"Maybe," Oleg said.

That was all Fralk needed to hear. He pointed his rifle in the direction from which the Omalo had shot, set the change lever to full automatic, and fired a long, satisfying burst. Ice splashed from the Omalo barrier.

"Do you think I got him?" he asked.

"Maybe," Oleg said again, this time in his own language. "As for what I think, *nichevo*. Soon enough you will know. If he does not shoot back, you got him. If he does, you did not."

Flash, boom—Fralk cursed.

Emmet Bragg was having fun, only slightly hampered by the fact that, as Irv had reminded him a couple of days before, he couldn't afford to do anything stupid. Had only his own neck been on the line, he would have worried a lot less. But four other people were depending on him to get them back to Earth. With Frank dead, he didn't even have a well-trained backup.

So he threw himself flat on his belly the second the Kalashnikov started barking and stayed there till well after the burst was done. The wisdom might have been forced on him, but it was wisdom nonetheless: a couple of rounds punched through the barrier to wound Minervans behind it. One might have got him, had he not hit the deck when he did—the snow and ice it kicked out froze the back of his neck.

More males fell from bullets that had clipped them above the level of the rampart. Still, Bragg thought, most of the rounds from the burst had gone high. That was bad shooting, worse than he had expected from the Russian. Maybe it was because Lopatin was KGB and hadn't got proper training.

"Isn't that too bad for him?" Bragg muttered. He was just glad Sergei Tolmasov was on the far side of Jötun Canyon. Tolmasov, he was grimly certain, would not have used the AK-74 like an amateur.

Staying low, Bragg scrambled twenty yard to his right, jumped up for a quick shot over the barrier, then dove onto his stomach again. A short burst chewed up the ice and snow almost at once, followed a few seconds later by a long one.

"Changed clips again, did you? Good," Bragg said, as if he were playing poker, not soldier, against the man with the rifle. "Now how many do you have left?" That was a question, all right. Lopatin, he thought, was shooting as though he had brought along a truckload.

This time, Bragg crawled a couple of hundred feet to his left, almost to the trees anchoring that end of the line. He popped up for three shots at Fralk's right wing. They might even have done some damage; the Minervans there weren't much more than a hundred yards away now, and they made a big target. Bragg didn't stay up long enough to look, which was just as well—the answering fusillade came hard on the heels of his last shot.

Reloading while on his belly was not a skill he had practiced much since basic-training days, but he managed. Still down there, he pulled out his radio and called his wife. "You all ready there?"

"Ready as we'll ever be." Louise's voice emerged tinnily. "Is that that damn gun I hear, Emmett? Watch yourself, now."

He chuckled. "I intend to, hon. Love you. Next time I call, I'll really need you. Out."

He started making his way back toward the center of the line and quickly forgot about Louise. He did love her, as he had said, but he loved what he was doing more. He had loved Carleen, too, come to that, but he had figured out early on he was never going to make it to Minerva married to a historian of ancient Rome.

Crazy, the stuff that goes through your mind, he thought. Carleen hadn't, certainly not since Athena touched down. He dismissed the memory of her once more as he got back to Reatur.

The domain-master said, "Well done. They're still coming, but with arms and eyestalks pulled in partway. They don't like being on the wrong side of your human noise-weapons any more than my warriors do."

Bragg jabbed a thumb at himself. "Not like, either," he said. Reatur's eyestalks wiggled. Bragg went on, "Now try to kill their human male with noise-weapon. Then we win—Skarmer lose courage when that male fall."

"A human does not have their noise-weapon," Reatur said. "It is the eldest of eldest of the Skarmer domain-master, the male called Fralk."

"Is it?" Bragg wondered what the hell Lopatin was playing at. Whatever it was, it explained the bad shooting from the other side. The mission commander shrugged. Maybe it made his job easier. "Try to kill Fralk, then."

"I want to tell you no," Reatur said. Bragg looked at him in surprise. The domain-master explained, "I want to kill him my-self. But you are right, Emmett. Slay him now, if you can."

Reatur was a soldier like none America had known since the

War Between the States, Bragg thought—he took his fighting personally. The pilot readied himself. He wished he had been a cop: some work with the pop-up targets the police used would have come in handy now.

He bounced up and shot with a two-hand grip, one round after another, aiming at the Kalashnikov. His attention focused so completely on the rifle that he had fired several times before he even noticed Oleg Lopatin a few paces away, and twice after that before he saw the rope around the Russian's neck. So things weren't all going Lopatin's way, he thought. Well, tough luck, Oleg Borisovich—serves you right.

The hammer clicked. The pistol was empty again. Bragg hit the dirt to reload. A moment after he did, the Kalashnikov started chewing away at the barrier in front of him. "Shit," he said. He was just glad Fralk couldn't shoot for beans.

Reatur's guess was a good one: Fralk did not care at all for being shot at. A bullet kicked up snow and dirt at his feet. Another two zipped past him, closer than he ever wanted to think about. And two more struck a male close by Fralk. He did not even scream before he fell.

"Get back out of range, you idiot, before you get killed and get me killed with you!" Oleg yelled.

Fralk needed a moment to understand the human, another to figure out that he made good sense. "Back!" Fralk called. Several males in his small band had not waited for the order. He would deal with them later. "How far can that cursed pistol shoot?" he asked Oleg when they had retreated a good way.

"This should be far enough," the human said, adding, "unless the man with the pistol there gets very lucky."

Fralk thought about retreating some more, but enough males around him understood human speech to make that look like cowardice. He fired several rounds in the direction from which the shots had come but doubted they would do much good. The human on the other side of that frozen wall seemed to have a knack for surviving.

"What I will do," Fralk decided, "is stay here and use the rifle to help our warriors on the flanks. I can reach the whole field from this place, and the pistol cannot. That still leaves us with the advantage."

"*Khorosho*, Fralk, *ochen khorosho*," Oleg said. "You are beginning to understand how to use your firepower. If you have more range than your enemy, you set up where you can hurt him and he cannot hurt you."

That made sense to Fralk, but he still felt peculiar standing off in the distance while his males and the Omalo first flung spears at each other and then began using those spears—and every other weapon on which they could lay their hands—at close quarters as the Skarmer tried to force their foes back from the barricade.

Several Omalo warriors stood very tall to thrust at Fralk's warriors. He fired a short burst. One of the enemy males tumbled away from the barrier, the upper part of his body a chewed, bloody ruin. The other Omalo warriors flinched away. A couple of Skarmer started to climb over the frozen wall.

Fralk shifted his aim from one end of the line to the other, squeezed the trigger again. He was not sure he hit anyone this time, but the Omalo flinched anyhow. Skarmer males started trying to get over the barrier there, too.

"If they can make it to the far side in any numbers, we have them," Fralk declared.

"*Da,*" Lopatin agreed. After the fighting was done, Fralk knew he would have to figure out what to do with the human, but now he valued his thoughts. Fralk felt pleased at regaining his equanimity: this was the first time since that other human had shot at him that he found himself able to plan for what would happen after the fighting was done.

Reatur flung a spear at one of the Skarmer scrambling over the rampart. It missed his target, but might have hit a warrior further on—the enemy was tightly packed at that part of the barrier. The domain-master shouted and waved his arms when one of his males killed the Skarmer with an ax.

But for every Skarmer who died, another—often more than one—did his best to climb over. "If they make it to this side in any numbers, we're done for," Reatur said.

"I know." Emmett dodged a spear. His long legs made him extraordinarily nimble, Reatur thought.

Off in the distance, too far away for Emmett to strike back, Fralk's noise-weapon began its deadly chatter once more. One Omalo male shrieked, then another, then another.

"They fight good," Emmett said. "Sometimes—often—human warriors run away from noise-weapons, first time see, hear them. Your males brave, Reatur."

The praise pleased the domain-master. "Where would they

run?'' he asked. "If they lose here, they lose everything. They know it. But"—he let his deepest fear come out—"I doubt even they can hold against terror forever.''

"You right, I think.'' Emmett took out his talking-box, spoke urgently into it in his own language. He put it away, dipped his head to Reatur. "We do what we can.''

Irv stuffed the radio back into his pocket. "You heard the man,'' he said. Louise Bragg nodded. So did Sarah. She had been limbering up every few minutes, ever since the battle started a few miles northwest. Now she started stretching in earnest.

"Let's give it one last check,'' Louise said to Irv.

"Good plan.'' They walked over to *Damselfly* together and went over it strut by strut, wire by wire, joining by joining. They checked the thin plastic skin of wings, tail, and cabin to make sure it hadn't developed any holes that could rip wide open in the air. They didn't find anything. Irv started checking again.

"Are we good?'' Sarah demanded. She was peeling off parka and long pants, hopping up and down to stay warm in the Minervan summer sun. "If we are, we don't have time to waste.''

"We're good,'' Irv said reluctantly. He gave his wife a fierce hug. "Be careful. I love you.'' Ending up in bed—or rather, on the floor—with Pat hadn't done anything to change that. It just made him feel like a hypocritical bastard when he said that to Sarah.

"Love you, too,'' she answered now. He wondered what she would say if she ever found out. He was full of scientific curiosity, but that was one thing he did not want to know.

He set the wide stepladder by *Damselfly*, helped Sarah climb in, then lowered the canopy. The sound of the hooks-and-eyes snapping it closed, shutting Sarah away from him, seemed dreadfully final. Shaking his head, he got down from the stepladder and carried it out of the way. Then he went over and took hold of a wingtip.

Louise had the other one. She also had her radio out. Irv took his out, too. "Testing,'' he heard Louise say. "One, two, three, four . . . how do you read *Damselfly*?''

"Read you five by five,'' Sarah answered. Irv heard her both in the speaker and directly. "How do you read me?''

"Loud and clear. Break a leg, kiddo,'' Louise said.

"Don't tempt me.'' Sarah started to pedal. "Let's get the batteries good and charged.'' A few minutes later, she said,

"Okay—here we go." She let the prop spin. *Damselfly* rolled forward. Irv and Louise ran with it, keeping the wing level.

"Airborne!" Irv shouted. Sarah took one hand off the control stick to wave, then gave all her concentration back to flying. Irv watched *Damselfly* slowly climb. "There goes the the funniest looking warplane in the history of—two worlds," he said.

"No arguments." Louise was on the radio again, on a different frequency. "Emmett, are you there?" she called worriedly. "Come in."

"I'm here," he answered. "Busy, but still here."

"*Damselfly*'s on its way now," she told him.

"Not a minute too soon. Out."

"Out." Louise turned to Irv. "Now we can only wait."

"The fun part," he agreed. "I'd rather be doing something, doing anything, than just standing around here."

"Me, too," Louise said. "I hate it when something that's important to me is out of my hands."

"Sarah said the same thing when Emmett was landing *Athena*. It's all in her hands now, though." Irv made sure his radio was on *Damselfly*'s frequency. "How you doing there, honey? How does the plane handle with the changes we made in it?"

"Doing all right," Sarah answered. "The extra weight isn't bad, about what I'd have if I were pedaling in my parka. And I'm not getting enough extra drag even to notice—gaining altitude shouldn't be a problem."

"Good," Irv said. "Out." He wanted Sarah as high as possible above the slings and arrows—to say nothing of axes and spears—of outrageous fortune. To Louise, he said, "Now what? Head over toward *Athena*?"

She was gathering up Sarah's discarded outer layers of clothing. "I think we'd better," she said. "We've never all been away at once before, and we sure as hell don't want to have to try to talk or fight our way through to the ship if—if Reatur loses."

"No," Irv said, although the odds of Emmett's getting free if Reatur lost were slim, and without Emmett, getting back to the ship didn't matter in the long run anyhow. Louise, of course, could figure that out for herself as well as he could and doubtless had.

They had only gone a couple of hundred yards when their radios crackled to life again. Ice that had nothing to do with the weather formed in Irv's midsection as he lifted his set to his ear—only bad news would make Emmett call back so soon.

But Pat was on the radio, not Emmett. She was in Reatur's

castle, checking on Lamra. "Has Sarah taken off yet?" she asked.

"A few minutes ago," Irv said. "Why?" He had a bad feeling he knew the answer before he asked the question.

He did. Pat said, "Because Lamra's getting ready to drop those budlings *now*, and I don't think she's going to wait around."

"Shit," Irv said softly. He could still see *Damselfy* off in the distance. Sarah was banking into a long, slow, gentle turn, the only kind the ultra-ultralight could make. He could still call her back—and most likely throw away the battle and Emmett with it . . . and Lamra and her budlings, too, come to that, if Reatur's males were beaten.

"What do we do?" Louise asked.

He kicked at frozen dirt, made his choice. "How are you at coping with gore?"

"I won't lose my lunch, if that's what you mean," Louise answered at once. "You want me to help you try to save the Minervan?"

"That's just what I want. Hang on to Sarah's clothes. She's got clamps and bandages in one of those pockets. Pat and I will coach you through as best we can. You've got to be quick and accurate twice. Each of us does, and if we are, we have a chance." Irv wished he were as confident as he sounded. It hadn't happened yet, not even once.

"I'm not the person you need," Louise said.

"You're the person I've got. Come on." They ran for the castle.

The world wheeled under Sarah as she began another slow, careful clockwise turn. The cold breeze coming in through the fresh-air tube helped take away the stink of the gunk sprayed all over the bottom of the cabin.

A great circle, she thought—surely this was the long way around to deliver a surprise to the Skarmer. It had a couple of advantages, though. For one thing, it gave her plenty of time in which to make *Damselfly* climb. She knew she had sugarcoated what she had told Irv. Even in dense Minervan air, the ultra-ultralight climbed like a fat man going up a tall ladder. It wasn't any worse now than it had been before they fiddled with it, though, so she hadn't really lied.

The route she was flying would also let her come up from behind the Skarmer, as far as the idea of *behind* meant anything when dealing with Minervans. This once, Emmett had argued—persuasively, worse luck!—it just might. Males in a battle ought to have sense enough to keep all their eyestalks pointed in the direction from which danger came—toward Reatur's warriors, in other words. They shouldn't spot her till too late.

Ought to, shouldn't, ought to, shouldn't . . . "If you're wrong, Emmett, I'll never speak to you again." Sarah panted. That, she feared, was no joke. Her stomach did flipflops when she thought about what a burst of Kalashnikov fire would do to *Damselfly*—and to her.

Fighter pilots, she realized suddenly, earned every penny they got, and then some.

"Never seen this place so deserted," Irv said, puffing. His footsteps and Louise's echoed down the hallways of Reatur's castle. On any other day, the noise of dozens of males would have drowned them out. Now he had only seen a couple, one barely full-grown and the other ancient.

"At the battle." Louise, also getting her breath back, was short with words.

The usual racket pierced the doors of the mates' chambers: mates were sheltered from worries about their fate. Or rather, Irv thought, they never got the chance to grow enough to understand what worrying about their fate meant. Maybe that would start to change today. Maybe.

The guard outside the doors widened himself as the humans came up. *He* was in his prime, standing by a post Reatur reckoned important enough to keep him out of the fighting. "What word?" he asked anxiously.

"I do not know," Irv answered. "The battle still goes on. Let us pass now, please."

The male unbarred the doors, shut them again behind Irv and Louise. Mates rushed from everywhere at the boom of the falling bar, then drew back, disappointed, when they saw only humans, not Reatur.

"Pat?" Louise called.

"In here." Irv shook his head when he noticed from which chamber the answer came. It was the one in which Biyal had died. He did not think of himself as superstitious, but he wished Lamra were somewhere else.

Lamra lifted an eyestalk when he and Louise came in. "Hello," the mate said. "Pat told me I should not say goodbye, not yet."

"No, not yet," Irv said soberly. Soon, though, maybe, he thought and scowled at himself. He could hear the unease in his voice when he asked Pat, "How's she doing?"

"See for yourself. The skin is splitting."

"So it is." Irv stooped and switched to the Omalo language. "Lift the arm by me, please, Lamra." Lamra did. The mate kept her fist closed, but Irv saw the gray-brown of Minervan wood between her fingerclaws: the precious toy runnerpest, he supposed.

He smiled at that a little and waved Louise down beside him. "See?" he said, pointing at the growing vertical slit over the bud. Louise nodded. "In a few minutes, as the opening gets longer and wider, you'll be able to see the whole budling, and how it's hooked on to Lamra by its mouth. When it falls away— when it's born, I mean—it'll drop off. That'll be that, unless we can clamp the vessel it was feeding from, and the ones for the other five, too. With two for each of us, we may have a chance."

"We can't afford any fumbling, though." Pat sounded as if she was talking as much to herself as to Louise. "We've got to be right the first time."

Louise got clamps, bandage packs, and rolls of tape out of Sarah's parka. "I'll do the best I can," she said. She didn't seem nervous; she sounded intrigued, like an engineer sizing up a new and challenging problem. Only fair, Irv thought—she was one.

"Let's take our places," he said. The budling's wiggling feet were already pushing through the opening in Lamra's skin. So, through the other slits, were those of its brothers and sisters. Irv slid over to Louise's right; Pat was on her left.

"What about the six vessels around each central one?" Louise asked. "Shouldn't we clamp those, too?"

"The bandages should take care of them," Pat said. "They're all small, compared to the one in the middle. That's the one— the two, rather—you've got to worry about. When the budlings drop, they'll go like a fire hydrant hit by a car."

Irv grimaced. That was a more graphic simile than he wanted to think about. He switched to the Omalo tongue again. "How do you feel, Lamra?" The mate, after all, was no experimental animal, but a person, too, and a young person, at that. She had to be wondering, worrying about, what would happen next.

"It doesn't hurt now," Lamra said after a moment's pause, perhaps for taking stock. "Will it hurt later, when you stop me from ending?"

"I don't think so," Irv said, as reassuringly as he could. Actually, he had no idea. He hoped he—and Lamra—would find out. He also hoped the mate was as confident as she sounded. *When you stop me from ending* . . . He knew that *when* was an *if*. If Lamra didn't, more power to her, for as much time as she had.

They would soon know how long that would be. The arms and eyestalks of the budling in front of Irv were twitching now along with its legs; its mouth was tightly clamped round the big blood vessel that fed it.

"Any minute—" Pat breathed. If she was going to add "now," she never got the chance. Lamra's budlings all let go at once. Blood gushed forth in a torrent that astonished Irv anew every time he saw it.

The clamps were on the ground between his feet. He seized the spurting vessel in front of him with one hand, snatched up a clamp, stuck it on. That flood slowed to a drip. He shifted leftward, grabbing for the second bleeder and the other clamp.

At almost the same instant, Pat shifted to her right. Just as he had, she had started on the blood vessel further away from Louise so she could deal with both of hers and be in position to help.

Irv fumbled with the second clamp, got it on at last. He looked toward Louise. "How you doing?" he asked. "Need a hand?" From the engineer's other side, Pat was using nearly the same words to ask the same thing.

"I'm done, I think," Louise answered. Like her colleagues—like the chamber—she was spattered and dripping with gore. She wiped the back of a hand across her face, which only made matters worse. With an engineer's caution, she went on, "Check me, will you?"

Irv looked at one of the vessels she had repaired, Pat at the other. Irv gave a thumbs-up a moment later; the clamp was on perhaps more securely than either of the ones he had done.

"This one's fine, Louise," Pat said. "Well done. I'm officially impressed."

"You told me what to do, and I did it." Louise seemed surprised anyone would make much of simple competence. "Shall we get the bandage packs on now?"

"Yeah, we'd better." Irv started to walk over to pick up bandages and tape, but almost tripped on one of the newly hatched budlings. All six of them were scrambling around like so many little wild animals—which, Irv supposed, in essence they were.

Their squawks were calliope-whistle shrill. "When we're done, we'll have to catch these critters," he said.

He was taping the first gauze-soaked sweat sock into place when he suddenly realized Lamra had neither said anything nor moved in some time. He could not afford to think about that, not until the other bandage was on. Then, with the emergency work done as well as could be, he took a step back—a careful step, so as not to step on a budling—to see how the mate was doing.

"Lamra?" he asked. She did not answer. All the eyes Irv could see were closed, and her eyestalks hung down against her body. So did her arms. They were not as limp, he thought, as those of the eloc mates he had failed to save. But the toy run-nerpest had fallen in the blood between her feet.

"Lamra?" he asked again. Still no reply.

"Now what?" Louise asked.

Irv shook his head, baffled, fearful, but still hopeful. "Now we wait. . . ."

"Progress at last!" Fralk shouted. At the eastern end of the fight, the Skarmer warriors had finally forced Reatur's males back from the barrier. But the Omalo, curse their stubborn ways, would not flee. They fought on, holding a line against Fralk's warriors. Progress it was, but not enough.

And from where he was, Fralk could not help make it more. His males stood between him and the enemy. He could not use the rifle, not without doing the Skarmer more harm than the Omalo.

"We shall advance," he declared. "From a position nearer the barricade, I will be able to pour a flood of bullets into the foe. They will surely break then, and our gallant males will be able to surround them."

"We advance!" the males with him shouted. They shook their spears and axes. Most of them, Fralk guessed, had resented being kept out of the fighting.

"The pistol—" Oleg said.

"Shut up, coward! Come on," his keeper growled, understanding the word the human had used before. He tugged on the rope. Oleg stumbled forward.

"Do not worry about the pistol, Oleg Borisovich," Fralk said in the human speech. "It has not boomed for a long time now. Surely the human who has it is out of bullets." He waited for Oleg's reply. Oleg only made the gesture humans used for a shrug. Fralk shrugged, too. "Toward the fighting!" he cried grandly, playing to the pride of the warriors with him.

"Toward the fighting!" they yelled back, and toward the fighting they went.

"He's in among that little bunch near the center. . . . There! He just fired a burst. See the muzzle flashes?"

"I see them, Emmett." Sarah wondered how Emmett's voice could come so calmly through the radio. The battlefield ahead looked like 200-proof chaos, nothing else but. Down there, she knew she would have been scared shitless—she was scared plenty up here. But Emmett seemed in his element.

He had read the Minervans well, too. So far none of the Skarmer had spotted her, though she was less than half a mile behind their army, flying straight down its line of march. A minute to target, maybe a minute and a half. Time to get ready.

Her left thumb clicked the POWER switch to ON. She would need all the help she could get from the batteries, because her pedaling was going to have to suffer now.

She reached down, peeled up a square of mylar that was only taped in place. Cold wind blew into her face. She pulled a butane lighter from the waistband of her shorts and flicked the little metal lever till it caught. She lowered the flame toward the wick on the gallon bottle that hung just behind her front wheel.

The wind blew it out.

She swore, flicked the lever again, and then glanced up to see if the Minervans had spotted her yet. Damn, they had! She would never get to make another pass. The lighter lit. Thanking God for the fire-retardant chemicals that were stinking up the cabin, she made the flame Bunsen-burner big.

The wick was not soaked with fire-retardants—very much the opposite. This time, it caught.

"Move, curse you, you worthless traitor," snarled the Minervan who had hold of Oleg Lopatin's leash. Lopatin had no choice but to move. He glared at the warrior. *If only I had you back in Lefortovo Prison,* he thought longingly, *you would learn just what an amateur at torment you are.* The KGB man knew how futile such dreams of revenge were. But they helped keep him going, anyhow.

Fralk fired again. His band was less than a hundred meters from the Omalo barricade. Any second now, Lopatin expected the American back of the barrier to prove Fralk wrong and with a little luck fill him full of holes. Lopatin would have saved a few rounds for another good chance at taking out the Kalashnikov, and he was sure anyone smart enough to make it onto *Athena*'s crew would also be smart enough to do the same.

Maybe, he thought with a sudden savage grin, the American would fill his kennel-master full of holes. *There* was a revenge that might be no dream.

One of the other high-ranking Minervans in Fralk's group let out a startled squeal—he sounded amazingly like a housewife spotting a rat. "A monster in the sky!" he shrieked. "Look! Three arms away from the battle—it's coming straight at us!"

Eyestalks writhed. Lopatin's head whipped around. He had never seen *Damselfly* before, but he knew what it was. The Skarmer did not. That first scream was quickly echoed by many more.

Lopatin's keeper had two eyes on the human, two on the battle, and two on the new flying horror. That left none to pay attention to the small green-brown bush by his feet. One of those feet brushed it. The keeper jerked, went limp. The rope slipped from his fingerclaws.

"A pestilence!" one of the other males shouted. "Nogdar just stepped on a stunbush! Grab that rope, somebody!"

Too late. Lopatin was free.

A spear, wildly flung, whizzed past *Damselfly*. Sarah did her best to ignore it; she couldn't do anything about it, anyway. Fortunately, most of the Minervans seemed too scared of the ultra-ultralight to think of trying to bring it down.

There was her target, dead ahead. She leaned down again, this time with a Swiss army knife in her hand.

Seeing the monster fly hissing toward him, Fralk wanted to void where he stood. He needed an instant to remember he was still holding the rifle. A rifle had chewed the krong to bloody rags. Anything that could kill a krong ought to be able to take out a sky-monster, he thought.

The cursed rifle was on the wrong side of his body to shoot at the thing! Fast as he could, he passed it from arm to arm.

Oleg Lopatin looked at *Damselfly*, looked at Fralk, and discovered, as so many had before him, one of the great flaws of international socialism: when faced with a choice between their own kind and an ideology, most people chose their own kind.

Lopatin did not pause to reason that out. He just yelled and jumped on Fralk.

The Swiss army knife cut the string that ran through the handle of the gallon jug filled with wood alcohol, naphtha, and butane. *Damselfly* seemed to leap higher in the air as the weight it had never been designed to carry dropped away.

The Kalashnikov bellowed, right under Sarah. She screamed, expecting to die in the next second. No bullets ripped through her. *Damselfly* did not tumble in ruins to the ground.

She couldn't even look back. She didn't have a rear-view mirror. All she could do was pedal and pray.

Then Emmett Bragg's hoarse voice came yelling out of the radio: "You can play in my league any day, darlin'! One extra large Molotov cocktail, right on target. Smoked 'em *both*!" He let go with a rebel yell that was almost too much for the little speaker.

"Both?" Sarah panted. She flew over Reatur's barricade, onto the side his males held. As her fear-induced adrenaline rush began to fade, she realized how tired she was.

"The Minervan and the Russian, too."

"Oh. Oh, Jesus. Didn't I see him fighting with the Minervan, trying to keep him from shooting me down?" If she had dumped hellfire on somebody trying to save her . . . She wanted to be sick.

But Bragg said coldly, "Well, what if you did? Hadn't been for Lopatin, that Minervan never would have had a rifle in the first place. And if he didn't, a lot of people—Frank maybe, a lot of Reatur's males for sure—would still be alive. Besides, nothin' you can do about it now, anyhow."

"You're right," she conceded, still wishing he had not told her.

"Look, if it makes you feel any better, we can turn the KGB bastard into a hero when we talk to *Tsiolkovsky*. Best part is, I guess it's even true."

"Yeah." It *did* make her feel better, less guilty. I'd never make a soldier, she thought. But then, she had never wanted to be a soldier. "Okay. I'm heading back for *Athena*."

"Good. We should have somebody minding the store. Now to win this battle—that's the point of the exercise, after all. Out."

"Out." Sarah pedaled on.

* * *

Reatur stared in mixed awe and dread at the flames consuming his foe. His watersmiths used fire, of course, to melt ice and pour it into molds for tools. Hot water could bore through walls or, dropped from above, scald attackers. But to turn fire itself into a weapon for war—the domain-master shuddered.

He tried to imagine how humans fought among themselves. Imagining a battlefield full of noise-weapons and fire falling out of the sky made him shudder all over again.

Only for a moment, though. He had his own battle to worry about, and enormous opportunity looking right at him. ''Come on!'' he shouted to the males around him. ''Their whole center depended on the noise-weapon. Now that it's gone, nothing's left there. We can split their whole army in half!''

He scrambled over the barricade. Yelling, his warriors followed. He heard a long series of roars from a noise-weapon, back where the Skarmer had forced his males to give ground. A pause, another long string of blasts. Emmett could shoot as he would now, without having to fear the enemy's more powerful weapon. Then came the sweetest sound Reatur had heard on the battlefield: his warriors cheering, going over to the attack.

''That way!'' he called. ''We'll cut off the Skarmer retreat.'' He hurried east, his males rushing with him in their eagerness to close with the enemy. Suddenly he stopped. He divided the warband with him in two, pointed to the larger group. ''You'll come with me.'' To the others, he said, ''You go west instead. Maybe we'll be able to surround each half of their army.'' That hope made his males shout louder than ever.

As the domain-master ran toward the much-battered rampart, his eyestalks started twitching of their own accord. He had never expected to be fighting from the *north* side of the barrier! Here he was, though, reaching across with a spear to thrust at the Skarmer on the other side.

The foe was frantic now, caught between the males they had pushed back and the barrier from which they had pushed them. Some started climbing over it, this time in the opposite direction from before. The arrival of Reatur and his warriors put an end to that.

''Surrender!'' the domain-master shouted in trade talk. ''We will not slay any male who throws down his weapons and widens himself before us!'' He waited to see if the Skarmer would yield.

They didn't, not right away. But after a couple of desperate attacks failed to dislodge Reatur and his warriors, Skarmer males began casting aside axes and spears and widening themselves.

When the first few who did so were not harmed, more and more followed their lead.

Reatur began telling off warriors to take charge of prisoners. Clamor to the west made him turn a couple of eyestalks that way. He cursed—the Skarmer there had broken out to the north, through his hastily dispatched containment force. Were they to swing back on his males now . . .

They did not. Instead, they streamed back the way they had come, all thought of fight forgotten. The western half of the Omalo army pursued. Reatur spotted Enoph close by. "Take charge of the captives. Let our males loot as they will, but they are not to injure the Skarmer unless they try to escape."

"It will be as you say," Enoph promised—and what Enoph promised, the domain-master knew, he would deliver. "But where are you going, clanfather?" the reliable male asked.

Reatur was already hurrying north. "To join the chase. I want to rid my domain of the Skarmer once and for all."

The western half of the Skarmer army, though beaten, was still a force large enough to disrupt his lands. And whoever led it now that Fralk was dead knew his business—knew it better, perhaps, than Hogram's eldest of eldest ever had. The invaders fought a series of stubborn rearguard actions to keep Reatur's warriors away from their main body.

"Curse them!" the domain-master shouted as his males finally broke through the third such delaying warband. "They'll escape, scatter, and cause us untold grief."

"Worse yet," one of his warriors said gloomily, pointing ahead to a defile. "A rearguard there will hold us off till sunset, and they'll be able to re-form on the far side at their leisure."

"You're right," Reatur said, and cursed again. Another battle to fight, then, he thought bleakly. Even winning would cost him the lives of males the domain could not afford to lose.

But instead of racing through the defile, the Skarmer piled up at its southern end. They milled about in confusion. A male, all his arms outstretched to show he carried no weapons, advanced from their ranks toward Reatur and his oncoming warriors. "Will you spare us if we yield?" he shouted in trade talk.

The domain-master was flabbergasted but did his best not to show it. "Aye, we will," he answered. "You have my vow on it."

"Good enough," the Skarmer said. He spoke to his males in their own language. They began throwing down their spears and knives and axes. The Skarmer widened himself to Reatur. "We would've gotten away if you hadn't somehow posted warriors in there to block our path. That was well done—I never saw them leave the battle, and I don't miss much. Juksal, I'm called.'' Juksal suddenly seemed to think of something. "Did you use tricks from the funny creatures to get them here?''

"The funny creatures?'' Reatur asked.

"Trade talk doesn't have a word for them. You know—the ones with two arms and two legs.''

"Oh. Our name for them is 'humans.' No, no human tricks,'' Reatur said, wondering just where the warriors—*his* warriors?— had sprung from. Only one thing occurred to him. He walked toward the defile. Some of his males came with him, in case the Skarmer decided to unsurrender. "Ternat?'' he called.

"Yes,'' came the reply, and the warriors with the domain-master started to cheer. "How do we stand, clanfather?''

"Well. Very well now, eldest, very well. The other half of the Skarmer army has already yielded to us.'' That brought answering cheers from Ternat and his warband. Reatur went on, "How fare you, eldest?''

"Also well. I have many, many massi with me, and Dordal as a captive, too.''

"Do you?'' Reatur said when the clamor among his males subsided enough to let him be heard. "*Do* you? Then, eldest, it is very well indeed.'' He thought about that, decided it was too small a thing to say. "Eldest, it is as well as I could have hoped.''

As soon as *Damselfly* touched down by *Athena*, Sarah knew she had made a mistake. If she didn't want to damage the ultra-ultralight, she would need help getting out, and it looked as though Irv, Louise, and the stepladder were still over on the other side of Reatur's castle.

She reached for the radio switch, then dropped her hand. All she wanted to do was sit and shake for a minute. Flying across Jötun Canyon had been tougher physically but had not left her drained and limp the way this bombing run had: terror was harder to take than exhaustion.

Cold started seeping into her bones as she rested. If she did too much of that, she knew, she would stiffen up and be sore for days. Her hand moved toward the radio again.

Something hissed through the couple of inches of snow out-side. Sarah turned to see what it was; she had never heard any Minervan creature make a noise like that. It wasn't any Minervan creature, as it turned out: it was Emmett Bragg, speeding up on his bicycle.

He slid to a smooth stop, waved. "Need a hand getting out of that contraption, don't you?"

"Yes, but doesn't Reatur still need you back at the fight?"

"Nope." He got off the bike. "For one thing, I'm out of ammo, so I'm less use to him now than one of his own warriors who really knows what to do with a spear. For another, he was moppin' up when I left. With you takin' out the Kalashnikov, the Skarmer didn't have anything in the middle, and Reatur broke 'em in two and defeated 'em in detail."

"All right." As usual, Sarah thought, Emmett had a good reason for everything he did. She laughed a little—he wasn't eight feet tall, though. "What are you going to get me out with? The stepladder's a couple of miles from here."

"I'll manage." He climbed up the chain ladder to the airlock and disappeared into *Athena*. When he emerged a minute later, he was carrying a large, square plastic-mesh box. He set it down by *Damselfly* and then climbed on top. "This ought to do the job."

"I think you're right." Sarah unlatched the ultra-ultralight's canopy and swung it open. She stood up on the pedals and reached out for Emmett. He more than half lifted her out of *Damselfly*'s cabin. The box made a crunching noise under the weight of the two of them. They jumped off it. Sarah stumbled. Emmett steadied her with an arm around her shoulder.

"Let's get you inside," he said. "Wearing that skimpy getup, you're gonna be a lump of ice in a couple of minutes." They walked over to *Athena*. He didn't take his arm away. She started to shrug him off, changed her mind. He was warm.

She sighed in relief when he shut the inner airlock door after them. "Till I got to Minerva, I never knew how wonderful the words 'room temperature' could be," she said.

"You know it." Emmett grinned a lopsided grin. "Of course, they take on a whole nother meaning when the walls of the room are made of ice." He turned serious again. "You did a hell of a job there, Sarah, a hell of a job."

"Thanks," she said, most soberly. "I don't quite know how I did it, but I guess I did. Right now I'm just so glad to be back here in one piece that I can hardly think about anything else."

"Glad to be alive. I know what you mean—do I ever." The grin got wider. Suddenly Emmett let another yell rip free. "Hot damn, girl, we did it!" he shouted.

He hugged her, tight enough to make the breath hiss from her lungs. Her arms went around his back. The solid feel of him against her was a welcome affirmation that she *was* alive. He tilted her face up and kissed her.

She was kissing him back before she wondered whether she ought to be. "Mmm," he said, back deep in his throat, without letting up on the kiss. Then his mouth slid to her neck; his teeth gently worried the lobe of her ear.

She closed her eyes and let her head loll back. "Nice," she purred. Perhaps because of her brush with death, every sensation, the touch of his tongue against the soft skin under the angle of her jaw, his warm breath on her cheek, seemed deliciously magnified.

His hands were on her hips, planted there as if without the slightest doubt they belonged. "Come on," he urged, nodding back toward the cubicles.

She did not hesitate. She had known for months that he wanted her and occasionally wondered how she would react if he ever did anything about it. Then the question had been academic, and easy to answer with a no. Now . . . "Why not?" she said, feeling almost drunk on excitement.

His hand guided her into Pat's cubicle. It was the one farthest forward, but afterward she wondered if he had chosen it because it held nothing that belonged to Irv or Louise and could set off guilt.

That was afterward. During, she only wanted him to go on. She stood while he quickly undressed her, then did the same for him. They embraced again. He steered her to the foam mattress and lowered himself onto her.

Low comedy briefly ousted desire. "Wait!" She wriggled frantically. "Get up for a second!"

"What the—" Frowning, Emmett took some weight on his elbows.

That sufficed. Sarah reached under herself and threw aside whatever it was she had been lying on. Her arms went around his neck and pulled him back to her. "Now!" she said.

Had she not already known he was a test pilot, she might have guessed it by the way he took her. He flew her as if she were some new plane, she thought before all thought vanished, trying this, trying that, seeing how she responded, what the limits of her performance were. Gasping, she doubted she had any limits.

He laughed when, at the end, she tried to sink her teeth into his shoulder. "Easy there. Shouldn't leave marks," he said, mind still in full control even as his body quivered and drove deep into hers.

That brought her back to herself faster than she wanted to return and brought her also to the beginning of anger. She suddenly suspected—no, she *knew*—the flying itself was more important to him than the plane he flew. Being just another test vehicle on which he could prove his expertise grated.

He sprang up from the mattress and bounded down the passage. "What the hell?" she squawked, startled out of annoyance.

"Radio buzzer." His words floated back to her. "I wonder how long it was on while we were busy here." Then she heard the insistent signal, too, and started to giggle. He had paid some attention to her after all. She heard him pick up the mike. Then he called loudly, "Sarah, you'd better come. It's about Lamra."

She raced to the control room. Only when Emmett handed her the microphone did she realize that they were both still naked. She didn't care. "What about Lamra?" she demanded.

"Hon?"

It was Irv. It would be Irv, she thought. Now she cared who she was standing with, and how. She felt herself go hot, then cold. But what Irv was calling about mattered more than anything, at least for the moment. *"What about Lamra?"*

Lamra looked at herself. *How funny I look*, was the first thought that went through her mind, well ahead of *I'm alive* and the surprise that accompanied it. Her bud-bulges, which had been so firm and full, were split open like ebster fruit and sagged down almost onto her feet. Great strips of the sticky hide humans used to hold things together clung to her skin. She supposed they were helping to hold *her* together.

She really was the most ridiculous creature imaginable. Her eyestalks quivered. The motion was less than she had thought it would be. For some reason, they didn't want to do what she told them to. But she was laughing.

"Lamra?" Three voices all at once, two sounding like people but oddly accented, the third deep and strange: humans.

She tried to talk. Her mouth didn't seem to want to work, either. She tried again. "Where's my runnerpest?" she demanded at last. The humans abruptly stopped paying attention to her. They yelled and screamed and, she saw when she managed to raise her eyestalks a little, jumped up and down.

"Where's my runnerpest?" she repeated, louder this time.

One of the humans finally handed her the toy. It was bloody. She squeezed it anyhow.

"How are you? How do you feel?" the humans all asked over and over again once they got coherent enough to talk sensibly.

"Tired," she answered. More thought produced, "Sore. Messy." She was thinking just clearly enough to know she wasn't thinking very clearly. "Hungry, too."

"Sore where?" Pat sounded anxious. "Hurt bad?"

"I'm sore where—I guess where—you put those *clamps*"— she used the human she had learned—"on me. No, Pat, I don't hurt bad. When you put them on, I hardly felt it at all. I hardly felt anything at all. It was funny." When she laughed this time, her eyestalks wiggled the way they should. "It was like being asleep and awake at the same time. Do you know what I mean?"

"No." Pat made the up-and-down gesture humans used for a shrug. "Glad you are not hurt, though."

Louise held up a couple of squirming, squalling . . . At first Lamra thought they were big runnerpests, but then she remembered seeing their like before sometimes, when Reatur would walk out after a mate had dropped. "Oh. The budlings," she said.

"Yes. You want to see?"

"I suppose so." Everything was interesting to Lamra, at least for a little while. But the budlings got boring fast. All they did was flail about and make noise. "That's enough. You can put them down now."

Irv spoke into his talking-box. The box, to Lamra, was much more interesting than budlings. She had started out wondering how humans made themselves small enough to fit inside, for their voices surely came out of it. Later she realized they didn't hide in there, but talked with each other at a distance. To her, that was more marvelous, not less.

Irv spoke into the talking-box again. This time, nobody answered. Irv shook the box, broke it in half—Lamra hadn't known it opened up—looked inside, made a human shrug, put the box back together. He held it to his mouth once more. He spoke louder now.

When nothing happened, Pat got out her talking-box and offered it to Irv. But just then, noise came out of his: another rumbling human voice talking. Irv answered. Lamra knew only a handful of words of human speech but recognized her name and Sarah's.

And sure enough, Sarah's voice came from the talking-box a moment later. She was talking about Lamra, too. Suddenly she started using words a person could understand. "Lamra, how are you? How do you feel?"

Lamra's eyestalks wiggled. "You humans all ask the same questions," she said when Irv held the talking-box above her mouth.

"Never mind jokes!" Sarah said sharply. "Tell me right now how you are!"

Lamra looked at herself again. "Ugly, I think. And the *tape*"—another human word she had picked up—"itches."

"Not what I mean!" Sarah sounded the way humans sometimes did when Lamra couldn't figure out what they wanted fast enough.

"Please don't be angry." Lamra wanted to pull in all her arms and eyestalks. "I think I'm all right, Sarah, except for the holes in me where the budlings were. Will they close up, or will I look like this from now on?"

"Not know, Lamra." Not counting a tiny hiss, only silence came out of the talking-box for a while. Then Sarah went on, "Sorry, Lamra, not mean to be angry at you. Angry at me."

"Why would you be angry at yourself?" Sometimes humans made no sense at all to Lamra.

"Angry because I not there when your budlings come," Sarah answered. "Want to be there to help you, but not can do."

"Oh. Don't worry, Sarah. It's all right," Lamra said. "Irv and Pat and"—she had to think for a moment—"Louise helped me very well. What could you have done that they didn't?"

Another silence, longer this time. Irv fiddled briefly with the talking-box and then said, "Lamra, Sarah thought of the way we used to save you. She showed us what to do. We were lucky to do it right without her here. If we make—*had made*—a mistake, she show us how to fix it." His strange voice held the gentleness Reatur used when explaining something to a new mate who was hardly more than a budling herself.

"Oh." Lamra thought about the tone Irv had used, about his words, and decided she had been silly. "Sarah?" she said. Irv put the talking-box above her mouth again. "I'm sorry, Sarah; I wish you'd been here, too. You must have been doing something important, or you would have been."

Still more silence. Then: "Not as important as you, Lamra; not as important as you. But did Reatur ever talk to you about Skarmer males on this side of Jö—uh, Ervis Gorge?"

"Yes, Sarah." Lamra squeezed the toy runnerpest again. "He beat them. I helped him beat them."

"That is important, Sarah," Lamra said. "If Reatur hadn't beaten them, then what happened with me wouldn't matter much, would it?"

"No, not much," Sarah said. "But still, curse it, Lamra, I wish I there with you instead!"

"All right, Sarah," Lamra said, thinking once more that even when humans used people's words, they didn't always make sense with them. Trying to figure out what they meant was fun, though, and now, she realized, she would have more time to do it. She liked that.

12

The males standing guard outside Hogram's audience chamber hefted their spears as Tolmasov and Bryusov walked by. Their eyestalks followed the two humans. Seeing a spearpoint twitch a couple of centimeters toward him, Tolmasov wished he were carrying his AK-74 instead of a radio. But no, he thought—an AK-74 had helped cause his predicament.

"They are not fond of us anymore, Sergei Konstantinovich," Bryusov said quietly. He could feel it, too, then.

"No," the pilot agreed. "I only hope they are not in the habit of blaming the messenger for the news he brings." He felt like some luckless boyar coming to Ivan the Terrible with word of a disaster against the Tatars.

The Minervans talking in the audience chamber fell silent as the humans entered. A couple of males ostentatiously turned all their eyes away from Tolmasov and Bryusov. "They deny that we have the right to exist," Bryusov murmured.

"Like turning their backs—but they have no backs. Yes, I understand, Valery Aleksandrovich." Even though the linguist kept stating the obvious, Tolmasov was glad he was along. Being able to speak the Skarmer tongue fluently ought to give him insight into the way the locals thought. And having another human close by was comforting in this room full of hostile aliens.

Hogram waited at the far end of the hall. Tolmasov approached the domain-master, bowed low in lieu of widening himself. Beside him, Bryusov did the same. Before, Hogram had always widened in reply, as much as he would have to one of his high advisors. The minimal widening he gave the humans now told how their status had changed.

"We have come as you asked us to come, clanfather," Tolmasov said. Let Hogram remember who needed whom now.

"Yes, I asked you to come," Hogram said. Tolmasov watched him closely, looking for any color change, but Hogram was far too wily to let his skin reveal his feelings. "I want you to explain once more, not just to me but to all my councilors here, how the rifle for which we paid such a great price failed to help us defeat the Omalo."

So you want to say everything is our fault, do you, Tolmasov thought. It made Hogram seem very human, but the pilot did not intend to let him get away with it. "Honored clanfather, am I wrong, then?" he asked innocently. "If we humans not come down in your domain, you stay on this side of Ervis Gorge, not send males across?"

Though Hogram stayed green, several of his advisors turned a furious yellow. "We thought we'd surely win with your weapon!" one of them shouted. "Instead—"

"Instead," Hogram broke in, "instead, those Skarmer males who are not dead are Reatur's captives, and Fralk, my eldest of eldest, is slain. As my eldest died years ago, the domain must now pass to Lorkis, my second, who is far from ready to take mastery. And I am old, so he may have to do so at any time."

"Honored clanfather, one of our males also died east of Ervis Gorge, a sixth part of all our numbers," Bryusov said.

"Sooner *all* you humans than Fralk," Hogram said. The rest of the Minervans shouted agreement. Tolmasov wished for the Kalashnikov again.

"Hogram, in war nothing is sure, not with rifle, not without," he said. He could not talk prettily in the Skarmer speech the way Bryusov could, but he knew he talked plain clear sense. "But you should be glad some humans still alive, on this side of Ervis Gorge and on other side."

"Why is that?" Now, when his words were quiet and controlled, Hogram did start to turn yellow. "Why should I not wish I had never seen any of you?"

Tolmasov took out his radio. "Because of this, honored clanfather. From this, we learn what happen to your army long before you find out otherwise, and what we learn, we tell you."

"And, because of this"—Bryusov pointed to the radio—"you can bargain with the Omalo on the east side of the gorge. What might Reatur do to your captive males if we, the other humans on that side of the gorge, and, through us, you did not speak up for kindness?"

The audience chamber grew silent. All Hogram's males were related to one another more or less closely; all felt the anguish of having so many of their kin at their enemy's mercy. None of them, Tolmasov was sure, considered that those males would not have been in that predicament had they not invaded Reatur's domain. Back on Earth, the Germans still whined about how their POWs were treated during the Great Patriotic War.

Hogram was green again. Tolmasov was sure his brief show of anger had been just that, a show. When he had summoned the Russians to come before him, he had ordered them to bring a radio. He knew he would have to dicker with Reatur and needed his underlings to know it, too.

Yes, Hogram was a wily one. How much that would help remained to be seen. Reatur held most of the cards, to say nothing of the Skarmer warriors.

"To save our males, I will speak with the Omalo domain-master, unless anyone here objects," Hogram said. He waited. No one objected. He waved a three-fingered hand at Tolmasov. "Please have the other humans summon Reatur."

"I will try, honored clanfather," the pilot said. He knew perfectly well that Reatur was not at the Americans' beck and call, let alone Hogram's. When the domain-master's summons came, he had asked Irv Levitt if Reatur would make himself available. Levitt had promised to try to arrange it. Now was the time to see if he had come through. Tolmasov spoke into the radio: "Ready with the relay, Shota Mikheilovich?"

Rustaveli was back at the orange tent; the more powerful transmitter there could reach across Jötun Canyon. "*Da*. Go ahead," he answered after a moment.

"Soviet Minerva expedition calling *Athena*," Tolmasov said in English; Bryusov translated for the Minervans.

The reply was prompt. "*Zdrast'ye*, Sergei Konstantinovich. Irv Levitt here. What can I do for you?"

Speaking English, Tolmasov did not have to try to remember Irv's patronymic. "The domain-master Hogram wishes to speak to the domain-master Reatur. He"—Tolmasov picked his words carefully—"seeks terms for ending the, ah, hostilities between them."

If Reatur didn't even want to talk . . . Tolmasov preferred not to think about that. It would wreck the leverage he had on Hogram.

"Reatur will talk with Hogram, Sergei Konstantinovich," Irv said in Russian. As the pilot felt a relieved grin stretch across his face, Irv went on in dry English, "We managed to talk him into it, because he feels he owes us one. But your fellow better not ask for much—he's not very happy about westerners right now."

The American anthropologist had style, Tolmasov thought, getting his warning across in a language none of the Skarmer could speak. Then Reatur's contralto came from the speaker, using the trade talk Tolmasov had trouble following himself. "What have you to say for yourself, Hogram?"

The old Skarmer domain-master waddled up to Tolmasov, who held the radio near his mouth. "Only that we tried and lost, Reatur. What else can I say? You hold my males. I hope—" He hesitated, then went on. "I hope you are treating them better than we might have treated yours had we won."

Some of Hogram's advisors went blue with fear as he said that. Bryusov gave Tolmasov an appalled look. The pilot kept his face blank. He knew Hogram was gambling but thought it a good gamble. Reatur would recognize and scorn false sweetness; honesty might sway him.

"They're not harmed, for now," Reatur said after a short, thoughtful pause. "It's up to you to persuade me to keep them that way. Put it like this, Hogram—why should I go on feeding all those males who are not mine?"

Hogram sighed. "Because I—my domain—will pay to keep them safe."

"How much?" That was one short word in trade talk, maybe the basic word of trade talk.

"How much do you want?" Hogram asked.

"How much do you offer? If it's enough, I may listen to you. If not—" Reatur let the sentence trail away. Hogram sighed again. Even Tolmasov, who had had scant experience bargaining before he landed among these capitalist aliens, could see the cunning behind that ploy. Hogram could not afford to be miserly, not if he wanted to see his warriors again—and, not knowing Reatur's price for certain, he would have to be doubly extravagant to make sure he met it.

"First, I will give you goods enough to pay the cost of maintaining my males from now until the flood subsides in Ervis Gorge. We can work out later exactly how much that is, but I will pay it."

"What do I care about goods later, when I have trouble coming up with food now to keep them alive till then?"

Hogram widened himself very slightly to Tolmasov, who

dipped his head in response. The domain-master spoke into the radio: "Since you now dominate the domain to your north, I trust you will be able to come up with supplies."

"You know that, do you?" Reatur started talking his own language, which Tolmasov did not speak at all. He heard Irv answer in the same tongue. The American sounded placating. Tolmasov chuckled, thinking, That's what you get for bragging to me about how wonderful your client is. The Omalo domain-master returned to trade talk. "Well, what of it? Still easier for me to rid myself of my captives than go to the bother of caring for them."

"That was only a token of good intentions," Hogram said, "to assure you that forbearance will not harm your domain. Above it, for my males' safe return I will pay—curse it, Reatur, I will pay that same amount twice more. May your eyestalks rot if you try to melt more out of me."

"It is not a small price," Reatur admitted. "Will you include in it, hmm, at least three eighteens of trade goods you have got from your humans, of at least, ah, nine different types?"

Hogram turned yellow. Tolmasov did not blame him. Reatur had all too good a grip on how the arrival of humans was changing Minerva. But the Skarmer chieftain said what he had to say. "I will."

"Now tell me," Reatur said, "why you want me to feed and house—and guard—your warriors until fall."

"Because when the flood subsides, by your leave we will stretch the bridge across Ervis Gorge once more. Our males can cross to our side, and we will send payment to you in return."

"Send the payment first," Reatur said promptly.

"I trust you no more than you trust me," Hogram retorted. "Send the males first."

"No."

Hogram turned yellow again. He did not answer.

"We'd best do something," Bryusov whispered to Tolmasov. The pilot nodded. The spectacle of Russians and Americans helping Minervans fight a war had done nothing for the prestige of the Soviet Union or the United States back home. Helping Minervans make peace might possibly repair it. But the silence was getting icy—a good word for silence on Minerva, Tolmasov thought.

"Suggest they takes turns," Tolmasov whispered back. "Do it in trade talk, so they'll both understand." Bryusov, by now, was fairly fluent in the local lingua franca.

"Honored domain-masters," the linguist said, "perhaps if some males are freed, then some of the payment made, then more males freed—"

"Perhaps," Hogram said thoughtfully. "A third of the males, a third of the payment, and so on."

"First you pay, then we release males," Reatur said. "And we will do it in six turns, not three. If we tried it the other way round, you could cheat us out of the last third of the payment and leave us with no arm of yours to grab."

Tolmasov waited for Hogram to get angry again. Instead, the Skarmer domain-master wiggled his eyestalks. He said, "You are wasted as an Omalo, Reatur; you should have been budded as one of us."

"No, I'm no thief, Hogram. My job is keeping thieves in line."

Irv Levitt quickly cut in, in English: "He's laughing. Is your boy?"

"Yes," Tolmasov answered, and switched to the Skarmer tongue to let Hogram know what the American had said. Hogram waved an indulgent arm—he had known without being told. Tolmasov felt annoyed, then resigned.

The Skarmer domain-master spoke into the radio. "Do we agree?"

"Yes, provided we can work out the cost of feeding the captives each day," Reatur said. "If not, I suppose I can always start getting rid of them."

If that was humor, Tolmasov thought, it was in poor taste. Hogram did not seem put out. "We will work it out," he said. "Are we finished, then?"

"I think so," Reatur answered.

This time, Bryusov interrupted without Tolmasov's prompting. "Honored domain-masters, while you talk with each other now, why not pledge not to fight each other anymore so long as you both abide by today's agreement?"

"What a foolish pledge that would be," Hogram said. "Reatur and I do not spring from the same bud. We are not friends. We may well go to war again, and we both know it. Why lie now?"

"For once we agree, Skarmer," Reatur said. "And who can say on which side of Ervis Gorge the fight may be? We can make baskets that float on water, too, you know, now that we've seen some."

Hogram made a whistling noise Tolmasov had never heard

from a Minervan before, one that reminded him of a teapot coming to a boil. "None of my males grasps the importance of new things as quickly as you do, now that—now that Fralk is dead. I wish you were of my budding, Reatur; I would name you eldest-designate."

"Dealing with *humans*"—Reatur said it in English; Tolmasov put it into Russian for the Skarmer—"has taught me more about new things than I ever expected to know."

"Yes." Hogram stepped away from the radio. He told Tolmasov, "That is all."

"Levitt, are you there?" the pilot called. When the American answered, he went on, "We have a success to report, it seems."

"Yes, they'll be relieved back home," Irv answered in English. "I don't think people back home could stomach a cold-blooded prisoner massacre." He let the obvious joke lie. Tolmasov respected him because of it; this was business. "Come to that, I'm not sure I could, either."

"Out," was all Tolmasov said. He and Bryusov bowed their way out of Hogram's presence and started back toward their big orange tent.

"Foolish, the Americans, foolish and soft," Bryusov said after a while. "One deals with whomever one has to deal with."

"They talk softer than they are, Valery Aleksandrovich. Never forget it." Tolmasov had had that same swift flash of contempt for Irv Levitt but changed his mind after a little thought. "For one thing, as you said, Levitt would go right on dealing with Reatur no matter what Reatur did. He may not want to admit it to himself, but he would.

"And for another, before you call them soft, remember what happened to Fralk and Oleg Lopatin. I am trained as a combat pilot, but I would not care to attack a Kalashnikov with a glorified hang glider."

Bryusov was very quiet for the rest of the walk. That suited Tolmasov fine.

Emmett Bragg was hurrying up the corridor when Sarah came through the airlock into *Athena*. He stopped and grinned at her with the peculiarly male grin that never failed to set her teeth on edge. "Will you stop it?" she hissed. "Anyone who sees you will know exactly what that stupid expression means."

The grin didn't go away. "Nobody here but you and me."

"Oh." That hadn't happened since the day of the battle. Since then, Sarah had stayed close to Irv most of the time, partly because they both spent a lot of time with Lamra and partly because it kept her from having to think about those frantic minutes on Pat's mattress. Irv seemed happy enough to be with her, too; they had probably spent more continuous waking time together since Lamra's budlings dropped than in all the previous months on Minerva put together.

Now she would have to think about those minutes. "Let it slide, Emmett, all right?" In similar circumstances Irv, she was sure, would have come back with a raunchy pun. Emmett just stood there, warrior-alert, and waited for her to go on. That her first thought was of Irv told her some of what she needed to know. "Not that it wasn't good while it happened, but—"

"But what?" He stepped closer.

"Emmett!" She heard her voice get shrill. That infuriated her, but she couldn't help it. If he went ahead regardless of whether she wanted him to, she would try to give him a dreadful surprise. But he was bigger, stronger, a trained soldier . . . Of all the nightmares she'd had about being cooped up on *Athena* with too many people in too small a space for too long, this was the worst.

Smooth as ever, he moved away from her. Then he started to laugh. "What's so goddamn funny?" she barked, angrier than ever.

"You, gearin' up to kick me right where it'd do the most good. You don't need to do that. Have I ever gone any place I wasn't welcome?"

"You'd know better than I would." But that wasn't fair, either. "Not with me," Sarah admitted.

"All right, then. Probably better this way, anyhow." That cool calculation of risk was Emmett to the core.

She did her best to imitate him. "I think you're right. For the ship and for—everything else."

"Suppose so." He cocked his head, studied her. "Do you really think you could've stopped me?"

"No," she answered honestly. "But I was going to give it my best shot."

"I noticed. Okay—can't ask for more than that. Now I'm gonna get back to work." He headed toward the control room, never looking back. For all he showed, he and Sarah might have been at the office water cooler, talking about the weather. She envied his detachment and had no idea how to duplicate it.

* * *

"Come on, Peri, throw me the ball!" Lamra shouted. "Throw it to me! It's my turn this time! I want to play, too!"

Peri threw the ball to another mate. Lamra hurried over toward that one, still trying to get into the game. "No, you can't have it!" the mate said. She threw the ball to someone else. "You can't play with us anymore, Lamra. You're too ugly."

"That's right," Peri said. "You've got holes in you from where your budlings fell out, and with them falling out, you shouldn't even be here. You should have ended, like mates are supposed to do. Who ever heard of an old mate?"

"Who ever heard of an old mate? Who ever heard of an old mate?" A bunch of mates, maybe even an eighteen of them, formed a jeering ring around Lamra. Sun-yellow with fury, she rushed at them, but they skipped aside, jeering still. And even if she had managed to catch one, what good would it have done? The rest would all pile on her before she could get any of her own back.

Sometimes she wondered if letting the humans save her had been a good idea. Down deep, she hadn't really expected them to do it. Before, when she had thought about what would come after, she just thought about going on as she always had, about running around and playing with the other mates without the big budling bulges getting in her way.

But the others didn't want to play with her, not anymore. "Who ever heard of an old mate? Who ever heard of an old mate?"

They were so busy making fun of Lamra, they hardly noticed the door to the mates' chambers opening. "What's going on here?" Reatur shouted. He was as yellow as Lamra, but his rage was not helpless like hers.

Some of the mates turned blue and ran away. Others held their ground. "We don't want her here," Peri yelled at the domainmaster. "She should go away."

"*You* go away, right now," Reatur cried in a terrible voice. He turned all his eyestalks toward the wall three arms away from Peri. Her bravado collapsed. She went from yellow to blue so fast she wasn't even green between, then fled with a squeak.

Reatur let his eyes look all around again. "That doesn't help, you know," Lamra said sadly. "You can't make them like me, Reatur. As soon as you're gone, this will just start again."

"Will it?" Reatur said. "Does it?"

"Every time." Lamra hesitated, then went on, "I thought it would get better. I mean, I'm not as odd-looking as I used to be. I don't have *tape* all over me, and I don't have those big *bandages* stuck where the budlings came out. But it isn't any better, not with the other mates. I guess I'm still too strange. I think my runnerpest is the only thing that likes me anymore." She opened a hand and looked down at the toy Reatur had given her.

"That is not true," the domain-master said. "*I* like you, you know."

"Yes, of course I know that," Lamra said. "After all, you made the runnerpest, and—and—" She stopped when she realized the size of the compliment he had paid her. Widening herself was the least she could do, and she did it. Then she blurted, "But you're not here to like me very often."

"That is also true," Reatur said slowly. "I cannot be here all the time, though, not if I intend to run the domain, too." He paused a while in thought. "Shall I gather all the mates together and tell them they have to treat you just like anyone else?"

For a moment, hope tingled through Lamra. She wondered if that would work. "I don't think so," she said at last, sadly. "They'll just be angry at me for getting them into trouble. And— I'm not just like them anymore, am I? I'm only like me, and I'm lonesome."

"I know you are. There's never been a mate like you before." Reatur thought again himself, then went on, "Which means the laws that hold other mates don't necessarily put fingerclaws on you."

"So what, clanfather?" Talk about laws meant nothing to Lamra. Mates lived as they lived, and that was all there was to it.

"So perhaps . . ." Reatur's voice trailed away. When he resumed, Lamra wondered whether he was talking to himself or to her. "So perhaps, just perhaps, now it might be all right for you to go outside the mates' chambers and live—well, almost as if you were a male, I suppose." He sounded surprised at where his mouth was taking him but went on anyhow. "Would you like that, Lamra?"

"I don't know." The idea was so alien to her, she could hardly take it in. She seized on the part of it closest to her troubles and asked, "Will males like me better than mates do?"

"I don't know," Reatur said. "Some will, some won't, I expect. That's the way it usually is. Some people don't like anything strange and different. But I think your chance is better now than it would be another time. What with the humans still being here, things are already so strange that you may be just one oddity among many."

"That's better than what I am now, here." Lamra thought some more. "You mean I'll be able to see and touch and smell all the things on the other side of that door?"

"As many of them as you want."

For all her life, that door had marked the end of Lamra's universe. She saw the outside world, faintly, through the sandy ice that let light into the mates' chambers. To mingle with those moving shapes, though, to find out what they truly were—

"Come on!" she said, and hurried toward the door. The slits of skin that had opened to let out her budlings flapped as she ran. They were healing together, slowly and raggedly; she would never have quite the same smooth up-and-down lines as before she had begun to bud, no matter how long she lived.

Reatur followed her. "Open," he told the guard on the far side of the door. Lamra heard the male lift the bar from the brackets that held it. Before the door opened, the domain-master said, "You can still change your mind, you know."

"Why would I want to do that?" Lamra asked. The door started to swing open. The first glimpse she had of the world beyond it gave her her answer. That corridor seemed to stretch on forever, though it was only a tiny part of the castle. And outside the castle was the whole world, unimaginably big, unimaginably strange. For a moment staying where she was, knowing everything—and everyone!—around her, felt like the only safe thing to do.

But strangeness had already come in through that door. Had it not, she would not be standing here turning blue with fright at the prospect of going out. Air hissed through her breathing pores. "Come on," she said again, not an excited squeal this time but determined even so.

"Let me go first." Lamra moved aside so Reatur could pass. The guard started to shut the door after the domain-master. "Wait, please, Orth," Reatur said.

"Sorry, clanfather. Did one of the humans go in before my duty started?" Orth poked an eyestalk around the edge of the door. "No," he answered himself, seeing only Lamra.

"No," Reatur agreed. He paused, as if he, too, was having second thoughts. But when he resumed, he spoke firmly. "This is the mate Lamra, the one the humans saved when she dropped her budlings. As you can see, she will not be ready to have buds planted on her again for some time, if ever. I am going to bring her out of the mates' chambers into the world. Treat her as you would a male of the same age."

"Clanfather?" Orth sounded so shocked, Lamra wondered if he would leave the door open for her. He did. Perhaps he was too surprised not to. His eyestalks kept moving back and forth between Reatur and Lamra.

She widened herself as much as she could, far wider than she made herself for Reatur these days. "Hello, Orth," she said. Barring humans, she had never talked to any male but Reatur before.

"Orth—" Reatur prompted.

"Hello," the guard managed to say. His eyestalks returned to the domain-master. "A mate out by herself, living like a male? Forgive me, clanfather, but not even a massi-herder living off by himself with a couple of mates would let them run loose. How could he? They don't know enough not to get into mischief, and then—" Orth suddenly seemed to realize Lamra was a person of sorts, even if a mate. "—and then they're, uh, done," he finished weakly.

"They die before they learn enough not to get into mischief, you mean, because they drop their budlings," Reatur said. "Lamra has dropped her budlings and isn't dead. She can learn. She has time to learn."

Orth stood silent. "Hello," Lamra said again in a soft voice. Orth didn't answer. He doesn't like me, Lamra thought—nobody likes me out here, either. She started to go back into the mates' chambers. With the mates, at least she could remind herself how foolish they were. But grown-up males weren't foolish. She knew that. If they didn't like her, maybe she wasn't worth liking.

But Reatur said, "Come along," and started down the corridor. She found herself following him; he was the one link with certainty she had left.

"What's *that*?" she exclaimed a little later, pointing into a small room. She had expected to see different things outside the mates' chambers, but none so different as the—animal? monster?—in there.

Reatur wiggled his eyestalks. "For years—for longer than you've been alive—I wondered the same thing. I found it in the hills not far from here. Turns out the humans made it. It's one of their gadgets, fancier than most."

"Oh," Lamra said. "Then there were humans so long ago. I hadn't thought of that."

Reatur looked at her. "I hadn't, either, not in that way. They certainly never showed themselves till this past spring. But you never can tell with humans."

"No, you can't," Lamra said, "because if you could, I wouldn't be here with you now."

Males walked by as Lamra stood in the doorway, peering at the human gadget. They peered at her, too. None of them spoke to her, though, or even to Reatur about her. She wondered if they were trying to pretend she didn't exist. She squeezed her runnerpest. The pressure of it in her hand reminded her she was real.

Then a male said, "Well, well, what have we here? You must be Lamra."

He was talking to *her*. She widened herself and stammered, "Y-yes, I am. Who are you?"

"I'm Ternat, Reatur's eldest. Are you, ah, doing well, Lamra? You must find this whole business about as odd as we do."

Someone who understood! Someone who wasn't Reatur or a human but understood! So that *could* happen! "I'm—better now, thank you very much, Ternat."

"Good." Ternat turned an eyestalk toward Reatur. "Why did you decide to bring her out, clanfather?"

"The mates were harassing her," the domain-master answered. "Males will, too, I fear, but they'll have the sense to obey me when I tell them to stop. And they're grown; they won't try to hurt her just because she's different. Or if anyone does, the example I make of him will show the others it's not a good idea."

Lamra widened herself to Reatur this time. "Thank you for thinking ahead and looking out for me, clanfather."

"You don't know how to look out for yourself yet, Lamra. I expect you'll learn. Some males get to be old and saggy-skinned without ever figuring it out." Reatur's eyestalks twitched. "In fact, there's one of just that sort I'd like you to meet." He started down the corridor, then paused to wave an encouraging arm to Ternat. "You come, too, eldest. I think you'll enjoy this."

The domain-master led Lamra out through an open door. Suddenly she realized no walls were anywhere nearby. She stopped walking and watched herself turn blue. "Is this— outside?" she asked faintly. She felt like a speck of dust floating in the middle of infinite space.

"Yes, it is," Reatur said. "What do you think of it?" He did not mention her color.

"It's—very big."

"So it is. Come on, now; we don't have far to go." And off he went, Ternat beside him. Lamra had a choice of staying frozen while the two people in the world who cared about her went away or of going after them. She took a step, then another and another. They came ever more easily. Reatur went outside all the time, she thought, and it didn't hurt him. It probably wouldn't hurt her, either.

But there was so *much* of it!

Several eighteens of males—more eighteens than Lamra could easily count—milled about in a large pen made of branches. Others, these carrying spears, stood all around the pen. "These are the males from Dordal's domain that Ternat captured," Reatur explained. "We'd send them back, but for some reason"—his eyestalks wiggled briefly—"Dordal's eldest, Grevil, isn't interested in paying for them."

One of the males, a large impressive one near the edge of the pen, was saying in a loud voice, "All this talk of *humans*"— Lamra knew mates who pronounced the word better than he did—"bores me no end. They're weird things, true enough, but what can they really do? I'm tired of hearing impossible lies and fables."

"Hello, Dordal," Reatur said. "So you want to know what humans can do, eh? Here, let me present you to the mate Lamra. The humans saved her when she dropped her budlings not long after Ternat captured you."

Dordal's eyestalks jounced up and down with humor that was obviously forced. "Tell me another tale, Reatur." Then one of those moving eyes lit on Lamra. "It *is* a mate," he said in surprise. "I'd not have thought even one like you would let them run loose. But why does it look so—tattered?"

"I told you, Dordal. You listen about as well as you plan. Lamra dropped her budlings, and the humans kept her from dying afterward."

"That's what happened, Dordal," Lamra agreed. "I was there. I ought to know." She reached down, pulled wide the still partially open flaps of skin that had once bulged over a budling. Dordal drew back in alarm. Lamra could not see why; only the *clamps* were still in there, and Sarah had promised that even they could come out in another few days.

"She'll live longer than you will, Dordal," Ternat said cheerfully. "A lot longer, if Grevil doesn't come up with your ransom soon."

"*Humans* did that?" Dordal muttered. He turned blue, hurried away from the fence. "Then they're worse monsters than she is!"

"Don't let him bother you," Reatur told Lamra. "He hasn't any more sense than a runnerpest, you know."

Lamra squeezed her toy. "I do know," she said, unruffled. "Some mates are like that, too, even ones who got older than I am before they started budding. I didn't think it would be true of males, too, that's all. Of course, the only male I've really known till now is you, Reatur." For some reason she could not fathom, the domain-master and his eldest started laughing at each other. "Stop it! What's funny?"

"Never mind, little one," Reatur said. To Ternat, he went on, "You see why I wanted to keep this one?"

"Because she can tell you're brighter than Dordal? A nosver could figure out that much."

"Disrespectful—" But Reatur's eyestalks were wiggling again. "No, because she thinks about the way things work. Don't you, Lamra?"

"I try to," she said absently. She wasn't paying too much attention to the domain-master. She was too busy looking at the wide, wide world, or rather, at pieces of it. If she examined one thing at a time, the wideness was less oppressive. She pointed. "What's that?"

"That's a lykao shrub," Reatur said. "Massi like the berries."

"Oh. What's that?" She pointed in a different direction.

"That's an eloc."

"Oh. It doesn't look much like its meat, does it? What's that?" She pointed again.

But instead of answering, Reatur pointed at her. "That is a mate who looks as though she'll be wandering around asking questions for the next year, now that she has so many new things to ask questions about."

"You're right," Lamra said happily.

"Good heavens," Irv said. "What happened to your calculator?"

Pat held it up. The only thing that held the batteries in was a big piece of duct tape. "Beats me," she said. "I thought I left the stupid thing on my bed a while ago, but I found it on the floor with the back smashed to hell."

"You must have stepped on it without noticing," Irv said.

"How do you not notice something that goes crunch?" Pat retorted.

"Speaking of not noticing," Louise said, looking up from a tape she was feeding into the computer for transmission back to Earth, "that calculator's been patched since—" She thought back. "I guess since the day Lamra had her budlings, the day of the big battle."

Pat nodded. "That's right. I remember having to fix it right after we all came back from Reatur's castle."

"Oh," Irv said. "Well, hush my mouth." He made as if to pull his head inside his shirt. Louise pretended to throw the tape cassette at him. He ducked. Everybody in the control room laughed. He spread his hands in defeat. "If that's when it happened, I give up. None of us will forget anything about that day, not if we live to be ninety."

"You better believe it," Louise said.

Irv remembered coming back from the castle, too, after Sarah had sped out there to make sure Lamra really was all right. He remembered drawing the privacy curtain to their cubicle afterward, so he and Sarah could celebrate her being alive, Lamra's being alive, everyone's being alive. And he remembered a pink-purple not-quite-mark, not-quite-bruise, in the middle of her left buttock.

At the time, he had thought nothing of it. He'd had other, more immediate things on his mind. But he remembered. And, it occurred to him now, that mark had been just about the size and shape of Pat's calculator.

So what had Sarah been doing that involved lying on a calculator, or maybe lying on one and then, say, throwing it to the floor? The only answer Irv came up with was the immediately obvious one.

And with whom? The answer to that was immediately obvious, too. Sarah liked men, at least in situations where—where one might be apt to lie on a calculator, Irv thought. The joke he tried to make fell flat, though he only told it to himself.

Another question filled his mind: What the hell am I going to do about this? Unlike the couple that had preceded it, that one had no immediately obvious answer. Confronting Emmett struck him as either useless or suicidal, depending on how much he annoyed the pilot.

Confronting Sarah—oh, that'd be real good, he said to himself: you'd even have to lie to claim the moral advantage.

He glanced over at Pat, then at Louise. So far as he knew, she hadn't done anything she wasn't supposed to with anybody. But if Emmett had, she was affected, too. "Great," Irv muttered. Two, count 'em, two unsanctioned belly-bumps and the whole damn crew was involved.

Or was it just two? On reflection, Irv decided it probably was. Since the day of the battle, Sarah had stuck a lot tighter to him than had been her habit before. Maybe she had all the same regrets he did. He hoped so, partly for the sake of their marriage and partly just because he wanted someone else to be as confused as he was.

The psychologists back home had warned about this kind of thing, for exactly these reasons. One of the rare times the psychologists were dead right, Irv thought, so of course nobody paid attention to them.

He laughed a little, under his breath. It *was* funny, in a French-movie sort of way. Then he sobered. In French movies, sooner or later everybody found out what was going on, and the fur really started to fly. That could happen here, too, from the same kind of accidental revelation he had just had. He hoped it wouldn't, but it could.

"And wouldn't that be wonderful?"

He didn't realize he had spoken more or less out loud until Pat said, "What?"

"Nothing," he said firmly. "I was just thinking, it ought to be an interesting flight home."

Snow swirled around Ternat. Fall was here early this year, he thought. Under most circumstances, that would have made him happy; he had no more use for summer heat than Reatur did. Now, though, he was looking for something, and the snow made it hard to find.

His feet scraped ice. "We're down to the very bottom of the gorge," he told the males with him. The frozen patch he was standing on, and others he knew to be nearby, were all that was left of the summer floods.

"How are we supposed to find the end of a rope in the middle of all this?" grumbled one of his companions. "We could look from now till the next flood comes through and washes us away."

"The Skarmer said it would be easy, when their humans talked with ours," Ternat said. "Of course, the Skarmer have been known to lie."

"They'd better not try it now," said the male who had complained, "not while we still hold their warriors." The rest of the band growled agreement.

"Exactly," Ternat said. "So we have to figure the cursed thing is around here someplace. Let's spread out a little and see what we can come up with. We have to try to keep each other in sight—we don't want to go straggling up the side of the gorge by ones and twos, as if we were so many of Dordal's males."

Eyestalks twitched. The loud male yelled, "If Dordal's males act like that, it's because he went home all by himself." The laughter grew. When Grevil refused for the third time to ransom the northern domain-master, Reatur had released him without payment. The civil war brewing between Dordal and his disloyal eldest showed the wisdom of the move. Ternat wondered if he would have thought of it.

The males formed a circle, as if they were warriors bracing to meet an attack from all sides. But this circle was wider, to let them search more ground and still stay in touch with one another.

They moved forward slowly, cautiously. People seldom went down to the bottom of Ervis Gorge, and of course it was never the same from one flood to the next, anyhow. *Anything* might be here. Ternat was glad he had a spear.

The male to one side of him suddenly stopped. "What's that funny noise?" he said, suspicion thick in his voice. Ternat listened, heard only the wind. He went over to the other male, who pointed and said, "It's coming from over there, I think."

Ternat listened again. Now he also heard the strange, rhythmic thump, twang, and tinkle. For a moment he thought of the beasts legend put in the depths of the gorge, beasts that could lure a male to destruction. Then his eyestalks wiggled in relief. "That's human music," he said.

"There's a human down here?" the male said incredulously.

"I doubt it," Ternat said. "They have gadgets that make music for them. My guess is that the Skarmer put one by their rope so the noise would guide us. A good idea, I must say."

"Pretty sneaky, if you ask me," the male said, as he would have about anything Skarmer. But then he shouted along with Reatur's eldest to let the rest of the band know what they had found.

Ternat's prediction proved good. The gadget sat on a large rock. Like a fair number of human gadgets, it looked like a box. Ternat wondered how the humans knew this box made music instead of, say, pictures. He let his arms and eyestalks shrug in and out: one more thing about humans he would probably never learn.

The box had a handle. Tied to the handle was a thin string. "This is what we came for," Ternat said. "We have to be careful now, so we don't break it on the way back."

The other end of the string was nowhere in sight. Ternat knew that eventually, back toward the Skarmer side of Ervis Gorge, it would join a cord, the cord a rope, the rope a thicker rope, and so on by increments until it linked to the massive cordage of the bridge that would once more span the gorge.

His small band, though, could scarcely have moved that massive final rope, let alone hauled it back to the stones to which it would be attached. Thus the lighter precursors: getting them to the attachment point, where a good-sized crew waited, would be easy.

"What are you going to do with the box?" a male asked.

"Keep it," Ternat replied at once. "It can be part of Hogram's first payment to get his miserable males back, and if he doesn't like that, too bad. Maybe our humans can tell us if it's good for anything besides their funny music."

"Me, I don't know that I want to be linked up to the Skarmer anymore, not after this summer," a male said.

"We can always cut the rope again, you know," Ternat said.

"Not till we get all those cursed hungry Skarmer out of our domain," another male put in. "I know we'll be fat this winter with what Hogram's sending us, but it's only right. We've been thin up to now, what with them eating up so much of our food."

"And Dordal's," said yet another, who had accompanied Ternat on the raid into the northerner's domain. "Let's not forget all those greasy-fat massi we brought back with us. Hogram's males didn't complain about the way they tasted."

"Hogram's males weren't in a position to complain about anything," Ternat said. "They're just glad we've fed them at all. And do you know what? They're lucky we have."

The band shouted agreement. Ternat still wondered if keeping the prisoners alive had been a good idea. Had the humans not urged otherwise, he was sure Reatur would have massacred the Skarmer. The ransom the domain-master was squeezing out of Hogram was more than enough to pay for the cost of maintaining the captives, but was it enough to compensate for having to look at them all through summer and fall, enough to compensate for remembering all the damage they had done, the lives they had taken?

Ternat did not know; where was the scale on which to balance such weights? Reatur had accepted. His eldest, trusting him, supposed that was good enough.

He lifted the string. "Come on. Time to go home."

"Here," Sarah said, dumping the jingling metal clamps in front of Reatur. "I, other humans show you now, many times, how to use to save mates. Wish I had more to give you. Use as you think best. Often, I hope."

Her shiver had nothing to do with the cold, though the weather was down to Minnesota winter and heading straight for Antarctica. Half a dozen clamps, as many as she could spare from her medical supplies. The thought of doing, say, an appendectomy in free-fall on the way home gave her cold chills, but far worse was the thought of what happened to all mates on Minerva, and how those six little clamps could help. She wished she had six thousand, or six million.

"I will use them, Sarah," Reatur said. "I have spoken with you of the sorrow of the mates, have I not?"

She nodded. "Yes, Reatur, you have."

"I thought so. Males have felt it for as long as there have been males and mates. Now I have a chance to get free of it, the first of all my kind. I will take that chance. I also wish you had more clamps. But perhaps it is for the best this way. These clamps will end by changing our world as much as the spring floods change Ervis Gorge. Like the floods, such changes should start slowly, I think."

Sarah nodded again, this time reluctantly. "Likely that is wise." To her, even one mate's dying without need was tragedy worse than the sorrow the domain-master knew when such death was inevitable. On the other hand, she knew that turning such a basic of Minervan life upside down overnight would bring plenty of dislocations of its own. If anyone could safely steer between extremes, she thought, Reatur could. He had a knack for finding the right questions to ask; maybe Lamra got it from him.

Now he came up with another one: "Might we also use these clamps to keep alive, say, eloc mates as well, to keep our herds large?"

Sarah rubbed her chin in consideration and discovered she could barely feel it. "If no mate—no mate of your people—will drop budlings before you can take clamps off animal, then yes. Otherwise no, if you want to save own mates."

"Ah," Reatur said. "That is sensible. Yes. Well, Sarah, I will say that all this has worked out better than I thought it would. Lamra has been, if not accepted, at least tolerated by my males. And the more mates we have who survive budding, the greater the chance the males will have to get used to them."

"I hope so," Sarah said. She had her doubts, though. Lamra was unique and, being unique, created scant antagonism. Some of Reatur's males, in fact, regarded her with almost superstitious awe. That would change when saved mates grew common. How it would change, Sarah was not sure. But if Minervans reacted like people, it probably would not change for the better.

The domain-master cut into her thoughts. "I understand you humans will be leaving soon."

"Yes, before too much snow drifts around, uh, flying house."

Then Reatur surprised Sarah. "Why not wait until the snow begins to melt next spring? I would like to have you stay."

She bowed. "I thank you, but no. Cannot do. Not enough of our food, for one thing. Also have to leave before certain time this winter, no matter what." Orbital mechanics, she knew, meant nothing to Reatur.

He sighed. "You do what you must, of course. But I will miss you." He widened himself to her.

She bowed again. "I miss you, too. All us humans miss you. But must go back to our home."

"Maybe you will come back one day?" Reatur asked.

Did he sound hopeful? Sarah wondered if she was reading too much into his voice. She didn't think so. "I like to see you again, like to see your eldest again, like to see Lamra again." That thought did warm her, despite the worse than icy chill of Reatur's castle. Then reality returned. "Other humans come one day, Reatur, I think. I hope so," she said sadly. "But not us, not me. Hard for us to come here—will be turn of other humans next time we do."

"Let it be as it will, then." The domain-master wiggled his eyestalks, catching Sarah by surprise. "Tell the humans back at your home that I am sorry I broke their fancy picture-making machine, all those years ago. When I saw it, I thought it was a monster. When I saw you humans, I thought you were monsters, too. But it is not so."

"I tell them, Reatur." Sarah felt tears come into her eyes. Angrily, she brushed them away with the back of her glove. They were worse than foolish, she thought—in this weather they were dangerous. Just what she would need, trying to explain to the domain-master how and why her eyelashes were freezing together.

"Good. Thank you once more also for the clamps, and for flying so bravely against the Skarmer with the rifle"—an episode Sarah would have been happy to forget—"and thank you for Lamra."

Sarah bowed very low this time, again fighting back tears. "Reatur, Lamra makes for me this long trip worth doing." Even if, dammit, she added silently, I wasn't there when the budlings dropped. She didn't think she would ever stop kicking herself over what she had been doing some of that time. Much too late to change it now, though.

The domain-master asked, "Can Lamra bud again, Sarah?"

She blinked. He *did* have a gift for the telling question, and she hadn't looked ahead in that particular direction. She gave him the only answer she could. "Not know, Reatur."

"Only a thought." He shrugged a Minervan shrug, with arms and eyestalks. "Even if so, I wonder if I should risk her again without you humans here to help care for her. But I like the idea of more budlings from her, could they be got in safety."

"Not know, Reatur," Sarah repeated. With a last bow, she went on, "Must go back to flying house now, to help get ready to go home." She almost hoped Reatur would want to talk more. It was freezing inside the castle, but it was freezing *and* windy outside. But the domain-master waved her on. Sighing, she fixed her hood so only her eyes showed, then trudged out into the latest blizzard.

The small sun shone bravely in the green-blue sky, glittering off endless miles of snow. The snow fell on *Athena*, no less than on the ground. Irv Levitt, who was sweeping it off the space-craft's left wing, leaned on his pushbroom and asked, "How long do they think the weather will hold?"

"Two days," Emmett said. "Which means our next launch window to rendezvous with the rocket motors upstairs is this afternoon. I intend to use it. We're early, but—"

"Yeah," Irv said. He understood that "but" perfectly well. Another storm like the last one, and *Athena* wouldn't just be covered with snow. It would be buried in snow—not ideal circumstances for liftoff.

He started sweeping again. His answer had been short for another reason, too: he still wasn't anywhere near comfortable around Emmett. It would have been a lot worse, he knew, had

Sarah seemed to want a return engagement with the mission commander. As far as he could tell—how far was that? a question often in his mind—she didn't. He kept his distance from Emmett, anyhow.

How well that would work once *Athena* was in space was another question. Everybody would be in everybody else's pockets again, and everybody, as he knew only too well, had good reason to be angry at somebody. They were all supposed to be very civilized people. He hoped the psych tests were right, because they were going to need to be very civilized, at least till they got home.

From the other wing, Pat called, "Done here."

"Good," Emmett said. He peered through snow goggles toward *Athena*'s tail, where Sarah and Louise were also busy with brooms. "Now we're getting down to what the de-icers can handle."

Irv saw the pilot glance his way but kept on pushing his broom. No, he thought, he was wrong: poor Pat didn't have a reason to be angry at anyone, except the Russians or the Skarmer or whoever had killed Frank. But, thanks to him, Sarah had plenty of reason to be mad at her, which amounted to the same thing.

One of the better reasons for monogamy that nobody ever talked about, he thought as he shoved snow off the wing, was how bloody complicated everything else got.

When he looked up again, the wing was clean. Sarah and Louise, brooms shouldered like rifles, were marching in step up *Athena*'s fuselage, laughing as they came. If Louise knew what he knew . . . Oh, shut up, he told himself fiercely. For a wonder, the internal dialogue did.

"Let's button this bird up," Emmett said. He waved the rest of them into *Athena* ahead of him. Irv was stowing his brooms when the airlock doors clanged shut, first the outer, then the inner. He had heard those clangs hundreds of times, but this time they were special. The doors would not open again, not on Minerva.

The crew trooped forward, into the control cabin. The seat Irv had used for months was again, suddenly, an acceleration couch in his mind. "At least we're used to gravity this time," he said. "Taking off won't be the hideous shock landing was."

"Shall we call the Russians and tell 'em good-bye?" Emmett said. He was not looking for an answer; he had already picked up the microphone. "*Athena* calling *Tsiolkovsky*, *Athena* calling—"

"*Tsiolkovsky* here, Rustaveli speaking."

Bragg switched to Russian. "*Zdrast'ye*, Shota Mikheilovich. Could you patch me through to Colonel Tolmasov? We are lifting off this afternoon; I want to pass on my respects before we go."

"So you give us the honor of staying longer on Minerva than you, eh?" Rustaveli paused, perhaps to think of more English words, perhaps merely to set up his reply. "You may as well; the only thing anyone will remember is that you landed first."

Bragg grinned. "Is that a kind thing to say?"

"No, only a true one. Do you deny it?" Rustaveli said. A moment later, he added in a different tone, "I have Colonel Tolmasov. Go ahead."

"Sergei Konstantinovich?"

"Good day, Brigadier Bragg. What can I do for you?" As usual, Tolmasov's English was excellent but bloodless.

"Not a thing, thank you. This is just a call to let you know we are lifting off this afternoon."

"Are you?" Surprise brought a bit of life to the Russian pilot's voice.

"Snow," Bragg said simply.

"Ah, yes, quite. The hills south of Hogram's domain have thus far shielded us from the worst of it, but I do not think that will last much longer here, either. The best of luck to you, Brigadier. I expect we shall have a good deal to say to each other, when we finally meet back on Earth."

"I expect we will." Bragg hesitated, went on. "Better to meet on account of this than in our planes, eh, Sergei Konstantinovich?"

"Yes," Tolmasov said at once. "And yet—"

"—you'd like to fly against me, anyhow. *Da*, you're a pilot."

Back where Emmett couldn't see him, Irv shook his head. Bragg and Tolmasov reminded him of a couple of big cats roaring at each other across a moat.

After Emmett signed off with Tolmasov, he turned that tigerish tone on his own crew. "All right, people, now we check this beast one more time, the standard preflight and everything else we can think of."

They did. When at last they were through, the pilot sounded almost disappointed as he said, "Looks green. Let's do it."

"Initiate turbojet sequence?" Louise asked crisply.

"Initiate," Emmett said. Her finger stabbed a button. For a moment, nothing happened. Irv glanced at the boards for red lights, saw none. Then, through the thick padding of his seat, he felt vibration begin; muted thunder spoke from *Athena*'s engines.

Outside the spacecraft, he knew, the thunder would be anything but muted. "I hope Reatur has everyone well back, the way he promised," he said.

"If they weren't a minute ago, I guaran-damn-tee you they are now," Sarah said. Irv nodded, at the same time wondering, *Guaran-damn-tee*? It sounded more like Emmett than his wife. But what if it did? After two years cooped up like this, everyone's habits rubbed off on everyone else. You worry too much, he told himself, and worried some more.

"Power buildup?" Emmett asked. He was watching the readouts as closely as Louise, but was too conscientious a pilot not to follow routine.

"Nominal," she answered, going through the ritual with him.

The thunder grew. "Thrust optimum for taxiing," Louise declared. Emmett shoved the stick forward. Irv had just started to wonder if the landing gear de-icers were doing their job when he saw the landscape start to slide backward in the monitor and felt the soft, irregular bumps that said *Athena* wasn't taking off from one of Houston's glass-smooth runways. Kicked-up snow made the VIEW AFT screen a meaningless white blur.

The snow ahead hid surprises, too. Far from being soft, one of the bumps made Irv's teeth click together. The whole spacecraft shuddered. "*Come* on now," Emmett said, as if gentling a restive horse. Like a horse responding to its rider, *Athena* leapt ahead, leapt—"Airborne!" Emmett yelled.

The ground dropped away in the monitors, but whumpings and bumpings went on. "Landing gear retracting . . . retracted," Louise said, simultaneously killing one of Irv's worries and making him feel foolish.

"Lord, I forgot about the stupid wheels," Pat said, relief in her voice. Irv grinned. Embarrassment, like misery, loved company.

"Heading one-two-two . . . one-two-five . . . one-two-seven," Louise reported as Emmett swung *Athena* around.

"Steadying on one-two-seven," he answered. That was the course the craft would need to rendezvous with the rocket motors waiting in orbit above Minervá. The noise in the cabin changed tone; part of it dropped away. "There's Mach one," Emmett said.

The monitors showed the sky a deeper blue-purple than it

looked even aboard the Concorde. As Irv watched, stars began coming out. "Seventy thousand feet," Louise said.

"And Mach two," Emmett echoed. "Still doesn't fly like a Phantom, but we're haulin'." He flicked switches. The turbines' roar died, to be replaced by a high, fierce whine. "Ramjet running."

"Readings within parameters," Louise said. Now the monitors that looked up and ahead showed star-flecked black; below, the Minervan surface looked more as it did in orbital photos than as if from a plane. The engine noise changed again, a little. "Computer adjusting ramjet opening for optimum combustion," Louise reported.

"Pretty soon it can adjust till it turns blue and there still won't be any oxygen out there to burn," Emmett grunted.

"Two hundred twenty thousand feet," Louise said, which was a more prosaic way of announcing the same thing. "Two hundred thirty thousand . . . two hundred forty thousand . . . commencing inboard rocket ignition sequence."

"Go for it, hon," Emmett agreed.

Irv didn't see Louise press the button. He just felt as though something kicked him in the ass even harder than he had been kicking himself lately. "Aren't you supposed to count down first?" he wheezed indignantly. He couldn't see the gorilla lying on his chest, but it was doing its damnedest to cave in his ribs.

In spite of acceleration, Emmett Bragg's voice never wavered. Irv remembered resenting the mission commander for that when they landed on Minerva. He tried not to listen. Then Emmett exclaimed, "Orbital velocity achieved!"

The inboard rockets died. Suddenly Irv weighed nothing at all. After that imaginary gorilla, he should have felt wonderful. Instead he gulped and swallowed spit—his stomach was certainly weightless.

"I have the external rocket pack on radar, bearing zero-zero two degrees, range twenty-seven miles and closing," Louise announced. "Nice burn, Emmett."

"Thanks, hon. Commencing docking maneuver. People, it's official—we're on our way home."

"Wonderful," Irv said. "Anybody have a Dramamine?"

"Right here." Sarah handed him one.

He swallowed it dry—she had pills handy, but no water. After a while, his stomach decided it was under control after all. By then, the big bells of the orbiting rocket motors half-filled the

VIEW FORWARD screen. "Home," Irv breathed, and started to believe it.

"It moves!" Lamra exclaimed through thunder as the flying house—walked?—through the fields. She hung on tight to her toy runnerpest. The din was terrifying, but somehow she was not terrified, maybe because she was too interested in what the flying house was doing.

"It goes up!" This time she could hear the disbelief in her voice. "And up and up and up!" Her eyestalks followed the flying house as it turned and dwindled in the sky. The roar dwindled, too. The long, thin white cloud the flying house left behind began to fray and blow apart, just like any other cloud.

"I saw it come down before." Reatur spoke louder than he needed to; Lamra supposed he was partly deafened, too, as she was. "I suppose I always thought that meant it could also go up again, but seeing it is a lot more impressive."

"I never saw it come down. I was still cooped up in the mates' quarters," Lamra said, a little indignantly. She thought back. "But I remember the noise! Nobody knew what it was. We all thought the castle was falling down."

"So did I, little one, so did I." Reatur turned a couple of eyestalks from the daytime star that was all that was left of the flying house to Lamra. "That would have been a little while after I planted your buds on you."

"So it would, Reatur," she agreed, consciously imitating his turn of phrase. She looked down at herself. She still didn't look the way other mates did, but the bud bulges were hardly bulges any more, and the scars that showed where the raw edges of skin had healed together were only light-colored ridges above her feet.

"All your budlings are doing well, I'm told," Reatur said.

"Good," she answered indifferently. She still did not care a lot about budlings. Seeing how grown males behaved was much more interesting: that was how she wanted to learn to act.

When Reatur spoke again, he sounded oddly diffident. "Do you think you would be interested in bearing another set of budlings?"

She started to answer, then stopped. One thing grown males sometimes did, she had noticed, was to think before they spoke instead of saying the first thing that popped into their minds. "I don't know," she answered at last. "Do you think you would be able to keep me from ending, the way the humans did?"

"I hope so. I think so," the domain-master said. "We'll have had a lot of practice by the time your budlings would be ready to drop."

"That's true," Lamra said. "Maybe we'll have more clamps by then, too. Do you think we could find some springy wood, say, that we can carve new ones out of?" She didn't know if there was any such wood, but the outside world, she was finding, had all sorts of things in it that she didn't know about.

"Maybe," Reatur said. "I've thought about that, too. Sooner or later, I guess we will need to see if we can make our own. Why don't you take a clamp and show it to one of our carvers?"

"Me?" Lamra squeaked in alarm. "He wouldn't listen to me!"

"To whom would he be more likely to listen than to the only mate in all the world who dropped her budlings but lived?"

"Well—" She hadn't thought about it like that. "All right, Reatur, I will."

"Good."

Lamra came back to the question Reatur had asked before. She had hardly thought about budding at all since Reatur planted these last six on her; she certainly hadn't thought about it since she had dropped them. But now, reminded, she recalled the way her body had driven her toward it. She searched herself for that same feeling.

She did not expect to find it. But she did—not with the urgency she had had before, perhaps, but with enough to be partial to the idea. "I suppose we can make budlings again," she said. "From what I remember, it was fun."

Reatur's eyestalks wiggled. "For me, too, Lamra."

"Well, then, let's go find someplace quiet and do it," she said, brisk once her mind was made up.

"Now?" Reatur sounded startled. Then he laughed some more. "Why not? There have to be a good many rooms in the castle that don't have anyone in them right now. Shall we find one?" They walked back together.

Afterward, the domain-master was not laughing at all. He widened himself to Lamra. "What's that for?" she demanded; she was still uneasy whenever he did it.

"Because over the years, I've planted buds on many eighteens of mates, probably more, and I've never felt sensations as strong as I just did with you." He mimed tying his eyestalks into knots.

"Oh." Lamra thought about that. "I was only remembering what I liked last time and trying to do more of that now."

It was Reatur's turn to say, "Oh." Then he asked, "Do you suppose it will be better still after you're healed from your next set of budlings?"

"*I* don't know," she said, flustered. That was further ahead than she'd thought.

Reatur was not listening to her, anyhow. He said dreamily, "Human males and mates both live to grow up all the time. What must planting buds be like for them, with so much practice on both sides?"

"When they come back, why don't you ask them?" Lamra said.

"If I live until they come back, I will. And if I don't live that long"—he looked at her with four eyes—"maybe you'll ask them yourself."

She thought it over. "Maybe I will," she said.

About The Author

HARRY TURTLEDOVE is that rarity, a lifelong southern Californian. He is married and has three young daughters. After flunking out of Caltech, he earned a degree in Byzantine history and has taught at UCLA, Cal State Fullerton, and Cal State Los Angeles. Academic jobs being few and precarious, however, his primary work since leaving school has been as a technical writer. He has had fantasy and science fiction published in *Isaac Asimov's, Amazing, Analog, Playboy,* and *Fantasy Book*. His hobbies include baseball, chess, and beer.

HARRY TURTLEDOVE

WORLDWAR: IN THE BALANCE

The Second World War has you've never seen it before. War seethed across the planet. Hostilities spread in ever-widening circles of destruction: Nazi Germany, Soviet Russia, Britain, France, Japan, Italy, Africa – the fate of the world hung in the balance.

Then the *real* enemy arrived. Out of the skies came an invasion force the like of which Earth had never known – and worldwar was truly joined. The invaders were inhuman and they were unstoppable. Their weaponry was overwhelming and their goal was simple: Fleetlord Atvar had arrived to claim Earth for the Empire . . .

In this epic novel of alternate history, the world's leading master of 'what if' fiction takes us to the adventure of a lifetime.

'Engrossing . . . totally fascinating . . .
Most highly recommended'
Booklist

'Turtledove excels . . . a feast'
Library Journal

'Vast . . . intriguing and panoramic'
Kirkus Reviews

HODDER AND STOUGHTON PAPERBACKS

HARRY TURTLEDOVE

HOW FEW REMAIN

A generation after the South won the first American Civil War, America writhes once more in the bloody throes of battle. Furious over the annexation of key Mexican territory, the United States declares total was against the Confederate States. And so, in 1881, the fragile peace is shattered.

But this is a new kind of war, fought on a lawless frontier where the Blue and the Grey battle not only each other but the Apache, the outlaw – and even the British Redcoat. For, along with France, Britain enters the fray on the Confederate side . . .

Once again, internationally bestselling author Harry Turtledove has created a thoroughly engrossing novel of alternate history. HOW FEW REMAIN is a stunningly original epic of blood and honour, courage and sacrifice, a mighty drama of conflict played out against the savage majesty of young America's frontier wilderness.

HODDER AND STOUGHTON PAPERBACKS

A selection of bestsellers from Harry Turtledove

Worldwar: In The Balance	0 340 61839 6	£6.99	❏
Worldwar: Tilting The Balance	0 340 64899 6	£6.99	❏
Worldwar: Upsetting The Balance	0 340 66698 6	£6.99	❏
Worldwar: Striking The Balance	0 340 68491 7	£6.99	❏
How Few Remain	0 340 71541 3	£6.99	❏

All Hodder & Stoughton books are available at your local bookshop or newsagent, or can be ordered direct from the publisher. Just tick the titles you want and fill in the form below. Prices and availability subject to change without notice.

Hodder & Stoughton Books, Cash Sales Department, Bookpoint, 39 Milton Park, Abingdon, OXON, OX14 4TD, UK. E-mail address: order@bookpoint.co.uk. If you have a credit card you may order by telephone - (01235) 400414.

Please enclose a cheque or postal order made payable to Bookpoint Ltd to the value of the cover price and allow the following for postage and packing:
UK & BFPO – £1.00 for the first book, 50p for the second book, and 30p for each additional book ordered up to a maximum charge of £3.00.
OVERSEAS & EIRE – £2.00 for the first book, £1.00 for the second book, and 50p for each additional book.

Name ....

Address ....

....

....

If you would prefer to pay by credit card, please complete:
Please debit my Visa/Access/Diner's Card/American Express (delete as applicable) card no:

Signature ....

Expiry Date ....

If you would NOT like to receive further information on our products please tick the box. ❏